THE EMPIRE OF THE BLACK SUNS VOLUME I:

CALL OF THE VOID

Acknowledgements

This book is dedicated to my adolescence, in which the story and characters were the centre of my imagination. This series explores its own understanding of spirituality, morality, friendship, and introspection, all of which I came to learn and explore in my teen years.

I'd also like to thank all early readers of the original edition of this book, whose honesty was integral in my critical evaluation and re-write of it. Of which, Imogen Holdsworth is of impeccable note.

Thanks also goes to my high school teacher and mentor-in-fantasy, Oliver Thomas, who helped me to become critical of myself and the world, and develop the ideas for this book.

Amanda Giannaros is also to be acknowledged. Thanks to her worldviews, eccentricities, and friendship, I was able to develop the characters, and build my confidence to write this series.

Ayesha Desai deserves my thanks for initially publishing this book's first edition and getting it out to the world. Her kindness was greatly appreciated.

The last proper acknowledgement goes to my editor, Joanna Gogos. Through her critical and literarily trained eye, I was able to vastly improve this story and my writing style. I'd have never known how properly terrible the initial drafts of this book were until she came on board and showed me my errors.

A special mention goes to the band *Fat Freddy's Drop*. It's not every day that a band gets an acknowledgement in a foreword, but the themes presented in their songs were the turning point in establishing key ideas of this series.

Thank you for choosing to read, and I hope you have a fantastic time doing so.

Yours truly,
Alexander Mackie.

Episode 1

How My Life Turned Upside Down

The walls were buzzing as music blasted through the rooms of the quaint house. I stood in the corner, glass of water in hand, as drinks, laughter, and stories danced from mouth to mouth about the centre of the living room's dance floor. This was going to be challenging.

Don't get me wrong, I like a good party. Just last month – on my seventeenth birthday – I had a bunch of mates around. Maybe sixty people showed up, danced on my deck and ate the plethora of snacks I had out. I spent most of my time dancing – that's where I came to life. People I didn't know too well? Meeting somebody new and making a friend? Not so much where I shone. I scanned the room, looking for a potential partner.

I'd never believed in destiny – fate, coincidence, divine circumstances, that sort of thing – although I'd hoped it would get me through this awkward ordeal before any of my close friends rocked up. I didn't judge people who legitimately believed in divine power. They clung to the idea that the universe was planned-out, and that you were just *meant* to do certain things, or that those things were just *meant* to come to you. To me, it seemed like a concept well grasped by those without motivation or inhibition, those who always saw holy intervention over coincidence in the most mundane of circumstances, and discredited the work of surgeons to the divine hand.

Still, I hoped for it. A man could dream that life would be handed to him. I remembered a conversation I'd had with my Dad about this, as he lay sprawled out on the couch after a long day of work, still in his detective uniform, with a glass of red in one hand and the dog curled by his feet. He glanced at me with his knowing eyes and smug grin and told me that there's no greater joy in life than being alone at a party.

To be quite honest, I never remembered how we got talking about being alone at a party, but that was Dad, always full of unsolicited wisdom. "You get to make whatever you want out of the night. Don't know anybody? Great, be totally yourself, be *whatever* you want to be. The world's an odd place, you'll find yourself pushed into the right corners. It works like that."

This corner seemed fine, at least until I gained some confidence. I peered outside. Through the window, the party continued in and around the pool. I'd considered going in, and the invitation even said to bring bathers, but I didn't see myself as cool enough to breach that crowd. It was Penelope Papas' 18th birthday, private school girl, very cute. Her friends were all way above my league.

The invitation had taken me totally by surprise. *To James Grey*, it had read. *I know it's been a few years since we've really chatted, but I'd love it if you'd come around to my eighteenth on the 10/1/1998. There'll be a few people from primary school there too. It'll be fun. Deliver your RSVP to this address.* I'd walked the journey to deliver the letter, welcoming the opportunity to procrastinate from this summer of homework. Penelope's house was in a much wealthier suburb than mine. The walk had led me into the broad, glimmering shade of wide European trees. On the walk tonight, the mid-summer breeze failed to tussle my hair thanks to the palmful of gel slicking it back. The fences were all high and white, with little speaker boxes by the gate that you had to ring to be let in. My best friend Tom and I used to play *ding-dong-ditch* with the buzzers on this street when we were little. I'd chuckled at the memory – he was the only one of us brave enough to do it, and it wasn't even a challenge for him.

Penelope's house was set apart from the others by the bouquet of balloons jailed to the front fence. I pressed the buzzer beneath them, and her gate opened itself, allowing me into the extravagant garden. It was an immaculate spectacle in the dying light of dusk. Various spotlights projected rainbows onto blossom and birch trees, which stood tall in the garden beds surrounding the path. I stepped onto the porch and waited.

I heard footsteps skipping towards the door, past the buzz of the bass rocking the house. When it finally swung open, I remembered why I'd had a crush on Penelope back in primary school. She held herself by her tiptoes on the door frame, teetering on massive heels. When she recognised me, her blue eyes popping behind her long, platinum hair, she shook into excitement.

"James Grey!" She proclaimed, wrapping herself around me. My hands froze and my face blushed red. I didn't know how to respond to the hug I wasn't expecting, and with every passing moment it became even weirder for me to lean into it. I couldn't afford a faux pa.

"Hey Pennie." I laughed awkwardly, pulling a hand into my pocket and searching for her card.

It wasn't there.

Hit with panic, I inspected my other pocket, then my back pocket, then the first pocket again. Finally, I resorted to the pocket of my left ass-cheek, the last place I'd ever put anything, and there it was. Well, if not reciprocating a hug in time wasn't awkward enough, handing somebody a birthday card which had been rubbing on your ass has got to be a close second. It was a hand drawn card, too. A little more sentimental, I seemed to think. Saved me money, too.

"Oh, James, you didn't have to." She smiled. "Here, come in." Penelope stepped aside, ushering me through. Her heels clacked harshly on the hardwood floor. "I don't think there's anybody here yet who you know, but give me about fifteen minutes to put this away and say hi to some people, and I'll be able to show you around."

"Thanks, Pennie." I damned my inability to show up to anything even casually late. If I was willing, or able, to be cooler, maybe I'd have at least an acquaintance here already instead of beating them all here. My breath became shorter, constricting. Sweat came to my brow. I would have to meet somebody new and go out of my way to be charming. I hoped Dad was right about the world.

That is how I found myself stewing in the far corner. I could have joined any group, really, I considered. In the centre of the room some people were dancing. How odd would it be to dance over and say hi? But no, it's more likely that I'd be some weird intruder. I'd be *that guy* – the guy who tried to outdance your group of friends. I hummed, looking to my watch. It had only been five minutes and my world was already collapsing. I sighed, and peered to the snack table. Nothing better to take your mind of crippling social anxiety than filling your face with garbage.

But there, I saw *her.*

Standing by a plate of fairy bread, guiding the sprinkle-coated treat to her mouth with the poise and restraint of a queen. Her dress was long and proper, and she held herself tall in it, standing fully but not pompously. She scanned the room my way, turning her face, revealing its sharp lines and bold features. She had an ancient beauty, not a girl you'd call pretty, but a woman you'd call commanding. Her face held power. On her chest, a gold locket shimmered in the disco lights.

I *had* to talk to her.

Her eyes passed over mine, assessing the crowd. Deep and blue, I felt myself fall into them, streaming into an endless, gentle abyss. Thrown into space itself. I soared past stardust, flying in the slingshot of a giant black hole, radiating in a soft, green glow. I reached out and touched its horizon, speckles off green lapping about and splashing off my fingertips. The world was a bliss glide. Here there was only happiness, and I was a part of it.

There was a clank, and something smashed into my ankle, wrapping around it. A chain had flung from the black beast's centre, yanking me back. I lost my momentum, I lost the sparkles of stardust, and I fell with the heavy, metal links into a stark oblivion.

I shook my head from the daydream. *That was crazy.* Not unusual, though. Often, I found myself drifting into strange dreams whilst fully awake. As I came to, I noticed her looking at me too. Her brow was scrunched, she gave me that look reserved for people who you knew, but you weren't sure how you knew them, or if you actually knew them at all. As soon as we'd caught each other glaring, we snapped our heads away.

I had to talk to this girl, but I'd gone ahead and made it weird. How could I approach her now that I'd been caught staring stupidly, and *creepily*? Girls didn't like creeps. *Hell*, I wasn't even attracted to this girl, but that's how I'd come off, right? I'd just be another weird dude for her night. No-siree, that would *not* be James Grey tonight. I'd have to think of another way to strike a conversation. Call me the king of hyperbole, but deep in my gut, in that space which drives the soul, I *knew* I had to talk to her, or my life would miss some integral meaning – even if it was only consequential for one night. I turned, wracking my brain for some answer, only to be confronted with a beaming, radiant smile.

"Ah!" I stumbled in surprise. Penelope flicked her long locks aside.

"Sorry that took so long." Penelope said, that smile still as strangely persistent.

"That's…okay." I fumbled the words, still picking myself up.

"I've got somebody to introduce you to, over there, by the snack table."

She pointed and I followed her finger, turning slowly, hoping to the dear Lord of Cheeses that she would be pointing to the girl I'd found myself staring at. Low and behold, where her finger and intentions met, the other girl was placed. Was this the strange operation of the world? Was this some strike of destiny?

This would be a story for Dad, if only he was alive to hear it.

Before I knew it Penelope was walking me over, through the crowd to the snack table. "Natalie!" She called, and my woman of intrigue turned. Her blue-green eyes darted between Penelope's and mine. She appeared just as shocked and nervous as I was. We must have been two stunned mullets – two deer driving cars, caught in each other's headlights. This would be a collision.

"This is my friend James Grey, I met him in primary school. James Grey, this is Natalie Athanas. She's a family friend." She pushed the two of us together, smiled, and proceeded to reach between us, dipping each finger in a cheese ring before skipping off. There was a pause, where we were each caught in each other's stare. My heart was racing, my forehead was sweating. I'd been pushed here, somehow, and I had no idea what to do with it.

"How do you do?" I asked, cringing as I said it.

"Very well, thank you." Natasha said. "James, was it?"

"Yes." I smiled. "Natasha?"

"Natalie."

"Oh…" I cringed twice as hard. "Lovely to meet you, Natalie." I burned her name deep into my brain. *Natalie!* "So, *Natalie*, how do you know Penelope?"

"Well, my Mum used to tutor her, so I was always around here in high school." She said. "How about yourself?"

"Just Primary school, really." I smiled, dragging my feet through the tension of nervousness. At least she was nervous too – or, she could have just been bored. It was hard to tell. Then I realised there was a silence. Was I supposed to go on? I didn't want to screw this up now. So much for *destined* conversation. "So…where do you go to school?"

"I just moved to Leslie Grammar." She said. "I moved from down by the beach to live with my Dad for year twelve." My jaw dropped, my heart raced, and I'm sure some stupid smile crawled itself to plaster across my face.

"Cheese! I'm from Leslie Grammar, I'm in year twelve!" I exclaimed.

"What?" She chuckled. "No way."

"Yes way." I beamed. "That's so cool." *It's almost like destiny*, I mused. *If you counted meeting somebody who you go to school with as divine intervention.* "So, what, do you live around here?" I asked, before I realised how weird that sounded. *'Because we could catch the train together, if you do.'* Was where I was leading, but that wouldn't have been obvious to her.

"Actually, I do." She smiled. "I mean, I'm on the other side of the train line, but I walked here."

"Ha!" I blurted. "I'm also from that way. I'm surprised we didn't bump into each other on the way."

"Oh, you got here *way* too late for that." She scoffed. "I was ten whole minutes early. Or, five minutes late, as I call it."

And she was uncool, too? This couldn't be. My nervousness had burst into elation. My otherworldly strong compulsion to talk to this girl had resulted in a maybe-friend!

"Are you catching the train to school, then?" I asked, and then before she could answer. "Because we could catch the train together, if you like?" She paused, considering the offer.

"That would be lovely, James." She smiled, and outstretched a hand to be shaken. Before they touched though, she withdrew. "Only if you get to school half an hour early. I'm not about turning up right on time, you know."

"Try an hour early." I smirked, and our hands met for a done deal.

We continued chatting, the party swirling around us. People came and went, buzzing through their evenings, churning between places and creating stories, but none of it mattered. The world moved on, but Natalie and I were caught in a stasis. We moved to the nearby couch, engrossed in each other's words. She used to live with her mother by the beach, but moved up to do year twelve at a private school, living with her father and maternal grandmother, whom she called her *Yamitse*. I didn't know what language that came from – nor did she – but we connected on having ethnic grandmothers. Hers being *Yamitse* and mine being *Baba*. She'd been dancing since she could walk, surfing from even younger, and spoke Greek at home. I tried to impress her with my early morning rowing, my stories of music and school, and my Italian-Macedonian heritage.

I checked my watch. "Lord of Cheese, it's almost nine-thirty, and I haven't had a dance." I gawked, standing. "Do you want to dance? I don't care if you don't, I'm going to anyway."

"To this music?" She huffed, rolling her eyes. "It's sing along garbage."

"And what did you have in mind?" I quizzed.

"You'll see." She stood. She strode through me, across the room, over to the cabinet by the sound system. She cut a path straight through the dancing girls, not a care in the world, and reached for a CD high in the stack. She pressed the eject button, right in the middle of the current song. My jaw went slack. Such a faux pa drew boos from the crowd, but they bounced off her skin. She pushed play.

Bass was plucking. Low and steady, and asynchronous. It jived, with the drums panning in over the top, right in each beat where the bass wasn't. My head clucked like a chook, my feet moving themselves. "Ooh!" I nodded, "Damn!" The groovy had me, entranced even before the guitar swooped in, spear tackling my soul. I was alight now, limbs moving.

"Damn Natalie!" I laughed, strutting into centre floor.

"I know." She said smugly. Her body moved fluidly, swaying between beats. She had inertia to her rhythm which was hard to ignore, like a tidal force. She swung her arms around.

Then there was a splash, my leg wet. I paused, and between Natalie and I, my cup of water had fallen off its perch. It wasn't unknown for my dancing limbs to make drinks fly, but I was certain I didn't hit it, and Natalie was nowhere near close enough. "I'll have to clean that up. I'll be back." I said. "But great music choice!"

"You know it." She bode me farewell, still entranced in the music. I turned to the kitchen, towards the hall, to see two very familiar swaggers strutting my way, my best mates Tom and David. I waved, elated to see their familiar faces.

My friendship with Tom and David was forged through years of schooling. Tom's grin, constantly plastered on his face, stood in the place of his soul. His feet moved with a jaunty bounce - his red, curly locks following with the same arrogance and cheek. David, next to him, looked to have just walked out of an op-shop change room. To his taste, vintage was the only description. If others couldn't have it, David wanted it. Unfortunately, he often lacked the confidence to demand what he wanted

– which was unusual for a handsome man of dark skin, great height, and a British voice.

"Mate!" I called to them. "My Cheese, I almost died. I had to *meet* people."

"Jimmy boy!" Tom called back and danced his way over, mimicking my style. He laughed, and we all shook hands.

Behind Tom, I noticed Penelope making her way down the hallway to us.

"I didn't think you would come." I said. "It's already nine-thirty."

"How long have you been here?" David asked. "It's still so early."

"Well, about an hour I think." I looked at my watch.

"Who've you been hanging out with for an hour? Fairy bread?" Tom asked, grabbing a slice from the table next to me.

I chuckled. "No mate, you think I could walk up to a tasty piece of fairy bread and start a conversation? That's too much pressure for me, man." I joked with him, grabbing a piece. "But no, I met the girl over there," I said and pointed to Natalie, who was still dancing to herself. "She's pretty cool. She's just moved to our school, so we'll see her around, I guess."

They each subtly glanced to Natalie, and turned back to me with shocked faces.

Penelope walked behind Tom, her arms grabbing him in a surprise hug. He coughed up sprinkles as she squeezed him tight, then slung her way around him, into our circle.

"So glad you boys could make it." She said, her gaze locked on Tom. "I'm going into the pool, but you should join me." And with her hand lingering on Tom for way too long, she pulled herself away, out the back door. David was gobsmacked.

"Man, it's the Tom and James show tonight, boys." He huffed.

"Knowing James, it's probably just the Tom show." Tom said, puffing his chest.

"Hey, I just made a *friend* tonight." I backed away from the implication. "Nothing more. Tom show it is. Don't let Pennie get away, *man of the hour*."

"Don't worry." He grinned. "I wouldn't dream of it." And board-shorts in hand, he ran out the back door.

The party wrapped up just past the turn of midnight, long after darkness had set on the late summer night. Natalie and I sat for most of it on the edge of the pool, teasing our feet in the water, talking on whatever else we could. I offered to walk her home, and she accepted, wanting somebody to be with through the moonless streets. We said bye to the birthday girl, and thanked her mother for having us over, before ducking into the dark outside.

We quickly came to the railway line. Natalie and I lived on the other side, and to get there we had to go through a cobblestone alleyway and into the old underpass.

We were walking by the tracks, on a street which was a busy thoroughfare by light. Shadows of trees crawled in the wind, darkness dancing across the houses on the left.

Natalie was tense, I could sense it. She'd been silent for a long way, now.

"What's up?" I asked her. My voice died strangely before my face, not even breaking the eeriness of the still-aired night.

"I don't know, something *feels* wrong about this. It's too quiet, you know?"

"It's also two in the morning." I joked, "I think that's expected." When I looked up again, I saw a shadow figure dart between two cars. It gave me such a fright that I ground to a halt, frozen.

"Don't you get that feeling when you know people are around?" She asked me, grabbing my hand to pull me along. I could see her hunching – stalking, even – as we toed towards the alley underpass. "I know people are around…"

Shoes screeched in the alleyway, followed by the dull thud of flesh on stone. A man grunted loudly, then men's voices started growling, their speech inaudible. Frozen, my first instinct was to run away, and I stomped my foot down to flee before my world fell in on itself. My very being screamed at the idea of running, squirming in my gut. Strangely, every urge, every *compulsion*, was telling me to stalk closer, to see what was happening. Just like that compulsion which guided me to meet Natalie, I felt that I had to obey it. Doing anything else would be wrong. The two of us, in unexpected unison, stalked closer, clinging to the corner of the alley. We peeked around.

There were four men in the alley, standing under the singular pool of dirty, orange light. One was being held up against the wall by two men in pinstriped suits. Another man in a red suit stood in the middle of the way, facing the hostage and growling. His nose was held high, his complexion dark and mysterious, his posture mighty against the frail victim.

"Do you know what family means, my friend?" He spoke in a thick French accent. "The Argols are about family. You don't want protection from the angry mobs and racists out there? That's your decision, but don't drag the rest of us down that hole…"

Argols? I shuddered. That was a name that my police detective father had taken home with him.

"Natalie, we shouldn't be here." I whispered, grabbing her arm. "These guys are in a dangerous gang. And they don't use guns, they use…"

The man reached across his body and unsheathed a sword. As he drew it, the leading edge erupted in flames, creating a wall of yellow fire down the blade's sharp side. The flame was liquid; it oozed and spewed from the tip of the weapon and dripped onto the cobbles. He swung it into the ground. It spat a line of fire directly between the victims' legs, the asphalt of the gutter melted, and tar bubbled at hostage's feet.

"...Flamethrowers!" I squeaked, but I couldn't bring myself to look away from the situation, let alone fathom leaving.

The big man in the suit swung the sword around his body – fire recklessly flying over the floor.

"Now tell me," He demanded as he stabbed the ground. The tar melted to make way for the hot weapon. "Why shouldn't we kill a rat like you?"

Movement in the distance caught my eyes. In the far shadows, lurking by the underpass, I saw a light blue glow – a pair of rectangular cyan eyes with a glowing partition between them, spying. As soon as I'd seen them, I noticed another pair, pink circular lights, onlooking from above the fence. Then I saw a purple pair, a darker blue pair, a yellow pair; all glowing eyes stalking in the darkness.

They were all moving, ducking in and out from behind the shadows, except the cyan pair, which stood their ground firmly at the end of the lane. They were bobbing up and down, as if the owner was walking closer. There was another eruption of flame from the hilt of the grounded sword. The blinding light was enough to distract me from the eyes, and when I went to look back they had all disappeared. The red suited man ripped his sword from the ground and held it to the throat of his victim, the flame illuminated the fear of death strewn across his face.

From down the alley there was a sound like something between swatting a tennis racquet and a laser gun. A cyan bolt of energy, like a rod of light with three glowing rings down its length, came careening through the air. It slapped the sword wielding man across his face; his head spun from its impact and his body followed. He tumbled to the ground. The sword's flame immediately extinguished, and the weapon smashed into the asphalt where it shattered like glass.

From a tree above the laneway a shadow-figure dropped and landed in the darkness with a metal clank. The shape was humanoid, but jagged – sharp, with spikes and hard edges. Its arm quickly entered the circle of orange light and grabbed the furthest of the pinstriped gangsters holding the hostage. It's arm and hand were armoured, its wrist was skinny, and its fingers too slender and long to be human. Before I could analyse anything more, the arm pulled away and the man fell into the shadows. The last gangster standing dropped the victim and drew his own weapon – a long, wooden staff which seemed to come from nowhere. Before he could use it, a shadow, moving too fast to illuminate, rocketed past Natalie and I from the street and grabbed him on the way through. The man was drug across the stones, into the darkness

The victim didn't look too much more relieved than he did before, as he was backing *himself* up to the wall for safety against the shadowed terror. The owner of the cyan eyes bobbed through the blackness, then stepped out into the edge of the light. Like the other figure, this one appeared humanoid, but covered in sharp and hard-edged armour. They had a large, silvery chest plate and shoulder coverings. On the ends of the shoulder plates were little lightning bolt ends. The same little bolts adorned its yellow helmet, like horns. The helmet was sleek, with a cyan partition up the middle which branched into eyebrows above its eyes. The line of its jaw continued outwards into two mandible-like spikes.

The man's eyes opened wide. He peeled himself from the brick wall and fell to his knees before the armoured man.

"Na Fara." He hailed. I didn't recognise the language.

"Yefarka di mis." The figure replied, *"Sur san Suneva."*

I finally had the energy to turn away from the scene.

"Suneva…" Natalie and I both whispered aloud at the same time.

I knew that word too. But where from?

Before I could express this to Natalie, I felt something behind me – like a disturbance in the gentle breeze. The shadow of a dark figure loomed over my shoulder. Reluctantly, I turned to face the demon-like being. Its bright, rectangular, orange eyes illuminating my face.

"I don't think it's safe for you here," it said calmly, with its smooth voice.

Natalie and I shrieked. We ran off down the street, back into the darkness.

Chapter 2
Skeletons in the Attic

Suneva, The Argols…I mulled it over before I went to sleep that night. It was obvious I was meant to stumble into that frightening scene with Natalie, if only to remember those words. But why?

I'd seen the image of the yellow armoured man before, too – the guy with the cyan eyes. I couldn't be certain, but I thought the image came from a little, red book Dad read once. I hadn't seen the book before or since, but I remember that striking figure being on the cover. I fell asleep with both the images swimming in my minds' eye.

We kept Dad's stuff in a box in the attic. Our house was modest. It had a long hallway, which connected the front door to the kitchen and dining room out the back. Mum slept up the front, and my sister, Simone, was with me in our own hallway. Halfway along the hall, across from the TV area, hung a string from the roof. If you pulled on it, the attic ladder would come crashing down to the floor. There were dints in the floor boards from where it kept landing.

That red book would be up there. It felt almost silly to chase these answers, especially this way. I had not been immune to the crazy and spectacular in life. There had been many occasions where I didn't believe my own eyes, so why did I believe last night so intently? Was it because Natalie was as scared as I was, or because I *felt* that it had to have been genuine? And why did I feel that I needed to know those words? What I did know was that in the bizarre night, a stream of intense gut feelings and compulsions, led me to meet a girl with whom I would witness something otherworldly. It wasn't the weirdest thing I'd ever seen, but I still felt that I *had* to know more about it. I couldn't leave those compulsions unchecked. Something was at work here, demanding my attention.

Still, Natalie and I didn't talk at all after the events we witnessed the night before. The whole journey home, we ticked our brains over just to keep our hearts pumping. I said goodnight on her doorstep, and she thanked me for walking her. We exchanged the pleasantries of *'it was wonderful to meet you'*, and then I went on my way.

I passed the study on the way to the attic. Simone, my elder sister by two years, sat hunched in the dark room over a bright screen. Her furious fingers typed away, tongue hanging out the side of her mouth, revelling in her grin. I could only assume she was making another blog post. Ahead-of-the-times, that was Simone. We were one of the only houses with an internet connection in nineteen-ninety-eight, and she damn well made sure to use each byte of bandwidth posting her opinion on far-left image boards, spurting paranormal madness on her connected blogsite. Feminism, demons and ghosts, those were her strangely disconnected points of expertise, plastered on an image board which covered topics from functional Marxism, social activism, all the way down to the paranormal and spiritual.

"Updating your loyal followers?" I asked as I passed.

"I'm on to something today, James." She grinned. "Evidence on the scale that we've seen."

"I'd like to see it, then." I said, and without a hint of sarcasm to the tone. Simone and I had a shared childhood experience which formed a contract between us – an infinite clause of belief. Never would we doubt each other's outlandishly crazy claims. It was well deserved, too. I'd never mock her for her beliefs – I did love her, after all.

"Oh, you'll see it, right after the world does." She yelled as I walked off. "They'll all believe us, James."

I got under the attic's trap door and pulled its release string. It took a forceful tug to undo the latch, but once it released I had to jump clear. The sliding ladder –

probably the most lubricated and well-engineered in the world – careened down its rails like a runaway train and crashed into the indents in the floor boards. It shook the house, summoning the family dog, Errol, right away. He circled around the base of the ladder as I climbed it, watching curiously.

The air in the attic was thick and unsettled. A shroud of darkness hung in the room – separate to the shadows which leaped between boxes in your peripherals. Not even the light from the singular, circular window could cut into the haze. The sun's rays were strangled once they passed the glass, and thrown to the floor like dead insects. Dust hung in the room like treacherous fog, dancing unpredictably and settling in a thick coating over everything.

I crawled past the many boxes to the back wall, where there was a large, wooden chest. As I made my way towards it, I couldn't shake the feeling that I was being watched. There were eyes in every particle of air and every shadow, all focussed on me. It was the same feeling which struck me each time I came here for Dad's stuff. It didn't surprise me anymore, but it was still creepy.

I pressed the button on the large, wooden chest's latch. The lid popped up pneumatically, just enough to get your fingers under the crack. I slowly swung it open the rest of the way, revealing items I had sorted through many times.

On top of the pile was his white golf visor, which he wore religiously every Sunday. Under that was his wedding suit, and some other clothes which he would lounge around the house in. In retrospect, it was weird to preserve his lazing around clothes, but looking at them always jogged my memory of him. It was comforting.

I could see the way that he would shuffle onto the back deck, wine glass in hand, and take his seat about the round table. Errol would circle the chair, trying to get him to throw his ball. John Grey wasn't a tall man, or an imposing one, but his strength radiated. He had a presence of command that extended as far as his love. *The last of the old bulls*, he'd call himself, patting his chest with a smart grin and a meaty palm.

Below his clothes in the chest was a layer of old family videos and photo albums. Usually, when I came up here to reminisce, I would grab out the tape converter and play them all through the TV, then flip through the photo albums. But today I was looking for information, not sentiments. I didn't feel like forcing myself through the memories.

To the right of the videos and albums were his trophies. There were a lot of them, and I knew them all. *John Grey - Best and Fairest for the League, 1977*; *Best and Fairest, St Leonards, 1976*; *Nationals U14 100m Freestyle 2nd place;* the list went on.

I always wished I could have lived up to his glory. I spent my childhood trying to be everything he was as a sportsman, but always failing. I couldn't run as far, or swim nearly as fast, or even throw a ball. I gave up, and just settled for doing my own things, like music, and drawing. I'd never know if he was proud of the decisions I made.

Finally, I got to his books. There were a few of his mother's cookbooks here, which I always found odd – why weren't they in the kitchen being useful? I loved Baba's cooking, but now she and Dedo had moved back to Macedonia. There were many autobiographies in the chest, each of which he had read over and over. Amongst autobiographies, there were some buddy-cop thrillers, a few books he bought for me, but only because he wanted them for himself, and a few sports almanacs. The little red book would have my answers, but it was eluding me. It wasn't anywhere in the stack. I grumbled, and started to dive deeper into the chest.

"Reminiscing?" a voice broke the silence behind me. I seized up and almost fell over myself. Simone was standing on the steps of the ladder, her head poking into the attic.

Simone wore a sweet, polite smile now, in contrast to her often dreary, offended demeanour. Clearly her work on the internet had proved successful. It didn't take a lot to stoke Simone's passions – no more than a casual misstep of words.

"Yeah," I regained myself, "a bit." I turned my attention back to shifting through the chest.

"I used to come up here a lot," she noted, wrenching herself up to sit on the lip of the entrance. "I still do actually."

"Looking for what?" I asked, not concentrating on the conversation.

"Memories." She said blankly, "Isn't it weird how you can construct a person in your head, run them through scenarios and memories and know how they would act down to the wriggle of their toes?" She asked.

"Yeah…" I mumbled, having processed nothing.

"Well I find that comforting. Like, if I'm still thinking about him, if he's still reacting to situations and making actions in my head, is he really dead?"

"Huh?" I looked up, intrigued. "What do you mean?"

"Well a person is just a consciousness, which is just a mind reacting to situations, right? So, if I can simulate Dad in my head, has he really died? I reckon he's only gone when the last person stops thinking about him."

There was a silence between us. They were lovely words, but I wasn't sure what I really felt about them – and it certainly wasn't what I came here looking for.

"I still think about him." I said, and smiled at Simone. "So, I guess he's not gone yet."

"What are you looking for?" She asked me after a brief pause.

"One of his books…or it doesn't have to be the book I'm thinking of…" I trailed off, getting deep into the chest again. "I know Dad had a lot to do with the Argols, but what about *Suneva*. I know he said that word." I looked up to her as I explained. Her eyes lit up.

"What makes you ask about the Suneva?" she quizzed, leaning closer. "Did you see one?"

"See one? I don't even know what it means." I coughed, "I heard an Argol mention the word..." A lie, it was the other figure with the cyan eyes that mentioned *Suneva*, but it was easier to say that than to tell the whole story. "Has this got to do with the stuff you spend all day talking about?"

"Has it got to do with my blog?" She scoffed, mocking me. "James, do you even know what I write about?"

"Yes." I rolled my eyes. "Women's rights and ghosts. Where do Suneva fit into that?"

She eyed me blankly, offended. "James, how long has it been since you read my blog?"

"I only read it once, okay." I squirmed. Simone huffed, shaking her head.

"How am I meant to educate if the masses don't read..." She sighed to herself, then continued. "Look, if you're in trouble with the Argols, or seeing Suneva, I'd go to the police. It's not something you'd want to be investigating."

"What? Why not?" I asked. "Come on, you can't just say *that*." I crawled over to the attic entrance, pleading with her.

"It's dangerous." She stood her ground.

"But not too dangerous for you?" I asked. "I might be younger, but I've got about a foot and fifteen kilos on you. I can handle it."

Her lips were pursed, but her face was conflicted. I pleaded with my eyes, until she cracked.

"Fine, wait a minute." She huffed, slouching back onto the attic ladder and running off downstairs. As soon as she'd left me alone, I felt the room playing its tricks on me. The shadows were thick. They condensed in on me, squeezing out my air. I held my breath right up until Simone's blonde mop appeared under me, a little red book in hand.

"Hey!" I exclaimed. "That's what I've been looking for."

"This?" She quizzed, climbing the ladder. She seemed perplexed that I'd even thought of it as she handed the book to me. It was a small novel, with a red, hard cover painted in a fanciful illustration. It had a figure on the front of it, painted in glistening golden armour. The shape resembled the being I'd seen last night, at least from my memory of them. Only, this picture had purple eyes instead of cyan, and golden armour to replace the yellow.

"I think I saw this guy last night." I said, pointing.

"Impossible." Simone said. "That's the main character, and this is a fanciful ill-reported biography from hundreds of years ago. They're well dead."

"Well, *somebody* looked like this." I huffed.

"Then they were a Suneva." She said, her voice croaking. Simone was not fond of Suneva, I could sense the fire in her eyes. I didn't dare to ask why.

"What did you see last night, then?" Simone asked "Well, somebody like this guy." I pointed again. "But men in suits with flame throwers, too. Those are Argols, right?"

Simone chuckled, head shaking. "Those weren't flame throwers, James. They were *Suneva weapons* and *Suneva abilities*."

"So, Suneva carry around flame throwers?" I quizzed. "Why should I worry about some flame-thrower jerks? Just stand out of range." Simone sighed, raising a hand of frustration between us.

"No, James, they don't carry around flame throwers. Some of them *are* flame throwers." She enunciated slowly. "And even still, there's more about them past their abilities which is dangerous, and makes them dangerous to pursue."

"Explain." I crossed my arms. Her lips pursed.

"You know ghosts, right?" She started.

"Sure." *That's an odd place to start.* I hummed.

"Well, actually, that was a stupid place to start." She cleared her throat. "Suneva are people with very special *auras*..."

"Very special *auras*?"

"I said to bear with me." She squinted at me. I knew that this look meant that I had to sit down, shut up, and let her finish her rant, lest I violate our secret contract of belief.

"Okay, people with auras." I repeated, "So how does that manifest into flame throwers, or something I should worry about?"

"They used to have Empires, back in the ancient times. Now they run in gangs, and..."

"How come nobody has heard of them, then?" I interjected.

"Because they had to be sneaky, James."

"Why?"

"Would you just let me talk." She glared at me again with her dangerous stare. I shut up.

"They have powers, James, like, real magical powers through their auras. They've been using them for centuries in secret societies to subvert governments and benefit themselves. They're dangerous, untrustworthy and selfish oppressors."

"So, they have magical *political* powers." I chuckled. "Simone, I think you've been listening too hard to those whack-jobs on the internet. Secret societies I could get behind, but magical aura powers? That's ludicrous. How do you suppose that would work?"

"Suneva worship black holes, they say that they channel the energy of them through their souls."

"Black hole magic?" I rubbed my chin, "Well, Simone, that still sounds stupid."

"You know, James, you could be nicer." She said, "I mean, you *saw* it, didn't you? How would you explain the flame swords?"

"Easy, gas-powered flame swords. Not everything needs a supernatural explanation. You've been talking to too many die-hard *experts'*." I rebutted. Simone rolled her eyes, stepping down a rung on the ladder.

"Just read the book, wise guy." She patted the little, red cover. "It's even translated into English for you. How nice of them." She continued her descent, with a very happy Errol barking and wagging by her feet.

I turned to the book, inspecting the glossy, red cover. *Diaries of Kyros Orion Olomb* it was titled, in simple, black lettering. I turned to the first page, to find that the title page was glued to the rear of the hard cover. Looking closer, it appeared that leaking pen ink had stuck them together. Compelled to do so, I pried them apart with a satisfying *rip*.

"Hey!" A distant Simone shouted, and trudged to the base of the ladder. "What are you doing to *my* book?" She stormed up the frail rungs of the ladder, the wood moaning under her. Franticly, I droned over the now separated page. It had a penned message.

> '*Maiki,*
> *May this book help you on your journey of self-discovery.*
> *When you're ready, come and find me and I will help you further.*
> *Your Friend — Kuvalik*'

Just as I comprehended the final word, the book was snatched from my hands. Simone gave me a dirty eye, then turned to inspect the damage. Her face immediately flipped.

"Sickening." She frowned. "The oppressive bastards even claimed this book."

"Who?" I asked.

"Suneva, James." She said, deadpan. "Kuvalik is *in* this book, but he dies early on so it's not the same guy. That other name sounds Suneva, though, from the others

I've heard."

"Right." I smiled, taking the book back. She reluctantly handed it to me. "And where'd you say that you got this book?" I asked. "I thought it was Dad's."

"It was Dad's, but he gave it to me." She smiled, taking some odd pride from the fact. "I didn't say, though. We got it from Mr Finneck's garage sale, back before he went hermit."

"That's quite interesting." I nodded. Mr Finneck was somewhat of a Neighbourhood celebrity. Living at the butt of the street leading to the train station, he was the friendly old man whom everybody knew. He volunteered at the school events, and even did electrical work and gardening for those who asked. Everything he did, he did with a smile, right up until he no longer came out. Dad was particularly fond of the man, hiring him for some odd jobs.

"If you're going to check anything out, be careful." Simone said. "I feel bad enough that I told you anything. I mean, I post things about the Suneva and the supernatural online where there's anonymity. In real life, you're exposing yourself. If you try and uncover them, they might kill you. They don't care about equality, or rights."

"I'll be fine." I passed her off. "I'm not exposing anybody, only taking a look." Although, secretly, my enthusiasm to follow this up had waned. I wondered what I had really found myself pushed into here, and whether it was worth defying my gut and its compulsions leading me to do brave and stupid things. Talking to girls was kind of extreme for me, anyway. Now I was chasing the supernatural, with their supposed secret societies?

I eyed the book. It wanted me to read it.

***

In a short few weeks I was back at school. I'd tried to get on top of my homework, but procrastination hit me hard as I started to read *The Diaries of Kyros Orion Olomb*. I barely got my reading for English done. That said, I'd never *not* do my homework. I was too scared of failure to let my grades slip. What would teachers think if I started slacking off? No, I couldn't have that. I was *James Grey*, the teacher's pet and high achiever.

I hadn't talked to Natalie at all through the weeks after our encounter. I didn't get her number and hardly remembered her address through the ordeal. I hoped she was coping with it all, but I was excited to share my findings with her. We'd walked into a conspiracy theory, according to Simone. There were fallen Empires – one of which was *Olomb's* – and evil magic powers. Even with the *Diary*, I had a hard time believing it all. It was a fine story, nothing more. My fading memories of the swords had not convinced me otherwise, it seemed.

That said, the strange coincidence of it all had me thinking. I felt compelled to talk to Natalie. Together, we had discovered a crazy scene, and then just as I was looking for information about it, it fell into my lap. I had the *Diary* with me as I got on the train to school. I figured that trains and busses were good places to read a book. Natalie appeared on the platform one stop after mine. Her face lit up when she saw me through the carriage window. She rushed past the morning commuters over to where I was seated, and plonked herself down opposite me.

"Hey." I smiled. "Lovely to finally see you again." Natalie fumbled to scatter her bags on the floor. She had a backpack, a laptop bag, and a sports bag, all full to the point of breaking. How much stuff could one person need for a single day?

"Hey…" she replied, tearing open her school bag. The inside of it was like a filing cabinet, colour coded and perfectly placed. She pulled out a white book from the purple area, thick like a textbook, and handed it to me. The front cover had a symbol on it that I'd never seen before. It was a white circle encompassed by black, radial flames. It resembled the shape of a Christian cross, but with eight arms instead of four.

"This describes what we were looking at the other night." She said, skipping all pretence of *how were your weeks off?* I smiled, giddy. "They're…"

"Suneva, I know." I said, "My sister is a self-proclaimed expert. She runs a paranormal blog, and frequents a paranormal, political activist image board."

"Gee, that's a mix." Natalie commented. "Well, I found this in my *Yamitse's* library. I had to sneak in there to get it, and it's half written in another language, but it explains enough. Go to page forty-six." She instructed.

I flipped through the book to get to the right page. It was old, with yellowing, cracking pages, and littered in diagrams. The one on page forty-six caught my eye. It was of a three-ringed bullet of energy, just like the one I'd seen in the alleyway.

"*Quatra*." Natalie explained, noticing my gaze, "We saw that in the alleyway. The book says it's energy they take from black holes."

"Cheese." I flipped on further. "Well, it turns out that my sister isn't totally crazy. I mean, she was talking about black hole energy, but I didn't believe *her* exactly. But a book? With that bolt we saw?"

"I know." Natalie said, "I didn't believe it either until I saw the diagram. There's some crazy stuff in this text."

"I think you're right." I said. "And if this is some conspiracy, somebody has gone to great lengths to make an old book and spread around very convenient clues." I inspected the book further, flipping to the front. The publishing date was from the tenth of July, 1951. From the feel of the tome, I'd believe it. "Why'd you have to sneak into your grandma's library anyway?" I asked.

"Huh?" Natalie responded. "Oh, she doesn't like me reading her books. Not that I can read much of this one anyway. Half of it is in another language."

"Really?" I hummed, flipping through the book again. Surely enough, another language emerged halfway through, and slowly took over the text. The writing wasn't in any recognisable letters. They were made of simpler shapes, with sharper lines and bigger curves. In the other language section, there was a large, annotated diagram. It was the outline of a human body, filled with a web of veins stemming from the neck, down the arms and legs.

"That's creepy looking." I handed the book back to her.

"Yeah, I don't know what it's meant to be, but it sure is interesting." She smiled.

"I did my own research too, and I came up with this…" I said, digging through my bag. It was a mess, stuffed with sports clothes, already breaking books, and a half-opened pencil case. Natalie squirmed in her seat and edged away from the disordered mess as I pulled out my little red book. I handed it to her.

"Doesn't that look like the guy?" I said, pointing to the cover.

"Yeah, you're right." She said, "Although this guy is gold, not yellow. And the eyes are the wrong colour."

"Well, sure, but still remarkably similar." I repeated.

"Definitely." Natalie agreed.

"It doesn't look as helpful as your book, and the stories in it could be fiction, but it's got something even better than information. It's got a lead."

"Really?" Natalie's eyes lit up. She leaned in over me.

"Look at the first page." I instructed. She opened it up to the cursive message. "It's from one Suneva to another. I know where my sister and Dad bought the book, so maybe we can trace it back to this *Kuvalik*."

Natalie smiled excitedly. Her green-blue eyes glowed. She handed me back the book.

"So, we're a team then? We're going to follow this up?"

"Sure…" I responded. It was so easy to say yes in the moment, but my mind skipped back to Simone's warnings, and to the real danger we'd seen in the alleyway.

"This could be dangerous." I noted, "My sister told me that these guys are in government-controlling secret societies…"

Natalie stared at me quizzically. "Somehow, that sounds stupider to me than black-hole-magic." She noted.

"Fair enough." I laughed, although I didn't appreciate the dismissal.

"Look, James, I believe everything happens for a reason. I've been thinking about this all week. I know that maybe I'm getting ahead of myself, but we didn't stumble across all of this for nothing. We were meant to look this up."

"You're right." I followed immediately. "This wasn't for nothing." I didn't want to mention to her the compulsion that I felt to talk to her. I was scared that she'd take it as my romantic interest in her, and I honestly didn't feel that way. I didn't want to start the friendship off on a sour note – and I didn't want to seem crazy either.

Not that our current proposition wasn't crazy enough.

I had made my decision, and with it, I felt a familiar tingle at the base of my neck. Comforting, powerful warmth spread all over my body.

"Let's do this." I said, "Let's see where else the universe leads us."

Chapter 3
Into the Abyss

Simone's account of the Suneva might have seemed fanciful at best, but like I said, we had an agreement to listen to one another. Reading more of the diary, of the odd life of Kyros, a Suneva man convinced by a ghost to lead an army, made me think of how our pact started. It was the one story of mine which never hazed with time. It was probably the only thing I experienced firsthand over the course of months and still barely believed myself, even when suffering through it. I kept forgetting, strangely, that my life was far from normal, and that my experiences really should have prepared me for the outlandish concept that was the Suneva. The story on my mind was the tale of our haunting.

***

The long, black fingers of the ghost – like legs of spiders squirming from a funnel – wrapped themselves around the door of my cupboard. Tendrils of darkness, vessels of fear, I saw them from my bed and froze like ice.

I felt cold.

The air was solid around me. My muscles were strained – I couldn't move, let alone shiver. The fire of fear in my stomach fermented. I remember seeing figure and smelling the rotting flesh on its skin, and realising that the dead could walk.

There's something truly horrifying about a haunting – or at least, a series of events perceived as one. Growing up, hearing stories of my Dad and his heroics, there was always the sense that problems and fears could be overcome; solved either vocally or physically – with Dad's stories more often following the latter method. However, when the threat was dead, deceased, departed, no longer physical, no longer living by the laws of nature you'd come to understand, or by motivations you had come accustomed to knowing, how did you deal with it?

I used to dream about the ghost. My mother accused me of dreaming whenever I'd seen him in my room. He would hunt me in my sleep, invisible, chasing me through strange places which felt familiar. Sometimes in these dreams I could fly – but it would never work as expected, and I would always fall to earth at the worst times. The sky would tease me, begging me to leap into its embrace, and sail through its blue mist. When I woke, I felt that if I jumped into the air, I'd never come back down.

Dad entertained my fantasies. It was his idea to move house when we did – to the one with the ghost. He believed me, if only to let me get it off my chest and not bottle it up. He, however, could never offer a solution that seemed real to me. How did you get rid of something you couldn't touch?

I talked to Simone about what I was seeing. I was eleven, a young and impressionable boy. She was thirteen – old enough to feel that she was too cool to believe in ghosts, or talk to her younger brother. Her room had stopped being a shrine to pink, and was now a temple to the great Gods of the decade – grunge rock bands.

"James, I think Mum's right." She said to me; and she was a teenager, so she knew more things than I did. "A ghost sounds stupid. Plus, when it happens, you can't move and you don't yell. Unless you're stupid, that's what happens in dreams."

After that analysis of the situation, I felt immediately invalidated, and decided to keep it to myself. If half of my family wouldn't believe me, then who would?

I started school at Leslie Grammar soon after, and I stopped seeing the figure. Still, home felt oppressive. The house was never welcoming. It creaked, and it moaned, and even the best of its lights couldn't scare away the corners of darkness which lurked.

I stopped talking to my family about how I felt, and emotions started to bubble. My inability to make friends at my new school had me feeling worthless, and at home I felt so cramped. I would go to bed early, wake up late, and still be tired all day. I had the appetite of any young boy, and would eat to fill it, but started to lose weight. I became thin, badly so.

Beyond that, my grades started to suffer, and not even my fear of authority could lift them. My need to do well was barking at me, but through a sound-proof wall. I couldn't force myself to do anything about it, or do anything at all.

The doctor told my Mum it was depression – and for what reason a child could become depressed, none of them could suspect. I knew it was the house, and I knew that the label was wrong. The ghost was doing this. I didn't know how, but I did know that the best solution was to be out of the house – away from the people who didn't believe in what I was going through.

I joined a plethora of activities, much to the surprise of my parents who believed that I couldn't muster the motivation to do anything. I would leave the house well before school every day, and return home well after I was expected. I regained weight, and even started getting my first scrags of muscle. I made new friends and acquaintances, felt happier, and despite my lack of time to dedicate to school, improved my grades. Each day when I stepped back in the front door, I felt my energy drain immediately. The fires in my stomach, which glowed hot with joy, became awesomely smothered. Each day, I promised that I would spend less time at home on the next, planning to only come home to sleep.

Mum and Dad stifled these plans, although it wasn't because they were concerned. They saw that I was happy, and that I was doing well – they just wanted their son around and safe.

I came home early one day, when I was fourteen. Band had been cancelled, and I was forced to arrive home on time. As I approached the house, I could hear yelling coming from inside. It was Dad, he was in a rage, his fury burning through the air. I stopped short of the door, looking to the drive way. Only he was home, and Simone had debating on at school. I didn't particularly want to enter, as I didn't like being in the house at the best of times, but I resolved to see what the issue was. If nobody believed my stories, the least I could do was entertain their issues.

I opened the door. A large shadow had pooled in the corner of the kitchen which I could see from the hall. Dad hushed to the sound of the open door. The shadow scuttled away, like thousands of spiders running in each direction. Dad eased his way towards the hall, and poked his head around the corner.

"You're home early." He said, surprised.

"Yeah, for once." I replied. His face flushed red, but he spoke no further of what had happened.

That night, he and Mum were to leave for a weekend trip to Sydney with their friends. They were to leave us for two nights to fend for ourselves. The pantry was full of food – Mum was Italian, and never left a cupboard unstacked – so it was expected that we cook our own dinners.

Dad looked apprehensive to leave. He gave me a knowing, guilty look as he got into the taxi. He made sure many times to give me the number of the hotel they were staying in, and told me to ring if we needed to.

Later that night, Simone was chopping up vegetables in the kitchen. The kitchen bench overlooked the lounge area, with the couches, T.V and fireplace. I walked from the bathroom, hands meticulously washed, back to the kitchen to help. Simone was rocking out, her headphones blasting full volume grunge into her ears. She was dead to the world, lost in a sea of distorted guitar.

As I passed the couch, I noticed a whistle from the chimney. Air chimed as it came down. It was a strong wail, and by the window next to the fireplace, I could see that it was a completely still night outside. My eyes stayed locked to the bizarrely whistling fireplace.

There was a great whoosh. A harsh gust burst down the chimney. A cloud of ash, thick and dark, discharged into the room. The black flakes danced, but among them, ones burned red and orange hot. They looked to settle, floating, but did not fall. I continued to stare, stunned that they could stay afloat. A chilling cold came over my body – not imagined – and my skin bubbled into goosebumps. I managed to crane my head towards Simone. Her eyes were on the vegetables, oblivious.

"*James Grey.*" A garbled voice groaned, like an asthmatic growling through an oily rag. "*You thought you could run to escape me. I'll have my payment.*" The voice was coming from the ash cloud, but bouncing perfectly off every surface. The echo sustained as the cloud congealed. The particles span around each other, in a vortex. They stretched high, and then into a form. The orange embers glowed fiercely within the garbled silhouette of a man. They projected evil and malice.

I screamed. What more could I make myself do?

I screamed Simone's name, but only a forceful whisper could escape my lips. I yelled again – desperate for her to hear me. Again, my throat betrayed me. Hot breath flushed out of my mouth, carrying only an inkling of sound.

This only happens in dreams. I snapped to the thought. But when had I gone to sleep? I'd lived the full day – the entire, uneventful day. *No, it's not a dream.* I held to my convictions. *Mum is wrong, this is real. Simone will see it.*

"*Simone!*" I cried again, my head snapping to her position. Her headphones blasted into her ears, she hadn't looked up yet, and she didn't look up now.

"*Simone!*" I gave one last, desperate attempt. The hot ashes swirled into a grin.

I did the next most obvious thing – I ran. I leaped off one foot, turning to pounce away, and hung in the air between strides. I expected my left leg to come forward, to hit the ground, and stride me farther away, but it didn't happen. I commanded my leg forward – as fast as it could move – I needed to *sprint!* But there it hung, swinging like a rope through treacle. I hung in the air bizarrely, barely falling, and barely moving forward.

Like running in a dream. I realised as my foot finally crashed onto the floor. My step was frictionless. My foot slipped on the hardwood, getting me no further, with no haste at all.

I snapped my head back to the ghost – that I *could* do without hesitation – and he glared at me with glowing ashes. His smirk thickened, and his form charged.

My breath turned furnace hot as I gasped between useless steps. My neck was burning, a fire building and raging in the biggest bone at its base. *You couldn't feel this pain in a dream.*

I clasped at my neck, easily able to move my arm. The skin was hotter than red coals. I grabbed it harder, but the pain became so intense that my dumbly-paced legs gave up under me. Suddenly, I fell to the floor, at a pace which was regular, but now felt five times too quick. My head slammed onto the wood. Finally, Simone looked up.

"*James!*" She yelled. Her voice was full, and frightened – a real yell. She threw her headphones to the bench. I could hear her feet scrambling, but I couldn't open my eyes to look. I was in too much pain. Magma, born in the core of the earth, was charging through my bones. Radiating from my neck outwards. I crumbled on the floor, a mess of sensations.

Overhead, in the hallway, a calm breeze formed, then gusted. Simone fought it to get to me. It bellowed down the hallway of the house, despite the closed doors, and knocked a lamp from its perch. Porcelain rained as its stand hit the ground.

Unable to bear the heat in my body, I passed out.

I awoke on the grass. It was dark, and the sky above was clear. I could see the stars in the sky, smeared across it and twinkling innocently. Looking into the void of space made me cheerful. Space was full of possibilities. Stars so distant, yet holding so much potential. Unreachable.

And the moon, which as I focussed on it, I could see shone as a halo, rather than a disc or crescent. There was an eclipse of the moon.

Eclipse of the moon?

Hang on. I jolted upright. Simone jumped. She sat near me, on the grass in the backyard, shaking. The house's portable phone was clung to tightly in her black, ashy hand.

"James!" She shrieked, startled. "Oh thank *God.*" She sighed, "You're alive! You're alive…" She hugged me tightly, practically grappling me into the ground. I could see the halo moon now again. I'd seen it before, if only once, but I never realised the impossibility of it.

"Do you see it?" I asked. My words slurred, I must have sounded delirious.

"*Did I see it?*" She shrieked, shaking me upright. "James, I'll never disbelieve you again. *That's* what you've been seeing?"

"No, not the ghost." I said, limply hanging in her embrace. My head tilted upwards. "The moon…" I pointed, but as I looked again, it was normal. Just a crescent in the sky.

"James, that's just the moon – I'll admit, it's pretty." She said. "But James, that *demon*." She spat the word with such intent. "I called Uncle Antonio. He's coming to pick us up."

She shivered on the lawn. I wretched myself up, and felt my neck. It was still hot. *What happened?* I wondered. I glanced at the back window of the house, and although I didn't see the ghost, I knew he was in there. I could feel him.

Change is coming. I seemed to hear it in my head, like the wind whispered it to me. That's what the two moons meant. Life was about to change.

Only a day later, when Mum and Dad came home from their trip, did Dad announce that we were moving. Change – *but would it stop the haunting?*

Simone and I made our pact, on that night, whilst we waited for Uncle Antonio to arrive. We would always believe each other, and stand by each other, no matter how ludicrous the situation. Simone could believe me about my ghost, having seen it, so I vowed to take her word on the Suneva.

Chapter 4
The Great Stitch-Up

Chemistry was my favourite subject, and the one that I excelled at. There were a few factors which contributed to this. The first was that I didn't study for it, so I had no reason to hate it. The second being that Miss Gordon was, without a doubt, the best teacher I'd ever had in all of my schooling.

Miss Gordon was young, but cool by her own accord. She was easy to approach, empathised with our problems, and actually cared for the mental wellbeing of her students. The course she taught was tough, but she made it easy. Her diagrams were perfectly built for my brain, and her wording was always what made the concepts click. Ms Gordon also had a more extensive knowledge of comic books, literature, movies and pop-culture than any kid or teacher in the school.

So, in the second week of classes, when Miss Gordon walked into the room with her new engagement ring – its diamond's glimmer casting all the girls' eyes in envy, the biggest I'd ever seen – we all couldn't help but be excited and simultaneously disappointed that she wouldn't be our shared wife.

She was swamped by the girls in the class, who piled around her to get a glimpse at the mighty jewel in its golden perch. They launched their grubby hands upon it to feel the stone – with the permission on Miss Gordon – like a swarm of rats. Natalie, who was also in my Chemistry class, sat uninterested with the boys. I persuaded her to accompany me as I had a look.

I'd always loved diamonds. As a kid, going through shopping centres with Mum, I'd find my way to the jewellery stores just to stare at the glimmering stones. They were mesmerising, not just in the way that they looked, but the way that they *were*. There was something so *neat* about diamonds.

I crawled past the ravenous crowd of teenage romantics to the beautiful hand of Miss Gordon. I rubbed my anxious finger across the shining stone.

This wasn't a diamond.

"That's not a diamond." I said my thought aloud, without thinking about what I was saying. The lunatic crowd of women immediately stopped their mad raving to stare at me – their spirits shattered and a sense of rage built between them.

"What was that, James?" Miss Gordon asked sweetly, although she'd heard me loud and clear. My cheeks flushed red. All around me, teeth were borne, ready for my answer.

"That's not a diamond." I repeated, meekly. The crowd remained hushed. "You know, can't you feel it when you touch it? It's like the difference between a grey-lead pencil and a coloured pencil. It's missing that extra…kick…"

Evidently nobody had no idea what I was talking about.

"Why would you say that, James?" Susie, asked me. Suddenly the whole crowd was in an uproar. Natalie's girl senses kicked in, and she dragged me out from underneath the pile of screaming women and back into my seat. Ms Gordon's face went red.

"Leave him alone, girls." Miss Gordon said, "His magic finger might be wrong, but I'm not sure it is…" She shrunk into her shell. Everybody returned to their seats, but projected hate upon me with their scornful eyes. I felt guilty for the duration of class, and continued to feel guilty afterwards. I had to make it up to Miss Gordon. I could do something nice for her, to show her that I meant well.

"I don't quite understand what happened." Natalie said to me at recess. "How did you even know? Why would you say anything?"

"I don't know!" I whined. "On both counts, really." I sat down, defeated, on the wall of the quadrangle. Natalie sat up next to me. "I mean, don't you just *know* when a diamond is a diamond?"

"No…" Natalie quizzed.

"Come on, it's like how red is different to burgundy. It's just…it just *is*."

"Sure." Natalie hummed. "You are a strange boy, you know."

"Yes, strange things tend to happen to me." I agreed.

"Maybe you should make her a sorry card," Natalie suggested at recess, "Or a *happy engagement* one?"

"Or…" I pondered, "Do both, but leave it as a surprise for her. Like, a message when she opens her computer. Something she totally doesn't expect."

"That sounds difficult." Natalie mused, "Why would your mind jump to that idea first?"

"Because I saw it on a show last night." I said, reminiscing my night spent avoiding language homework, my feet nestled high in front of the television. Simone had even joined me, it was the first night in a while she'd spent out of the study – her nerd dungeon. "Except the boy left it for his crush…anyway, I'll make it up, then take the image to Tom. He'll figure it out."

I'd arranged to meet Tom in the school library's computer labs the next day at recess. I brought Natalie along with me as an opportunity to show her around the place. The library was in the north-east quarter of the senior-school block of buildings. A large, north facing glass wall opened the reading area to the light of day. In the windowless back section were the rows of computers. Tom sat in front of a computer, whose monitor faced the back wall, his red hair a mess and his tie only half done. He had with him a muscular boy with an ugly face and a serious attitude, Rhys Cameron. I begrudgingly made my way over to him – not wanting to walk within ten feet of Rhys.

"James," Tom greeted with open arms, "And you've bought the new girl. You know…" he addressed Natalie, "they're strict on the uniform, but not *that* strict. Although you wouldn't learn that from James."

I glanced over to Natalie. She wore her hair in a high ponytail, with a white branded, school ribbon. Her dress went down to the knee, not a millimetre higher. Her socks were pulled up. I guess I didn't even think it was odd. When I turned back to Tom, he pulled me in.

"I thought I told you to come alone, man." He whispered to me, becoming serious.

"I need to show her around. I thought you said it would just be you and me, what's *Rhys* doing here." I asked him, glaring.

"I get more than one business proposal in a day, Rhys is actually paying me." He winked. "Now," He said for Natalie to hear as well, "take a seat. I'm here to kill two birds with one stone, just sit back and relax."

Natalie and I pulled up a chair and gathered around the monitor. I made sure to stay on the opposite side of Tom from Rhys, and I kept Natalie the furthest from him. Tom rustled through his bag whilst Rhys and I eyed each other off in our peripherals.

"You know, James." Rhys said through his thin lips, "The girls want to tear you apart for how you embarrassed Miss Gordon. Them beating you up is about the most action you'll ever see."

"Shut up, Rhys." I groaned. "Why do you need Tom's help? Too thick to find where you've saved your files?"

Before Rhys could answer, Tom interjected, floppy disc in hand.

"Rhys might be computer illiterate, but so are you…compared to me." He said, "And he's payed me good money for something top secret." Tom inserted the disc into the drive. The computer buzzed, it's black command screen popping up and sprinting through thousands of lines of code.

"I wrote this myself. When this baby reboots, we'll be kicked into the admin side of the system. From there, we can get some *personal* information about a few select teacher's accounts, then reboot as them and alter some details."

"Wow, you wrote that yourself?" Natalie asked, "That's incredible."

"It's nothing for Tom." I said, "He's a buff at this stuff."

"Thanks, Nat. I try." He grinned, focussing on the lines of flying code. "Coding is better than insulting a teacher's engagement, or needing to fix your grades so you can look smart enough to play footy…"

"Hey!" Rhys hit him in the shoulder. Tom did not waver.

"Whoops, sorry man. Well hey, you could have just studied like everybody else and not made me risk my reputation. Not that I'll ever get caught doing this. The IT guys are totally hacks…not the good kind."

The computer screen turned black, and it rebooted. It logged straight into the admin side. From there, Tom went to two folders. The first was for Mr Whetherby, the second for Miss Gordon. In each, he executed some command, which caused more code to run down the screen.

"Okay, Rhys first, given he's the paying customer." Tom said, and executed one of the files he'd just created. The computer logged out and logged back in, this time through Mr Whetherby's account.

Tom searched through the files until he got to the grades for Mr Weatherby's Year Twelve English class. He opened the spreadsheet.

"I'm lucky that I'm only a few marks down." Rhys said, "I'm sure he won't notice a change in some of my class tests, or the essay."

"Whatever you say, man." Tom said, "We could even it out over a few teachers. It's easy enough to open their accounts."

"No, I only need three extra marks." Rhys said. "Just put one extra in the practice essay, and one in each of those prose analyses." He pointed to the files, as if Tom couldn't work out what he meant. Tom simply smiled and nodded.

"You're the boss." Tom said, and changed the marks accordingly. He noted the previous time of modification, and after saving the document, restored the modification date to its former value.

"Okay, that was easy. Now for you, James." He said, "Did you make your card? Were my instructions about paint clear enough."

"No need to condescend, friend." I said, and pulled my own disc from my bag. "I can make pixel art. It's right here." He plugged it into the secondary slot, and hacked his way over to Ms Gordon's account. He created an executable file which summoned the image, to open it when she opened her computer next.

"Somehow," He noted, "That was more difficult. Not by much." He grinned. "Have fun explaining how or *why* you made that one work when you next see Ms Gordon."

"It's a nice gesture, okay?" I huffed. "I saw it on T.V…"

"Far out, I just can't believe how well you did that." Natalie commented, interrupting my flawed logic. "Where did you learn?"

"I'm self-taught." Tom explained, "Just picked up some coding books one day and started to read. It's not that hard once you understand the language." He smiled, "Now, everybody scram discreetly. I'll clean up this operation, but we've already drawn enough attention."

Natalie and I headed out after Rhys. Rhys bumped me on the way through the door, but thankfully neither of us exchanged words. We walked off into the rest of our recess.

At lunchtime, Natalie and I returned to the computers. We'd agreed to meet and research.

"We should use the internet whilst we have access to it." She said to me during physics, "And see if we can find out anything about *Suneva* from it."

"I've got internet access at home." I said, "And my sister can tell you *all* about the internet's opinion. It's not great."

"Well, I don't" Natalie retorted, whispering as we drew the attention of the teacher, "And you've probably taken a *boy look*. Let me do some searching,"

We walked swiftly into the library, tucked our sandwiches into our clothing, and logged in on one of the furthest computers. I opened Internet Explorer before Natalie pushed me aside and took command of the keyboard. She directed the buzzing, boiling circuits of Windows 98 towards Yahoo, and wrote in the search bar "*Suneva*". She hit enter.

"That's totally a boy look. That's what I would have done." I protested. She stuck her tongue out at me and we waited for it to load. I set a piece of paper and pencil in front of me while the browser loaded, and I started a drawing.

Only one result pinged onto the fresh screen. It was *fairysmogsblog.org*.

"One result?" Natalie remarked.

"And what do you know, it's that site my sister goes on." I smugly grinned, "Told you that's all we'd find."

"Okay, fine. It's still worth the exploration." Natalie said. She clicked on the page.

It opened into an image board layout. There were multiple threads visible on the first page, and a lot of room to scroll down. Along the top there were links to hosted boards: *Paranormal, Ghosts, Demons, Communism, Alt-Left, Progressive Opinion, Women's Rights, Suneva.*

Down the left some were other page categories. We were on *discussion forum*, but there was also *fairysmog's blog* and *writer's blogs*.

I took control of the mouse.

"*Hey…*" Natalie protested. I clicked on the *writer's blogs* links, and was taken to a page with a few streams of text split by columns. On the left-most column was an article dated the 2nd of February 1998, by user *Simone23*.

"See, I told you this is the place Simone visits. There's her blog." I pointed to the username.

"That's great." Natalie said, "But I don't think a daily blog will help us. I saw a link before that said *Suneva*. Let's look at that." She stole the mouse from under my hand and clicked on the link to the top right of the screen. There was another minute of load time, in which I got a little further through my drawing, until the *Suneva* image board came up.

There was a paragraph of text titled *Board Sticky – Read Me First* which took up most of the screen. Under that there was a picture of a weapon on a table, taken with an offensive level of camera flash, with some comment next to it. The sticky read:

Welcome to fairysmogsblog.org/suneva. Here we discuss sightings, meetings, attitudes, and all things Suneva.

We absolutely do not encourage anybody to find Suneva in real life. Suneva are dangerous by nature. They eject energy in the scale of terawatts, able to turn your body from flesh into gas. They tout high morals, but very rarely show them. Suneva have proven to be arrogant, condescending, racist and vigilant in discussion. They very rarely see the harm that they do to others through their intimidation. Be warned, and stay safe.

Fairysmog.

Natalie scrolled down as I was still finishing the last line. In the centre of the browser now was the first thread, the one with the bad photograph. The first comment said:

>*found this*
>*what is it*
And there was a reply:
>*Suneva weapon, do not touch, it could shred ur hands.*
>*Or do. That would be funnier. Post pics.*

"Gee, this doesn't seem so innocent." I said, "Did you read the level of vitriol in that sticky note?"

"It's bullshit." Natalie said confidently, "I don't believe it. I won't base my opinion on some…on some ghost-hunting political activists."

Inside I fumed. Natalie might have known something about political activism, but I'd had my haunting experience. I wasn't so readily able to throw aside somebody's opinion based on their belief in the paranormal.

"Well, they sure seem to have more experience than we do." I noted.

"As if." Natalie let the notion slide, "These people rake forums all day. They probably live in their mum's basement.

She closed the browser, stopping me from reading anything further. "Let's not worry about this. I think we need to follow your lead."

"Don't throw these people's opinions aside so easily." I said, passing *her* off this time. "They're all saying the same thing."

"Single minded groups have circular knowledge spread, James." She said bluntly. "One idea exists and soon they all follow it. Outsiders get shunned. That's how in-groups work. I wouldn't take their word too seriously."

Fair enough. I muttered to myself. She was right. "What about what we saw in the alley, then? I'd say it verifies the in-group."

"You can't pin the actions of a few on the attitudes of many, James. That's just bigoted logic."

"You're just full of good points." I smirked. I didn't know how to rebut that.

"Look, based on my *Yamitse's* book, there's more history to the Suneva than some modern gang fighting. I don't believe that we're putting ourselves in danger. They seem more like hippies, from what I read."

"Hippies, really?" I chuckled. "You'll have to show me what you read."

"That'll be next, after we follow your lead." She smiled.

"Right." I remembered. "My lead, the Kuvalik guy, and Mr Finneck to get to him."

"That's the one." She said. "I'm in if you are."

"You can count on me." I smiled back to her.

***

"Now, despite the overall positive theme of this week's assembly, I do have some serious trouble for one student." Mr Dempsey, the principal of Leslie Grammar, spoke. His voice turned coarse as he pretended to sound angry – like a man choking on his own vocal chords and whatever wisps of hair sat upon his head. "We've had a very *serious* incident, where our IT systems were compromised by a student, and grade values were altered. We know it was a student, and if they do not come forward to us in the next ten minutes, all of you will lose access to the computers this term."

There was a resounding wail and moan amongst everybody in the senior school assembly. Mr Dempsey, a small, yet commanding, and incredibly politically-incorrect man, stood with his disapproving gaze. He eyed the crowd, but specifically lingered over Tom, David, Natalie and I, who sat next to each other. Against all good judgements, the force of disapproval got to me, and my eyes widened with guilt as he glared over us. I could tell that he caught my signal.

Other students continued to mumble.

"We didn't do it!" One student said loudly, "Why the hell do we get punished?" The question was left unanswered. Mr Dempsey continued to gloss the room over smugly.

"I think I have to stand." Tom whispered to me, "He has to know I did it. I can't let everybody down."

"Are you sure, dude? I can't imagine what shit you'll get in."

"I kept my receipt with Rhys." He said, "I made him sign a contract. He's coming down with my sinking ship, don't worry."

"Dude, really…we can all take this punishment for you."

"That's selfish, and stupid." Tom said. He handed me his jumper and song book so he could stand.

In the other corner of the room, on the raised section of seats, Rhys Cameron stood up. There was a gasp from the audience. Mr Dempsey was taken by surprise.

"Rhys?" He questioned, in genuine astonishment.

"It was James Grey." Rhys pointed down to me. "I saw him do it."

All eyes in the room turned to me.

"What?" I burst, not standing. I craned myself around to face Rhys. "That's…that's…"

Tom stood up.

"I did it." Tom said, "Rhys paid me to change his grades. He was too dumb to make the footy team."

"Hey, what the hell!" Rhys shouted down from his podium. Tom shrugged back at him. "James can barely log onto a computer, let alone write code. I hacked the system."

Tom wore a smug, satisfied grin. He put his hands on his hips and absorbed the silent accolade of his peers for his programming abilities. I turned back to look at a very angry Rhys Cameron. He was not happy with Tom and I at all.

"Tom Cory and Rhys Cameron, the two of you will come with me to my office immediately after this assembly, is that understood?"

Tom saluted the principal, then took his seat again. Rhys begrudgingly nodded and depressed into his chair.

Natalie, David and I waited for Tom outside the principal's office. We took up all of the chairs by his door, sitting in silence in an attempt to eavesdrop. Feet shuffled and footsteps came to the door. We quickly jostled into position to pretend to be talking instead of listening. The door opened, and the two IT techs came out followed by Tom. Tom closed the door behind himself. Rhys was not let out just yet.

"How was it, man?" David asked, "I don't know how you fessed up to that Mr Dempsey is a scary man."

"It was fine." He smiled, putting his hands on his hips, "Nothing gets good ole' Tom Cory down."

"So, what's the verdict? Suspension?" David asked.

"Nah, just a detention." Tom smiled, "I made a deal. They could have my code to see where they went wrong and fix their system, and for this, I'd just get a detention."

"What about Rhys?" I asked.

"Oh, he's in *deep* shit." Tom chuckled. "He hired me to do it. He's not playing any football this season."

"Oh, that's so satisfying." I squealed. "But, hey. If you gave them your hack does that mean you'll never be able to get back into the system?"

Tom slyly grinned. He looked the hallway up and down, and even though it was empty, still ushered us off the chairs and walked away. Once we were a fair distance from the office, and totally silent, he pulled out his disc pouch from his bag.

"You don't think I'm prepared for that, James? Then you underestimate me." He pulled out the floppy disc he'd inserted into the computer earlier. "A good magician never reveals his tricks. In fact, this magician just gave them the wrong code so he could implant more ways to bypass their system. But, this time, they'll never detect me."

His grin was enormous. He slotted the floppy disc away and swung his bag around onto his back.

"You are a genius, man." David said.

"Tell me something I don't know, dude." Tom winked. We all walked off together to get lunch.

Chapter 5
The Girl and The Agent

Celeste ran into the dark storage room. There were stacks of crates on either side of a narrow corridor, bordered by a perimeter walkway. She slipped down the centre aisle, cast in the green glow of the exit sign, and skidded to a halt behind the cover of the last stack of boxes. She didn't dare look back to the door.

She caught her breath, and pulled a list from the pocket of her skirt. She crossed out the next two names in line, adding them to the collection of expended contacts. *Only two names left.* She thought to herself, *Why couldn't the old man write any faster?*

Celeste felt the *quatra* energy as it coursed through her veins. It came from her thread, the connection between her body and her black hole, *Veritas*. The energy pooled in her hands, begging her to use it. It gave her the power to extend her influence on the world. It would not help her right now. Her attacker didn't need sight to find her, they could sense the energy in her body, and this would be her downfall. She shut out the sensation of *quatra*, meditating through her nerves.

The entrance doorway opened – moonlight spilling into the room. She gasped, softly, and resisted the temptation to look. She heard it creak shut, and she heard the metal footsteps of her stalker. They clanked on the concrete floor, edging up the left-hand walkway.

Her mind buzzed. She could feel her heart thumping in her chest and through her throat. The energy of the black hole pooled again in her hands, but this time by her command. She could stay here in fear and hope that the attacker didn't find her, or she could use the power she was given by the universe to fend them off as she ran again.

Running. Always running.

The shadows of her attacker's long talons were thrown across the left wall, cast in a corona of green light. Celeste watched the blackness stalk closer from the corner of her eye.

Before she saw the attack, she could feel it in her soul. A bolt of bright indigo quatra – a bullet of energy surrounded by three rings – illuminated the room in dazzling light. Celeste extended her left hand to the attack, absorbing the energy through the veins in her arm. She passed the bolt through her torso, and out her other arm, into the ground. It dissipated into the concrete – it's three glowing rings spreading out radially, melting and bubbling the concrete, until their light died. She leaped to her feet.

Celeste stared down the barrel of her attacker's weapon – an umbrella, with a glowing purple end. The attacker stood tall. Their glowing eyes hidden behind a floppy hat, and their metal form covered by a long trench coat – the only hint of their Suneva power being their bold, energetic presence and their metal, high-heeled feet.

"I didn't expect Iva Argol to be so easy to catch." They said. Their voice ran silky and sultry. They advanced on Celeste. "I also didn't expect you to run so easily. You have a reputation…"

"Iva Argol *isn't* this easy to catch." Celeste spat in her thick, French accent. She flicked her wrist and her sword was thrown into existence. Its blue hilt rested snugly in her grasp. Its tip extended, growing from the hilt to meet the butt of the umbrella. "You found *me*, not her. But you'll *wish* that you did find Iva Argol, because I'm the *Ivaer* who built her reputation…"

Celeste felt her soul's grip, and using quatra from the black hole *Veritas*, she powered it. Her crimson lips grinned. From her free hand erupted a plume of dazzling blue fire. She swung the tendrils of hot, dripping plasma at the Umbrella Lady. The fire was the extension of her powered soul – her connection to the universe. The surrounding boxes burst spectacularly into flames. Black smoke amassed quickly, burning bright over blue light.

The Umbrella Lady stumbled against the heat of the attack and was blinded by smoke. Celeste kicked off the floor, and launched herself into the centre clearing. She swung herself around the corner crate, sending it toppling into the opening. *A good tripping hazard*, she thought.

She sprinted towards the green light of the exit sign. Plumes of thick smoke creeped behind her. A bolt of indigo quatra – that she had not sensed through her adrenaline – zipped past her head, singeing her chestnut hair.

She threw her hand backwards, and fired a bolt of her own, blue, quatra. It hopelessly missed, she could tell, as she hadn't aimed it. Another indigo one came, but she sensed it, and dropped to the floor, letting it fly overhead.

She rolled on the concrete and sprung back to her feet. The footsteps behind her were close, and the door was still seconds away. Her mind panicked, but she had one last idea.

She summoned quatra energy in both of her hands, and using it to manipulate her soul beyond her body, blasted jets of hot, blue fire from her palm and sword. She painted the aisle of boxes in thick, deadly flames. The jets reached far across the clearing. Immediately, the smoke in the room thickened, and obscured all sight. The room was an oven. A Suneva could sweat through their armour in this.

Celeste lunged at the door, and threw herself out of it. She slammed it shut behind her, and took a tiny, intense flame to the door's lock. The Umbrella Lady charged down the aisle on the other side. Her footsteps rang into this hallway. Her body thudded against the door, which bowled Celeste over in fright. She dropped her sword as she fell, but recovered herself. Curiosity kept her from running. The doorhandle jiggled, then shook violently. They pounded their fists on the door.

Melting the lock can't hold them forever. Celeste realised, as the door shook so violently, that it might give way. She sprinted down this hallway, and through the front door.

She burst out into the busy night-life streets of Melbourne city. People bustled in the large crowds, moving like a river along the sidewalk. She put her sword back where it had come from, and ran into a taxi. She handed the driver the list from her pocket, with the two uncrossed names and their address. He could take her to safety.

***

An Argol gang member was strapped into a chair in a white room. The chair was bulky and metal, like a dentist's chair, and the straps were thick and made of dark leather. The man, tall and strong, banged against the restraints. His hair, wet from sweat, slapped his face as he struggled to free himself.

Just weeks ago, he was ambushed in an alley by agents of *Fara Hesslik*, Suneva from *The Empire of the Black Suns*, but he had escaped. Their trackers were good, better than any he'd ever seen. They'd found him, they'd captured him again, and when he had woken from his drugged stupor, he was in this chair.

He yelled into the void beyond him. His thread – the connection between he and his black hole – had been neutralised. He could not draw on its power to get him out of here.

Next to him, on a metal surgery bench, was an array of space-aged looking instruments and life monitors. The wall in front of him was made of one-way mirrors, and on the left side of the wall was a bulky metal door. It's lock clacked, and it opened.

An armoured figure emerged from the opening. The light shone off their metal plating, of colours silver, teal and gold. Their joints were inhumanly thin, and their fingers long and gangly. Their helmet looked eternally angry, with two, green glowing eyes and a triangular grille where the mouth would be. Two pipes extended from it to a tank on their back. They strutted over to the constrained man, and stood before him in a power stance.

"*Vestas!*" The Argol man groaned, "Argol will hear about this…fuck it, *Hesslik* will hear about this."

"*Fara* Hesslik approved this." Vestas retorted in his posh voice. "One way or the other, you will be a useful Suneva to the cause of your *brothers and sisters*. So far your actions under Argol and his lead have eventuated in the separation of *our people* from society. I'm giving you a chance to change. You can switch your allegiance to Hesslik and the Empire – who will do *good* for Suneva relations – or you can protest and I will use you for my studies. Either way, you further the advancement of Hesslik's cause. Choose wisely."

"I know what you do." The Argol man spat, "Don't hide behind a veil of moral good. I'll never bow to a bunch of pushovers like you."

"You'll regret that." Vestas warned. "But I suppose you'll do more good for us like this. You can't imagine the technological advancements I'll make from the data in your thread…" The Suneva went to pick up one of the instruments – a thick white device with two probes on a spinning head.

"Where's Olomb?" The Argol gangster asked. "He wasn't mad like you nuts – he was a reasonable leader."

Vestas laughed, revving the device by pulling its trigger.

"Olomb was a coward, and a traitor to the Suneva people." He said, "He led us here when he gave up on his position, and Argol picked up the pieces of Suneva society and drove our name into the ground. Hesslik is the only hope for good Suneva in the world, and he's doing better things for the *Empire of the Black Suns* than any Suneva could. It's because of people like you that we're hated, and that a bigoted idiot with a name like *Fairysmog* has credibility."

Vestas reached for the man's shirt with his long, cold fingers. He delicately unbuttoned it as the man squirmed under his grasp. From the life monitor, he affixed eight cold sensor pads to the man's chest. The computer sparked with signals. Then, with the spinning device in hand, he walked around the table and behind the man. Vestas pointed the device, with its rotating, flaccid prongs, at the biggest bone in the man's neck. The Argol man wriggled against the constraints. Vestas grabbed the man's throat with his creepy fingers. They pressed on his flesh.

The door opened, Vestas lowered the instrument. *The Umbrella Lady* stepped into the room. She stood her umbrella near the door, and hung her coat and hat on a nearby hook. Their armoured body was minimalistic. It was highly mechanical, and all made of shining silver plates. On her smooth head, usually hidden by her floppy hat, were eight small, purple eyes.

"Ah, *Tona Narsus*, come in." Vestas instructed. "You're just in time to witness the data collection."

"I've got news for you, Vestas." She said, pausing close to the door. She eyed Vestas and his tools with disgust. Her voice, to Vestas, could only be described as sensual. He had to put down the instrument to concentrate.

"News?" He inquired; finally finding his words.

"Iva Argol is in Melbourne. I've been tracking her."

"You mean, *the* Iva Argol? The lost daughter of the *Green Dragon* himself, *Naxaer Argol.*"

"Exactly." She stated. "The child claims not to be Iva Argol, but then, how often does a real fugitive accept their title?" She strutted towards Vestas now that he'd dropped the odd implement, her footsteps calculated to twist her metal hips, her heels clacking. She stopped just before the chair.

"And there's more. I came across the signals of two new, somewhat strange Suneva. One of them seemed quite powerful. I think you'd find them of extremely interesting to study."

"Yes, of course." Vestas was sweating through his armour. "And, Iva Argol too. Not only would a Suneva of *that* blood line provide some brilliant data points, but she would fetch us a good sum of money with Argol himself. Do you know the bounty on her head?"

"I know it." The Umbrella Lady spoke.

"Good." Vestas composed himself. "Bring the three Suneva back to me, then. As soon as you can. I'd be keenly interested in them all."

"As you wish." She said. She turned to leave, then paused.

"What about the other Argols from the alley?" She asked.

"Don't worry." Vestas smiled through his helmet. "I have *Lion's Foot* on them. He gets results."

Whilst Vestas had been preparing his victim, a Suneva covered in bronze and iron coloured armour, with gleaming red eyes, had walked out the front door of the Empire compound. He was tall and incredibly bulky; the face of his helmet was flat, and unemotive. They did not like what Vestas did to the Argols they bought back. They never stayed around to witness the studies.

The bronze Suneva stepped into the carpark. They removed their armour and donned their riding leathers, making sure to store their heavy, iron chain under the hulking black jacket. They put on their helmet – a matt black mushroom helmet with full face mask, and mounted their vintage racer bike. Its single headlamp burned the road alight as the bike's engine roared into life. The bronze Suneva, known as *Lion's Foot,* dropped the beast into gear and ran it through the backstreets.

Vestas had a tip-off midweek to the location of a fugitive Argol. The Empire had a vast network of Suneva in Melbourne who would submit tips, and Vestas had designed his own frequency scanner devices to intercept law-enforcement chatter. The combined information told *Lion's Foot* that the fugitive would be in the container fields by the docks. Once there, *Lion's Foot* would have to sense the Argol's presence to track him down. All Suneva could, at some level, connect to the quatra field which permeated everything. Suneva left signals in the field when they used quatra, and these could be detected to track a Suneva's movements. If they were smart, this Argol man would not be using any quatra, but *Lion's Foot* didn't take him for a thinking man.

His bike raced past the city and its late-night lights. The lines of colour smeared across his helmet as he soared past the glowing silhouette of Melbourne's skyline. He reached a sea of containers, stacked into high towers right by the dockside. He slalomed his steel horse between the high-piles of metal boxes, under cranes and beneath the purple, moon-lit night. He could sense the man here. They were using their abilities, without care for who might feel their presence. He followed their trail to a contractor's hut in the centre of the dockyard.

He parked the bike behind the nearby rolling crane, and strutted his way over to the building. Stealth wasn't the Bronze Suneva's greatest asset. He subsequently didn't bother to try. He was revered by Hesslik for his efficiency.

There were multiple men in the shack, and they felt a disturbance all together at once. *Lion's Foot* could see them shuffling around through the window. One man peeked out of the blinds, throwing lines of yellow light across the Bronze Suneva's motorbike helmet. *Lion's Foot* reached behind his neck, and pulled out the iron chain he'd stored in his leather jacket.

The peeping man yelped in surprise. His eyes bulged, he manically pawed at the blinds to make them shut. The men scattered around the room – a storm of panic. Glass smashed, metal fell from tables. The Bronze Suneva smiled – this man was frantic.

The Argol man squabbled for the door, falling out of the contractor's hut with a polished, wooden staff in hand. This was the man from the alley.

"I heard you work for Argol." *Lion's Foot* said in his modulated voice.

"Yeah, I do." The man croaked. He cracked the wooden staff against the ground. Sparks of electricity sprayed off on impact. A constant arc crackled from the pole's end into the asphalt. "What's it to you?"

Lion's Foot remained silent. The chain unfurled in his hand, snaking onto the ground.

"Get out of here before this gets serious." The Argol member warned. The bronze Suneva once again did not speak. He tightened his grip on the chain's links in his hand.

The mobster shouted. He raised his staff and blew a bolt of green quatra from its end. The Bronze Suneva raised his left hand to the bolt. He absorbed it through his arm, and directed it away from his head, through his torso, and out through the chain.

The mobster's wooden staff erupted with sparks of electricity, forming an arc of blinding plasma. It cracked through the air towards *Lion's Foot*.

Quatra flowed into *Lion's Foot's* body, and he used it to extend his soul's reach into the earth before him. He could sense the shadow of his hand extend beyond his physical limits, and anchor into the asphalt. *Lion's Foot* braced, grappling at the ground, and heaved upwards. The asphalt between the two men breached the road surface, erupting from the ground to form a rocky wall. The violent lightning was absorbed into the earthen stack.

With a push of his influence, *Lion's Foot* sent the dislodged wall of road hurtling towards the Argol mobster. They rolled out of the way, and tried to stand, but were thrown off their feet when the mass of rock smashed behind them.

Lion's Foot tensed his grip on the chain. Through his soul's connection to it, he could feel every atom of iron in every link. He could control their position in space, and the bonds between them. He cracked the long chain like a deadly whip. It smashed against the asphalt, then hovered in the air at his soul's command. The Argol man finally got to his feet, and stared at the floating metal linkage with terror.

Lion's Foot cracked it again. This time, it lunged and whipped around the man. The linkages of the chain tied the mobster's hands to his sides. He dropped his wooden staff, and fell to his knees, squirming to break free.

Lion's Foot strolled over to the man, who lay constricted in the metal python. He raised a casual hand to the man's head and commanded a bolt of quatra energy through his arm. The red, three-ringed bullet emerged from his left hand and hit the mobster in the back of the neck - where the thread to his black hole connected to his body. The staff on the floor shattered and sublimated as the foreign energy was absorbed by the man. His thread was neutralised.

Lion's Foot loaded the man onto the back of his motorcycle. He took the man back to Vestas.

I called Natalie after dinner on the day that Tom got into trouble. It was always a nerve wracking experience calling somebody's phone, especially around dinner time. You never knew who would answer it, and how angry they would be that they'd just sat down to eat and you'd rudely interrupted them. The dial tone kept buzzing into my ear. I considered hanging up the phone, and pulled it away from my face when a voice come through.

"*Yassas.*" A croaky voice rang through the receiver. It had a strong accent, much like my Baba used to sound when I remembered to ring her. *I really must ring her*, I felt a stab of guilt. The voice I heard was jubilant to be answering a call, much to my elation.

"Oh, *hello.*" I said, hoping for dear life that I'd gotten the number right. "My name is James Grey, a friend of Natalie. Is she there?"

"Eh, you want-eh Natalie, eh?" The only lady chuckled. "Yis, I will get her."

"Thank you." I smiled into the phone. I became aware that I was trying to look polite into the phone, and immediately stopped.

"Natalie, there is handsome sounding man in the phone for you." The old lady shouted into the house, loud enough that I could hear it.

"*Yamiste!*" Natalie yelled back, clearly embarrassed. The phone shuffled between hands, and finally I could hear Natalie's breath. It took her a few tries to catch it before she could speak.

"Hello?" She called into the device.

"Hi Nat, it's James." I smiled again into the phone.

"Oh, *James.* Why didn't you tell my *Yamitse* that?"

"What? I did. I didn't tell her I was handsome! She came up with that on her own."

"Oh, poor James." She cooed, "Anyway, what's up?"

"Well," I started, "There's a party on this weekend, for Freddy Gold, not sure if you've met him…"

"I have…" She replied begrudgingly. I think I remembered their introduction, too. It would have been at the first school assembly. He'd leered at her from the impressive perch awarded by his inhuman height and slouched, sloth-like posture. His eyes glazed with sleaze, he'd tried to ask her on a date right then and there, without more than an introductory sentence. Natalie's face had quivered in response, its muscles uncertain whether to set on disgust or offence. Instead of walking away, she called him a caveman right to his face. He only rolled his eye to the attack, lumbering his massive, towering body away from the scene. I cringed at the awkward memory, laughing nervously into the receiver. "Oh, well I asked if I could bring you along. Did you want to come along?"

"I wouldn't have accepted *his* invitation." Natalie growled, "But I can't refuse yours."

"Not his biggest fan?" I bit my lip.

"He didn't really prove himself a gentleman, when I met him."

"Yeah, he's a dick." I agreed, "Or, just oblivious - but he throws a good party. I'll pick you up after dinner on Saturday."

I'd have withheld higher moral standards and refused Freddy's invitation myself, but a party was a party, and it was nice to get invited. I couldn't speak for liking crowds, but I'd never give dancing a miss, nor a chance to hang out with friends.

Admittedly, I asked Natalie to come before I asked Mum if I could go. I approached her about it that night. She was in the kitchen, slaving over the hot stove as if cliché was in her job description. I felt guilty. I never asked Mum for much, and I always felt bad asking for *anything*. I meagrely approached.

"Hey, Mum…?" I inquired as I rounded the corner. She peered up from a pile of chopped tomatoes.

"Oh, there's my son!" Mum joked, turning back to the tomatoes, "I'll call off the police search, we finally found you."

I rolled my eyes. Mum could sense when I did this. It triggered the automatic response of gravitating her fists to her hips.

"Well, James, I never see you at home. You're always out, always busy. When will you have time for your mother?" She asked. "Sometimes I think that when you move out – and don't do that to my heart just yet – that you'll forget to visit."

Mum's clairvoyance knew no bounds. I cringed.

"Yeah, okay, so I'm not around much." I laughed nervously. I felt even guiltier now. "But if *you* didn't go out every Sunday night, when I'm home, maybe you'd see more of me."

Mum grumbled, her whole face frowning. I felt my soul retreat into my gut, face grinning stupidly. I'd called her out, and somehow hadn't expected her to get annoyed by it.

"You know that I'm out every Sunday, James. Sunday night drinks are a weekly tradition. But you? You never tell anybody where you are, or where you're going, you just never happen to be around." She paused, radiating her dissatisfaction. I winced, preparing to speak, when she bulldozed over the silence. "I mean, it's *okay* because you never get into trouble, and you've never tried anything remotely adventurous in your life, but I'd like to know your movements, is all. Think of my heart."

I pursed my lips, my own heart weighing on me. I'd almost have turned around and refused Freddy's invitation there and then, so not to disappoint my mother, but my requirement to dance in the week, and my commitment to take Natalie to this party, selfishly outweighed my need to impress my mother.

"That's why I thought I'd tell you, then, that I'm going to a party on Saturday…" I said, sheepishly. Mum tilted her head to me. "I mean, *can* I go to a party this Saturday?"

Mum huffed, but turned back to her chopping board. "When would I say no to that?" She asked.

"Probably now, if ever." I coughed. "You just told me that you hated me being out!"

"I hate you being out and not knowing where you are." She clarified. "It's fine if you tell me, James. Plus, I like knowing that you're having fun, Lord knows you need more of it. It's better than your sister, who's always on that damned computer. Where are her party invitations?"

"I don't know that the friends she has would throw the best parties." I squirmed. I still wasn't sure how to feel now. Mum had told me not to feel bad about it, that I'd done the right thing by her, but I still felt like a disappointment. Her shunning was effective.

"You're probably right." Mum hummed, nodding. "Weirdos on the internet. Anyway, if you're taking drinks, there's some in the fridge. You can take six cans, but I don't want you having more than that."

"You think I'll get through six?" I coughed. "How big do you think my stomach is?"

"That's a lot to you?" She chuckled, laughing for the first time. "Oh well, take less, that's fine by me."

"Thanks Mum." I smiled, I went in for the hug, wrapping my arms around her. I could feel her smile as she leaned into it.

"How many more of these parties are coming up, anyway? When should I schedule in our next meeting?" She asked, returning to cutting vegetables through my embrace.

"I don't know." I said, "I'll let you know when I do."

"Good." She said. "I look forward to conferring with your secretary on them."

I huffed a chuckle. There was work to be done, but I didn't move to do it. Instead, I stayed by Mum, chatting all the way past dinner.

***

On Saturday night, Mum agreed to play the part of taxi-driver.

Our car pulled up outside Natalie's house – a respectable red-brick cottage. The upstairs balcony and the front fence held a railing supported by white columns; over the windows hung those classic, faded green and yellow sun shades. In the middle of the garden, behind rows of knee high hedges protecting a herb patch, was a sandstone water fountain. The noises of the trickling stream bounced off the bricks and created a peaceful aura. It was a classic Greek household.

I stepped up from the garden to the balcony and banged on the heavy wooden door. After the sound of footsteps across carpet, Natalie opened the door and hugged me hello. She looked very nice, with white semi-platforms and a modest-length, flowy, floral summer dress. Her hair was left long and wavy. I wasn't sure if I was meant to tell her that she looked pretty. She could have taken it the wrong way.

"You look nice," I said it anyway and gave a friendly smile.

"Thanks." she said and smiled back the same way. "So do you."

I was wearing a tight shirt, a colourful bomber jacket, and black jeans. This was a classic combination for me - mainly because I hadn't gone out to buy new clothes in a while.

I walked her down the pathway to Mum's car. They made pleasant introductions, and we drove small talking between the three of us. On the way to the party we packed the car to the brim, with Tom and David getting a lift also. It was the party car.

We got there at a fashionable time, not too early but just on the border of the first hour. This caused Natalie to sit like a board in the car, almost to the point of an aneurism, but it was David's request that we be *'fashionably late'*.

We entered Freddy Gold's house through the open door. The music was blasting outside, and nobody seemed to be hanging out in the house itself. We walked down the long hall, out into the kitchen and lounge-room overlooking the backyard, to see the outside packed with partiers. Those inside were sprawled motionless across couches.

Tom, David and I went to put our drinks in the kitchen fridge. Natalie didn't have any with her. We each grabbed a drink, and Tom took two.

"Do you want one of my ciders, Natalie?" He asked.

"No, that's fine." She smiled, looking out over the party. "I don't drink."

"That's the right idea." Tom grinned. "James only started this year, and it definitely didn't make him any cooler, right James?"

I frowned. Tom patted me on the shoulder and nudged my elbow.

45

"Say, David, where's your exchange student tonight?" Tom asked.

"Celeste?"

"Yes, the hot French girl, who else?" Tom quipped.

"Hot French girl?" My eyes lit up. Natalie gave me a scornful look.

"She didn't get an invite, and Freddy didn't let me take her along." David sighed. "She would have liked a night out, but she's too hip for anybody here. Her fashion is so *good*." He was mesmerised by the thought.

Tom rubbed the bridge of his nose, grunting to the remark. "Of course *that's* what you noticed…"

"You should have told Freddy that she was hot." Natalie said. "I'm *sure* he would have let her come then."

We shared a hearty chuckle.

"I like your style, Ms. Athanas." Tom said, "Anyway, James and I will go and find the birthday boy. We'll save you two the trouble of having to talk to him, hang tight."

I raised an eyebrow to Tom's suggestion. Natalie interjected.

"It would be rude to come to his party and *not* say 'hi'. I'll come too."

"No!" Tom blurted, perhaps louder than he had intended, and flung his hand to stop her. Natalie gave him a sharp look, forcing him to clear his throat awkwardly and readjust himself. "Really, it's fine." He coughed. "Freddy'd be too far gone by now to realise that you're even here. James and I will chart a path around him for the rest of the night." Tom said, and walked off finally, ushering me along.

I shrugged to Natalie and David and jogged to catch him. He held the back door open for me, and I followed him outside into the party.

"What's that about?" I asked. Tom stared out over the field of intoxicated teenagers, and put his hands upon his hips.

"You're not trying to get with Natalie, are you?" He asked me. His face wore a grin.

"No, man, really." I said. "She's a friend, that's all I want."

"Pretty unlike you." He scanned the crowd.

"Unlike me?"

"Yeah, man. I've never seen you not attach to a girl who's payed you a bit of attention."

I blushed, shrinking into myself. Tom sensed my embarrassment, and quickly spoke on.

"Anyway, look, I had to draw you away. David is interested, and he should be making a move any second now."

"What!" I exclaimed. I turned around in horror to stare through the window.

David and Natalie were talking. I could read the body language – he had shrunk himself, and her feet were faced away. She wasn't replicating his stance in the slightest. She wasn't interested, and he was a terrible flirt. I could see the staggered conversation stumbling out of his mouth, jumping for life but falling flat on the ground, leaving a trail of awkward corpses.

"Tom, come on, she's my only female friend. I can't ruin that by having her think I'm setting her up!" I spun him about, hands on his shoulders.

"Leave them." Tom said. "It'll be fine. Let's find Freddy."

"No." I insisted. "I'm not going to lose her as a friend." I marched back towards the door.

"Don't block David, man!" Tom called, jogging to get in front of me. "You're overreacting, it'll be…"

We both stared through the glass, stunned, stopped in our tracks. A charming young man, of model height and proportions, with dark caramel skin and golden, curly hair had approached Natalie from the left flank. A gold earring sparkled in his left ear. His stride was majestic and light, like a levitating man holding himself to the ground. He cut between David and Natalie, reaching for Natalie's golden locket as he passed. Natalie recoiled initially, but then, amazingly, leaned into the interaction as he spoke. Golden-tipped words sprayed from his tongue, somehow throwing her guard. Natalie seemed, even, to strike up further conversation, leaving David to squirm away whilst he could. The Englishman stared over to us, his eyes dead. He made a neck-slashing motion to Tom, calling in for conversational reinforcements. The mystical, gypsy-looking boy ushered Natalie away to a couch, and they sat down together.

"Looks like somebody beat you to blocking our man." Tom grumbled. David, defeated, slouched across the lunge room and came out the door to meet us. "That's got to be the greasiest boy I've ever seen, that weird guy." Tom said to me. "Fancy just walking up and fondling somebody's necklace like that. Fancy *Natalie* going with it…"

I couldn't help but disagree with Tom. That golden-skinned man had charm, and an air about him. Just from sight, he possessed that magic that some people simply had. It was in the way he subtly swung his body, clearly in the words he chose, and how he'd held himself so tall and yet so loose. It would be hard to reject that advance, even for a girl like Natalie.

"Let's find the birthday boy." I suggested. "Forget about that other guy for now."

We pulled up a line of deck chairs and sat around the outside spa, chatting between ourselves and those swimming in it. Freddy was splashing about in the blue-lit water, making a real arse of himself dunking other guests. Beers and ciders now made half of the water, bubbling warm alcohol-smell into the air. It was almost nauseating.

"You know, David." Freddy tried to school him, leaning over the edge of the spa. "Girls can pick up on your nervousness. They know when you're scared, man. You've just got to be totally confident. Totally in charge." He said with a sly grin. Tom gave a loud "Pah!", waving his hand at the drunk birthday boy.

"No, wrong." Tom said. "Just hang out with your mates and don't acknowledge girls. If it doesn't look like you're keen, and you're not pushing interest, people open up way quicker."

"Really?" David hummed.

"Yes, really." Tom smiled, patting the boy's back. "Plus, you're unique. Use your fashionable indifference to blow them away."

David smiled somewhat, but resigned his jaw to rest on his hands, eyes staring far off in thought. Past him, through the door, I noticed the gypsy-looking golden boy eyeing me. Natalie had left their conversation at this point and was instead chatting to some other Greek girls in the year level. Natalie seemed to, despite her prude and calculated nature, fit in with almost anybody, and make friends twice as quickly. I envied the way she could just go up to some of the most popular people in the year level and strike up deep conversation. She smiled away, sipping on apple juice or the like, drawing laughter from her new friends.

I focussed on the golden boy's glances. His stares were fleeting, yet subtle. I'd locked eyes with him constantly whilst sitting out by the spa, and each time, he would let his gaze assertively linger before forcing his eyes to wander away. From a distance, he radiated this strange, dangerous smugness. Yet, his eyes were so alluring. His stare had depth to it – a little like Natalie's when we first locked eyes. How did he have that?

"You getting the next round?" Tom broke my trance. I shook my head.

"Huh?" I asked.

"Next round. Freddy here needs a beer, I need one, and David *absolutely* needs one. Hop to it, servant!" He clapped, ordering me away. Others around the spa chuckled, and I stood to my subservience, only to realise one thing. The golden boy was near the fridge.

I froze up, gazing back in his general direction to find him missing. Just like losing a spider on your bedroom wall, the sudden absence of danger only created greater anticipation. Losing a spider only meant you had to worry more about where it was. Slowly, creeping, I stalked past the back door, toeing my way through the now-packed dancefloor, and into the kitchen. Noticing the clear coast, I threw my hand straight for the fridge. Grasping at the handle, somebody else's hand came out to meet it, with skin of a golden olive glow.

Like a rusty gate, I creaked my frightened gaze slowly up the arm to its source.

"Hi James." Natalie's smiling face greeted me. My legs fell, melting my body into the fridge door.

"Sweet cheese, Natalie. You scared the hell out of me."

"Really?" She coughed. "What were you expecting?"

"That boy you were talking to." I said, wriggling my limp body back into the fridge, palming for beers. "Odd looking dude. He's been catching my eye all night."

"Odd? No, he's amazing." Natalie said, her voice lifting, becoming dreamy almost. "I came over to tell you to talk to him, actually."

"Why?" I asked, deadpan. I scooped up the precious cargo I needed all in one arm – four cans. "What's so cool about him?"

"He told me all about myself. Just needed to look me in the eye to know who I am, even things I've never expressed about myself. He said that there's some great, spiritual discovery in my future. I know that sounds stupid, but I *feel* that way, you know?"

"I don't." I admitted. *So, the boy's a hippie.* "But it sounds like a lovely experience anyway."

"You should talk to him." She said, undeterred by my dismissive tone. "Trust me, it's worth it." And with that, she turned to skip away. I watched her leave. She looked to be going over to Tom and David outside. *And without helping me with these drinks?* I shook my head. She *was* in a curious mood. Quickly, I stood, regaining my legs, and tracked across the dancefloor.

I shuffled across, monitoring the beers like babies wrapped in my arms. Each was a precious gift, to be protected from trauma before reaching thirsty lips. I danced cautiously between revellers, until I was struck from behind. One beer, one sacred sheep of my flock, flew from my arms. It crashed to the floor, shaking violently, on the verge of explosion already.

"Damn!" I cussed, and squatted to pick it up. Another hand beat me to it, it's golden skinned, slender fingers grabbing the can and placing it upon my stack. Slowly, I moved me gaze, and met the eyes of the golden skinned boy. I shot up with surprise.

"You've got to be more careful, there. Somebody is in for a nasty surprise." They said in a voice so soulful and lustrous that it must have shone from a golden tongue. It was hard to be fearful of such a voice when so close to its majesty.

"Thanks, man." I said, shifting the beers. A lack of fright, however, didn't indicate a willingness to talk. I politely nodded and tried to step around, only to be blocked by the boy.

"Simon is my name." He introduced himself.

"James." I hummed, nervously. I could feel his gaze penetrating me. His eyes looked past me, *into* me. I tried to avert our now locked eyes, but it was difficult not to fall into the trance.

"I was drawn to your friend's eyes." He said, and it sparked my attention. "And they told me a story. Your eyes, too, tell a story."

"Do they now?" I asked, forcing myself to look away, but unable to comply with my own demands.

"Oh yes, a story of success, of great loss." He said. "You've had to change recently to fill a great void, but its like plugging a colander against a flow of water. You can't be everything that you need to be."

"Excuse me?" I hummed, almost more offended than amazed that he knew I'd never be a man like my father.

"But you've got great leadership in your future. Weakness, too. Lots of that to overcome, and you won't beat most of it. And acceptance is there also. I'd warn you to trust your gut, and act in ways that you think are *right*." He smiled, resting a hand on my shoulder.

"Excuse me?" I asked again. "How…what makes you say that?"

"I can see it in your eyes." He nodded. "They're a green that you don't often come across. Luminescent, jade green."

"Luminescent green?" I hummed. My eyes were a deep brown. I scoffed shaking my head from the trance. "Alright then." I regained my scepticism, rushing into me like hot blood. "Thanks for the psychic reading, but I've got beers to hand out."

"*Soul* reading. That's what I do." He said.

"I bet." I noted, storming past him. As I reached the door, he must have perched upon his tippy toes to yell:

"It was nice reading you, James. Just remember, *sur san Suneva.*"

"*Sur san Suneva?*" I croaked, stopping dead before the door. I flung myself around, searching for Simon, and noticing his tall head of hair receding into the crowd, jogging off. My mind raced to Natalie. We had a lead, we had to chase him.

I threw myself out the door, running up to the spa side and throwing a beer at each guest. Each caught with a skilful hand. "Natalie!" I shot my gaze at her. She met my eyes and read my panic. "A moment?"

"Sure." She stood immediately.

"What's up?" Tom asked, rising. "What did that creepy dude say to weird you out? Are you okay?"

"Nothing, dude." I said to him. "Nothing at all, I just remembered…something. I need Natalie."

"Hey, dude, we're all ears." Tom stepped in closer. "Anything you need."

"Really, it's alright." I stammered, peering over my shoulder. Simon was getting away, disappearing into the front hallway, raking towards the exit. "The weird guy just…stole Natalie's drink right out of my hand." I said, grabbing Natalie's hand.

"Natalie doesn't drink." Tom said, hands on hips. Natalie and I paused, eyes darting awkwardly.

"She does now." I blurted. "Come on." I tugged her again towards the door, running.

"Hey, thanks for the beer!" Freddy called after us, immediately followed by a girlish scream as an untabbed, shaken beer made a freezing fountain into his face. I threw Natalie and myself through the door, dragging us into the crowd.

"Wait up!" Tom wailed, following.

"What's up?" Natalie asked, muffled by a head of hair which flew into her face.

"*Sur san Suneva.* The tanned guy said it."

"What?" She gawked.

"He's a lead. He's a Suneva." I panted, my hand shoving through the dense field of dancers. The floor was packed to the walls, a chaos of shaking limbs. Marching through it was as tedious as wading through treacle. I'd lost Simon's head to the corner, but I still endeavoured through, dragging Natalie behind.

"Why didn't he say that to me…" Natalie trailed off.

"Probably because you didn't dismiss him like I did." I broke us free from the crowd, clear into the hallway. From here, I could see the front door close its final inch. Our lead had to be on the other side.

"Come on!" I urged. Natalie and I sprinted for the exit, barging against the door and busting it open. It flung us into the warm night, and we tumbled into the garden.

A hand shut the front gate, the body had already disappeared behind the front fence and its tall hedge. Footsteps ran on concrete, up the street.

Natalie threw her heels aside and we launched through the gate.

He ran up the hill, into the blackness. We chased, and were gaining ground. The wind rushed by us. The pounding of bass continued from the party, muffled in my head by my laboured breath.

Simon, out of the view of street-light, stopped in his tracks and pivoted abruptly to face us. His eyes glowed bright yellow, like T.V screens. They deformed, becoming rectangular and edged. His arms grew longer, his spine stretched upwards, cracking violently and piercing the night. His head enlarged and squared off, his entire body shape changed into the shadow of something else. Spikes towered over his shoulders. He had sharp definition; his form was cold like metal.

A pinprick of pain grew in the base of my neck, quickly becoming an inferno of agony. The light breeze transformed into a gale which gusted stronger as my pain intensified. I was in too much agony to move, even if I tried. I was sweating bullets, gazing at this demonic creature of the night - just like the ghost many years ago.

With a silent flick of the wrist, the shadow man produced a sharp blade which shimmered menacingly in the lamp-light.

"You will no longer be lost in the day." It boomed in a deep and crackling voice, "Blackness does not betray; it embodies all light."

The creature turned swiftly. It ran, and before it crested the knoll, I'd lost it in the darkness.

The wind died off sharply. I regained control of myself, the pain went away. I crawled to my feet, and stumbled up the hill.

"Come back, man!" I yelled, "I just want to talk…"

Of course, he was gone – a good lead was gone.

I turned to Natalie, who was kneeling on the ground, one hand flat on the pavement, the other groping her neck fiercely. She moaned in pain. I ran back to her.

"Gee, are you okay? Did he hit you?" I knew that wasn't possible, but I might as well have asked.

"No, its fine James," she cringed, and took her hand from her neck to examine it. The skin of her neck was burned and red. It glowed in pain where the hump of the bone was.

"Pain at the base of your neck?" I took an educated guess, "Like fire in the bone?"

She looked at me quizzically. She tilted her head, to make sure I was being serious. She was about to open her mouth when Tom's voice pierced the night.

"Told you he was an odd dude?" he smiled, standing just outside of the gate. "Stole somebody's first ever drink, what a sly character. Shouldn't have let him talk to you. You saw those eyes. He was shifty." He waltzed proudly on over. "You alright?" He asked, offering a hand to Natalie. She declined his offer, and lifted herself up. Sweat dripped buckets from the palms of her hands. "Christ, what did he do to your neck! Your skin is glowing red!" Tom exclaimed.

"Nothing," She assured, giving me that look again that we were on the same wavelength, "Just a bad sunburn."

"Sunscreen, love. I thought a beach girl like yourself would be on top of that." He was about to pat her on the back, but remembered the glaring red burn and decided against it. He turned, and led us back into the party.

"I get the pain too." I whispered to Natalie, "I had it just then."

"I haven't had it in a little while…" she trailed off. "What do you think it means?"

I closed the gate behind us and looked up into the sky. Instead of the circular moon, peeking from behind a cloud was a white ring in its place. *Not a ring*, I realised, *An eclipse, of a black moon over a white one.*

"James?" Natalie shook me out of my trance. I blinked and the moon was normal again.

"I think it means changes are coming." I noted neutrally. We followed Tom back into the house.

Chapter 7
Cross My Heart and Hope to Die

Luminescent green eyes? I pondered as Natalie and I drew back into the party. We stayed at least five steps behind Tom, shuffling wordlessly between ourselves.

Where have I seen luminescent green eyes? I had an answer to this. It was the use of the word *luminescent* which had triggered something in me. I could see them, too. Glowing bright, somewhat boxy rather than natural. The headlights of a machine, maybe? I toddled off towards the kitchen, intent on a glass of water to clear my head. There was a memory trying to emerge, something hidden away, deep down, or something so obscure I'd only dreamt it.

Nearing the kitchen counter, two boys fought over a roll of bread. It was the strange thing which could only happen with intoxicated teenagers. The roll looked stale, anyway. It crunched beneath their fingers. Once one boy had a hold of the treasure, he launched it at the kitchen wall, causing it to explode.

"That shit is stale, Mark!" they said. "I'll find you a better one."

The other boy nodded, wearily, and they went back to searching. On the counter under the impact zone there was a half of a bread roll, and a steady coating of crumbs.

Crumbs… I gasped. The green eyes, they were *that* memory, weren't they?

***

On the 5th of November, 1996, there was unrest in the Grey household.

I'd had a fight with Dad. Such fights would always begin when he wanted five things done at once and expected them all to be done a minute ago. The worst being when he came home from a day of work just five minutes after you'd come home from a day of school, and somebody had left a mess.

You'd only been in the house for five minutes, but the dog hair on the floor from this morning was your fault and nobody else's, and those leftover dishes were scattered straight from your royal arse across the kitchen sink, and you shook the leaves off the trees in the back yard, and how *dare* you not have had the house presentable for his majesty when he trudged himself through the door.

And the worst part? You'd put your best effort into cleaning everything else as best as you could in the time you had, but he still found one minor, insignificant detail which wasn't done. There was never praise for the job completed, only anger at that left to do.

So, when he got angry that night, I just couldn't be bothered dealing with it. I'd spent my half an hour at home sprucing up the lounge room, folding and putting away Simone's clothes, cleaning up the glasses in the sink which he *hated*, and fixing each cushion on each couch perfectly. But I'd missed the *crumbs*. Crumbs of toast scattered lightly by the toaster. Their existence was clearly the work of a madman set to derail my father's day. Their even, light spread across the counter was a fierce attack on his livelihood, on the very value of the house which he and my poor mother had sweated and toiled to earn. Crumbs, the total and utter symbol for the spoon-fed, dole-bludging children and their entitled attitudes who had fortified their spot in his abode some seventeen years prior. It was five crumbs, for fuck's sake. I let him know that there was a screw missing in his brain if he thought five bread crumbs was the epitome of entitlement. I yelled that a screaming match was no way to solve the issue of crumbs, that it had been *his* mess from this morning, and if he wanted a perfect house, he knew *exactly* where the sponge was to clean it up.

That earned a sponge to the face.

The wet sponge melted on my red cheeks. I kicked the fridge so hard the thing nearly fell over, then in a pang of guilt and fear, I ran from the house. I ran to Tom's.

Tom was family friends with the songwriter for this new and upcoming indie band. He had tickets to a gig where they were the opener to a blues ensemble. He was meant to be taking Penelope, but she'd let him down and he now had a spare ticket. When I rocked up on his door step, he handed me the ticket and told me that he "had the perfect plan for tonight." I agreed, happy to do anything.

We had caught the tram into St Kilda; the beachside Melbourne suburb home to many bars and clubs. We were both severely underage at the time, being 15, but had no problems getting in with our VIP tickets. The feeling of skipping a line, and doing something we otherwise couldn't dream of was elating. Standing in the venue surrounded by adults and lovers of new music, I felt so sophisticated and cool. Tom and I tried to shoot shit with a few other patrons as we sipped on raspberry-lemonade, but our youthful talk of silly things would have given us away as kids.

It took a while for the band to get set up on stage, but when they started, they were unbelievable. The members were so clued in to each other and had such dynamic chemistry. They stole the energy from the audience and delivered it back tenfold. I didn't think much of their album, but as a live show, it was a different experience.

"Pretty good, hey?" Tom bragged after the first few songs. He had to say it directly into my ear about five times before I could hear him, because concert venues love blasting solid soundwaves through your skull.

"Yeah man. These guys are *tight*. And so *groovy*."

Their style wasn't funk, or jazz, or soul, or disco. It was something indescribable and new. It was their own sound, and for the next hour of my life, I became lost in its rhythms. The hypnotic, rock-bossa drums and funky bass consumed my soul.

We even got to hang out backstage with Tom's friend Jason, who wrote most of the songs. I couldn't bring my mouth to be articulate when talking to him, making an idiot of myself as I tried to display my admiration for his work. He took my idiocy well, however, and was a real pleasure of a dude. He was a genuinely selfless *'do it for the love of music'* kind of guy, which was rare in the self-obsessed music scene. I joked to him that I played trumpet, and that if he even needed another man on the horn, he should give me a call.

He never did call me, though.

By the time I got home that night, Dad, Mum and Simone were all in bed. My legs were sore from all of the standing and dancing, and my ears rang like static. I fell into the warm embrace of my bed, and plummeted into a deep, effortless sleep.

I woke to the sounds of loud yelling, muffled, but coming from inside the house. Groggily, I rolled over and waited for it to stop. It got louder. I groaned, and flipped over again. My alarm clock showed that it was three in the morning.

Who the hell has a fight at three a.m? I moaned to myself, *What can you even fight about at three in the morning?*

Stuffing my face into the pillow, I tried to ignore the sounds, but the argument became more intense.

Surely they can figure this out. I thought. Apparently, they could not. *God damn it, this family...* I huffed and threw the covers. I stormed down the hallway, stomping my feet as I marched towards the commotion. It was coming from Mum and Dad's room. The door was open, light and noise were spilling out. I flung myself through the door frame.

"Okay, who the *fuck* has a yelling match at this time?" I yelled into the room. The scene was not what I expected. Simone was on the phone, Mum was frantic, and Dad was on the bed. His eyes were wide open, staring at me – through me. His mouth hung open like a stupid fish, and through it came deep, yet rushed, breaths. They were sporadic – too far apart to be normal breaths, and disturbingly noisy.

"Wake up!" Mum yelled into Dad's unresponsive face. She slapped him with her open palm, once, twice, thrice. His expression did not change – not even his eyes blinked. The breathing continued.

"Yes, his eyes are open." Simone calmly said into the phone, "He just took a breath. And there's another one."

"What in sweet cheese is happening?" I asked. My heart rate spiked. Mum stared at me with a tearful and desperate face. Simone gestured to the phone.

"Mum, what is happening?" I asked Mum specifically. She managed to articulate her thoughts.

"He's not getting up. He fell on the bed and he's not getting up!"

"What?"

"We need to get him on the floor, now!" Simone demanded. Mum and I rushed over to the bed. I took the weight of his torso, Mum picked up the feet. In her frantic inability to do anything useful, she dropped the feet and I stumbled with the rest. His body thudded against the carpeted floor. I stopped his head from hitting the ground but at this point I didn't know that it mattered. He was so blank. I'd never looked into the eyes of a person and seen *nothing*.

"We need to do CPR." Simone said. "James, you know CPR."

"I do?" I asked. It should have been clear to me that I did, in fact, know CPR. One of my endeavours to emulate Dad's greatness led me to a season of surf-lifesaving. I knew a lot of first aid.

"I don't remember what to do." I said, before I realised that the statement was true.

"He's forgotten…" Simone said into the phone. The paramedic chatted to her, the squeaky voice dragging for an eternity. Dad was dying by my knees.

"Okay, get both your hands. Put the balls of one on the breastbone, and…"

I put the first hand down and it was clear what I needed to do. I put the other one top and I compressed the man's chest as hard as I could.

Break a rib. Was all that ran through my head. I remembered learning about CPR, and hearing that people never pushed hard enough, so patients died. You couldn't be too scared to break a rib, because people don't care if they've got a broken rib if they don't die. I pummelled into his chest as hard as I possibly could. I was too nervous to push whilst he was breathing. The paramedic on the line told Simone that we shouldn't breath for him, but I didn't want to squeeze out his breaths.

When I'd done two-hundred and fifteen pushes, counted by Simone, she nudged me aside to do her set. But she wasn't pushing hard enough, or in the right place. Adrenaline pumped my body.

"Man the phone." I demanded, and shoved her aside. I railed into Dad with all of the strength I could muster. Still, I felt like it wasn't enough.

Mum, on the other hand, was running up and down the street like a headless chicken, screaming for help. Nobody awoke to her calls, not even the doctors across the road, who we found out had taken their holiday.

The ambulance arrived, Mum leading them frantically into the room. Firemen heaved at the heavy bed and pushed it aside. A young female paramedic told me she would take over at the next breath, and when it came, I passed Dad on to her.

We were corralled into the kitchen by a fireman as paramedics and their equipment cascaded into the bedroom. I watched them jog between the master bedroom and the front door, acting as couriers between the ambulance and the scene. A fireman tried to talk to us, but we mostly sat in silence, watching the minutes tick over on the kitchen's clock. It was excruciating. Despite the organised chaos ensuing in the house, each second took its own lifetime.

The emergency servicemen and woman went from jogging to running between the bedroom and front doors. The fireman tried to distract us, to talk about absolutely anything else, but we were too intrigued. In that moment, I understood that Dad might not make it. I hadn't come to that conclusion before. I couldn't handle it.

I felt the pain again, that sharp prick of heat and discomfort in the base of my neck. This was not the first time I'd ever felt it, but it was the most powerful. As I felt my neck flare, I could feel another odd sensation. I held my Dad's breath in the palm of my hand. I could feel it as it poured in and out of his mouth. I could see it in my mind's eye, a whole house away, drifting aimlessly between the room and his lungs. The feeling was bizarre. I knew that his breath was not between the fingers on my left hand, but it was there that I felt it run cold over my skin; like I was reaching out to him.

His breath pooled in, and pushed out. Pulled in, and pushed out. Like the tide at the beach; waves lazily rolling over the sand.

The air moved weakly, continually so. More dominant in my senses was the air that came from the compressions, now forcefully escaping his mouth. They were pressing harder, and he was breathing less.

I'm just day dreaming. I said to myself, still keen on the sensation. My neck throbbed intensely now. I fell to my knees on the floor. I could hear people yelling

at me from all around. The fireman got down to my level, but I couldn't communicate
with him. I was stuck in my thoughts and feelings.

*I'm just dreaming. He's not dying. He can't. He's made of stone – the last of the old bulls,
the strongest man I know. A fitter man doesn't exist. Come on, breathe! You arrogant bastard!*

In my hands, I felt his last breath. It petered into nothingness, drowned out by
the intense compressions.

I went into an awesome hot flush. From my neck, heat radiated throughout my
body. I was instantly sweating, my skin beet red. Time slowed down, and I my ears
rung so intensely that I couldn't hear anything. My chest turned to fire, and my breath
to hot smoke as it poured out of my lungs. I couldn't comprehend what was
happening, and what I was feeling. Reality came down on me like a crushing weight,
and I faded out of consciousness. My vision went to black and I fell face first into
the cold, wooden floor.

I awoke to the sound of gentle waves crashing into sand. I could hear the water
foaming, the air escaping it, and it being dragged back out to sea. My face was cold.
My body was cold. I could see in front of me a large vegetated sand dune, and above
it, a violent grey sky. I wrenched myself off the ground, to see the beach before me.
The sea was dark, and the waves much rougher than the gentle sound they made.

The waves were at least six feet tall. They moved away from the shore, crashing
out to sea and rolling into the horizon of churning ocean. It was king tide rolling out.
The waves out at sea were growing, and blindly crashing over themselves.

I pulled myself off the ground and brushed the sand off my body. It got stuck
to me, the way that sand gets stuck to wet skin. It irritated me.

There was a man standing on the beach near me. He wore a blue and green
robe, and had a darker complexion. He was standing too far down the beach for me
to see his face, but his presence wasn't ominous. He made me feel safe.

Looking out to the ocean, I got a feeling that I often had. I felt that if I reached
out I could touch the sky. I could pull myself through it, and soar in the air. Freedom
lay before me.

On this feeling alone, I sprinted towards the water. I leaped off the wet sand,
my body hanging over the outwards-rolling waves below. I pushed my hands down.
Like swimming in the air, I was propelled upwards by my push. The sky had me, and
I would not fall.

I kicked with my feet, and spiralled through the atmosphere – riding a jetstream
like a corkscrew, high into the sky. I was at least one hundred feet high, looking down
at the ocean. I halted myself, held my hands out, and tilted down to the water. I dove
straight down. Air cascaded through my hair. I could feel the salt spraying up from

the tumultuous sea. It bombarded my face as I raced into oblivion. At the last instant, I commanded the sky under my body, and I pulled up. My stomach dropped through my pants, like the drop of a rollercoaster. I swooped away from the water's surface, flying upwards.

I looked back towards the sand, from my place high in the air, and saw the robed man leaving. He crested the dune, and bobbed out of sight. A sea breeze built up as he did so. It started lightly, and once he was gone, it was a proper ocean wind.

There was a new figure on the beach where I had woken up. They stood tall, covered in armour. They had a squarish, silver helmet, adorned by a large fin on the top, and a spatula-like chin protrusion. They stared at me with their large, green eyes – like glowing screens.

They had silver chest armour, and a green and black, mechanical body underneath. Large spikes rose from their shoulders. They had bulky, silver feet, and unusually thin joints. Their hands were silver, and their fingers were ungodly long.

I had seen this figure before. He appeared in other dreams of mine. I couldn't decide if they looked malicious.

It flicked its wrist quickly, and a rod sprung into its grip from nothing. From the rod ejected two prongs, forming a fork, and a long, green blade which ran parallel to the staff, connected to the leading prong and supported just below the hand.

My belief that I could fly was suddenly suspended. I felt the heavy pull of gravity on my body, and I felt the air dissolve around me. It felt stupid to believe that I could hold onto it and push myself through it. I fell immediately.

Down, down into the swell churning below. Down, down into the dangerous, dark water. Wind swirled around my ears and arms, I was falling feet first into the sea.

I was cast in immense pain as I crashed onto the ocean's surface. I felt my whole body bruise on impact. I sunk into the water. It was too dark to see, I was too hurt to move, and too far from air to breathe.

I forced myself to move. I broke through the surface and opened my mouth. A wave crashed over my face. I fought my way out of its tumble and surfaced, but water rushed into my desperate mouth. I spluttered violently as the wave passed.

I heard a rumble from the shore. The silver and green bulky figure had blasted off, he soared on a stream of air straight towards me. He was closing in quickly, his predatory green eyes locking onto me, his staff head glowing green between its prongs.

I braced for impact. I closed my eyes and listened to the sound of my breath against the churning of the waves. The world was crashing around me, and I could hear him coming for me. I did not know what the figure wanted from me.

Nothing happened.

All sounds faded out, leaving me with just my panicked breaths. I was no longer bobbing in the churning sea. I was face-down on flat ground. The fireman was pulling me up, and I struggled off him. I rubbed my head, it hurt.

A paramedic was walking down the hallway towards us. Her face was sour. She had bad news, but I already knew what it was. My father was dead.

And what was my last word to him? - the man who built me from a boy to a man, the man who inspired me to be active, to do sports; the man who I, with all of my heart, could not more deeply aspire to? Was it "I love you"? No, I told him to go *stick it* about some crumbs left in the kitchen and his insistence that I clean it up.

I loved him, and he died without telling me the same, all because of some bread crumbs.

Mum cried on Simone's shoulder. I rejected their embrace, or the words of the paramedic. I went to the sink, took the sponge, and wiped the bench down. I held the crumbs in my hand, and I threw them into the bin.

I could cry now.

Chapter 8

The Emperor of the Black Suns

Natalie and I left the party early; not long after all of the commotion. Tom was annoyed that I'd taken Natalie home so soon into the proceedings, not even giving David a chance to talk to her after the golden-skinned boy left. David would have his chance later, but Natalie and I were on to something potentially important, and according to my constant visions of the moons, life changing.

"What do you think it is," I asked her, "when our necks hurt like that?"

We were sitting on my bed. I perched myself on the edge and she sat cross-legged on the bed centre. I had recently upgraded to a queen-sized bed, which I couldn't be happier about.

On the wall by the foot of the bed were shelves lined with posed action figures. To the right of the display was my closet, which I had closed to hide my slobbery from Natalie. To the left of the bed was the door, and between the door and the bed was my study desk, which didn't have any room for studying over the other crap I had there. It's no wonder, say any of my friends who had visited, that I didn't have a girlfriend nor successfully taken a girl home. I'd put both of those down to severe social ineptness, but the décor didn't help. At any rate, I had enough decency to hide the model trains.

"I have no idea," she said, "I just think it's amazing that I found somebody else who it happens to. Nobody ever believed me about it."

"You told other people about the pain in your neck?"

"Why wouldn't I?" she responded reasonably. "Didn't you tell your parents when you were in pain?"

"Yeah but…" I had to think about it for a minute, "I don't know, I guess I just never mentioned it. It's only happened less than ten times…"

"Ten times?" she gave me a curious look, "Not every second day?"

"God, no!" I exclaimed, "You get it that often? How do you get through the day?"

"I'm used to it, I guess." She sighed, "it still hurts like all hell, though."

"You poor soul," I sympathised, "I mean, it only happens to me when I'm really scared or in danger or something bad is happening…"

"Oh, same here." She clarified, "That's when it happens bad, but otherwise I'll still feel it a few times a week."

"Damn, that's crazy." I tried to sympathise. She gave me a faint smile, and sighed.

"So, what exactly did Simon say to you?" I asked her, changing the direction of our debrief.

"Well, he said that I am stubborn, but a good planner and organiser."

"That's nice…somewhat." I smiled.

"But he also said that I was overwhelmingly *spiritual*, that he could sense that I was connected to the world, and that I had broad senses."

"Well, do you?"

"I don't know. It seemed like such a strange thing to say." She explained, flustered, "I mean, I'm not religious, never have been, so I don't know how else he could mean *spiritual*."

"Maybe he meant internally. Like, you meditate or something."

"But I don't. I mean, I have a good understanding of myself, but doesn't everybody?"

"I know what you mean." I said, "But without painting myself in pity, I feel his assessment was strangely accurate of me. He called me weak, and said I was struggling to fill a void. It had to be my Dad's death he was referring to."

"James." Natalie grumbled. "Don't beat yourself up like that."

"*But,* he said I had green luminescent eyes – which I don't. So he was wrong there. I've seen a figure in my dreams who does, though."

"Really? He said my eyes were orange, but *I've* never seen orange eyes in my dreams. Although, I've always felt like I *am* orange, you know?"

"No, I don't really know about that one." I teased lightly.

"I guess the similarities had to run out somewhere," she noted.

"I can't believe this is all coming together, anyway." I said, "Like, we're actually finding real Suneva. I didn't even believe anything about them before."

"I know." She said, "It's crazy."

"We have to go to Mr Finneck's house tomorrow, then." I said, "You know, the guy who sold my Dad the *Diaries of Olomb*. He'll lead us to *Kuvalik*, or *Maiki*…and then think of where we could take this!"

Natalie sat silently.

"Is something wrong?" I asked.

"No, I just realised that I can't do tomorrow. I'm seeing my Mum."

"Can't Mum wait?" I asked. My mind was racing.

She grasped at her golden locket. I immediately sunk down.

"I don't get to see Mum all that often. We're going surfing. *This investigation* can wait, surely." She asserted.

"Okay." I backed down. "What about Monday after school then?"

"You're rowing, I'm dancing until late." She said. "We'll have to wait til Tuesday."

"Okay." I sighed, "I'm sorry, I'm just so excited."

"I know." She said, "And I'm sorry to get jumpy, but family always comes first." She smiled wanly, trying to lift the mood.

"You know, out of everybody you know, I should be the least likely to deprive you of time with your parents." I said. "I mean, if I had another day with Dad…"

She grabbed my hand. It was unexpected. I blushed. Surely, she didn't think of me like that. I didn't want her to. I removed my hand.

"It's not a pity call." I joked. "You enjoy your day with your Mum. I should walk you home now though, it's almost twelve."

She agreed, and we set off. I walked her home through the darkness in runners and my gym gear. Gym gear because once I was there, there was no way I was walking back, not with everything that'd been happening. I practically sprinted home and into bed.

For the first two periods on Monday, I didn't see Natalie at school. I found Tom and David at recess at our usual hangout overlooking the soccer fields – they hadn't seen her either.

"Maybe she's still riding waves with her Mum." Tom suggested, "But it didn't seem like her to skip a school-day for *anything*. She's too straight."

"Yeah, I know." I added, trying to hide my concern. I knew there was nothing to worry about, but I just had a bad feeling building in my gut.

"She must love surfing - almost as much as David loves it." Tom teased, and gave David double pistol fingers.

"Surfing is pretty hot…" David admitted, turning red.

"Hey, look. I'm sorry your chances got bummed out the other night," I apologised to David. He smiled. "That other guy totally set off the mood, but if you actually want to get to know *her*…" I put the emphasis on *her*, "…then I can set you up…"

"Really?" He blurted,

"…at a price." I continued.

"Name it."

"What can you offer me?"

"I can make it a double date. You bring Natalie, I'll introduce you to my French exchange student. She comes to school next week, but you can get the first introduction."

I immediately forgot about my worries of impending doom. My heartrate spiked. My pupils dilated. This was a very good offer, and my delight was written across my face.

"You've got yourself a good deal, my friend." I said, and shook his hand.

"I like where this is all going!" Tom grinned, slapping a meaty palm on our backs, "Can I fifth wheel?"

David and I glared him down. He didn't ask again.

I was excited that afternoon. I'd locked in a date with a French girl – possibly not to her knowledge – I was in the middle of a top-secret investigation, and I was high on rowing endorphins, albeit totally exhausted. Being so close to the Head of the River, my coach had us doing one of the hardest sessions yet. I just about fell out of the boat when we landed. It was absolute agony, but in the end I got through it. That's the amazing thing of a rowing team, I'd found over the years. No matter how impossible the task would be by yourself, it's always doable with seven other guys.

For two days, though, I'd been busting to check on old Mr Finneck to see where he got that Suneva book from. It had taken all of my restraint to not simply run off and do it myself – the thought of disappointing Natalie was much worse than the joy in what I might find. Just one more day, I told myself.

I fell through the door at home, three bags orbiting my body, my wet rowing suit hanging on by tendrils of dried sweat. I was in a state, totally dead to the world. I stumbled down the hallway, to see Simone peering her square eyes around the corner of the study's doorframe. The side room was lit only in the blue glow of her screen, her dishevelled sloppiness concealed in hazy shadows.

"Hey-a James, you're in late." She smiled and waved. I trudged myself through the hall giving her a weak wave as I passed.

"Hard session." I said. "Where's Mum?"

"Out with Kathy." Simone said, toeing over to me. I made a sharp right heading for the couch and falling onto it, bags and all. I let my body sink in, every muscle relaxing, happiness ensuing. Errol panted up and licked the sweat on my legs.

"Is there dinner?" I asked.

"Yeah, there's lasagne." Simone stood over me. "But before you do that, you're walking the dog."

Walking the dog? My eyes shot with blood, wide. My legs fell out of their sockets to free themselves from pain. A deep, hunkering dissatisfaction bubbled in my gut bursting through my mouth in the growl of a wolf.

"Walking the dog?" I roared.

"I walked him this morning, and last night, and ten out of fourteen times this week." Simone huffed. "You're always out, you never do it."

"You're always in, of course you do it!" I moaned. "Do I look like I'm in any condition to walk the dog?"

"You damn-well better be." She retorted. "Look at him, he's desperate." She pointed to the dog. In the heat of yelling, he thought he must have been in trouble so sat up carefully on the carpet, eyes and smile wide, trying to be as inoffensive as possible.

"You're coming then." I said to her. "You'll have to pull me along."

Between losing the wet clothes, throwing my bags into the centre of my room and putting on some shorts, I came to a realisation. If I had to walk the dog, then I had to go and venture out into the world. Would it be so unforgiveable, then, if I were to lead Simone and Errol by Mr Finneck's old house? If I could just look at it maybe I'd satiate my curiosity to investigate, which also not disappointing Natalie. It seemed perfect – I'd take a look and see if there was anything weird about the place then report back to Natalie and venture out together. I was filled with rejuvenated vigour, and emerged to sweep Simone and the dog out of the door.

"So, how are…things?" I asked Simone as we rounded the entrance to the underpass. Errol stopped to sniff at the scorch marks left in the rocks. I tugged him along, drawing Simone's attention away.

"Usual." She said. "Or, I don't know. My sociology lecturer is a real piece of work. Real opinionated prick, making me hate the unit."

"That's rough." I nodded vacantly. I could see old Mr Finneck's house now right at the butt of the street we emerged onto. It's windows just peeking into view from behind the corner. "I mean, that was your favourite subject, right?"

"It's my major, now." She said. "I'd just hate for it to be ruined by a teacher."

"You're not the kind of person to let others get them down, though." I noted. "What's got you hating them? Surely you can talk it out?"

She laughed at my suggestion, spinning about with a mad smile. "Oh Jamesey…" She said. "Oh, how I've tried."

"What have they even done?"

"They wouldn't even *credit* my argument about minority-driven hierarchical structures in my last essay." She huffed. "I had evidence, I had ways to link it to current societal structures. I swear, when people get too deep into doctrines…" She shook her head, mumbling more nothings to herself. I let her stew silently, not really wishing to hear the full argument.

"I guess that's the danger of getting too involved in anything, right?" I said, but Simone simply rolled her eyes, surely taking some extra meaning that I hadn't intended. We walked towards Finneck's house in silence, now.

"What about that boy you were seeing?" I asked her, trying to shift the mood.

"Men are trash." She said bluntly, but her face dropped when she saw my expression. "Not you, though." She apologised. "Or little Mr Errol, here. I mean, just *this* boy. He came off really nice and new-thinking, but in the end, he was just so typical. Couldn't empathise with anybody, totally self-important…" She trailed off again, and I let the conversation die.

From a distance, Finneck's house looked amiss, and up close, about to cross the road, I could see clearly what was wrong. The place was abandoned. Beyond the chipped front fence, the weatherboards of the bungalow house had started to fade and rot. A broken window bestowed the front bay, its curtain flapping in the light breeze. The garden had run amok, consuming most of the brick path and the foot of the building.

I went to tug Errol across the road, but he would not step towards the house. He dug his paws in.

"Come on mate." I urged. He stood staring, and I followed his gaze from the road, up the fence, to the bay window. The curtain rustled, and behind it, a shadow watched with glowing eyes. Eyes that held a galaxy behind them. As soon as I'd seen the shadow, it's lines dissipated into the blackness.

That was my calling. I rushed the rest of the walk, turning Simone around with stories of how she'd hate Tom and David for their views on romance, if she ever really got to know them. Once I reached our house, I feigned dropping my wallet on the walk, and threw on some gym clothes to go running after it, instructing Simone to man the house and get it looking nice for Mum to come home. It was almost on the edge of becoming dark now, with the sky beginning to show its yellow glow. Under the railway line I ran, and up the street to the abandoned house.

Staring at the house again, its curtain flapping ominously around the broken glass, I contemplated why I'd come back. I'd felt called to adventure, but was this worth upsetting Natalie? Something lived here alright. I'd seen their shadowy figure and glowing eyes. Strangely, this enticed me more to enter than it frightened me away. Still, I could hear the conversation I'd have tomorrow about this. "Why did you go without me? All you had to do was wait a single day!" Natalie would moan, and I'd have no answer to it. How could I justify a selfish act to satiate my own impatience?

Maybe I wouldn't have to, I reasoned. This really could be nothing but a vandal, who perhaps I should have been scared of. Looking at the decrepit house, one thing was apparent – Finneck no longer lived here. If we were chasing him for a lead, we wouldn't find it here. So, then, maybe it was worth me finding where he went, so that Natalie and I could more efficiently chase him up?

Yes, that was a perfect excuse. I pushed through the gate.

The hinges gnawed at their mechanism, screaming in a rusty growl. A stiff breeze buzzed past me, cold in the yellow-pink light of the dying, summer day. On the plot of the land, I could feel something at the heart of the house calling me in. There was a glow to the frightening, decrepit building. Quite literally, I could see it as I rounded the overgrown trees which had previously covered the front door. Through the obscuring glass, there shone a pale, almost imperceptible blue haze. Now at the door step, I tried to peer past the scattering glass, but could see nothing. I tugged on the door instead, but it was either permanently stuck in place, or needed a key. I glanced about.

The porch had a rusting vintage racer bike and an old park bench. On the bike, hanging out of the saddle bag, I saw the glimmer of a key. Curious, I noted, that such an obvious key should withstand the test of time. I stepped over to grab it.

The door opened as I turned my back.

I swung to it immediately, despite my pounding heart. It took my brain a minute to catch up with my eyes, which scanned an empty doorway and wall before me. Blood pumping hot, I peered past the open door, into the dark, dank hallway beyond.

The blue glow had disappeared, replaced with blackness. The heart of the house was smothered.

"Mr Finneck?" I called in feebly, "Mr Finneck, are you here?" I stepped past the boundary, into the blackness. The broken light fitting by the entrance seemed to buzz in my presence. I paused, watching the filament weakly lick orange. "Do you know anything about a Kuvalik?" I asked. Suddenly, the broken bulb roared and flickered, flashing on.

Then the next bulb flashed, and the next, and the next, until the hallway was flickering with orange, unstable light.

And now, drawn to see the hallway's end, I spotted the source of the blue glow, which now returned with rejuvenated energy. The glow belonged to a pair of squarish, cyan eyes, cresting a partition atop a yellow helmet.

"Hello, Maiki." The yellow armoured figure greeted.

***

I had been here many times before with Mr. Finneck, but today was different. Gone were the cheery decorations, the smell of herbal tea, and the wonderful old man. In its place was a scene from the post-apocalypse. The ceiling was hanging on by wood fibres and the floor had part rotted away. A half-sunken bookshelf lay in the corner of the room, its books scattered everywhere. The TV set was engulfed by a vine that snaked its way out of the kitchen. A hole in the roof let some of dusk's pink light cast a beam through the dust to the floor. To add further to my discomfort, there was water stuck in my ear, and no amount of head-shaking could get it to come out.

The figure with the cyan eyes paced before me. They were tall and armoured. Most of its body was yellow, but it had black, silver and purple plating scattered on the joints, with a large grey-metal chest plate and collar. On his chest and on his large cape, he had printed the same symbol from Natalie's book – the white circle with black, radial flames, like a cross. I recognised this figure easily as the leader from the alleyway. In the light, they were strangely handsome, with a pointed chin and a partition up the centre of its helmet which split and formed eyebrows above its rectangular eyes. It had strong looking spikes protruding from its jaw on both sides of its face, and little metal lightning bolt horns.

There were three others in the room too. One was in slick, black and dark grey armour with pink, circular eyes. They had long, thin limbs, and their helmet gave them the appearance of a barn owl, or a raven. They sat stiffly in an adjacent reclining chair, eyeing me with their beady, pink stare. Their armour crumpled and creased under their body as naturally as skin. Another, the tallest in the room, had amour of silver, teal and gold. His helmet was angular, his green eyes forming a constantly displeased expression. Tubes connected from his back to a large triangular grill which took up the helmet's mouth space. They were far less pensive than their counterpart, lounging tall over the scene.

There was another armoured figure that lingered in the outskirts of my vision.

I didn't get a good look at them.

"So what you're telling me is that you had no idea you're a Suneva." The yellow figure paced on the other side of the coffee table.

"Yes, that's exactly what I'm telling you." I said, "How did *you* know my name before I did?" He'd called me *Maiki*. Maybe it was a mistaken identity, as they'd clearly been expecting visitors, but that put my possession of the Diaries of Kyros Orion Olomb and its handwritten message down to no sheer coincidence. It was orchestrated.

Natalie was going to *kill* me.

The figure stroked their chin. They turned to the lounging man with the displeased face and triangular grille.

"Vestas, what do you make of this?" He asked.

"It's strange." They said, "*Tona Narsus* said that one of them was powerful. *Saraker* noted the power in his eyes. I can't see how they *wouldn't* know."

The yellow figure turned back to me.

"Who were you *expecting* here tonight?" I asked. "Are you sure it was me?"

"We weren't expecting anybody, really." They said. "You just happened to stumble into our meeting."

"And you just happened to know who I was?"

"All new, unexpected Suneva are of my concern." They said, a strange smile forming beneath their helmet. I wasn't sure how I could tell their expression underneath, but it shone true. "It's important to know that all new Suneva know how to *respectfully* use their talents."

"Look into my eyes, please." He instructed. I did as I was told. He mumbled as he stared into my very being.

"Saraker was right. I see the leadership in this future, but maybe not the same power. This is a strangely clouded aura. I'm surprised that he reported much clarity."

"Would you please tell me what's going on here?" I asked. "I don't understand any of this, and I still don't know how you knew my name before I did." All of the figures in the room turned to each other, as if deliberating silently between themselves. Then, the yellow figure smiled.

"Destiny tells us many odd things. Its compulsions can lead us to conclusions we're not capable of making on our own. You must have felt the hand of destiny by now, and the compulsions it forced you to follow. Included, sometimes, are names. Much like the fact that your parents had a name for you before you could even comprehend it, this universe knows things about us that exist independently of influence. A Suneva's name is *A priori*." They grinned, squatting to my level. "This must be a confusing experience for you."

"Definitely." I nodded. I had felt the compulsions, clearly. It was strange to call them destiny, but I had nothing to attribute them to. Could my name really exist before *me*, though?

"Introductions are in order then." They said, extending a hand. "I'm *Fara Hesslik*, although, please just call me *Hesslik*. I'm the leader of *The Empire of the Black Suns*."

"Great. I'm Maiki, or so the universe tells you." I responded, glad not to have to use my real name. I reached up to shake his hand. His long, metal fingers were cold to touch, and threatened to stab mine at any moment. "So, you rule over an empire?" I asked.

"It's a deceiving name." He said. His demeanour was much cheerier than it had been ten seconds ago. It put me off, somewhat. "We're not an *Empire*, we're a community for Suneva, and a *religion*. The name is for tradition's sake."

"A religion?" I noted. "I didn't think I'd find religion involved with real magic." I hummed, then turned. "Are you *really* sure that I'm who you say I am? I couldn't possibly be a Suneva, right? Let alone the guy referenced in this *one* book." I held out the book which I had taken with me. Hesslik reached out for it, and I gave it to him.

"You have a thread to a black hole. You have a soul, and destiny has named you. You are a Suneva, Maiki." He smiled, turning the first page. He examined the note.

"If you read these diaries, then you know about the Suneva, at least?" He asked me.

"I know very little." I admitted, although I wouldn't have admitted to having only gotten two-thirds through the tale and given up. Old-timey narrators told awful stories without much in the way of plot structure. Reading Olomb's diaries was a chore. "The idea of the Suneva has been hard to swallow, despite having seen many. I just can't take black-hole-energy at face value. It seems too made-up." Although, it was mind boggling to think I might be a part of something so fantastical. I could barely comprehend what it meant for me. What did this make me now? Would I change, or was I always different?

They chuckled lightly.

"I was like you, Maiki. Unlike my fellow associates, I did not come from a Suneva family. I had to discover this all for myself. Granted, I discovered it at a much younger age, where I was more willing to believe it all. Yes, it all seems crazy, but part of being a good Suneva is opening your mind to the possibilities. If you don't believe in anything so far, believe in this…"

He squatted down to my level, and held his two, gun-metal grey hands between our bodies. There was a crack of electricity, and a bright spark which caused me to close my eyes. When I opened them, there was an arc of light coursing between his two palms.

"I don't think I can do that…" I squirmed from the arc. As pretty and mesmerising as it was, it was still a deadly zap. In the back of my mind, the thought of Natalie was nagging at me. Each detail I learned right now was something I'd either have to explain to her or hide from her. Through my excitement to learn, there was insane guilt. How could I do this?

"Oh, of course not." Hesslik chuckled. "No, you're not a *liktas* like me. You can't control electricity. Amasos no!"

"What can I control then?" I asked. My next question came to my mind, and it was the question from which there was no turning back. "I mean, I barely believe that I could, so *how* could I do it?"

Hesslik looked over his shoulder to the armoured figure with the eternally disappointed expression.

"Vestas, maybe you should explain this."

They nodded, and the figure known as Vestas pulled up a stool from the kitchen and sat opposite me.

"Hi," he said. He talked fast, and in a smart, London accent. "I'm Vestas, I'm a *quatra* scientist. I study Suneva and their energy. Everybody in this room is a Suneva including yourself. Have you got that far?"

"I have now." I replied, although I still wasn't sure that I could comprehend this. What had just been fantasy, or a possible elaborate hoax to fool two kids, was now very real, and something that explained my own past experience. Accepting that these armoured figures were Suneva, and everything that came along with that, was a leap of trust.

"Great. Let's go from the start." Vestas sped on. "*Suneva* comes from the words *Sun*: Black sun, and *Eva*: children. *Suneva*: Children of the Black Sun. Those words are from a language called *liktan*, which we use not because it's fun, but because the language holds many Suneva concepts that don't translate well. You lose too many connotations when you, say, translate *quatra* to *black hole mass energy*. It holds more meaning than that. *Liktan* is a language which has remained relatively unchanged for over two thousand years."

"Okay, that's very interesting." I noted, "But how does the power work?"

He looked at me blankly.

"You receive quatra from your black hole. You are connected – I can tell just by your eyes – to Omercronius. Everybody receives a unique set of wavelengths of quatra energy through their *thread*. The thread, like most Suneva concepts, is debatably tangible. It connects to you in the biggest bone in the base of your neck."

He rubbed the back of his own neck to indicate where he was talking about. It was exactly where Natalie's skin had glowed red on Saturday night, and where she said she had always had pain. Then something else occurred to me.

"That's where *I've* been getting pain." I remembered aloud. "Is that the thread?"

"It could be." He huffed, "I'm a scientist, not a chiropractor."

And so it was *maybe* confirmed – Natalie was a Suneva too. And, how couldn't she be? With all of our shared experience, with the amazing coincidences of *destiny* in our journey so far, how could I suspect otherwise?

How the *hell* did I break this to her? Would she accept it as easily as I did?

"Are you familiar with the conservation of energy?" Vestas swiftly moved on.

"Yes." I responded, my mind racing from future anxiety back to my lessons in chemistry and physics. "Energy which goes into a system must equal the energy which goes out." Ms Gordon had taught me well.

"Good: energy in is energy out. It's the same concept with Suneva. You receive quatra, which has an incredibly high energy density, and convert it into the energy to manipulate the world around you, through your *soul connection* to the world. Hesslik and I are *Liktas*: our *soul connection* is to electricity. *Boekidin* over there…" He pointed to the large, bird-like Suneva with the beady pink eyes. "Is a *Kidin*. That's a little bit different to most Suneva abilities in that it's not so easily quantifiable. It boils down to mind reading. I've been working hard to quantify the soul connection in terms of energy frequencies and other *real* numbers. So far, we have correlations, but nothing set in stone."

Mind reading? My lips pursed shut. I eyed the mechanical bird. Was he listening now? His silent gaze became much more imposing. I couldn't be sure if I was safe in my own head. "Thank you." I said to Vestas.

"You're welcome." He cut me off.

"So, what are my abilities, then?" I asked.

Vestas looked to *Fara Hesslik*.

"Isn't that quite the question." Hesslik chortled, and made his way over to me. "A soul connection is something you will have always felt, and been aware of. Just like colour-blindness, you'd never know you had it until you could see life through somebody else's eyes. Luckily, a Suneva can experience life as a pure human for a short time."

He held his grey hand in front of my chest. His first two fingers were up, like a peace sign. His thumb was held out, and the third and fourth fingers faced forward of the palm. In my gut, I knew that this gesture was dangerous. Every fibre of muscle was screaming at me to move away. I was more stunned than I was brave to sit still in its face.

"Would you mind Vestas taking a frequency reading?" He asked me. Vestas now held in his hand an instrument which could only be described as a digital donut.

"No, that's fine." I squirmed, hiding my strange, unsolicited fear. Vestas made his way behind me and held the donut above the base of my neck. This was also viscerally uncomfortable. I shrunk into the couch.

"Got the reading." Vestas said.

"Alright, Maiki. This might sting. You also might feel like vomiting, but that's normal."

"Really?" I squeaked. Before I had time to protest, a three-ringed blast of energy in bright cyan – a blast of quatra energy – came from Hesslik's posed hand. It collided with my chest. It felt hot on my body. It entered my very veins, and soared through branches of arteries towards my neck.

A blindfold was draped over my senses. I could still see, hear, touch, smell, and do everything perfectly, but something was missing, something *huge*. My spatial awareness fell flat; plummeting to nothing, I was suddenly aware that I must have had a very, very keen sense of the world around me. I couldn't feel where everybody was in the room, nor how big it was, nor where open doors were.

Beyond that, it was easy to notice the lack of energy in my body. Now that it was gone, I could tell that there was always a baseline buzzing of energy at the bone of my neck.

There was also this missing *fullness* to the world. It was the same fullness which made grey-lead pencils feel more *full* than coloured pencils, and Mrs Gordon's engagement ring feel less *full* than a diamond. This feeling of density used to exist all around me. Was I feeling *carbon*?

"Carbon." I said aloud, realising I hadn't been listening to anything happening over the sensation of the dull world around me. The realisation of this new sensation was exciting – enough to make me forget how tense this whole experiment had been. I really *was* connected to the world.

Now I'd have to deal with the consequences of it.

"*Maikess* goes within the two-twenty-five Hertz range." Vestas noted. "I picked it up."

"*Maikess* is carbon." Hesslik noted.

"And four-fifty-five Hertz, well, that matches up with *Muhrakiin*. I'd say he's a *Kiin*."

"*Kiin*?" I asked.

"Air." Hesslik responded. "*Maikess Kiin, Maiki.* Carbon and air."

It all made sense. When my neck throbbed at the thread, wind would pick up around me. I'd never thought that the gusting wind was important until now. Were my dreams of flying were an expression of this connection?

"A *Kiin* of *Omercronius* no less. Muhrakiin only left us a few years ago. We thought that he was the last *Omercronian Kiin* to grace the earth. I'm glad to be proven wrong."

"This is all incredible." I uttered, "I can't believe that I never noticed any of this before. Am I stupid?"

"Not stupid," Vestas said, "Simply human. We were all there, at some point."

"Anyway, with revelations aside…" Hesslik marched on, "I did come here for business, not to educate you on all things Suneva. Maiki, I would like you to join my Empire community. With leadership in your future, I have no doubts that you would quickly rise to a high rank in my council – which is ultimately where I see you. I would also like to ask you to participate in Vestas' research. He's been searching a long while for interesting quatra users such as yourself – those who were introduced to abilities later in life."

"That's quite an offer, Hesslik." I said, stunned. I wasn't sure that I trusted these Suneva, yet. Would I really get involved with them so easily? "Would you teach me how to use my abilities?"

"I will teach you how to be a better *Suneva*, but I cannot teach you much about *kiin*. You are the only one left, after all. *Kiin* is now but a dead art."

"So, what's the point of joining you?" I asked, "I mean, what could you and the Empire offer me if not lessons?"

"Community." Hesslik stated, "Community, so that you're not alone in this growth of yours, and teachings of ethics and Suneva philosophies."

"Right." I noted. Community sounded somewhat wholesome – guidance through this *would* be nice.

"These things are important, Maiki, for the world we live in today. After the fall of the last Suneva nation, Olomb's Electric Nation, we lost community and guidelines. When Suneva yearned for the *good old days*, and wanted to be a part of society again, families like the French Argols rose to power as centres of community and established the idea that we had to abuse those around us to gain respect. They forced the idea that we are separate from human society, and will not integrate, but rather be a force of reckoning. I want to integrate Suneva back into the social world, and I want to do it peacefully. We should not be feared, and we should be allowed to be ourselves in all situations.

"I took the teachings that Olomb fought wars to attain, and modified them for today's Suneva. With the community I'm creating, no lost Suneva like yourself will have to question who they are and find no answers – or worse still, find their answers with *evil* men who seek to exploit their powers.

"A greater awareness of the Suneva and our teachings of introspection, peace, and justice will give young Suneva like you and me a place to connect with others and understand ourselves, our destinies, and our place in the cosmos. With strict ethical codes, people will know what to expect from us, and we will always have a defence against those who call us *'devils'* and *'evil'*. Only through cooperation, not destruction, will we rise to be a part of the modern world."

Hesslik flicked his right wrist. In it appeared a blue handle, and from the handle grew a curved sword, in the shape of a stylised lightning bolt. He held it firmly by his side.

"If you join this community, Maiki. You can become a realised Suneva, and together, we shall all rise."

There was silence in the room. I found it strange that now, without the connection I'd apparently always had, I couldn't tell the emotions behind the masks. I was staring at blank helmets. Before, at least, I had some idea of a smile under the armour. I wasn't sure how to respond.

"Do you take my offer, Maiki?" Hesslik asked.

"I'm not sure." I said. In truth, I couldn't commit to anything here or now. Not without Natalie. *Oh fuck, Natalie.* How in the great holy-hell for cheese would I explain all of *this* to her? This was no scouting mission, this was solving the whole bloody mystery right behind her back! I couldn't move on without her, not when she, in all reality, probably was a Suneva too. "It sounds good, it really does." I wasted time. "In fact, it's aimed at people like me…"

"*Suneva* like you." Hesslik corrected.

I thought of Kuvalik, whose note indicated that my first Suneva duty was to find him. He had answers for me, and Natalie too. Maybe that was my first *'place in the cosmos'* that I needed to be after Natalie handed my ass to me. "But still, I don't think I can afford to get into this stuff right now. I'm in the middle of year twelve. I need this year to study, you know?"

Hesslik nodded.

"And I'm really not sure I'd be much use to your research, Vestas. I mean, I wasn't even aware of my own Suneva…ness until today."

"Oh, you're exactly what we're looking for. *Believe me.*" Vestas said. Without knowing his expression, it sounded somewhat sinister.

"It's okay, Maiki." Hesslik said, "We all understand. Still, you're such a promising young Suneva, I know this isn't the last time we'll meet." He extended his hand to me, I shook it again. "I'll be watching your progress closely, and with great interest, Maiki." He said to me. There was no guiding smile or crooked expression for me to see, nothing to frame his intentions except for a flat, glowing face.

Then, I felt my body flush insanely hot, like boiling water had been poured into my blood. My body seized, my lungs filled, and all of my senses returned. The *fullness* to everything was back, and my spatial awareness was entirely restored. In my neck, I could feel the energy buzzing.

Through his helmet, Hesslik wore a sly smile.

"Anyway, I must be off. I can't stay in Melbourne too long, and the night is setting. I get most of my work done at night." He joked.

"Wait." I said, frantic now. "How long are you staying here? I have a friend who I think needs to meet you."

"I'm leaving tomorrow – I'm not sure what time." Hesslik said. "But Vestas is staying. If you come back here tomorrow, I might still be around."

"I'll have to do that." I noted. I could still act like I hadn't been here. I could get pretend-surprised at all of these revelations tomorrow night. I just had to make these Suneva would play along with the charade.

"Take this, just in case." Hesslik said. He handed me a pamphlet. The picture on the front was the image of the white circle with the black radial flames. The pamphlet flopped lamely in my hand. Surely people with black-hole-magic could make a cooler infographic than a pamphlet.

"That's the symbol of the Suneva, and of my Empire." Hesslik pointed to the picture. His voice inflected with glee, like he was proud of this work. "There's not much to this, just our aims, and a simplified outline of our moral code. Still, it's important information."

I opened the pamphlet. It, indeed, had a bit of writing in it. I didn't feel like reading it all now.

"Thank you." I said.

"You're welcome, Maiki." He returned. He extended his hand to help me up. I took it. "As I said, I will monitor your progress closely Maiki. This is a goodbye for now, but certainly not forever."

"I hope to see you again." I said, and what I meant was '*I hope that you're here tomorrow so that I don't lose my new best friend.*' He escorted me through to the door, then closed it behind me. The water which was stuck in my ear finally dripped out, and the feeling left me very satisfied.

As I walked home, I could feel the gentle breeze rustle through the trees, and I was now aware that this wasn't normal. I still couldn't believe what had happened to me. There was no choice in this, only being thrown a life-changing trait and told to run with it. Worst of all, how would I hide this from Simone?

I am Maiki. I have a soul connection. I thought to myself, the breeze rustling through my fingers. *What I do with this?*

Episode 2

How to Get Your Heart Broken in Three Easy Steps.

"I only went out to the building to scout, you know? Had to see that old Finneck was there, and…" *No, that's stupid*, I grumbled. I sat on the early train to school the next morning, on my way to band practice. I thanked the lucky stars that Natalie wasn't going to school early to get homework done, which she usually did, because then I'd have to face her now. This *destiny* thing was giving me extra time not to screw this up, and I had to be thankful.

I had the pamphlet that Hesslik had given me in my bag. I palmed it again, peering at the radial flame symbol of the Empire. I could feel my thread buzzing now that I focussed on it, and I could sense the energy that it had always given me. When the train doors opened, I could feel the air rush in to the train cabin. There was also that familiar *fullness* to everything around me which I could sense through my palms. I couldn't do anything with the energy, but there was something strangely comfortable in the validation of these senses I never realised were quite there. It was like finding a part of yourself you'd forgotten, deep in that box of things you kept in the garage. Although, strangely, maybe I *had* held my father's final breath in my hands. That was scary.

Either way, this knowledge of myself *felt* right. Holding the air in my hands gave me a silly elation. Hopefully Natalie would feel the same way. Maybe that's how I could phrase it…

Oh cheese… I moaned again to myself. I had no idea how to break this to her. I could see my future now, painted before me as a terrible daytime soap opera. Either I admitted full fault and Natalie became very angry in my impatience, or I lied to appear better and the whole truth ended up coming out, tarnishing my image in her eyes. Should I kiss her ass or lie to hide my wrong doing? Which way best preserved me?

I had plenty of time to keep playing over scenarios in band. With each gut wrenching simulation of taking a backhand to the face, another layer of nerves was plastered onto my already jittering mood. I considered not telling her at all, and just going back to Finneck's house to find Hesslik again, but what if he wasn't there? And I didn't have a chance to corroborate with him on a false set of events. He'd either sell out my lie unknowingly, or if he wasn't there, I'd have to explain the whole thing to her in a creepy, abandoned house.

Dread looming over my day, I finally mustered the courage to leave the music buildings and head back to the senior school. With any luck, Natalie wouldn't show up like yesterday. Yes, I could live on that hope.

I waddled through the senior school under the weight of my physical and emotional baggage. The only thing that kept me moving beyond the stress of having to preserve my image to my friend was this strange elation of the soul. I was keying into feelings that I'd always had, but now knew that they must have been related to the air around me. That odd sensation of weight on my palm, maybe that was increased pressure? The distractions let me get to my locker, whereby I picked up my bags and mashed them into the small cupboard without thought. I drew out the next two period's mangled, dishevelled books, when I sensed a disturbance behind me, like a shadow over my shoulder. I closed the door lightly, dreading what I might see, and turned slowly.

"Jesus, James." Natalie said, her face cringing. "You do *not* keep a clean locker. Far out."

"Ah!" I yelped at seeing her smiling face. I backed myself right into the locker door, vying to gain control over my body and face. This moment had come *way* too soon. I was stunned.

"So, do you want to…"

"I've got a meeting with Ms Gordon!" I blurted, catching my words as they fluttered from my brain. "I've got to go, I'll see you later!" I rushed past her, bolting for the stairs. I barely caught my breath by the time I crested the flight. I could sense how laboured it was, that feeling teasing me. Natalie would *have* to know of my, and *her* abilities sooner rather than later. I ran off to Ms Gordon's office. I didn't actually have a meeting, but I could just go there to chat, maybe.

"James, I thought you were better than this." Ms Gordon said sternly, her glasses hanging low over her nose. She rocked back in her chair, shaking her head. I'd told her that I had to reveal to a friend that I'd broken an agreement of trust because I was too impatient. "It's very selfish of you to ruin a plan like that." She noted. "And I don't think you're in the right mind frame if your only concern is *protecting your image.*"

Ouch. It did sound bad put that way, didn't it? I squirmed into the chair she'd given me. Other teachers shared this office, and I could feel their judgement cresting upon me.

"I just don't want them to be mad at me. I don't know what to do! Every path leads to that."

"Then that means you've done something you *know* is bad, which is arguably worse." Ms Gordon frowned. "What about all of that philosophy we discussed late last year? Do you remember looking within to find your own validation?"

"Yes…"

"So, forget what Natalie thinks…"

"I didn't even mention her name!"

"Oh, who else would it be?" Ms Gordon sighed. "Forget what she thinks and internalise this. Are you proud of your actions? Would you be proud to hide their extent to save your image?

"No." I hummed.

"What about your integrity?"

"Yes, I get it Ms Gordon." I sighed, feeling the immense guilt she'd managed to make me load on myself. With it though, weight was lifted. I knew I had to tell Natalie, now. I had to be proactive, because being honest was the only way to be proud of my actions. "Thank you." I resurrected from the chair.

"Any time, Mr Grey."

And so at recess, right after getting out of Maths, I put my books away and ran over to Natalie's locker. I soared up two flights of stairs, all the way to the top of the blue tower. Rounding the corner five minutes into the break, I expected to have missed her. The locker bay was empty except for one stirring soul. Rhys Cameron. His untucked, creased uniform came into view just as I crested the last set of stairs. Blood flushed into my system. My face went hot. Me and him up here alone? I didn't see this ending well. I tried to sneak onto the linoleum floor, but he turned to the noise anyway. I froze up. He frowned.

"James Grey." He grumbled.

"Rhys Cameron." I stuttered. Rhys Cameron was a big boy. His enthusiasm for gym over studying was what forced him into paying Tom for a grade change. Since his encounter with the principal some weeks ago, his muscles seemed to bulge even larger under his already tight shirt.

"What are you doing up here, dick-for-brains?" He pulled some books out, then slammed his locker door shut.

"I'm here to talk to Natalie." I said, prying myself tall. All I had to do was *look* imposing. In my palms, I had a sense of the size and *fullness* of the room. I wished there was some way it could help me here.

"She must be the only person you talk to past sucking up to teachers, mate." He leaned on the locker door. "I tell you what, Jimmy. Tom's an alright bloke. He stood up for you where I don't recon he should have. The second he does something wrong, I bet you'd rat him in."

"I wouldn't, man." I said.

"Mate…" He laughed, and strutted his way over to me. He rolled up his sleeves, revealing stupidly toned, rippling forearms. I squirmed at my bag straps.

backing away. My heels hung over the ledge of the first stair, and I wobbled. "You're an absolute rat, and a total idiot. Don't lie – you got me and the lads suspended last year."

"So?" I coughed. I didn't care to piss Rhys off, but I wouldn't be dismissed for doing the right thing. "You drink on a train in school uniform, expect to get in trouble. This institution is bigger than you." I tried to sound tough, but it was hard to keep focus with his mammoth shadow cast over me. "Don't shit on the image it creates. Your parents pay good money for it."

I tried to stand tall, teetering on the step's edge. He laughed in my face.

"See, that's the problem I have with you." He said. He grabbed my shirt between the buttons and hoisted me high. I tried to resist, but was useless against his strength. Rhys turned, and slammed me up against the wall. My bag was crushing into my back. My arms struggled to hold to something, *anything*.

"You think you're above all of us, but you're *that* concerned with image and class. You're a wanker, mate. But you'd never admit it. You sit up there with your high grades thinking you're better than everybody. Well, I know you're a fuckwit. Do you?"

I didn't have a response. I wasn't going to call him out again on his disrespect for the opportunity his parents had given him. I wasn't going to call him out for being entitled enough to believe he didn't deserve consequence for breaking rules. I wasn't going to call him a prick, in general. I had nothing to say.

"I thought so." He said. "You think I'm going to hit you? I might be thick, but I'm not that stupid. I already got suspended once."

I breathed a sigh of relief.

At that moment, I saw a head of thick, wavy hair bobbing up the stairwell. Natalie Athanas emerged under it. She had a very full bag on her back and arms laden with books. Rage built in her crystal blue eyes like fire to kindling. She roared up the steps, expertly sliding her bag across the linoleum floor of the locker bay and marching her way over to Rhys and I.

"You put him down this instant, you thug." She demanded of Rhys. Her expression was ruthless. Her stare could kill. Her hand held power in its grasp, and Rhys sensed it. He eased his grip.

"I was just finished with my lesson." He mumbled, lowering me to the ground. "You're lucky your girlfriend showed up…"

I blushed. Natalie grimaced.

"You dare call me that again, Rhys Cameron…" She scowled.

"And you'll do what?" He asked, letting go of my shirt and shoving me for good measure.

Natalie didn't have a response. Her face went red. She kept her finger pointed at him and growled. Her stare and scowl were intense, her gaze piercing, like a witch delivering a curse. Despite his cool face, Rhys still backed off with hands in the air. He collected his books, and made a wide radius around Natalie on his way to the stairs.

"Should I hang a *'do not disturb'* sign on my way out?" He called over his shoulder as he descended the steps. Natalie picked up her plastic water bottle from her bag and pitched it at the back of his head. The shot was perfect. The bottle exploded on impact – as if by her command – and drenched his back. He paused and turned while the water steamed off his cool face. He picked up the bottle, teased it over the railing, and dropped it down the centre of the stairwell. He continued his way down after it.

"You're pretty amazing, you know that." I uttered to her.

"Yeah, sure." She said going over to her locker and fiddling with the combination, "He's in the locker next to me. I can't stand him. I defend you every day."

"You do?" I asked. The guilt that I was about to let her down hit me, but I couldn't let it stop me from telling the truth.

"Yeah." She said. "I mean, you'd back me up, right?"

"Of course I would." I said.

"Good." She said. She opened the locker door.

"How was spending time with your Mum?" I asked. "I didn't even run into you yesterday."

"Yeah, it was great." She said, "I really love spending time with Mum." Her voice dropped.

"What's the matter?"

"Don't worry. It was genuinely a good time. The waves were great. I spent extra time with her and came to school late."

"Sure." I squirmed, "Sounds good then. Caught up on work?"

"I caught up in lunch time yesterday." She said, "You should know me James." With her books in hand, she closed her locker. She flicked herself around, letting her hair fly in my face. She gestured for me to follow her.

"So, what did you get up to last night?" She asked.

"I, uh..." I hummed, coming to a pause. She stopped on her step, peering up at me.

"What happened?" She asked. I could see her concern, but I could also sense her glare penetrating me. She was trying to read me. Best I was quick about letting her down.

"Look, let's take a seat somewhere." I said, and scanned the vicinity. There was a bench overlooking the cafeteria, right on the mezzanine walkway. "Over there." I pointed, and walked past her. She followed curiously.

"Is something wrong?" She asked.

"No." I said, then reconsidered. "I mean, *maybe*. It depends on your point of view."

"What is it?" She asked. I slid myself onto the bench and she followed. She was so concerned, I could see it in her gentle face. She was ready to back me through anything, so keen to help out, and I'd totally broken her trust. My lip quivered.

"I'm a Suneva, Natalie." I said.

"I…" Her brow turned. "Excuse me?"

"And so are you. You have to be."

"James, have you been hiding this from me?" She asked. Her voice had a growl to it. She wasn't hurt, she was angry. This was exactly as I feared. My eyes shot wide, it was time to activate this bicycle's backpedal.

"No, no!" I objected. "I only found out last night. I swear."

"What did you do without me?" She huffed. "How could you possibly know that? What makes you even suggest it?"

"I investigated the Finneck lead last night." I said, and the completion of my sentence caused her eyeball to burst a vessel.

"James!" She growled.

"But the old man wasn't there. I would have turned back, but there were actual Suneva in the building." It looked as if she was going to object, so I rushed to get my words out over hers. "They were the leaders of the new Suneva world. The *leaders*. And I'm *Maiki*, the guy whose name is in the book. The message was to me. It was all meant to happen.

"And, I *know* that you're a Suneva, because you get the pain in your neck. It's your Suneva thread, that's what the scientist Suneva told me. Plus, you've been so involved in all of these coincidences, it had to be destiny."

"So the *universe* wanted you to break our plans, James? The *universe* tells me what I am?" She mocked, "God, don't pin some divine plan on your selfishness. Didn't you know that I was excited to find everything out? Why should I hear this from you?"

"I knew you were excited, Natalie. I did! And I'm sorry." There were tears coming to my eyes now, I couldn't handle this, and I damn-well *hated* getting teary. It only made me more emotional. "I thought I was just scouting the place, then the whole thing fell out of control, and I couldn't leave it. I had to talk to the Suneva. I discovered something about myself that has explained so much about my life. And it will about yours, too.”

“Well, I’m glad I was there to hear about it.” She scorned. I’d tried being remorseful, even reasonable, but she still chose to hate. That got me worked up.

“They might not even be there tonight.” I protested, turning red. “I stumbled into a chance meeting of, apparently, some of the best people to talk to. In fact, I was *drawn* there.” Maybe I sounded too righteous, that wasn’t helping my case. “Look, Natalie, you *are* a Suneva.”

“And what do I do with that information?” She asked, baffled. “What does it even mean?”

“I don’t know.” I said. “But they might be there again tonight. *Something* will be. Some clue. You have to come with me. I have to make it up to you, and find out *who* you are.”

She sighed, long and loud. I could see the gears turning in her head. She was mad, but she was considering my concession.

“I even found this.” I gave her more food for thought, reaching into my backpack. “It’s a pamphlet that Hesslik gave me – he’s the leader, the guy with the lighting-bolt helmet. It’s all about what it means to be a Suneva, or something. I was saving reading it to read it with you…” I couldn’t feel the pamphlet anywhere. I pulled out my books, and still I couldn’t see it. I tipped the whole thing upside down, letting my mess fly. Natalie wasn’t impressed.

“I’ll find it…” I said, well aware that I’d now lost it. *How could I lose something so important?* “But it had that symbol on it. The one from your book, with the radial flames. Like a cross.”

“James, quiet.” She demanded finally. I zipped my lips, sitting tall to her command. “I’m mad, James, but it sounds like you’ve honestly done well. You were selfish, and *awful* to go behind my back – don’t get me wrong – but I can see that you really do care about how I feel here…somehow.”

“Thank you.” I uttered, but she held a hand to my mouth.

“*Never* deceive my trust again.” She warned, a finger pointed to my eyes. “I will not tolerate being stepped over, is that clear?”

“Yes, Natalie.” I nodded.

“Tonight, we’re going to that house as planned.” She demanded. “You will meet me at my locker at three thirty-five. We’re going straight from here, and you *will* show me everything I need to know. I’m after some answers James.”

“You’ll have them.” I said. “I promise it.” Although, I really had no way to guarantee it. I just had to step up to the strange challenge.

“Good.” She nodded, rising “I’ll see you then.”

“Where are you going?” I asked, rushing to follow. She walked off.

"I need time to think, James." She said without turning to me. "You just told me *a lot*." And with that, she sauntered off. I depressed back into the bench, my mushy brain swimming in its cavity, glad to be through with that interaction.

I wasn't sure if it went worse or better than I expected.

***

Natalie and I disembarked from the train station and made our way through the underpass. I noted Natalie's expression as she passed the marks left by the Suneva encounter. Where I had gleaned over them and moved on, she crouched down by a scorch mark.

"They must be powerful." She said, running her finger through the melted groove.

"Well, it *was* fire." I noted.

"Yes, but regular fire doesn't do that to asphalt." She said. "I can see why your sister is so scared."

"Sure," I said. "But it's *us* now that she's so scared of. That doesn't feel great."

Natalie nodded, standing. "I'm sorry for getting mad before." She changed the subject. I hummed.

"No, no, you were right to be mad."

"I know." She said, shutting me up. "But I'm excited to see where this goes. *If* I am a Suneva, I can define myself apart from *this*." She pointed to the fire stain. "If I'm a Suneva, I know I'm not violent like the men we saw, so I know I shouldn't be scared of what we might be."

"Huh…" I nodded. "You've clearly thought of this."

"I have." She said. "Now, let's go." She gestured me on, and I lead us over the crossing, and down the street to the house at its end.

I opened the gate and gestured her through. She took the first steps across the weed-overgrown garden. She tip-toed carefully between the tall grass and spider webs sticking up between the brick path. We pulled ourselves up onto the veranda, coming to the door.

I couldn't help but notice the lack of *glowing*. There was nothing *drawing* me into the abandoned building today, no cyan glow. I felt a tension rise in my stomach – I was going to disappoint Natalie. I'd promised her answers, I'd have to deliver. I looked to her, and she seemed content – excited even – to be standing outside the spooky house. I was glad that she wasn't mad, at least. I reached across to the bicycle where I'd seen the key yesterday, and pulling it out of the attached bag, I slotted it into the door's lock.

85

I shoved the door, which was heavier than I'd expected, and it creaked open slowly. The house groaned, and something fell in its depths. The hallway was empty. A beam lay across the back doors. Light poured in from a hole in the roof at the back-right of the house. I couldn't see much from the front door, but I immediately had the sense that we were being watched. There were eyes looking at me. They weren't coming from a direction, but rather all around.

"Do you feel that?" Natalie asked.

"The feeling of being watched?" I asked. She nodded.

I was going to follow my instincts and turn around, but she grabbed my hand and walked through the entrance. She pulled me into the house, then closed the door behind us. Darkness set upon us. Dust floated in the still air. Moans and groans of timber and metal echoed softly. Somewhere in the structure, water was dripping. There was a hole in the floor in front of us. There was still the intense feeling of being watched.

"Charming place." She said, and swung her bags down by the door. I followed suit.

"It used to be better." I noted, and took in the sights again. "I guess Hesslik's not here."

"But somebody is." Natalie said. "I've never felt so *seen*, and I can feel them here…"

"If you say so." I said. I ducked my head into the room immediately to our left I let go of Natalie's hand, but she searched for it and grabbed it again. There was nothing in here except for a bookshelf missing most of its books, and a few pieces of antique furniture. Glass was scattered on the floor by the bay window. Graffiti covered the bay.

"Nobody in here." I said, turning to Natalie. The lights behind me flickered, painting the room in splashes of yellow light. Neither of our hands were on the switch. I spun back around, to see the lightbulb burn white hot. It blew up, and glass sprayed onto the floor.

"Uh…" I mumbled.

"They're not in here." Natalie rushed, with a straight face. "Let's keep moving."

"Yes, good idea." I agreed.

She led us out of the front room and down the hall. Vines grew freely from the roof. They hugged the walls where the light from the roof's hole reached. Sporadically along the wall were tags – lazily done graffiti *'art'* by losers like Rhys Cameron. It was marking your area with all the intellectual complexity of pissing on a tree. I sneered. Natalie tutted.

"Glad we're agreed on that." I said.

"Even graffiti artists are agreed on that, James." She said.

She stalked past the living room and kitchen, towards this person she knew was present. I followed her lead. To the right was the couch on which I had sat and Hesslik had introduced himself to me. We walked under the open roof. The structure around the hole was charred, like it had been burned through. A main beam in the roof had been cut. I was surprised that the ceiling hadn't fallen in.

She opened the sliding door near the end of the hall. Its bearings were rusty, it howled as it was forced aside. I frantically scanned the living area for anybody who might have heard the sound – like nails across a chalkboard. Nobody had heard, of course, but I still felt the omnipresent gaze.

We ducked into a secondary hallway. There was a door at the end, towards the front of the house, and a few on the side.

"They're down the end." Natalie said.

"Are you sure?" I asked.

"Yes" She said, entirely serious. "I don't know if I'm leaning into some false sense, here, but I can feel it." I wasn't about to deny her the right to new sensations, so I nodded and followed. We stalked down the hallway, being sure to take light steps. The house creaked and groaned behind us, however, it was silent underfoot.

My heart thumped as we came towards the door. I reached for it first, resting my hand on the handle. I looked to Natalie, and we breathed in unison. We mouthed, *three, two, one…*

I turned the handle and pushed. The door moved so smoothly, and we'd put so much weight against it, that we fell into the room together, landing in each other, becoming tangled on the floor. We scrambled to get out of each other's limbs.

Bare wooden boards with loose nails made the floor that we'd fallen upon. To our right was a bed frame, and at the back of the room was a closet and a standing dresser. On the door side of the bed was an old sword, in a stand, and on the opposite side of the bed was a chest of drawers. A large open window by the drawers let dull light shine through the room. The day was bright outside, but the light streaming through the glass was so grey.

"I understand holding a hand for comfort…" I teased as we pried ourselves apart.

"Shut up." She smiled, pulling herself to her feet. She extended a hand to help me up. I took it.

"Maybe it's the wrong room?" I suggested.

"No, this is right." She said, and scanned the room. "I just don't get it."

"No shame in trying to follow your instincts, even if nothing happens." I said.

She grunted, and turned from me to stalk around the room. She opened the wardrobe, then made her way around the bed.

"You think they're hiding?" I chuckled.

"I'm just looking." She said.

The standing wardrobe caught my attention. There was something etched into the inside of its door, which Natalie left open. Upon closer inspection, there was a message, carved with a knife, in a foreign scripture. It looked almost like the language in Natalie's book. It could have been the language that Vestas mentioned to me.

"Hey, come look at this." I said to her. "Do you recognise this?"

Natalie creeped her way over, making sure not to step on exposed nails from where the carpet had been ripped out. She leaned over me, tucking her head between mine and my arm to get a look at the writing.

The door to the room behind us slammed against the wall. The room shook. Natalie and I screamed, and jumped out of our shoes. We whipped around, still yelling, and backed each other into the dresser.

"*Boo!*" Laughed Rhys Cameron, standing in the doorway. He strutted into the room with swagger, pulling up a seat on the bed frame, and ripping a bite from his apple. His grin was from ear to ear.

"Cheesus H. *fucking* Christ!" I yelled. My face ran from white to red. I scrambled off the dresser and pulled Natalie up after me. "What the *fuck* are you doing following us?"

"Not illegal." He grinned, "I wanted to see what the two love-birds were up to in an abandoned house. Between you and me, James, I think I entered at the wrong time."

"Shut up and get out." I demanded. I'd never been so forceful in my life, and a grin of satisfaction irked to join my face because of it.

"Oh, you don't get to make the rules here." Rhys said, rising to stand over me. "You see, this isn't in school. Principal won't do anything about what happens out here. Plus, you try and tell somebody else, you'll have to justify being here." He rolled up the sleeves of his jumper, and undid his tie.

"Rhys, get the hell out." Natalie said, storming up to him.

"Back off *Athanas*." He spat. He put his meaty hand out and shoved her right in the chest. She stumbled backwards into the back wall.

I wound up a fist and swung it across his face. It impacted with the combined weight and destructive power of a sack of feathers. I must have punched wrong too – it was the first punch I'd ever thrown, and my fingers hurt like all hell.

He barely flinched.

"Ah, *cheese*." I grabbed my fist with my other hand.

"You're fucked." Rhys said. He gritted his teeth and wound his own fist. I piled into my gut. Amazingly, I didn't fall, but I did keel over like an idiot. He shoved me hard, and I fell back into my arse, slamming into the dresser.

He stomped towards me. I scrambled to get up. Natalie was regaining herself in the corner. My feet couldn't seem to make me stand – they wailed, frictionless on the hardwood underfloor. Rhys wound his foot, preparing to drive it through my skull.

The lightbulb flickered on. The door slammed shut. Something flew out of the dresser faster than the eye could see. It slammed into Rhys' chest. Broken glass slopped from his jumper onto the floor.

"...the fuck?" He uttered. He groped at his now wet jumper, then turned to the door.

The curtains didn't close, the light didn't change, but the shadows in the room did. A small purple orb formed at shoulder height, just in front of the closed door. To it, the moving shadows lifted and flocked, like black smoke drawn into a vent. A body of pure blackness formed, with the orb at the centre of its neck. From the orb stemmed a network of purple veins, and in the head, they grew into two rectangular eyes. Its form was jagged, like armoured Suneva we'd seen. Its edges were fuzzy, and undefined – like its body never ended.

"Holy…what the…" Rhys went to say, but thought better than to be articulate. Instead, he screamed, and pushed past me, kicking me out of the way to get to the window. He slid it up and climbed through, all in one smooth movement. The window slammed after him, and Natalie and I took that as our cue to start screaming.

The ghost looked just as surprised as us. Whilst we scrambled into the opposite corner of the room, it slicked itself up against the door, trying to get away from the noise. Its ethereal, smoky hand reached by the bedside. It grasped at the rusty sword with a serrated inner edge, set in its stand. It drew the sword above its head.

I felt my thread burn hot on my neck. It was begging me to use its power, but I could barely move. Natalie, squished into the wall behind me, groaned in her own pain and fear.

The ghost threw the sword down, stabbing it into the ground. Natalie and I jumped and shrieked as the floorboard split. Purple radiance pulsed from the orb in the ghost's neck and through its arms. It plunged through the sword, and three rings of purple light burst from its tip. The room was cast in deep violet as the rings expanded across the floor, and climbed up the walls before dissipating.

"H…h…holy…" was all I could choke out.

"Who enters the house of *Kuvalik*?" The ghost boomed over me. Its voice was wise, and it echoed with great power. Its tongue rang like a trumpet.

"W…what?" I chuffed.

"Which Suneva threaten the great leader Kuvalik?" It asked. "Do you come here to vandalise?"

"What?" I choked again. Natalie shoved past me, standing between the ghost and me. It didn't move, it didn't threaten us. Natalie figured out that it's questions weren't rhetorical. It was actually interested in us.

"That other guy wasn't with us, great leader Kuvalik. He's a dick." She said and turned to me. "The sword in the ground is a Suneva greeting, James. It was in my book."

"I see." The ghost replied.

I was flawed looking at it. *A ghost is dead*, the thought bounced in my mind. *Dead, deceased, gone from this earth yet still thinking.* I saw its black figure and smoky outline. I could sense the rot of its flesh, dripping from its cold soul. I had a hard time handling it, despite having seen a ghost before. When dead men walk, all is truly false.

"James, wake up." Natalie waved her hand in front of me, snapping me from my disgusted trance. "This is *Kuvalik*."

"I know." I said. "And I'm Maiki, but Kuvalik is dead. *Long* dead. I've read his death. It's in Olomb's Diaries."

What did it matter if he's dead? I found myself asking. Of course a ghost was dead. That still didn't make it any less frightening.

"Why the hell aren't you frightened by a ghost?" I asked Natalie, my gaze flickering between her and the ethereal being.

"Because it's not trying to hurt us." She said, and she was right, this thing wasn't threatening. In fact, a moment ago, it had been just as frightened as I was. I took a moment to let my heartrate drop, and sucked in a deep breath to peel myself off the wall.

"Hi." I squeaked, looking around the room. "…sorry for the mess." I stumbled towards the ghost. It sparked memories of my childhood haunting, of long fingers wrapped around a cupboard door, of depression and anxiety in every corner. I pushed the sensation aside, I had to, and made my way past Natalie. If this was Kuvalik, I had to talk to him. He was the whole point of coming here. "I…I'm James Grey. I think you know me as *Maiki*."

The purple in its orb buzzed with excitement. The misty form of its body grew in height. A smile came across its black face.

"You've found me. You must be ready to learn." Its voice radiated equally from its entire, undefined being.

"Yeah, well, I don't know how you expected me to find you." I said. "You didn't exactly leave an address."

The ghost smiled. "This first lesson is the one you learn on the way here. As a Suneva, your instincts and feelings are the most valuable tools you have. You are awarded many extra senses with a connection to a black hole. You used them, and you made it here. Congratulations Maiki."

I frowned. I'd used very little to find the ghost today, despite my earlier habits of stumbling into important situations.

"Actually," I said, "It was Natalie who knew you were here. I was ready I pack up and leave when I didn't find Hesslik." I gestured to Natalie. She grinned.

"What is your Suneva name, Ms Natalie?" The ghost asked.

"Am I a Suneva?" Natalie asked, "I might be, but we don't really know yet."

"Undoubtedly, yes." Kuvalik said, "For somebody not yet using quatra energy, your presence is so strong. Do you have somebody to teach you?"

Natalie hummed, nodding to herself. "Well…that's that, then." She didn't quite know what to make of it. "A strong presence?"

"A *very* strong presence. You've got quite the aura."

"I see." She hummed again. "Will you teach me what this means, then?"

"I cannot." The ghost replied. "I made a promise to *Muhrakiin* to train the next *Kiin*, as I was one of the last men to shake hands with the ancient air king. But, I cannot read threads or eyes. I won't be able to help you unless you know *who* you are."

"I see." Natalie sighed. "Do you know somebody I should go to, then?"

"Your presence is familiar. What is your full name, Ms Natalie?" The ghost asked. He wafted through the room, passing by me to rest close to her. His form was electric. The black smoke crawled with static.

"Natalie Athanas." She replied.

"See your Yamitse." He said, without a second thought. "Tell her that Kuvalik sent you. Tell her everything about how you came to find the Suneva. She will teach you, and she will do a very meticulous job of it."

"My Yamiste?" Her eyes shot to fear. "Oh no, I couldn't tell her that I was looking through her books…"

"I promise it to you, she will not care." The ghost said. He laid his dead hand on her shoulder. "She will want to see you grow. Go to her." He said, and Natalie started to smile.

"Okay." She agreed.

"So, Maiki." The ghost turned to me. "You have come to me. When would you like to start learning?"

"A soul connection is a powerful feeling, Maiki." Kuvalik said to me. "You are connected to this world in a way that others might only imagine. Given your source of power, you can reach out to the elements beyond you, and *grab* them." He extended his ghostly arm in front of him. Purple light pulsed down his incorporeal veins, and from his fingers erupted sparks of electricity.

We were in his living room, under the hole in the roof to the afternoon sky. Natalie had gone home, but I stayed on for my first lesson. Standing here, about to learn the use of real powers, I could only feel excitement. Natalie was fulfilled and my lie made-up for, there was no longer guilt tied to this knowledge of who I was. How could I not be excited to expand my possibilities? Like Natalie said, we are only what we make of ourselves. I didn't have to be scared by Simone's perceptions. This was a new world.

"You understand the soul connection, do you not?" He asked me.

"I think I do." I replied. "Hesslik took away my power yesterday. He did it with quatra-"

"Yes, this is known as *destructive interference*. It will be one of your most useful self-defences. Absorbing another's quatra energy will 'block' your thread for a short time."

"I could feel all of the senses that I'd had all of my life and never realised. I can feel the *fullness* of carbon in things, and the sense of space through air."

"And *where* do you feel these sensations?" He asked me. I focussed on them.

"In my fingers, and my palms…and my arms, and my chest, and my ass…in that order."

Kuvalik chuckled.

"Would it be accurate to say that you feel it in your *being*?"

"Yeah. It does feel like that." I agreed.

"Then you know the *soul connection*." He smiled. He floated around me in a circle, standing by the well-kept couch. I followed him with my gaze.

"The sensation of the soul and its connections are granted at a base level quatra use. To do anything more with your gift, you must call on the energy to do so. The first thing to know, however, are the rules for being a good Suneva."

"Are these like the ethics that Hesslik mentioned?" I asked.

"Yes. Hesslik has taken one stance on the traditional rules. They come from *your* people, the ancient *Kiin*. Like all ethics and morals, they're fluid and imperfect.

but these rules are widely followed and adhered to." He explained.

"The first rule is that one must not to use quatra, or quatra abilities against a person, unless you are met with a threat. You may retaliate only with power equal to the threat. Even then, quatra must only be used defensively. You should *never* attack anybody."

"Okay, it wasn't my first thought to attack somebody, but good to know." I noted.

"The second rule, is that quatra is a tool of knowledge and self-discovery, first and foremost. Those who believe, or try to convince you otherwise, are lazy or lost. The third rule, is that quatra is a dangerous energy, Maiki. You must treat it with respect. The fourth rule, and somewhat the *most* important one, is that quatra should never be used to kill. That is the ultimate dishonour and misappropriation of the gift."

"So: act defensively, seek knowledge, treat power with respect, and don't kill. Sounds to me like 'don't be a dick'."

"Yes, but these are serious rules, Maiki. You must tread very carefully. You may find it easier to break them than you believe."

"Then I will aim to tread as lightly as possible." I responded.

"Now, to manipulate your soul connections, you must channel and use quatra energy. The most basic form of this is expelling it through your body."

He held a hand out. His fingers drifted in the gentle breeze coming from the roof's hole. He held them like Hesslik had done to my chest – the first two fingers up like a 'V', the second two forward of the palm, and the thumb orthogonal. He angled his palm down and in slightly, and summoned energy. It ran from his thread, down his arm, and out of his palm. The three-ringed bullet of purple energy soared through the living room and collided with the wall between the two hallways. Its rings emanated, and then dissipated, just like they'd done before.

"Did you feel the energy?" He asked me.

"I could see it." I said. "But I didn't *feel* it like I felt the other sensations."

"Strange." He rubbed his non-existent chin. "Then this may be more difficult for you."

"Great." I grinned.

"I want to you try and summon quatra energy." He said.

"And how do I do that?" I asked.

"You are a *Kiin*, Maiki. You will find it easiest to focus on your breathing. Many *Kiin* would say that quatra circulates in the body like the flow of breath. In and out, and it moves through your system like the wave of air. Focus on your chest. Let it draw the energy in and pump it around your body. You must be aware of where your thread is."

"Sounds hard." I noted.

"It will be on the first go, but it will become second nature. I promise you that." He smiled. "Just, be careful where you aim your arms. If you hit me, I'll die. I'm holding my consciousness together through my thread and its quatra. If my thread was blocked, that's the end of me."

"Yeah, I'll make sure not to kill you." I wheezed at the implication.

I focussed on my breathing. Air rushed in, air came out. Like a tide at the beach or wind through a tunnel. I felt the energy at the base of my neck, it buzzed.

"Look *through* your thread. It is your connection to the great black hole *Omercronius*."

When I breathed and emptied my mind, I could feel past the mouth of the thread. The energy was there. I exhaled, and it became obvious how to command it through my body. It *would* move with my breath. When I exhaled a second time, I drew it in, and forced it through my body. The energy, hot and fast like turbo gasses charged through my neck and into my arm.

It burst from my hand, and I jolted from the recoil, which although minimal, I wasn't expecting. The energy came out bright green, and at an odd angle. It flew into the floor, and ran its rings until they dissipated.

"Very good." Kuvalik said. "How did that feel?"

"It felt easier than I expected." I said. I turned my hand up and stared at my palm. "Although, now, looking at my hand feels dangerous."

Kuvalik chuckled.

"How do I aim the bolt?" I asked. "You put your hand into a pose when you did it."

"Ah, yes." The ghost said, making the peace-sign gesture again. "This is a good gesture, but much more useful for reading the quatra field – which you won't be able to do yet. Each set of fingers aligns with an axis, with the palm acting as the fourth spatial dimension which we don't perceive."

"You believe in a fourth spatial dimension?" I quizzed.

"I'm a living consciousness kept alive by black hole energy. I opened my mind long before this stage. You would do well to open yourself to new possibilities, Maiki."

"Yes, right." I blushed.

"Using a pose like mine will not be useful for firing quatra until you're more experienced. But *this* pose will help you..." He said. He drifted closer to me. I became immediately uncomfortable as his smoky body drew near to my breath. I might have accepted who I was as a Suneva by now, but it was still strange to accept that dead men lived.

He held his hand in front of me and aimed to my right. He formed a fist, with his thumb pointed out to the side.

"The thumb is used to create a perpendicular reference direction. Curling the fingers inwards will limit the other directions the quatra could go. The bolt will come from the palm."

I studied his hand, then replicated the open fist. I aimed my left hand away from the ghost, and set my sights on the handle of the sliding door. I concentrated on my breathing again. This time, it was much easier to summon the quatra, which pumped from my neck pneumatically. It burst from my arm, coursing a straight line to the door. My aim was off, but the idea was right.

"Very good." Kuvalik congratulated me. "Mastering these basics is important. Do not be frustrated if we spend whole days on basic practices like these."

"Well, you're the teacher. I'll try not to." I said. "Thank you for helping me."

"You're doing well. Patience and an open mind will help you go far."

For the next hour, Kuvalik had me practice the art of drawing and firing quatra. He had me stand and breathe to draw quatra from my thread. He gave me targets to aim for, and had me fire from both hands. This was the art of patience and perfection. My aim didn't get much better, but my ability to call on the energy did.

"Do you have any more time today?" He asked me at the end of the hour. "It might get dark soon."

"It'll be fine. Mum would just think I'm at a rehearsal or training for something. Let's move on."

"Okay then, Maiki." Kuvalik said, but squinted at me with the eyes of a discerning parent, knowing I was overstepping my boundaries. "Then I will move onto your *quatran* – the abilities you gain from quatra. I'll start with *kiin*, although, you should not be frustrated if it does not come to you as easily as anything else has. This could take time to develop, and might not work every time that you want it to."

"I think I had to expect that. Patience and an open mind." I tapped my head. He smiled.

"Yes, you'll learn that lesson quickly."

"Now, how best to teach this…" He pondered. He let his shadowy body circle me, floating around the living room. I could feel the wake which swirled behind him. Vortices shed and waned in his trail.

"Do you ever get the feeling…" He asked me, "that if you reached out into the sky, you could touch it. That if you leaped, you could grip into it and you would never fall."

"Yes." I answered, remembering back to my dreams. "I get that feeling a lot."

"Okay, good." He said. "We're going to use that feeling. Using a *quatran* should be easy like that – the feelings are natural. The hard part is using quatra to manipulate your soul."

"Yeah, that does sound like the hard part." I noted.

"I want you to focus on the feeling, Maiki. Reach out with your hand and grab at the air in front of you. Feel your ability to do so through your soul connection."

I put my left arm in front of me. I focussed on the far corner of the room. I could feel the energy of the air in my fingertips. I could feel my grasp on it. I flicked my hand, but it did not follow.

"There are two ways to think about your abilities." Kuvalik commented, "If you have trouble thinking about the soul connection, and powering your soul to move their air – which can be a difficult concept - you can think about the conservation of energy. You receive energy through your thread, and you can deliver it to the air. As with *welle* - water, and *raduk* – earth, you can give the air *kinetic energy*, and a directional velocity. This is the power you have over air, to give it kinetic energy. This is not the same as your connection to carbon, but we will get to that later. If it helps, focus on transferring your kinetic energy to the air, through quatra."

Right, just like Vestas said. I thought to myself, *Energy in, equals energy out.*

I focussed again on my breathing, to feel the energy flowing into my body. I focussed on the air in the corner of the room, and the grasp I had on it. *Give it the energy*, I reminded myself. I gripped with my hand, and summoned quatra energy from my thread. I swiped at the air, to transfer my kinetic energy to it…

The bolt of quatra came straight out of my hand. The air remained still. I groaned.

"A common issue." Kuvalik noted. "We could be here for a while before you can actually move the air."

"So, what did I do wrong?" I asked.

"You missed the transfer. You meant well, but the quatra was not absorbed into your soul, and so did not transfer to your grip on the air."

"And how do I make sure that happens?" I asked.

"I can't really tell you that. I've forgotten what it feels like to not be able to do it." He chuckled. "But if you practice, you will get there."

Right. I grimaced, determined. I set my sights again on the air. I let my hand float by my side, collecting my grip on the air in the room. It slung over my pocket, fingers twitching, like a cowboy ready to draw. I summoned the energy from my thread. It coursed through my veins, and when it came to my arm, I drew my pistol. I flung my arm up, and grasped at the atmosphere, gripping in, and focusing on what I wanted the energy to do. I could feel the transfer. My grasp was powerful, it was *full.* I swatted with my arm, and a gust followed my movement. Dust stirred in the corner of the room. My face lit up.

"Hey, I did it!" I gleamed.

"Indeed you did. That is a good first step." Kuvalik noted. "You did not need to ask me *how* you would move the air beyond giving it energy, such as motions or thoughts or bodily positions. You trusted your gut, and you allowed your soul to connect in the way that you wanted it to."

"I did?" I asked.

"Yes, you followed your intuition, and this is always the good step. In time, with practice, the amount of movement you will need to command the air will become minimal. Right now, you're inefficient. Further along, maybe decades from now, a simple flick of the wrist could send you flying into the air."

"So quatra can amplify my movements?" I asked. "It almost certainly should." Kuvalik stated. "But of course, you will get better. That was your first movement of the air. Let's keep practicing."

I continued to practice. I couldn't move the air every time that I tried, but little by little, I felt myself improving. Even then, having just picked up the skill, I could feel deep inside that there was so much more I could do with this. Tantalising possibilities sat on the tip of my tongue, waiting for me to gain the proficiency to perform them. I was filled with excitement, the magnitude of which I don't think I'd ever imagined feeling. I didn't care what Simone thought, or what others might think of Suneva. Expressing this part of myself made me happy, and I grinned from ear to ear.

Is this my life now?

***

I spotted Natalie on my way to my first class the next day while traversing the long pathway to the language department, through the thick brush of gum trees the school had planted.

I'd spent all night practicing my abilities with the air – or *kiin* as a Suneva should know it. Mum was not pleased with how late I'd come home, but there was some lie of another activity I'd taken up, said without much guilt for the elation I felt. I spent my time in my room experimenting with small blasts of wind. I found the ability to push outwards and have a gust soar past my palm, pushing me backwards. I played with circulating the air above my head and around the room. It took all night to get anything remotely cool or interesting to happen, and even though I was under slept today, I didn't care. I was excited to show Natalie.

Natalie walked taller than I had seen her before, her head lifted, her skin glowing. She held one hand by her side as she stepped away - her fingers in the peace-sign pose that I was told I couldn't do anything with yet. I sleuthed up behind her but she knew I was there and turned just before I could surprise her.

"James!" She greeted cheerily. "Wow, this really does work…" She stared into her palm.

"Careful you don't shoot yourself in the face." I said. "That's like, a real issue now."

"Ha, I guess it is." She smiled.

"I'd take it your Yamitse helped you out?" I asked.

"Yeah, I can't believe it." She glowed, "I mean, she is also a Suneva. She was waiting until I discovered it myself to teach me anything."

"Well that's…interesting?" I quizzed. "Surely you would have been better off knowing your whole life – like Hesslik seemed to believe."

"Maybe." She said. "But she was right, in that if I was always different, I could have been treated differently. She just wanted me to feel normal as a kid. I like that. Although I don't appreciate being lied to me whole life…"

"That's rough." I hummed. "So, what are your Suneva abilities?"

"Water and Hydrogen." She said. "*Zamen* and *Welle*, which makes me *Zamelle*."

"Huh, that feels pretty close to mine." I said. "And, there are plenty of other abilities, right?"

"Sure." She noted. "I guess it is a little strange. But I didn't focus much on them last night. My *Yamitse* taught me all about the soul, and how you use quatra to power it. She taught me about control, and the field, and things about the eye colours and the auras. There's so much to it, James."

"I know. How exciting is it?" I rhetorically asked. "You look radiant."

"For as ridiculous of a thing this is, I really do feel great." She smiled. "I feel *complete* finally, like this was always missing from my life. You look better, too."

"And I feel it." I smiled. "I wonder who else is missing out on something they always had?"

"Strange to think." She smiled. "I want to show you something cool I can do, but…" She glanced around, scouring the surroundings for onlookers. She looked to the scrub next to us, and pulled me in by my arm.

"You know this is the kissing bush, right?" I asked, peering over the leaves. "Gee, if Rhys Cameron caught us…"

"Fuck Rhys Cameron." She scolded, "look at this…"

She pulled her drink bottle out of her bag and placed it on the floor. She removed the lid and tossed it to me, which I expectedly dropped to the dirt. She grasped at her element with her hands. She waved them in and out, in circles around each other, keeping her fingers in the Suneva peace pose.

"My Yamitse told me that quatra flows through the body like blood. It moves like a stream into the soul. Its flow appears gentle, like a winding creek, but can be as forceful as a tsunami."

Her hands danced, and the water was charmed from the bottle, like a snake. It slithered out and gushed around itself, gently dancing into the air as a rope of water. I was stunned.

"But, Kuvalik told me you could only give elements like ours kinetic energy. How are you holding it like that?" I asked. All I could do was push air around – if I could push it at all. I couldn't hold it in place like that. This was madness.

"It's *easy*." She said, "I'm giving the water velocity around itself. You know, like I'm wrapping it up."

"Right." I said. "I thought you didn't even practice water with your *Yamitse*."

"I barely did. This is beginner's stuff."

"Oh, sure." I flushed red. "I guess it all takes *an open mind* and *patience*, right?" I recited Kuvalik's message.

"Huh? No, this was, like, the second thing I did with water." She smiled.

How is she so amazing at this with no practice? I grumbled. I could feel a spark of envy.

"Show me something you can do, James." She smiled, using the snake of water to wash her dropped bottle lid. I froze up.

"Oh, I can't do anything like you can…" I mumbled.

"No, really, I'd love to see it."

"If you insist." I faked a grin. I summoned the energy from my thread. My hand was held by my chest – in its fingers, I could feel my connection to the air. The digits of my soul dug into the atmosphere. I pushed my hand forward, like an open palmed punch. A trickle of air rushed past my body. Natalie's hair blew about gently.

"Oh…" She blushed red, "That's neat, James."

"Yeah, neat." I laughed nervously.

"Plenty of time for us to learn." She noted.

"I was thinking about it, and for what?" I asked. "I mean, I'm eager to learn – Kuvalik told me that the powers are a tool for knowledge and self-discovery – but what will we use them for? I don't think you can really use them in public…"

"Something will come our way, James." Natalie said, "I can already feel it. There are other Suneva presences around, too."

"If you say so." I said. "But how do you know about other Suneva?"

"Oh, my *Yamitse* taught me how to sense others in the quatra field. She said I picked it up really quickly. You can't sneak up on me anymore." She winked.

Cheese, of course you figured it out in a second.

"Anyway, I've got to get to class, James." She said. "I'll see you later, yeah?"

"Yeah, I'll catch you later." I smiled wanly. Natalie extracted herself from the kissing bush and scurried off to class – eager to be five minutes early, as usual.

I casually pulled myself from the scrub, brushed myself off, and looked up to the sky. The two moons had been there a few nights ago, foretelling changes for me. *Is this it, or is there more change to come?* I questioned, looking up at the clouds.

When I came back to earth, I saw Rhys Cameron walking the other way down the path. He didn't even look at me as he slid past. His eyes told a story of terror. I grinned.

Chapter 11

Double Date

I had seen Kuvalik almost every day this week, much to the dismay of my mother.

"James, I swear." She'd tell me as I would enter the door during the hours of dusk. "If you don't come home and sit down for a minute, your brain will explode. You can't keep doing everything." Fists-to-hips, her concern was always levelled as annoyance towards my contrary insistence.

"I'm fine Mum. My grades haven't died yet." I said each night, before wandering into my room.

"But you'll drop from exhaustion. You just watch." She warned, watching me walk away.

I'd been visiting the ghost after or before school when I had nothing on, and he would invite me into his living room where he would have tea ready. Kuvalik was a *Liktas* – he could manipulate electricity. I understood how he powered a kettle, but where we got the water and tea from, I would never know.

I drank his tea – some mix of a few flavours – and sat down on the cushion before the coffee table and couch. On the second day of our training, I complained to him about being so much less developed than Natalie.

"How does it come so naturally to her?" I asked. "She made it out as if she didn't even try, yet here I am barely able to blow her hair around."

"I don't think you should be caught up comparing yourself to others, Maiki." Kuvalik said. "Zamelle will be powerful in different areas than you will be. She is very spiritual, and I could sense that she had been connected to her soul long before she knew anything about being a Suneva."

"Yeah, but it's crazy just how bad I am…"

"Patience and an open mind, Maiki, is what it will take to gain strength in your abilities." Kuvalik spoke over me. "You are not bad, she is simply very connected. Becoming spiritual is a large obstacle, which she has already dealt with. Where she flourishes, you might not. Where you flourish, she might not. Two separate souls and personalities will take two separate approaches to using quatra."

"Fine." I huffed. "As long as I can be as useful as her."

"That you will be. Every person has their own skills and uses. For everybody's uniqueness, there is a purpose. You must focus on your spirituality - on your soul, and believe more in yourself."

I took Kuvalik's advice with me throughout the week. *I have to progress spiritually*, I told myself, *but what does that even mean?*

I took the chance to do something that I had never before considered – meditation. I cleared space on the floor of my room, and sat down in it to clear my mind. I tried to drown out the sounds and stimuli of the day with my thoughts, then drown out my thoughts with silence.

I found it very difficult to think of *nothing*, though, and soon my mind wandered without me noticing. It wondered to the activity in the room. With my eyes closed, my mind was more open to the sensation of air currents. I could feel it moving – the whole mass of the atmosphere in the room. I could feel the eddies and vortices which swirled slowly around my collection of figurines. I could feel the fullness – that sense of carbon – in the plastics which surrounded me. In my mind's eye, carbon was smeared across my vision like warmth on a heat map.

The air swirled fastest around the room at the top and by the window, where the sun's rays danced, and slowest above the floor. I extended my hand to these currents, and drawing quatra from my thread, was able to connect to them. I pushed with my hands to give them energy. Their flow became more erratic, causing turbulence in the once calm room. Every push I did would create entropy in this way – as if I was fighting the air, and not a part of it. I could tell that this was not correct, and expressed this to Kuvalik.

He praised my sight.

"For now, be satisfied with your ability to influence the air around you." He said. "The observation of entropy is an astute one to make. I'm not sure that many *Kiin* in history have tried to solve that issue. Maybe you'll be the first." He smiled at me.

"But now," He started, "I would like to introduce you to *maikess* – carbon - and have you make your first proper connection to it. Did you bring pencils, like I asked?"

I went over to my bag and pulled out a collection of too-short graphite pencils.

"Can you feel the carbon in them?" He asked me.

"This got me into trouble once," I laughed nervously, "I can definitely feel it."

"Great. We will expand your connection to carbon from *sensing* to *manipulating*." Kuvalik started. His ghoulish, black body sat down on the couch, over the warmth of his tea. The steam coming from the cup simmered right through him.

"Real elements will not move like air. You will not be able to give them motion in the same way." He explained. "You can telekinetically control their position, and you can change their shape, but you cannot give them the same *kind* of movement. It's precise, and delicate."

"So, what. If you're changing the structure, you're changing the bond energy right?" I asked.

"Yes, that's true." Kuvalik said, "and probably the thing you will find easiest to do. But remember, Maiki, talking about conservation of energy was a guide. In order to understand all of your abilities through *quatran*, you must open your mind to what your soul *feels* it can do."

"Yes, patience and an open mind. I can't forget it by now." I noted as I grabbed the pencils in one hand. They had the familiar *fullness* of carbon.

"Uh…" I was about to ask what it was that I should do to grab at the carbon and change it, but figured that Kuvalik would never give me a straight answer. If I wanted to progress spiritually, I had to take this initiative.

I controlled my breathing to draw on quatra in my thread and body. As it always did, it moved with my breath. I could feel my grip on the carbon, as I could with air. I could feel the way that my soul could touch it, and change it. I felt that if I reached out for it, I could mould it, and call it to me.

I used the quatra energy to extend my grip. I wrapped my hand around the lead of the pencil, and fuelled my hand with energy. I could feel my grasp on the atoms of carbon – I almost had a sense of each individual one. I had the power to change how they interacted with each other, I could move them, and alter their connections. I used my connection, gripping to the atoms intently with my left hand from a distance. I had prepared for a tough pull, but the core slid out easily. I bowled myself over and smacked face first into the rotted wooden floor.

Kuvalik chuckled in his golden, ghostly echo as I stood up. I laughed it off unconvincingly as I re-connected. It was surprisingly easy. Without much thought, I could telekinetically hold the little rod of *maikess* in place. I grabbed it in my hand and it melted to the touch of my fingers. I squashed it into a ball, rolled it out into a snake, and formed a donut. It was like pure carbon putty. Next thing, I'd be pushing it through a big squeezer to get fibre-glass spaghetti.

"When you can power your soul's connection more efficiently, you'll be able to perform higher-energy feats, such as creating diamonds." Kuvalik explained. "There's a lot you can do with carbon right now, but many more possibilities are to come."

"I can feel that." I said. "I can feel that with the air too. Hopefully I improve quickly." I smiled.

"I think you will." Kuvalik said. He gestured to my tea, which was becoming cold, and I sipped it. It helped me to relax, and let my mind wonder into connections and possibilities.

Natalie wasn't pleased about the double date David had organised for Sunday. David was nice, but he wasn't her type – he was just so softly spoken and unsure of himself. Natalie needed somebody who owned their own sense of authority, who had enough sass to defend himself from her strong personality. She needed a man who was logical, witty and strong, yet reserved. Not David.

Despite the fuss, she still agreed to come along – if only to meet The French Girl herself and try to set me up with them. Tom had also crashed the night, turning the double date into a triple date by bringing Penelope along. All parties involved agreed that a diluted date would increase ease of conversation, but David feared we would take Natalie's attention away from him. I told Tom this would only work in his favour. Natalie wasn't interested in him, and this would be an easy let down.

I didn't know what to expect of David's exchange student, and that made me nervous. Moreso, I knew exactly what to expect of myself: social ineptitude, inability to detect flirting, and inability to flirt myself. I was hopeless with girls. If it wasn't for destiny pushing me into Natalie, I'd never have talked to her, even though I wasn't romantically interested.

The magnitude of my self-doubt was an enigma. *I would bore them, wouldn't I?* I thought to myself. *I mean, I know nothing about French culture, or people. What do I say to this girl? What about me is interesting enough to hold a conversation?* I looked at myself in the mirror, dressed nicely and with my shaving razor to my face. I grazed it against my chin, painfully removing the stubble.

Hopefully she's not that hot. I consoled myself. *If she's not intimidating like that, maybe I'll be able to talk to her.*

The thought of her potential bad looks lifted my spirits, weirdly. I was dressed nicely, at least. *Maybe it will make up for my lack of hot personality.* I hummed and cleaned myself up.

"Where are you going now, looking that handsome?" Mum seemed to coalesce from the shadows to catch my every movement. I smiled a wide grin despite my nerves for the night ahead.

"I'm going on a *date*." I beamed. The pride of telling my mother I had a date was much more uplifting than the act of going on a date.

"Is that what you've really been doing all week?" She asked me. My face dropped.

"You think I'd ever get more than one date?" I asked. "Heavens, no."

"Well, who's the girl?" She swooned up to me, tugging on the collar of my shirt and pulling at the sleeves. "Jesus, James, you couldn't have ironed this, could you?"

"Come on, Mum." My nerves spiked, did I look terrible? I didn't know how to iron, that was Mum's job. "She's a French exchange student, anyway."

"Fancy." Mum smiled. "Good luck then, James. Do tell me in advance next time."

"Yes Mum." I nodded, and turned to leave.

I got on my bicycle. I was glad that Mum liked my clothes, because I'd gone shopping midweek with Natalie and Tom to choose them. Tom was, antithesis to his rampant, cool, disregard for the opinions of others, a great shopper, but with often poor taste. He convinced me to buy my shirt – a somewhat slim fitted number with a floral pattern; not quite Hawaiian, but not far from it.

Tom tried to convince Natalie to buy something – just for the sake of going in a few stores himself, but she refused. She told him that she had as many clothes as she needed at home – she was always practical, but never failed to dress well despite it. Even out to the shops, her casual look was upmarket-reserved, with long, flowing dresses and skirts, closed shoes, conservative shirts, and hair down. She didn't wear make-up either, which made me wonder if there was ever an occasion she considered right for it.

Soon after setting off from home, I arrived at the house of a very flustered David. His exchange girl was still getting ready when I was let in. I would have to wait to meet my date.

"Man, I'm not going to lie, I'm pretty nervous." He squeaked as he paced his kitchen. I sipped apprehensively on a glass of water, hoping to *Omercronius* – the black hole of mine – that my breath didn't smell or that I hadn't missed anything.

"Mate, you'll be fine." I patted him on the back, but he rolled his eyes and continued to pace about.

I tried to think of something to say to calm his nerves. His house was large but entirely retro. The walls were wood-panelled straight out of the seventies, with entirely grey carpeted floor to match. The furniture was stuck in all years between, a mismatch clearly the result of only buying new furnishings when the old broke.

"I guess if it makes it any better, we're both about as screwed as each other." I said. "But you've got a London accent. That's about as charming as they come."

He grinned, and chuckled to himself.

"Aren't you nervous?" He asked me. "Because you don't look it at all."

"Really?" I asked. A grin came across my face. "Well, that's a relief."

"Is this really James Grey before me; the same James who would get nervous talking to a brick just in case you were bothering it?"

"The very same." I agreed. "But maybe we've just got to have fun with this, you know? You'll get nervous and go nowhere if you're too serious. Sit back, relax, and let the good conversation flow."

The words came out, and I'm not sure where in my brain they came from, because they made sense. David was taking a drink of water, and caught my gaze down the barrel of his glass. His expression changed, as if he'd had a lightbulb moment.

"You're right, James." He admitted. "I'm missing the fun. This is just meant to be fun." A smile grew across his face, and it followed onto mine.

"Oh, also, what *is* the exchange student's name?" I asked, realising that I'd forgotten it.

"Celeste, man. You left that pretty late. That could've been awkward for you."

"Yeah, it could have." I laughed.

Then the doorbell rang. David's smile all but faded.

"Oh, gee. I better go and get that." He coughed. I walked behind him to the door, making sure that his stumbling, panicked body made it. His open palm collided with the door knob, his fingers tightened on it to engage unlocking sequence, and he hesitated. His hand twitched – there was a system malfunction. He took a deep breath in, and amended the technical difficulty. He turned the knob and opened the door.

Natalie looked stunning, standing on the other side. She was just in jeans, a blouse and a jacket, but she made it look elegant. She smiled sweetly at us as we opened the door, then shyly ducked her head to get through the doorway – not that she needed to – and stepped past David and I. David looked halfway about to faint, halfway about to explode out of his skin. She turned to hug as each, and David tried to contain himself.

"How are you doing, Natalie?" David asked her. "Welcome to my abode."

"I'm doing very well thanks, David." Natalie smiled politely. She examined the furnishings around – clearly taken by the mismatched homewares.

"Let me give you the grand tour." He offered.

"Sounds good." Natalie smiled again. He went to grab her hand to show her around, but she politely pretended that she had not noticed his hand, and so could not take it. She followed him into the house. David submerged his hand deep into his pocket and didn't dare remove it.

I decided to leave them alone to let David soak in the social torture of a one-on-one interaction. I could hear his helpless mumbles echo up the stairs as he showed her the top floor. Maybe he'd leave me alone with Celeste later in the night, and I could learn from the same anguish.

I went into David's room to make sure that I was looking alright, and to put on some more cologne. He had a vanity table with a crystal-clear mirror, covered in his sister's old boy-band stickers. The room used to belong to his sister before she moved out, and the vanity table was included in David's room upgrade package. Tom, David and I laughed about it. We agreed that he'd at least be more likely to bring a girl home than I would, with my action figure collection.

The rest of his room was lusciously stylish, an antithesis to the rest of the house. It was filled with paraphernalia, from soccer trophies, to photos, old action figures, and a collection of protein powders. His bed was retro in all the right ways, and the head of it contained a built-in radio. On his white and crème walls hung artwork and famous records.

I made my way over to the vanity table and took a whiff of his cologne.

Eh… I fanned my nose. *Why did I think this would be a good idea?*

As I moved my hand around, I had subconsciously connected myself to the air around me. A small breeze brushed back and forth across my face. I grinned, and glanced over my shoulder to check that the door was closed. It was.

I stood up and adopted a fighting stance. I could feel the size of the room through the air, and, with my advanced spatial sense, the line of action figures sitting on his bed's head. I jumped up, pivoting on my right foot to face the bed.

"Bad guys should watch out…" I narrated to myself with a grin plastered over my face. I directed my open-palmed fighting stance towards the row of figurines. "Because there's a new hero in town. And his name is *Maiki.*"

Gripping into the air in the room, I summoned quatra from my thread. I pushed my left palm forward like a punch, and a jet-like gust of air followed its motion. The blast hit the target with incredible accuracy, and dealt a devastating blow to the assorted action-men. I followed through with a right jab. A blast of air flew past me. The fallen men of the bed-head were pushed hard, and scraped along the wooden surface. I blew on my hands like a cowboy across the barrel of his smoking gun. My grin was insatiable.

"I love this." I jauntily swayed back around to face the door, my smug smile radiating. The door was open, the knob held by a hand, whose arm I followed to find a tall girl of red lips and shirt. She stood tall in the doorway, her chestnut eyes glaring at me through the flicked wing of eyeliner. She was gorgeous, her nose posh, her lips bold, her face slim and defined, with little ankh jewels hanging off her ears. I'd spent moment admiring her features before I realised that the face they formed was totally unemotive. Scarily so. They stepped into the room – their gait accentuating the movement of their hips, which revealed her form and her tight, white jeans. I was too smitten to be shocked that she'd caught me in a magical act. At this point, I was trapped in a room with a hot French girl. This was slowly becoming a fantasy. Her eyes were deep, they locked onto mine.

"You…you must be Celeste." I gurgled. "I'm James." I extended a nervous hand for her to shake, even though she was halfway across the long room. Her expression narrowed, a slight grin forming on her luscious lips. Her head shook. She looked like a cat ready to pounce.

The fingers of her right hand twitched. She flicked her wrist, and the hilt of a weapon materialised in her hand. A whole sword erupted from the hilt, making a sound akin to a rip in space. Two nozzles popped up on the swords hilt, and from them a helix of blue flames burst, encircling the blade. My mouth hung open, I backed up, stalking past the vanity table. She advanced on my every step.

"Holy shit…" I uttered. "Where does everybody get these weapons?"

"You've made a *big* mistake, coming here." She said. Her accent was strong. It was undeniably hot. There were lots of things in this situation that were objectively hot.

"I don't know what I've done." I squealed, "But…"

"Shut up." She ordered. Her flames danced on the sword. She pointed its end to my neck. I gulped. "I know you're a hunter, or an agent of Hesslik. You were after Iva Argol, but you found *me*, and I'm about to make your life infinitely worse."

"Please don't." I begged. I glanced hastily around the room for an escape, but there was none bar shattering the window. I could feel the heat of her flame's helix on my face. I was sweating now, and saw only one way out. I gripped into the air, twisted my body, and flung my hand forward with all of my might.

Nothing happened.

We both looked at my hand, both slightly confused. I tried it again. And once more, nothing happened.

"Heh…heh…" I laughed nervously.

A frown slithered across her bold, red lips. I panicked, and tried again, then again. My mind ran. *Just convert the energy. It's easy. Quatra into kinetic. Convert…convert!* It was like flicking a lighter and only getting a spark with no flame. I couldn't transfer the energy. I couldn't do it.

"You're kidding, right?" She asked. "I *almost* feel bad about this…"

Her sword glowed an electric blue, and from it burst a bolt of bright blue quatra. Instinctively, I raised my hands to shield my face. I stumbled down as it happened, tripping on something behind me. My right hand caught the blast of quatra energy, and I could feel it pressing through my veins like hot gas. The force of it knocked me back.

I couldn't let it reach my thread, or I'd be dead. Those split nanoseconds of fear kickstarted my connection. I drew on as much quatra as I could. The invading bolt got almost to my neck before I'd flushed my system. It flew from my left arm into the ground as a mottled blue and green bolt of quatra. I landed square on my butt. With my connection established, I bounced straight to my feet.

Celeste gritted her teeth. The flames on the sword – whose point was still aimed at my throat – burst into a plume. A great jet of flames poured from the sword. I leaped backwards, and my feet connected to the air around them. They blasted air downwards subconsciously as I leaped. I was flung on jets of air into a backflip over the bed. I slammed my hands down and blasted a cushion of air upon which to land. I was surprised at my prowess in the face of danger.

The immediate peril, and my sudden, strong connection, opened me up to a new sensation. I felt the quatra surging in my thread. I felt my breathing, not in my body, but in my soul. From somewhere in my thread, in the realm between *Omercronius* and me, I felt an object. It was a disturbance in the pipeline, like a lump under the skin. I *'itched'* at the feeling in the void, and realised that it was in my left forearm, just beneath the veins.

The disturbance was bulky, and thick. My realisation of the sensation made my skin crawl. I flicked my wrist, as if that would make it go away, and it worked. The sensation of the object shot through my arm and out of my palm. In my hand, I now held a grip, and from the grip erupted an impressive staff. It ended in a twin-pronged fork, and had a razor-thin green blade which ran the entire length of the front face. This was the blade from the figure in my dreams.

Simply by holding it in my hand, my senses were magnified ten-fold. It acted like an amplifier, channelling my soul connections to the elements around me and strengthening them. My mind was blown trying to comprehend the instant feeling it gave me.

I was so entranced that I almost didn't notice the plume of bright blue flames barrelling towards me. I connected to the air around me through my pronged staff. The connection was instant, and more concentrated than I could have previously imagined. I rammed the four-foot, pronged pole in front of me, like a magical pike, and a powerful jet of air followed it. The flame split over the dome of wind, encircling me but not touching me.

The door creaked open behind the French girl. She snarled and pivoted to face the intruder. I held my staff ready to strike again. Natalie poked her head through the crack, then burst her way in. She slammed the door shut behind her and glared at Celeste with eyes of scorn. She flicked both her wrists, and two swords, like retro-futuristic cutlasses, appeared in her palms.

Of course Natalie can already do that. I sighed. She pointed the weapons at Celeste. The French girl backed away from the two of us, right into David's dresser. Her sword's flames thickened as they encompassed the sharp blade.

"What the hell is going on here?" Natalie asked. Her voice was hushed; she wasn't trying to draw attention to the scene.

"I knew it." Celeste scowled. "Agents, the two of you. You've heard the rumours of me, I'm sure of it. You know what happens to Suneva who try to capture me…"

"Hold up…" Natalie demanded. She opened her grip, and the swords dissolved back into her arms, back to the void from whence they came. I looked at my hand, *How did she do that?* I opened my hand, but my staff dropped to the floor. I quickly recovered it.

"…who the hell *are* you?" She asked. "Should we know you?"

"You're Celeste, aren't you?" I asked. The girl looked confused. The flame on her sword simmered down.

"No, I don't believe that. I'm not that dumb." She spat. Her eyes darted between Natalie and me. "That's the oldest trick in the book. You know exactly who I am. I'm not going with you anywhere."

"Fine, who do you think *we* are then?" Natalie pestered.

"Funny." The girl scorned. "You're agents of *Fara Hesslik*, or *Naxaer Argol's* mobsters. You've come for the bounty on *Iva Argol* — but you've come to the wrong place."

"Who is *Iva Argol?*" I asked. Without the ability to put the weapon away, I put it down across the bed as a sign of good faith. Celeste seemed even more confused. Her fingers twitched on her sword's grip.

"*Who is Iva Argol?*" She mocked my question. "You've never heard of the missing Argol daughters?"

"I've only heard of *Suneva* for a few weeks, period."

"We only fired our first bolts of quatra a week ago." Natalie added.

The girl's gaze darted between Natalie's eyes and mine. The spark of her rage fizzled, as she pulled our honesty from our expressions. She stumbled on what to do next, the flames on her sword spattering.

"You're being serious, aren't you?" She asked. "I can see it in your eyes." She let the flames encompassing her sword vanish. "I'd believe that *you're* new – you had trouble connecting." She said to me. I blushed red. "But you…" She pointed at Natalie with a paranoid finger. "You're more connected than a week old Suneva."

I frowned. Natalie smiled.

"So I've been told." Natalie passed off the compliment. "My name is Natalie Athanas, or Zamelle. I'm a student of *Lilawelle*. This is James Grey, or Maiki. He's a student of the ghost Kuvalik."

"Students of *Lilawelle* and *Kuvalik*?" Celeste asked. She dissolved her flaming sword back into the plane of her thread. I stared at my weapon, lying on the bed, hoping that maybe it would dissolve itself if I did nothing. "I don't think I can afford to be in a room with two high profile Suneva like yourself. Sorry, I have to leave."

Natalie blocked the entrance.

"High profile?" She asked. "What are we missing here?"

"*Oui*, high profile." Celeste repeated. She was sweating now. Even in her anxiety, she was beautiful.

"They're just an old lady and a ghost." Natalie said.

"More like the most connected Suneva alive, and the past king of the electric nation. No thanks, I'm not hanging around for that kind of attention, even if you're oblivious to it. If you're telling the truth, Hesslik better not know who your teachers are. You'll be a high priority on his radars."

"I've already talked to Hesslik, actually." I added in. "Plus, if our teachers were high profile, surely we'd have met a few more Suneva by now?"

"Great." Celeste laughed. "This only cements your inexperience. You must let me leave, now." She demanded of Natalie, but Natalie would not budge.

"I passed Hesslik off. He's moved on." I said. "There's nothing to worry about."

"Hesslik would never move on." Celeste stated. She glared at Natalie. Natalie remained determined not to move – the stare between the two girls intensifying. Celeste grumbled, and summoned her sword again.

"How long have you been doing this alone?" Natalie blurted. Celeste scrunched her face, her head knocked back in the recoil of her expression.

"What kind of a question is that?" She asked.

"A good one." Natalie frowned, "I don't think you should leave. It sounds like you've got a lot of troubles. What if we could help you through it all? You can't get through life alone."

I abandoned my staff on the bed, and leaped over the furniture to be closer to the two. Celeste fidgeted at my movement. She was about to flick her sword towards me, but constrained herself.

"Sorry, that's not how this works."

"Why not?" Natalie prodded.

"You're week-old Suneva – there's no way you're prepared for what I've been facing."

"You almost didn't believe we were a week old. Why not let us prove ourselves?" Natalie demanded.

"Because it's too dangerous!" Celeste yelled, then caught herself. The room was silenced, bar her heavy breath. I could feel it between my fingertips. She was anxious, her fear building – and I didn't think it was us whom she found frightening.

"Too dangerous for one person alone." Natalie said, and stepped aside. "But you'd know it more than we would. Sorry for blocking your way."

"Thank you." Celeste said hurriedly. Her voice wavered. She dissolved the sword in her hand – once again, as if to tease me with how easy it was – and stumbled boldly through the door. She left it open as she passed. Natalie and I shared a glace. She frowned, and I shrugged.

I turned back to the bed, to the action figures I'd knocked over and the great, massive, pronged staff I'd left upon the doona cover.

"You don't know how to put away your *shath*, do you?" Natalie asked behind me.

"My *shath*?" I asked.

"Your weapon."

"No, not really." I admitted.

The door to the bedroom closed, and I turned to face it. Celeste had come back in the room. Her face was drawn – her eyes, I could see now, had bags under them. She looked both taught yet relieved.

"I'll take your offer." She sighed. "You're right, it's dangerous, and I need help."

Natalie grinned widely. I wasn't quite sure how to respond. I hadn't suggested helping at all.

"But." The French girl continued. "There are two things before I let you join me. The first, is that *Veritas* help you, you may never cross me. I've had enough of being let down and used as a pawn. If you *dare* use my trust against me, I swear to the great black hole that you will pay for it."

"Noted." I squeaked.

"Secondly, if you are truly ignorant of my situation, which at this point I believe, you should know what you're walking into."

"We want to help, tell us everything." Natalie smiled. She had a way of speaking – the tone of her voice, the way she positioned herself – that could put anybody at ease. As I well knew, she could also turn around and do the exact opposite. Celeste appeared to calm.

"Seven years ago, Naxaer Argol, *the Green Dragon*, Mr Argol – whatever you call him – lost his two daughters. The eldest, Amalie Leroux, was not a Suneva. The youngest, Celeste Leroux – *Iva Argol*, was a Suneva of *ivaer* and *genar* – fire and oxygen. He lost his daughters the day he murdered my father."

Natalie gasped, but Celeste did not stumble on the words. She was numb to them.

"I have the same connections as his daughter – to *ivaer* and *genar*, and share a first name with her. Since the bounty was placed on her return, I have become a target, seen as a walking pile of money for hunters who have mistaken my identity.

"The only person who was ever good to me was a Suneva priest in Paris. Everybody else has tried to sell me for a bounty."

"Good lord, that's awful." Natalie said.

"Right now, my biggest threat is from Hesslik's agents. He's joined the search for the Argol daughters, and his trackers are the best in the world – but they've set their sights on me instead."

Celeste sighed. Her story made me nervous. She was ready to murder me just before, on the *slight* chance that I could have been a threat. She's hardened, well beyond anybody I'd met before. We were about to take a merry stroll into peril - fights which were potentially way above our skill level.

"We'll be able to help you." Natalie said. "I know we will. It's the three of us now." She put a hand on Celeste's shoulder, and the girl accepted it, although was reluctant to smile brightly and let down her guard.

The three of us. It rang in my mind. *The three of us against what?* I remembered Celeste's agonised breaths in my fingers. I started to pale.

"Please, though, do *not* break this trust I have given you. I'm tired of it. I'm so tired…" Celeste flopped herself onto the bed. I pulled aside my staff just in time so that she wouldn't lay on it.

"So, if you're not this *Iva* character, who are you?" Natalie asked. Celeste glanced up to give her a pointed look. I could see her considering whether to answer but she sighed and relaxed.

"Celeste Bouvé, *Genive*."

***

In his handheld device, the bronze Suneva watched a video message from Hesslik. He'd been handed this message before he came to Melbourne. He let it play

112

through – the instruction to him which outlined the three Suneva he was to find and present to the *Fara*. Once it played through, he tossed it onto his bed. He stormed out of the compound - marching past Vestas, whom was conducting experiments, and into the warm autumn night.

Lion's Foot gripped into the earth by his feet with his soul connection. Running forwards, and heaving upwards, a block of asphalt was launched up from under his feet, catapulting him into the air. He connected to the iron in the light overhanging the compound's gate, and *drew* it towards him without altering its bonds. Given that the atoms could not escape their alloy in the lamp, they anchored him to the post. He drew them in, subsequently pulling himself onto the pole. He slammed into the light, then pounced off it, over the gate into the night.

Landing in a crater of asphalt, *Lion's Foot* brushed himself off and removed his Suneva armour. Underneath, he was wearing his riding leathers, and his full-face mask.

His roadster roared between his legs, carrying him down the streets of Melbourne's suburbs. Wind whipped past his face and exposed wrists. *Lion's Foot* dug into the asphalt on turns to dipped into curves, smiling beneath his mask.

He bought his roaring beast to a halt outside a modest house. Its exterior was made of ugly, shit-brown bricks. He sneered at the architecture - the whole house looked to be pulled through a time portal from the seventies. There were Suneva inside, he was sure of it, but he wasn't sure how many. Two of them, though, were the Suneva he was looking for.

Lion's Foot turned his bike off, just outside the driveway. He sleuthed around the side of the house, to where he sensed the active threads. Using his control of earth to mask his footfalls, he was almost silent. When he was close enough, he crouched to the ground, and mashed his palms to the floor. He listened to the voices through the earth.

"*Celeste Bouvé. Genive.*" He felt a young woman say. That confirmed his suspicious, and he continued listening.

As the evening's sounds drowned out to a movie, he retired to the door, where he penned a note from paper he'd stored in his jacket. He left it on the doorstep, and walked away. *Lion's Foot* believed that he had done enough. Now was not the time to escalate. It was a Sunday night. It was a night of peace.

Watch out, the letter read, *Hesslik is after the three of you. He is coming, and you won't be able to hide.*

***

Natalie and Celeste showed me how to dissolve my staff back into my thread. It wasn't difficult to do, but I didn't get it on the first two tries. It involved the *feeling* of sucking it up your arm and into your thread. I suppose that's the best way to describe it. I had to stop thinking about what I was doing, and feel it instead. To practice, I summoned the weapon and dissolved it again. I grinned at the new skill, but Natalie seemed unimpressed.

Penelope and Tom arrived, and the night kicked off. We ordered pizza, and went to sit down by David's projector T.V to watch movies. David, the sly dog, had decided that a horror movie would be the best choice.

"Hey." Celeste said to me as I grabbed us each a plate from the kitchen. "I'm sorry about before. You know, attacking you probably wasn't the best introduction." Her hand lingered dangerously close to my arm. Her red nails, poised, hung near me. I followed her hand, along her arm, and to her face. This girl was beyond stunning. I couldn't help but realise it again.

"Hey, that's alright." I said. "It's good to not paint yourself as the damsel in distress, you know?"

"Ha. Me, a damsel in distress?" She laughed. "James Grey, you have a *lot* to learn about me." She chuckled. She stepped close to me – close enough that her breath lingered on my cheek. Her eyes sparkled, observing my face as I squirmed. She winked, then slapped my butt. I shot to attention, gobsmacked. She gave me a momentary, steamy stare, and with that, she strutted off. I almost dropped the plates in shock.

Butterflies raged their tempest in my stomach. I rushed down to the den to bring her the plate I had acquired, and eat pizza.

For the remainder of the night, I could barely capture her attention, whereas Tom and David had her falling to the floor in stitches. Her hand was casually misplaced from time to time, touching a leg here or a shoulder there of my friends, but not of me. She gave everybody an equally steamy stare. I considered scooting closer during the film, to try and close the gap, but I couldn't bring myself to do it. She was too good looking, she couldn't want me. She was flirting in the kitchen, but she's clearly just flirty.

You got too nervous, dude. I thought to myself, as the rumble of a loud, inconsiderate engine outside drowned out the movie. *You got too nervous and you blew it – for tonight at least.*

I looked over to Celeste on the couch next to me. Her hand was placed between us. My hand was next to it. The movie was winding to an end. I twiddled my pinky – how easy it would be to crawl my hand atop hers. I extended my little finger outwards, like an ant's antennae, feeling for any hints of interest from her. I looked at her big, red lips, at her strong gaze. Her eyes were deep, in the same way that Natalie's were. My heart was pounding, I was about to make the move. I let my hand crawl over to hers. My pinky outstretched, about to touch her skin, about to cross the boundary to the point of no return.

I withdrew. I couldn't commit to the move. I felt so weak, and stupid. *If Dad was our age, he wouldn't have messed that up.*

I wasn't the only man to fail in his mission to woo that night. David had, predictably, not had much luck persuading Natalie to have a romantic interest in him. Tom, however, already had Penelope under his spell – or was already deep in hers. He kissed her goodnight when she left.

Penelope was the first to leave. She had a meeting at school early the next morning. She bent down to adjust her shoe on the doorstep before continuing home.

Natalie, Tom and I left shortly after. I hugged Celeste goodbye, and she held onto me tightly for our brief contact.

"Goodnight, James." She said to me, in her smooth, French accent.

"Goodnight, Celeste." I said to her. I smiled, she smiled back, but there was no magic in her eyes.

Maybe I had to let this one go.

Chapter 12
Armour of the Soul

David, Tom and I gathered in our usual spot the next day at recess. We sat on the concrete steps overlooking the soccer pitches, eating away at our twenty-minute break.

"So, last night was not a success." I said. "Or, maybe a mild success for you, Tom."

"Eh, I don't know about that." He slumped down onto the step next to me. "I might have kissed her goodnight, but I've been doing that every time we catch up. Penelope was just so off last night."

"Really?" I asked. My stomach grumbled. I rammed banana into my face.

"What, you didn't notice?" David asked, standing before Tom and me. "I was knee deep in nerves, and even I noticed."

"What was she doing?" I asked.

"Well, for one, she left super early…" Tom said.

"She had school early." I protested.

"Sure, but she didn't tell me that. And she barely said a word all night. Not a 'thanks to David for having her over', or a 'thanks Tom for paying for my pizza'. I mean, that's just not on." He scowled. "And she's totally not like that when it's just us together, but she goes all silent around my family too. I'm sick of it." He huffed.

"Gee, I think we hit a nerve." David winced.

"You're not, like, *going out*, are you?" I asked him.

"No," He sighed. His head sunk between his knees. "I think I'm learning my lesson, boys. She's just so *basic*. Like, she's such a classic hot-white-girl. I need somebody with manners, who has some good interests and hobbies. Somebody *intellectually* stimulating. I mean, the sex is great…"

"Wow, too much information!" David coughed.

"…But she's terrible. I think I did a bit of a 'dick-think' on this one. She's way too crazy."

"Well, hey, that's a mature realisation." I smiled. "But does a lack of manners constitute being called crazy? Entitled, maybe."

"Oh no, that's only the start of it." Tom laughed. He craned his head of red hair up to face me. "She *is* crazy. She's right into conspiracy theories, and the paranormal, just like your sister."

"Hey!" I rebutted.

"You got my gist. Penelope's a nut. She's closet crazy. When I ask her questions about herself, or want her to open up about her interests, she never does. I'd never have known she was deluded if she hadn't have asked me to fix her computer. Thing went totally kaput, so she gets me over and makes out with me until we land on the machine…"

"*Nice.*" David grinned.

"Anyway, she leaves to make us lunch, and I dive into her stuff. Man, some weird shit came out of it. Like, ghosts, daemons, the rise of an alien race. It's crazy. She's crazy, and I think I'm going to have to break her heart."

David and I fell silent at the implication. It was clear that he was fed up with her.

"Is it stupid…" He asked, "that I just want to stick it out for the physical stuff?"

"No." I said. "It's not stupid, but it's not doing you or her any favours. You could mentally check out, but it's not very nice on her, and you'd have to pretend that you were in it altruistically. It's not worth it, man."

"Yeah, you're right." He huffed. He filled the void of his mouth with an apple and munched down. We watched the soccer in silence.

"So," I said. "What did everybody think of Celeste?"

"Crazy hot." Said Tom between his existential sighing. "Like, not ridiculously hot, just hot and crazy. Not my thing any more, I guess."

"You think she's crazy?" I asked Tom.

"I've been living with her for over a week." Said David, "And she's definitely…I don't know, like, twitchy? But then she's so laid back too. Very *chic*, when she wants to be."

"No, I don't mean twitchy." Said Tom, "I mean that she's *way* too flirty. I recon she'd be a freak, but maybe not a girlfriend."

"Gee, fellas, I don't know." I hummed. "I was blown away by her. I don't think I've been more physically attracted to anybody else in my life."

"There'll be other girls." David said.

"Yeah, but, still." I sighed. "I can't believe I blew my chance last night. I had so many opportunities to make a move, but I just flopped like I knew I would."

"And there'll be other opportunities." Tom noted. "Not that I think she's worth much trouble."

"No," I protested. "I really feel something, but if I leave it too long the chance will go. She probably already sees me as just a friend. I'll never crawl away from that label."

"Don't be so fatalistic." Tom whined. "You can crawl out of that zone if you do it now. Just go talk to her a bit more and lead on that you're interested."

"And what if she rejects my advances?" I asked.

"Why does it matter?" He asked, wiping a hand over his face, "She's an *exchange* student. She'll leave in a month or two. You could only have a fling at best, anyway."

"He's right." David said. "It's totally low pressure."

"You're right, fellas." I said. I gathered up my rubbish in one hand and eyed off the bin. "I'm going to find her right now. I'm going to talk to her *right now*."

"That's the attitude I wish I had." David said. "Go and do it." He handed me his rubbish, and Tom apathetically slid his apple core into my banana peel. I went over to the bin, then continued into the quad in the centre of the senior school.

I stood in the centre of the quad and examined my surroundings. There were lots of kids around, but my eye immediately snapped to Celeste. She was outside the green house locker bay, talking in a large group. Celeste was in the younger year level; she was sixteen, and as such was surrounded by a bunch of other year eleven kids — the popular ones, anyway. Her eyes glowed. She was laughing with them, and absorbing their attention.

My heart sank, my hands gravitated to my pockets. I wasn't popular. These dudes were all friends of Rhys Cameron, or at least liked him better than me. There was no way I had anything to say to any of them. I couldn't imagine a way to breach the group.

I stood there for a good minute, bouncing back and forth between my feet, staring at her smile. It took me that whole time to realise how creepy I looked.

I turned away, pivoting on my foot to find Natalie. In the past week, she'd stopped hanging out so much with Tom, David and I, and had made some new friends in some of the other Greek girls of the year level. I powerwalked over to the tree where they all sat, on the edge of the football oval, on the back side of the senior school.

As I looked at this group of girls, I felt it again – that sense of not belonging. Even though I knew Natalie better than anybody else who sat with her, I couldn't think of a way to breach the circle of friends. I pulled my feet through the sludge of my self-doubt, edging closer to the group in spite of my fears.

I didn't even have to say anything as I sheepishly approached. I was called to.

"Hey James!" Christi Nanos called to me. She had olive dark skin, and dark brown hair, which made her classically good looking, and as follows, intimidating to me. But, she was also one of the nicest people in the year level. Her smile was so cheery, and she was never mean spirited.

"Are you coming to my party this Saturday?" She asked me.

"Oh, yeah, definitely." I squeaked with a growing smile, "I thought Tom told you."

"He did." She smiled, "I just wanted to make sure he got it right."

"Oh, okay." I smiled. "Well, yeah, I'm going to be there. I've been looking forward to it."

"Tell David to come talk to me at lunch." She said. "I want him to bring his exchange student."

"Oh, really?" I tried to hide my excitement. "Yeah, I'll get him for you after English."

"Thanks, James." She grinned sweetly. I turned to Natalie.

"Hey, Natalie, could I talk to you for a minute?" I asked. I gestured awkwardly to the side of the building, where there was some privacy.

"Oh, uh, sure." She said, getting up and following me away. Behind us were hushed giggles. I led her to the side of the building, on the driveway to the teacher's carpark. We talked under the shade of the trees there.

"What's up?" She asked me, crossing her arms.

"Look, I just need some advice." I said, slumping down. "I mean, I think I really screwed up my chances last night by being too nervous to make a move. Even now, I saw Celeste hanging out with a bunch of popular year eleven boys, and I couldn't think of a reason to approach. If I don't step out of the friend zone now, I don't think I'll ever be able to. But I I'm just so…boring. Last night she laughed way harder at everybody else. Just now, I saw her having a great time with a bunch of other guys who are way cooler than me. How can I possibly compete, I…"

Natalie held an index finger right up to my lip. I went cross-eyed trying to focus on it. My lips immediately sealed.

"James, don't spout nonsense." Natalie said.

"But it's *not* nonsense." I protested. "I'm not good enough, or social enough, and…"

"No, that's stupid." She put it bluntly. "Firstly, stop putting yourself down, it doesn't get you far. Secondly, why are you trying to be something you're not? Other boys, like Tom and those popular guys, have charisma and humour. You have…well, you're James Grey." She said. "You're awkward, full of hyperbole, intelligent, and you're well rounded. Somebody will like that."

"But Celeste doesn't, and she's who I'm trying to impress."

Natalie rolled her eyes.

"Okay, let me finish then." She rubbed her nose. "Look, you're desirable in other ways, James. You might be oblivious to it, but I know a few girls that have a crush on you."

"*Really?*" My face lit up. That one comment went to my head faster than blood could make it to my brain.

"Hey, don't be like that." Natalie said. "You've chosen your girl. Don't chase somebody else because you think they're easy. What kind of a person does that make you? A dickhead."

"Okay, sure." I agreed.

"But look, if she doesn't see what there is to see in you, she's not worth the hassle of being romantic with." Natalie said, patting down my arms. Her smile seemed earnest. "Plus, Celeste's our Suneva friend, you have every reason to chat with her. Why don't you ask her for some help with something? Have you summoned your *alis* yet?"

"My *alis*…what is that?" I asked.

"That's your armoured form, James. That's Maiki."

"I couldn't even put away my staff." I chuckled. "But, we have our armour already?" I asked.

"Yes, of course." She huffed, "James, haven't you seen all of the other Suneva? They're covered in armour."

"Yeah, but they put it on, don't they? Where'd you get the idea that they *summon* it?"

"Because I've done it. The armour is a part of the soul, James. Just like your weapon."

Of course you've done it.

"Look, just ask her about how one retrieves their Suneva armour. Take her to make-out-bush, or wherever I pulled you into last week. You'll have a good reason to talk to her and be one-on-one. You'll both be vulnerable, and she'll get to see your character. I think that will work."

"That's a good idea." I said. "Thanks Natalie." My smile grew. Natalie patted me on the shoulder.

"You're a funny one, James." She noted. The bell rang over her voice.

At lunch, after English class with David, I set out to find Celeste. I made it as fast as I possibly could from my locker to the green, ground floor bay, where Celeste's locker was. I skidded to a halt by her door - the location of which I had procured from David.

She turned up not long after me, a plethora of books in hand. She smiled with her bold, crimson lips as she peered over her stack of items at me.

"James." She said, her voice inflected. "Hi."

"Hey Celeste." I smiled back. "Sorry to surprise you..."

"No, you're okay." She said, bustling past me. "Just let me put my stuff away."

"Yeah, of course." I said, standing aside. She cracked the code to her padlock and I opened the door for her.

"Thank you." She said.

"Look, I wanted to talk to you earlier, but you were surrounded by friends."

"James." She turned to look me deep in my eyes. "You can come and talk to me any time." She smiled, holding me in a brief trance.

"Sure." I snapped out of it. "But it's about Suneva stuff." I said. "Probably not something I could say out loud."

"Gosh, it really is different in this country, isn't it?" She noted, closing her locker. "What did you need to ask?"

"Can you show me how to summon armour?" I asked. "Natalie told me that the armour isn't a thing you put on like clothes. I didn't know that. In fact. I didn't even know that the weapons came from the thread."

"You didn't know that?" She raised an eyebrow. "What has Kuvalik been teaching you?"

"Only the basics." I blushed.

"Right, well, there's no Suneva around school. Let me show you a thing or two." She grinned. "Do you know any secret places?"

I didn't take Celeste to make-out bush. Not only did I not want to have to explain the name, but it also wasn't that secretive of a location. There was one place in the school where barely anybody went. It was the old smoking spot from back in the day. It was an isolated space, between the back of the art buildings and the school's boundary. There was a strip there, covered by tall gum trees, where teachers could park. The trees shed branches often, and Mr Moon's car made a shining example of why one shouldn't park under them.

I took her around the side of the art buildings, and right into the centre of the mysterious smoker's carpark. She strutted across the dirt, flicking a small blue flame into existence between her index finger and her thumb. She pivoted on the loose stones to face me.

"Are you sure nobody comes here?" She asked.

"Absolutely sure of it." I said.

"Okay, good." She eased up. A large blue flame lit up in her palm. She sustained it, letting its tendrils tease the sky. "So, you want to get your armour?"

"Yeah. I've got absolutely no idea how though. I didn't even know it was a *soul* thing until today."

"How didn't you?" She quizzed.

"I thought everybody just owned a set of armour." I repeated my reasoning.

"Right." She pondered. "James, how do you use your powers?" She asked. She strutted over to where I was, swaying her hips.

My eyes followed the pendulum, my mouth running a brainless *"um…"*

"Okay, good answer." She teased, and stopped before me. She grabbed my left wrist in her non-lit hand. Her grip was firm, and her hand was hot. I flinched at the idea of somebody grabbing my wrists, but eased up when I saw her face.

"You got stuck trying to attack me yesterday." She said. "Why?"

"I was trying to transfer the energy of quatra to the kinetic energy of the air. I just couldn't do it though. I had my grip, but the quatra didn't transform. I tried to breathe to make the quatra come, but it wouldn't."

"Hmm…" She pondered. Her hand crawled its way from my wrist down to my fingers. Her fingers gently caressed my skin. "How long have you been a *Kiin*?"

"I've been controlling the air for a week."

"Right." She rubbed my hand. "I think it's time to expand your mind a bit. It's okay to think about *quatran* as an energy conversion, but it's also stupid."

"Stupid?" I asked.

"Yes. You're limiting yourself. Quatra isn't about science, it's about feeling." She stated. I looked at her, puzzled. "Okay, maybe there's some science aspect, but you open yourself up to so much more by feeling, and using your soul. It's not quantitative, is what I mean. Maybe it's easier for me – I've been a Suneva from birth and grown up in a Suneva family. I've grown into my powers, and I grew up knowing how to use them and all aspects of the soul. It's not hard. You think it, and you do it."

She took her hand from my arm, and held it between us.

"I think I can make the flame. I feel the flame in my hand…" with a *whoosh*, a blue flame bubbled in her palm. "And the flame forms. I don't think about the energy, or do some stupid breathing exercises to make the quatra flow. I just think about what I know my soul can do."

"Right." I said.

"So, just do it." She said. "I want you to push the air. Just put your hand out and *know* that it will move. Think it, and do it. Or, better: *feel* it, and do it."

"Okay." I bit my lip, concentrating. *Feel it, and do it.* I could feel my grip on the air. I didn't think of drawing quatra, or breathing in to summon it, I just held on to the air and pushed forward.

A powerful gust of wind rushed past my body – more powerful than any I had summoned previously. The force of it pushing against my hand sent me stumbling backwards.

"See, it's that easy." She said.

"Wow, that is easy." I said, finding my footing again. "I didn't even have to think."

"You shouldn't *have* to think." She said. "It's the natural way our bodies work. We're Suneva."

"So, what about armour, then?" I quizzed.

"Right." She grinned. "That's harder to explain. Your armour is in there. It's a part of your soul, and a part of your connection to your black hole. *Feel it and do it.*" She repeated. "Just imagine it coming over your body…"

She winked at me as her face disappeared from sight, covered by gleaming red armour. It erupted from the point of her thread, crawling over and locking onto every space of her body. It constricted her joints to unnatural thinness, as if her body didn't exist under it. Her helmet was bright red, with mean, blue eyes. It had two angled fins, like antennae, extending from the back of her head over her face.

The rest of her was a mix of gunmetal grey and bright red plating, with blue spiked shoulder guards and knee pads. Her figure was sharp, and mean. Through the helmet she smiled, and from her back erected four insectoid wings. I stumbled in fright as they unfolded before me.

"Wow." I uttered.

"This is *Genive*." She said. "When a Suneva wears their Suneva armour, you call them by their Suneva name."

"Sure…*Genive*." I said. I pointed to the wings. "How did you get those? Can you fly?"

"It's not uncommon for Suneva to have extra appendages." She said, pulling a wing around and stroking it between her bright red, frighteningly long fingers. "But no, I can't fly. They can, however, soften a landing."

"Damn." I uttered. "That's so cool."

"Thanks." She beamed. "Anyway…" The armour peeled itself from her body, rushing back into the mouth of her thread in an instant. Underneath was the same French girl who I had seen before – no deformed joints.

"Try it." She instructed me. "You should be able to feel it *in there*."

"Alright." I said. I concentrated hard on feeling anything at all. All of this soul searching recently left me dizzy, trying to 'find' magical items in magical places. Truth be told, I couldn't *feel* anything at all.

"I don't think there's anything in there." I said.

"Don't be silly." She said. "It has to be in there. Don't you feel like your bones are thick? Like there something they're holding and want to let go of?"

I'd never considered how my bones felt before. They liked to dance, I knew that much.

"Okay, where did you find your staff?" She asked.

"It was in my arm, but also not…I'm not sure how to explain it." I admitted.

"Was it in your arm, but also up *there*…" She pointed upwards, "between your body and the black hole? In the *void?*"

"Yes, exactly that." I said.

"It's the same for the armour." She said. "It's a part of your soul, but it's a figment of quatra, and your connection. It's in you, but also between you and whatever else there is in this world. *Feel* it."

I focussed on the feeling, and became acutely aware that I could feel my bones in my body. This was not a sensation I had known before. In keying into this, I became aware of another sensation – the sense that I felt my bones somewhere else, in my thread. I tilted my head back, and I found myself staring up the pipeline of quatra. My vision danced through the void. I could see my connections, like a web of magic. There was a reflection of my whole body in there – where I felt my staff was held, whilst simultaneously being jammed into my left arm.

"There it is." I said. "I can see it."

"I knew you could." She said. "Now, I don't know how you'd think about doing it – I've never thought about it at all, but summon it."

"Okay, I'll try." I said.

I held onto the image of my reflection, floating there in the *void* of energy. I tried to reach out to it. With each breath I could feel my ethereal fingers edge closer to one another. My bones rattled, as if they were about to crack open. The sensation was euphoric, rather than painful. Powerful warmth spread through my body. My reflection was outstretched, trying desperately to hold my hand and be dragged through the thread. Our fingers touched, and the mirage collapsed in on itself in an instant. I was yanked out of the vision of my reflection and thrown back into the waking world. The force of the illusion ejected itself from my body in a disturbingly powerful burp. I coughed and spluttered.

"Very charming." Celeste noted, stepping back. My face flushed red and hotter than her fiery hands.

"I thought I had it." I laughed uneasily.

"That wasn't it." She said.

"You don't say." I brushed myself off.

"You really are an odd Suneva, James." She said. "I've never known anybody *not* to understand the armour and the sword."

"Thanks?" I quizzed. I extended my hand, latched onto the air and swiped across my face. A gust of air pushed the involuntary burp away.

"You'll get it, soon." She smiled, and patted me on the shoulder. I smiled wanly back. I became acutely away that I'd failed to be flirty at all, and if anything, I had just disgusted the poor girl.

Leaves and stones crunched underfoot around the corner of the building. Both of our ears pricked up at once, and we span on the gravel to face the sound.

Three people walked around the corner, each with a smoke in hand. Rhys Cameron led Jason and Sam – two of his good friends – to their apparent favourite smoking spot. They twirled the cigarettes in their fingers as they strutted around the building. They glanced to Celeste and me.

My eyes were as wide as a rabbit under an eagle, but Celeste was calm and collected. She took my hand firmly in hers and spun me around to face her – away from Rhys and his friends. Her eyes stared into mine, and for a second my heart melted into my veins. My blood ran hot as she stared past my soul with a look of total, physical desire. My mind froze, my brain aghast and confused.

She wrapped her arms around my neck and pulled my head in. Her lips diverted from their collision course with mine, and she kissed my cheek. I could feel my pulse in my eyelid as it twitched from excitement.

A cheesy grin cracked into place across my paralysed face. She quizzed me with a squint. I had no idea what it meant, but it stopped me smiling right away.

"Damn, you can do *way* better than James Grey." Rhys Cameron called from the other side of the dirt patch. Celeste peered around my body to stare him down. She removed her arms from my shoulders, and I turned to face the scene.

"What was that, *darling*?" She asked in her French inflection.

"He said, you can do way better that *him*." Jason scoffed, pointing at me with the end of his cigarette. Rhys' free hand plunged into his pockets, fumbling for a lighter.

Celeste strutted away from me, tracing a red acrylic nail down my arm as she did - letting it linger before stepping away. She pulled her own cigarette from the pocket of her blue school dress, and snapped her fingers on its end. It lit up in a dazzling blue flame. The boys were too occupied watching her waist sway to notice. She put it in her mouth.

Celeste stepped close to Rhys, her face almost at his. She grabbed his smoking arm with her right hand, and plucked the cigarette from between his meaty fingers. She let go of him, and held the cigarette between their line of sight. She flicked her index finger up the inside of her thumb and created a blue fire which rested atop her nail. She used this to light the cigarette, which she delicately placed between his lips. He was gobsmacked. Celeste smiled at him with a lustful gaze.

"Light-up nails." She explained to the stunned man as the flame died out. "All of the girls have them in France."

Her hand lunged for his throat, but stopped short of grabbing at it. Her nails clenched at the base of his jawbone, and she pulled her hand away, tracing his jawline. As her fingers cleared his chin, they snapped together, fostering a flame between them. She quickly extinguished it, and wordlessly turned to walk away.

Rhys Cameron was expressionless. His mouth hung agape as the lit cigarette dangled limply from it. Celeste teased them with her gait as she came back to me. She dropped her cigarette and stomped it underfoot. White smoke rose from between her rosy lips, and an orb of white solid lifted from the cigarette's extinguished end into her grasp – a wad of pure oxygen.

She grabbed me by the hand – which I didn't have the time, nor brainpower, to reject, and walked me around the corner of the art building. I smiled smugly back at Rhys. On the outside, I was satisfied, but I knew we were both as confused as one another. Once we'd cleared the corner of the building, she dropped my hand.

"That," she said. "Is how you have fun with mean boys."

"Yeah…right." I tried to gather myself. "You smoke?"

"No, I keep that as a prop. You never know when you get to freak somebody out." She said. "But you shouldn't have been surprised if I did. Have you met other French girls my age?"

"None." I replied lamely.

"Well, they smoke. That's about it." She said. "Anyway, let's go eat something, I'm starving."

"Sure." I nodded my head in agreeance.

We walked off together back to the senior school. She didn't grab for my hand or my body again, and I had no idea where that left us.

Chapter 13
Square Eyes

Simone had logged on to the family computer just after breakfast while Mum and I stirred lazily in the house. The machine whirred into action, and she forced the struggling beast to open Internet Explorer to get her to the fairysmog message boards. Whilst the disturbed circuits growled to load her requests, she palmed through documents she had in her hand. They were Police reports on Argol activity and they were to be the topic of today's chat.

The chat room finally opened, and curtains closed, Simone adopted her screen name of *Simone23*. As the clock ticked over seven-thirty, the agreed upon time for the conference, three more users entered the chat. These had been Simone's friends for at least a year, even if she had never met them. They were *Pondxtr86*, *XxRocker* and *Sportsboy2*. Reading the names brought to Simone a physical illness – she hoped that to the outside world she didn't appear as cringy as a near-grown woman adopting the name *XxRocker*. Still, these were people she trusted, they waited on her word.

Sportsboy2 was typing, Simone could see on the messenger window. "Anderson says that Iva Argol is in Melbourne." He said, and there was a pause to his typing - likely his internet cut out.

"Iva Argol iz in Melbz?" *XxRocker* replied. Simone grumbled at the awful use of shorthand spelling.

"Things are about to get a lot more dangerous in Melbourne, then." Simone said to herself, before typing it to the chat.

"U take Andersons word for it?" *Pondxtr86* asked. Simone hummed. Only a few months ago, Anderson had been just an anonymous tip to the *fairysmog* message boards. A warning that Hesslik's scientist would move his operations to Melbourne and draw Suneva attention to the city. After that became confirmed, and the Empire of the Black Suns had a base of operations in the city, Simone had no doubts about the man's word.

Simone also had no doubt that the presence of Iva Argol in the city had spurred the violence which I had come across. She pondered it now as the chat fell silent. Should she have tried harder to convince me against my convictions to chase Suneva leads? Surely it was too dangerous for me to chase these beings. Had she led me into danger?

"Of course I take Anderson's word." Simone typed to the chat. "He's got insider knowledge."

"How tho?" *XxRocker* asked. Simone wished she was more critical, but without having talked to the man, she just *believed* him. It was a strange choice.

"Because he's always right." Simone replied, and the chat lulled once more.

The thought of my meddling continued to nag Simone's thoughts. Humans can't see quatra bolts, which meant that I shouldn't be able to. She thought it likely that any day now I'd find myself between two Suneva, and a bolt of the deadly energy would sail straight past my face, and I'd have no idea I was in incredible danger.

The image was caught on a loop in her head, the bolt narrowly missing my face for one hundred repeats until finally it collided, and my head exploded in a shower of blood and brains.

Simone cursed, growling, forcing herself from the nightmare. Simone couldn't escape them though. Ever since she'd discovered the Suneva, she knew that she had to be the one to protect regular people. The people on this message board believed it too, somehow. It was an unhealthy messiah complex, the arrogance of which was not lost on her, but it was warranted.

Because Simone could see quatra.

Her mind wandered away from the chat, which seemed to have moved on, to the first time she'd seen a bolt of the energy. Simone was about fifteen years old, sitting in the Police station with Dad. In what must have been totally against protocols, she found herself beside Dad on the right side of a one-way mirror, watching an interrogation. Lost to Simone was the reason why she was there in the first place – something about being sick, maybe? The man behind the glass was an Argol gang member, being interrogated by another detective. The Argol sat stiff in the interrogation chair, their eyes aflame in rage, their fists curled to breaking. They roared, banging at the table. The detective spoke.

"Look, Michael, we have you at the scene. Your prints are on the weapon, we…"

"You don't have *shit* on me. I haven't touched a weapon in years!" They yelled, palm slamming on the table. From it, three bright yellow rings emanated across the table surface, bathing the room in a cool glow. The man then punched at the air, a three-ringed bullet of yellow energy screaming from his hand. It thumped against the glass, rocking the mirror in its frame. Simone threw herself back in fright, clutching to the back wall as yellow rings cascaded across the mirrored screen.

She remembered how calmly her father turned to her, and how pointed of a look he gave her. Nobody else in the room even twitched a muscle. That was when she knew her sight was inhuman, and it was when she started her research.

"Wat did u call the meeting 4 tday?" *XxRocker* asked Simone in the chat. Simone flicked through the files again in her hand. These were her father's own cases. She'd stolen them, and she'd found them shocking.

"There's intense Police corruption, or some kind of collusion, for cases involving Argol gang members." Simone typed to the chat. She wasn't particularly in the mood to defame her dead father, a man who could not defend himself, but she found her revelations important none-the-less. "I've got a number of complete Police case files relating to Argol gang activities on hand, and in each and every report, there is a calculated effort to remove any mention of the Suneva and mentions of Suneva abilities. There's a lie to account for almost every supernatural action."

"That's not good." *Sportsboy2* added.

"No, it's not." Simone continued. "That means that the Suneva really *do* have some control over the legal system. It's worse than we feared, they've already got their roots. Who knows what they can do now."

Simone shivered just thinking about the possibilities. Then a curiosity hit her, how had her father even apprehended any Argols to begin with? It's not like they'd neutralised them to bring them in - she'd seen a stray bolt of quatra fly in an interrogation room. Wouldn't the dangerous Suneva have weapons and abilities which would make them impossible to catch? Weren't they impervious to bullets, also? With super-strength to boot?

"There must be Suneva in the force, too." Simone theorised to the chat. "Otherwise there'd be no apprehended Suneva in the first place." Yes, that was a correct thought. Dad probably worked with these corrupt cops, too. Clearly he had by his writing. That was sickening.

Simone was sure anyway that she was not a Suneva – everything she learned had taught her that. She had no connections to the world, no *sense* for quatra or Suneva, and no soul or weapons, or hippie spirituality which many of them boasted. She'd tried on many occasions to prove herself wrong. Certainly, it would be easier to fight the Suneva if she was one herself, but she was not. Simone was normal, she just had better eyes than most.

And so Simone had to be the saviour, as she was the only person who could see the danger. She was the only person who could know about this level of corruption.

"This is going deeper than I ever imagined." *Pondxtr86* added, with a surprised emoticon. "I feel so powerless. What can we even do when they're controlling the police? Their crimes don't even get persecuted. When will we have justice?"

Simone wished she knew the answer. She slumped back in her chair, face pouted. She might have been able to see flying bolts of quatra, but it didn't help her to stop the Suneva responsible. Right now, awareness was her target. A solution would come.

Hopefully.

The door to the study creaked open. Simone's eyes bulged. She threw the documents aside, not wanting to be seen fondling stolen Police reports – she was sure that it was a terrible crime to be caught with – and minimised the tab on her browser. There was nothing more suspicious than a plain desktop, but it was better than what she'd just had on the screen.

"Hey Simone." I said, entering the room. Simone spun in her chair to face me, sitting tense in the chair. Could I see those documents lazily thrown aside? She hoped that the room was dark enough to conceal them.

"I'm off to school. Just thought you should know that I took the last banana." I smiled, holding up the curved fruit.

Of course you took the last banana. Simone huffed, wondering what she was going to take to University today, now that I was going to abscond with half of her intended lunch.

There was something off about me, recently, Simone thought. Maybe I *had* stumbled across the Suneva. Maybe I'd been close to fatal danger, and been totally aware of it. That would scar a person.

In my eyes she saw a sparkle, and she wasn't sure what to make of it.

"Okay." She said to me. "That's fine. I'll see you later."

"Catch-ya!" I said, and swung the door closed. Simone heard me leave.

She sighed, swivelling back to the computer screen. She reopened her tab, to see that the chat had soldiered on without her. Had I been scarred by what she'd led me to see? The idea haunted her. Simone was meant to be the saviour, did that mean exposing people she loved to things they'd rather not see to direct their fears? It sounded obvious that people *needed* to know of the Suneva, but she wasn't willing to hurt anybody. Perhaps that's why she'd been holding back this whole time.

Maybe she'd hold back a little longer, she decided. There was still so much more to know.

"You've come a long way Maiki, in such a short time." Kuvalik said to me. I sat again around his coffee table with a cup of tea near my hand, like I had almost every night in the past two weeks.

"To summon your staff on intuition alone is a large feat, and a great step in your development. To *toxicate* a bolt of quatra this early is unheard of."

"Sure." I said, tapping the mug with a frustrated finger. "But I couldn't put it away without help – and what's toxication?"

"What you just described to me." He said, "combining another's quatra with yours in an act of redirection. For many, this is harder than straight redirection."

"So, what's straight redirection?" I dug further.

"When you accept a foreign bolt of quatra and pass it through your body without letting it touch your thread – usually from one hand to the other."

"Sounds   useful."   I   said,   "can   you   teach   it   to   me?" The ghost paused.

"It involves closing off quatra pathways. You haven't opened all of yours yet. I'm not sure you're ready to redirect."

"Great." I sarcastically chuckled. "I'm only advanced enough to summon *burp.* and my staff. I guess I'll never be qualified for *anything* as a Suneva."

"The burps are a strange side effect which I've never seen before." Kuvalik rubbed his smoky chin. "But this isn't the ceiling of your power, and you shouldn't fear, Maiki. In time, all will come to you if you keep trying."

"Well, I've been trying with the armour for days, and I'm getting nowhere." I huffed. I crossed my arms and abandoned the tea on the coffee table.

"Patience and an open mind." Kuvalik repeated for the umpteenth time this week. "Celeste helped you achieve an open mind. You must have some patience."

I groaned.

"I'm just so *shit*." I ranted. "I mean, Natalie can already do the swords *and her alis*, and I wouldn't be surprised if she could redirect too. She apparently already knew that the armour was a *soul thing*, and that Suneva weren't going out in flocks to buy armour from some guy who apparently made all of the sets."

"Your conclusions on things are often humorous." Kuvalik chuckled. "You really believed that Suneva bought and put on their armour?"

"Nobody else told me any different." I glared at the ghost. "Anyway, it's logical enough, right? How did Natalie know the truth?"

"She is moving faster with her powers, James." Kuvalik noted. "Her *Yamitse* would have taught her how to summon it when she was ready. Evidently, this was early. Natalie is very gifted, and she *lives* with her teacher. You should not be comparing yourself to her."

"It's hard not to." I continued raving. "Her and Celeste are so much more powerful than me. I can't even imagine what would happen if we came across one of these agents Celeste goes on about. How useless can I be?"

Kuvalik sighed. His ghostly, flat eyes rolled in their shells. Smoke ebbed and flowed from his body.

"James." He said calmly, holding back. "I don't think you've put everything in perspective. Celeste is from a Suneva family. She is sixteen years old – or so you told me. She's had sixteen years to work on her quatra and a whole family to teach her about it. Natalie comes from a very strong lineage, even if this was hidden from her. As you were told by Celeste, Natalie's Yamitse, *Lilawelle*, was at one time *the* most powerful, connected Suneva using quatra. You, however, do not come from a Suneva family or lineage. It's only foreseeable that you weren't born with a connection, and that you received your thread through a destined hit of black hole radiation."

"Hit by a black hole?" I moaned.

"Yes, James. That's how it works. If you're not passed down a connection, then you were chosen by the black hole to receive their thread. It's the honour of destiny, rather than the gift of genetics. For all you know, you only received your connection two months ago. You have a massive hurdle of spirituality to overcome to be anywhere near par with Zamelle and Genive. Your progress *really* is amazing."

"Fine, *Fara* Kuvalik" I gave up arguing, "If you're so sure about it."

"I am." The ghost remarked, "And you should be too - but do not call me that name. The position of *Fara* is long gone for me. It has been stripped from me many times, by men who wrote slanderous things of my life, and one who ended it."

"I'm sorry, Kuvalik." I hushed. The ghost bore over me. His presence building in the room. He wafted back, giving me space to breathe.

"It is okay." He said. "Now, we must meditate further. You must continue to open your quatra pathways if you want to become a better Suneva. More pathways lead to more ways to connect. Greater connection leads to greater spiritual strength."

***

It was the Saturday night of Christi Nanos' party. Tom, David, Natalie, Celeste and I were in the city, having just finished eating dinner, heading down Swanson street towards Flinders Street train station. Storm clouds gathered overhead on the humid night. They hung low in the sky, and threatened to rain, but had not yet.

David, in fitting with his retro and hyper-hip stylings, was a food lover. His parents were extravagant chefs, and at each special occasion, they would take him to enjoy the plethora of food that Melbourne had to offer. Down each alleyway in this city were places serving meals beyond comprehension, packed with insufferable people of equally pretentious opinions. David wasn't pretentious about food, but he liked to make sure that we were well travelled in our palettes.

"So, what did we all think of Thai-fusion flavours?" David asked excitedly as we trekked towards the train station. Christi lived in Brighton – a rich, beachside suburb, to where we would catch the train.

"It's all pretty good, mate." Tom said, "But, I don't know. Why does it have to be so *out there*? Couldn't there just be Thai-fusion steak and veggies?"

Celeste let out a burst of laughter at the remark, then closed her lips. Her cheeks went red.

"Ah, so the French girl finds it funny that I'm not a *foodie*." Tom remarked giving her a nudge. "Well, it's alright. You go home to your lobster, or whatever French people eat. I'll go home to my steak and steamed veggies."

"See, Tom, this is why I have to take you out." David said. "If you're going to live, or, rather, *grow-up* in this city, you've got to be attuned to its ways. I mean, forget that Penelope doesn't say anything at dinner, what would you say if her parents cooked you some amazing meal and you had no idea what it was?"

"Yeah, Tom." I agreed. "Penelope's a fancy private-school girl. That's some expensive taste."

"Her parents have good taste, sure. But, she's just as bad as me." He half smiled, "but about her…" He mumbled, going quiet.

"Oh, see…you boys and your banter." Natalie softly scorned, throwing her arm around Tom's shoulder. I noticed Celeste in my peripherals. She walked behind the line of us now, hunched down into an unassuming posture.

"No, it's alright." Tom said, picking Natalie's arm up and replacing it by her side. He flicked his red hair. "I let her go, you see. I mean, I was discussing this with James and David, but she was just *rude* when I tried to do nice things for her. I had to let her down over the phone…"

"Over the phone?" Natalie redirected her scorn to Tom.

"…and she cried on the other side of it for a whole hour. It was devastating to do. I had to keep looking back at Mum to realise why I was doing it. You know family is more important than some good sex."

"Eh…" Natalie cringed in disapproval. "Well, I'm glad you saw that in the end. The fact that you didn't at the beginning, though…"

"Yeah, well, you live and you learn." Tom said.

"I'm proud of you, man." I said to Tom. "You really showed some good character, you know."

"Yeah, right?" He cheered up, "And now I get to be back on the prowl. You wait till you see me tonight James. Christi hasn't got a boyfriend, has she? Because I forgot to get her a present, but I can make up for it…"

"Oh, gee." David groaned.

A warm hand grabbed my arm. Alarmed, I turned, but my arm was squeezed.

'Shhh…' Celeste whispered into my ear. It was her right hand holding me, with her left on Natalie. She pulled us closer in, and talked to us in a hushed voice.

"Don't be alarmed, and *do not* look around, but we're being followed."

"By who?" I asked. "Do you know how many people are on this street? Nobody is following us."

"We're being followed by a Suneva." She reiterated, "I call her *The Umbrella Lady*."

"I thought I felt a presence before…" Natalie said. She extended her hands in the peace-sign pose by her side, and closed her eyes. Celeste gripped at her arm.

"That gesture marks you out as a Suneva. Never do that if you're being followed." Celeste scorned. "I was the only target, now they might have sights on you too."

"So, who is it?" I asked, swinging my mass to look around. Celeste let go of Natalie, and gripped into my arm with both hands worth of red, acrylic nails. I yelped.

"I said, *'don't look around'*." She seethed, "They're in a large, floppy brimmed, brown hat, with a silver face and a long trench coat. They'll have a silver umbrella in their hand."

"Right, sorry." I apologised. She let go and stepped back, changing her stride into a relaxed stroll.

"Now," She continued, "You two go off and distract David and Tom. I'll deal with this."

"Are you crazy?" Natalie choked, "No way am I letting you fight them alone. Right James?"

I spluttered, and did a double take. "Yeah…right." I wheezed.

"Look, Celeste, we said we'd help you out…"

"You pretty much made me agree to that."

"No," Natalie insisted, "I showed you the *power of friendship*. We won't let you down. Three on one is so much better odds, Celeste. We'll get out of this."

Celeste huffed, and scrunched her brow. "Alright." She sighed. "But know what you're getting yourself into. This isn't going to be a walk in the park. This is real danger. I don't know what they'll do if we don't defeat them."

"Why do we have to fight?" I asked sheepishly, "I mean, we're not gladiators. This is civilised…civilisation. We should just call the police if we're being followed."

"The police won't find her. She's smarter than that." Celeste said. "And she'll attack when we're first alone. If that's at the party, so be it. It's too dangerous to have her following us any longer."

"So, what are some Suneva fighting tactics?" I asked. "What should we expect from a fight?"

"Well, the point is to disable her thread and then run away. It's harder than it sounds, though. She doesn't have any *quatran* abilities, which means that she is *very* practiced with straight quatra. Even if you land a hit, she can redirect it. You'll have to catch her off guard to disable her thread."

"Is there any use in using our abilities, then?" I asked. "This seems like a lot of quatra stuff."

"*Quatran* can distract, subdue, or interfere with your enemy. They're always useful."

"Okay, so she has to find us alone…" Natalie pondered, looking around. "Any one of the alleyways on this street should do. We just have to district David and Tom."

Celeste's hand lunged for mine. She wrapped her fingers around my golden ring – the one that Grandpa passed down to Dad – and plunged it into her pocket. My face flushed red with immediate anger. I was about to yell. Celeste poked Tom and David.

"Hey, James lost his ring…" She said.

"I…*Yes*," I seethed, steam blowing from my ears, "My golden ring. You know the one – the one that my Dad used to wear. The priceless *family ring* that I only wear on special occasions and barely take off to eat. I can't believe I misplaced it."

"Yes, very clumsy." Celeste added.

"Oh, shit!" Tom gasped. "Oh man, that's terrible. When did you last have it?"

"I *distinctly* remember having it on at the restaurant."

"And when you left?" David asked.

"I'm pretty sure it was on."

"Damn." Tom scrunched his brow. "That takes a real tug to get off, too."

"You don't say." I eyed Celeste, who feigned her innocence.

"Natalie, James and I will try to look for it." Celeste said. "You boys should go to the party. Get it ready for us."

"Are…are you sure?" David asked. "I don't mind being late."

"No, really." Natalie said. "You boys go off. We've got this."

"Alright, if you say so." Tom raised an eyebrow to me. I was still angry, which was lucky. Celeste had no idea that I couldn't lie. If I wasn't preoccupied being so enraged, I'd have given us away.

"Tell Christi that we're not far off." Natalie smiled. "We'll go to the restaurant first." We turned, and walked briskly back the way we'd come.

I saw our stalker now – it was easy to spot her large, suede hat in the crowd. She livened her pace. Celeste rounded the corner to the alley first, and Natalie and I ducked in after her. Once out of sight of Tom and David, we started sprinting.

"Wait, guys!" Tom called from the distance, "You need the next lane…" I could hear his footsteps jogging to catch up.

He was right. This laneway was a dead end. It was a back alley. It had a central gutter paved in blue stones, and was flanked by two, tall brick buildings. Backed up to the buildings, on either side of the alley, were large bins. The alley ran downhill for the length of a shop, and ended in a tall, concrete wall. We were trapped.

Natalie and Celeste ran down towards the end. Celeste ducked behind a bin, and Natalie hid behind the one opposite. I flailed into the lane, scrambling on the oily asphalt to join Celeste behind the left row of bins. I craned my head under the dumpsters, and watched the laneway entrance in anticipation. From the three of us, there was only silence.

"Guys, you've got to…" Tom rounded the corner of the alley. He danced on one foot, then stopped dead. "Guys?" He hummed, then stepped cautiously into the lane.

Celeste's hand nudged my shoulder. I looked up to it, to see my ring. I snatched it from her grasp and put it back on.

"I'm sorry, James." She whispered. "I didn't know it was special."

"Look, it's fine." I said.

"If you're sure." She said.

Without a sound, gleaming red and gunmetal armour flung itself from her thread and around her body. I looked across the way to Natalie, to see armour solidifying around her body too. It was sky-blue, with brilliant silver chest and stomach plates, and teal green accents. Her helmet was sleek, with arrow-ended horns that looped around like a ram's, and a 'T' shaped slit for the eyes and face. There was no face, however, under the slit – only an orange, swirling void. Her twin swords appeared in her hands, too, and I was left wondering how useful I was going to be tonight.

"Can you redirect quatra?" Genive asked me as I summoned my staff. I was, once again, taken aback by the amazing connection it afforded me.

"No." I said. "Kuvalik didn't think I was ready to learn."

"No armour, either?"

"Afraid not." I said "But, I can *toxicate* quatra, apparently."

"That's good enough." She sighed.

"Where the hell did they go?" Tom asked himself, trying to peer over bins and around corners from the alley's entrance. Two harsh, metal footsteps clanged behind him. I ducked under the bin to watch.

The feet – like two toed, silver stilettos – strutted into the alley. I didn't think that Tom heard them striking the asphalt behind him. "Maybe they didn't go down here at all…" he muttered to himself as his feet twisted.

He turned himself right into the path of the *Umbrella lady*. She strode through him, unaffected, as he lost his balance and stumbled into the wall of the alley.

"Jesus Christ." Tom huffed, "Watch where you're walking, love." He picked himself off from the wall and dusted his sleeves. "Oh man, that's a stain…"

"You should leave." The Umbrella Lady instructed him. "This isn't the place for you." I could see the tip of her Umbrella resting by her feet, as if it were a cane. She did not turn to him to talk. Under the bin I could see up to her waist, and I could see her hands by her side, analysing the quatra field.

"Not the place for me?" He snarked, "Do you know who I am, darling?"

"Do you know who *I* am?" She turned, smacking her umbrella down.

"Yeah, a total *bitch*." He remarked. "Telling me where to be. Piss off with that kind of shit."

"I'm being serious." She warned. "I'm not inclined to hurt humans, but this is a dangerous place to be right now, without a *connection*."

"*Connection?*" He quizzed. "Shit, is *everybody* in this city crazy. God, you're sounding like the crazy blogs my ex reads. I'm not leaving here until I find my friends."

"I gave you a last warning." The Umbrella Lady hissed. Her armour cracked – the sounds of clanking muffled by the trench coat. Her hands split down the palm, then her arms seemed to hiss at their seams, breaking in two. The velcro on her sleeves ripped apart, revealing her four arms. In the top right one, she held the Umbrella.

"Oh my *fucking*…holy…" Tom uttered. He slowly backed away, not daring to take his eyes from the mechanical, four-armed lady before him.

I'm with you, Tom. I said to myself, my eye twitching in fright. I desperately looked up my thread, between my body and *Omercronius*, to the reflection of myself. In my fear, I reached for it, grasped onto it with my soul's hand, and dragged it out of the thread. This time, instead of burping, my armour hissed and crawled over my skin, locking into place.

The sound of the plating crawling into position caught the ears of the Umbrella Lady, she turned down the alleyway. Genive leaped from behind cover to face her. Her sword was drawn by her side, and it burst into its helix of blue flames. The asphalt bubbled and spat under its influence.

"What the *holy fuck*!" Tom gasped.

"We'll handle this bitch." Genive assured him. She put on a voice to do so – weirdly enough, an English accent. "Run." She instructed. Tom nodded and ran off, around the corner.

I examined my new body. I was breathing. I had a heart rate. I could feel the ground under the soles of my bulky, silver feet, and the wind over my metallic skin. In fact, I could feel the wind at least twice as well as I could with my bare hands. I could feel a richer *fullness* to everything around me. My senses of my soul's connections were vastly enhanced. With the staff in hand, the difference was phenomenal.

I thought it odd that I was still breathing, because I couldn't be sure my body was under the armour. My joints, like other Suneva, were frighteningly thin, but did not feel wrong. I had ungodly-long, silver hands, and a black body with silver and green armour over the top. I was the figure from my weird dream, on the night that Dad died. I was the green and grey Suneva with the large head fin, menacing, green eyes, and chin blade. I was *Maiki*.

"Iva Argol." The Umbrella Lady addressed Genive. She stalked down the alleyway, her heels clicking elegantly on the asphalt. Her voice was seductive, like the mistress in a bad noir movie. "You're got quite the bounty on your head. Vestas wants you…"

"So, if you want me, come and get me." Genive ordered. "You'll be disappointed when I fetch you nothing. Argol knows that I'm not the daughter who left his house."

"Oh, but there's a bounty for all three of you." The Umbrella Lady continued. My eyes almost burst out of my helmet. I could see the green light that they cast upon the dumpster's wall. "Oh, yes. Vestas will pay handsomely for three strange Suneva, each with a strange thread."

"Strange thread?" Genive quizzed, "I'm a perfectly fine Suneva."

"An *Ivaer* of a blue flame as hot and bright as yours is something to be considered *strange*. It would be even *stranger* if you're not an Argol, as you claim. You're worth money to me either way. Your time is up."

"No it's not!" Zamelle yelled, giving away her cover. She stood tall next to Genive, her twin swords resting against the ground. Puddles of air-conditioner fluid quivered as she asserted herself.

"Ah, yes, the strangest thread of the three." The Umbrella Lady noted. "Do you know that you're leaking quatra?" She asked Zamelle. Through her helmet, and her flowing, insubstantial orange face, Zamelle looked shocked. "You use the energy so *inefficiently*, that I'd be surprised if you could fire a bolt at all. It works for me – you left a fat, orange trail which led me straight to the three of you. Iva Argol proves hard to track, but you? *Hardly*."

"Now," She continued, "You can come with me easily, or you can play games. Either way, you're leaving this alley with me."

Nobody had a witty reply. Genive fired a bolt of her bright blue quatra and the madness started. The bolt missed, soaring into the street. The Umbrella lady raised her umbrella and another hand. She fired two indigo bolts – one for Zamelle and one for Genive.

Genive unleashed a torrent of blue flames to blind the assailant. Zamelle leaped back behind cover. Indigo quatra bolts sailed blindly through the wall of fire. Zamelle collected fluid from the alley, preparing an attack. I had a moment to think of what I would do.

There has to be something I can do with air. I thought. *What did Celeste say? Something about distracting, or disorientating?*

Genive and Zamelle fired bolts of quatra from around the corners of their dumpsters. Each bolt that cascaded down the alley was reflected back – just missing the girls' helmets as they peaked around to fire the next.

Zamelle spun her body and whipped a slew of air conditioner fluid from a rank puddle towards the Umbrella Lady. Genive let another jet blast of flames between the bins.

For a moment, there was no action. We could see nothing beyond Genive's blue flames. Then, the flames split. The Umbrella Lady strutted through the onslaught, all the way up to the back of the bins. Genive and Zamelle backed away. I flailed away into the corner of the dumpster and the wall. Hesslik's agent smirked. She raised one of her four arms to me, and fired a bolt.

Air streamed from my bulky, silver soles and my long, gangly hands. I blasted into the sky, twisting around mid-air. I pounced to at least four times a normal human jump, and dug my claws into the wall behind me, like a sacred cat.

The Umbrella Lady didn't take her eyes off me as two of her hands moved to absorb Genive and Zamelle's quatra blasts. Zamelle's orange bolt was redirected straight towards me. Genive's went into the ground, shot from the remaining hand.

I yanked my claws from the wall and pushed myself off with a blast of wind. I soared overhead, across the lane to the other wall and towards the entrance.

She's got four arms, which means she can only re-direct two bolts at once. I noted mentally

I clung into the wall, my fingers wrapped around the brickwork's mortar. I was uphill of the action now, and had inadvertently closed Hesslik's agent in.

Maiki is a master tactician. I smiled beneath my helmet. I leaped from the wall and rolled across the floor to a safe landing. I flung my staff around my body, and used it to extend my soul and grasp at the air around me. I threw the air as my torso swung around. The jet of wind blasted towards the battle.

A leaf fluttered along the ground.

Under my sleek, silver helmet I scrunched my brow. I extended my soul through my staff once more and stabbed it in the direction of battle. A gust of wind rocketed past me and towards one of Genive's blue plumes of fire.

The leaf moved. A single tendril of flame changed direction. The Umbrella Lady was totally unaffected.

Aw, what the hell. I sulked. One of the four arms contorted around the Umbrella Lady's body to face me. Zamelle's orange bolt entered her bottom left hand, and exited in my direction. I jumped out of the way, blasting air from my feet and staff to land on the left wall.

The Umbrella Lady turned on her side now, to keep everybody in her field of vision. Each one of her hands held a peace-sign pose. Quatra came in, was redirected through her body, and came out. She redirected a blue bolt from Genive towards me. She was just acting as a channel now, to direct our attacks toward each other. I launched myself across the gap. The quatra bolt hit the bricks behind me, and their rings emanated through the surface. The mortar bubbled.

I landed uphill on the adjacent wall. I barely had time to comprehend my position before I saw the next blast of quatra flying my way. I pushed off again, summersaulting through the gap back to the first building.

They'll redirect another to me when I land, I thought.

Instead of gripping into the building, I bounced straight off and upwards in a flip, firing a bolt as I did so. She did not redirect a bolt to me. Rather, she waited to receive my bolt, then turned it to Zamelle, and fired a bolt of her own on me.

But it wasn't aimed at *me*, it was aimed at where I was leaping to. Not the wall where I would land– that would be easy. It was aimed in my path of flight. If I kept on my path, I would collide with it, and I would lose my power. My armour would disappear, my fingers would turn to flesh, and I would not be able to grip into the bricks. I would break them trying to grab onto the wall, and I would fall from a great height and break my legs.

I reached the turning point of my arc across the gap, hanging upside down in my flip through the air. I focussed on the bolt racing towards me. I could save this still. I didn't have to break my bones today. I extended my staff to the careening streak of energy and outstretched my limbs, slowing my tumble.

My heart rate spiked. The bolt crawled towards me in slow motion. I reached for it with my staff as my body flipped over its path. It slipped through the gap between my staff's prongs, and soared towards me.

It collided with my chest. It was burning hot. My whole armoured body was a quatra path. It raced into my veins and ran through them like hot, pressurised gas. I could visualise it moving through my system. I summoned as much quatra as I could manage, and just as the invading energy came to my neck, I flushed it out and through my staff.

The proceeding bolt of purple-green, toxicated quatra was not well aimed. I saw it fly on a straight path which would lead to the floor behind the Umbrella Lady. I finished my summersault, my long fingers digging into the wall.

Zamelle's whip of dirty water slapped Hesslik's Agent across the face. Her floppy hat was knocked from her head, and she stumbled back to catch it with one of her arms.

She fell into the path of my misplaced bolt. It slammed into her armour right by the thread. She screamed, and fell to her knees. Her armour did not shatter and fall off like it did for the Argol man in the alley. Rather, as she fell to her knees, it smoked off her body – rising off her skin like dirty fumes. Her head of blonde hair rolled around limply on her neck, and she fell backwards onto the asphalt. Her eyes were shut. She appeared unconscious.

I climbed down the wall and jumped onto the ground. I ran over to the woman. Celeste and Natalie, out of their armour, surrounded her with me. I searched for the button to retract my armour, and amazingly, found it. I willed it to go away, and it scurried off my body, back to the void between *Omercronius* and I. I scrambled to my knees and felt for a pulse in the woman's neck.

"She's alive, James. Don't waste your time." Celeste said. "But great work on that bolt."

"Great work?" I quizzed. "She's unconscious. Is that meant to happen?"

"No, but toxication is strange." Celeste noted, "The body can't reject its own quatra the same way that it can reject foreign quatra. When you mix the two together, the foreign one gets absorbed, the thread stays blocked for longer, and the *toxi* foreign quatra makes them weak."

"Oh, gee." I cringed. I stood to my feet. I could see her chest inflating and deflating. I could feel the air rushing into her mouth. She wasn't dead, that I was sure of.

"…but this isn't any regular toxication." Celeste continued. "Let's get out of here before she wakes up. She will not be happy."

"Why not?" I asked.

"She lost her thread." Natalie said, her eyes wide open. Her hands were held by her side in the peace-sign pose, twitching. "How did that happen?"

"It's a one-in-a-million toxication, I guess" Celeste hummed, "That happens sometimes – the two of you really pulled off that hit, though. Now, quickly, let's get out of here before she wakes."

"We can't leave her like this." Natalie defended, standing tall over the French Girl. "She needs medical assistance…or something."

"No, she'll be fine. Trust me." Celeste said, "If we stick around, *we* won't be."

"I'm with Celeste." I squeaked.

"Fine." Natalie huffed, looking over the woman's body. She sighed.

Celeste and I walked towards the mouth of the alley. Natalie took the time to lay the woman out on the ground in the recovery position. She jogged up the hill to meet us, and we slunk towards the train station through the dark of the muggy night. Natalie rubbed her golden locket between her finger and her thumb.

Tom and David were waiting for the train when we got there. We were just in time to catch it with them.

Chapter 15
Party's Over

The door slammed. The Umbrella Lady's shoes squelched on the hardwood as water flowed from their soles. Her jacket was slopped on her form, hanging with the smell of a thousand wet dogs. Her hair, by now a mop, framed her red, enraged face. Steam bubbled off her cheeks.

The armour of Vestas consumed his body. He put aside the book he was reading and turned to face the door. The sight made him stumble back and grip into the bookcase with his long, sharp appendages. He held in with sheer fright.

"Tona Narsus?" He squeaked.

"Not anymore." The Umbrella Lady growled, ripping her coat off and slinging it across the room. Her fists balled so tightly that her fingers threatened to break themselves. She stormed up to Vestas' desk and slammed a polaroid photo upon it. Vestas peeled himself from the bookshelf to inspect it. He crawled his hand across the table and gently flinched at the photo.

"A one-in-a-million hit, Vestas." She raged. "Iva Argol and those two inexperienced *vassan* stripped me of my identity. That's them in the photo. The darker boy is fine. The red-haired kid is a dickhead, though."

"I can't possibly understand your loss." Vestas tried to say, only a whisper escaping his lips. "But this could be a great opportunity to study the effects of…"

"Shut up with the studies!" She demanded. She swiped her arm across the desk and a pile of papers was transferred to the floor. Vestas' hands strained in mourning of the afternoon lost organising those. "I don't care if it's out of Hesslik's agenda Vestas, I want *vengeance*."

"The *Fara* doesn't look kindly on vengeance, Holly." Vestas called the woman by her English name. "I think you need to take some time to calm down and abandon your anger."

She stifled a deep and mournful breath. Her fist released its death-grip on itself. Her eyelid twitched.

"What will you do for me, Vestas?" She asked.

"They're already on my list." He said calmly. "Hesslik gave me the go-ahead to convince them to partake in our studies. I wish I could say that your action as a lone agent was my oversight, but it's not. You refused the help of my other agents in chasing these three Suneva. The work you've done in tracking them, however, means that we cannot possibly lose them now. You've done good work, and it will all come together in the end. We'll have Iva Argol, we'll sell her back to *The Green Dragon*, and split the profit." He put his cold, metal hand on the woman's shoulder. She shrugged it off.

"And what will you do to the other two?" She asked.

"Their strange threads will prove useful – although, not to them for much longer." Vestas assured her.

"Good." She huffed.

The Bronze Suneva was in his quarters. His bulky, metal legs sat crossed on the steel-framed bed. His long, chunky fingers wrapped around a black device. It was one of Hesslik's inventions – a mobile phone shaped device which could record and playback video messages. Hesslik was a talented inventor.

He fiddled with the device in his palm. His breath was strained. He tried to feel the earth at his feet to calm his mood, but all around was plaster and steel. He growled in frustration and squeezed his balled fist. The device's shell cracked. He released his grip, and let it fall to the floor.

There was a knock on the door. The Bronze Suneva pulled his headphones out and rushed to open it. Vestas lay in wait on the other side.

"Do you have a moment, *Lion's Foot*?" He asked.

"Yes, Vestas."

"You have done well in tracking down Argols and other small-time, deviant scars on society." He said, walking past the Bronze Suneva and into the room. "I don't know what Hesslik's orders for you were, but I have talked to him, and I have a new mission for you."

"A new mission, *tano*?" The Bronze Suneva asked.

"Yes. You're coming with me to track down Iva Argol. This overrides any previous instructions you might have had – and this comes from Hesslik himself. Is that clear?"

"Absolutely clear." The Bronze Suneva replied.

"Good." Vestas rolled his shoulders back. He stood tall, and marched out of the room. The Bronze Suneva rolled his eyes over the crumpled device by the corner of his bed. He snarled – a frown growing behind his helmet.

***

Tom, David and I gathered around the kitchen sink at Christi Nanos' house. I got myself a glass of water. Outside, rain was pouring down. The whole party had shifted inside and the house was absolutely packed. There was a group of people playing drinking games on the dining table, with others jammed in watching, and even more in the T.V room.

"You know, man…" Tom said to me from behind a bottle of beer, "It's awesome that you found your ring. I mean, it's like you to lose things, but that ring? Old man John Grey would come back as a ghost and kill you for losing that."

"Yeah, I know." I sipped my water. "I was lucky to find it. I rarely ever take it off, but I did when the honey lemongrass chicken came out. I didn't want to get any of the thick sauce all over it."

"Honey lemongrass?" Tom quizzed, "You mean that wasn't honey soy?"

"Tom, do you even have a palette?" David hummed.

"At least he eats the food when he doesn't know what it is." I said.

"Yeah." Tom agreed. "I'm already one step up on Penelope. Man, screw her. She wouldn't have even touched a plate tonight if I took her. I'm so much better off."

"Here, here." I cheered. We clanged our glasses together.

A finger tapped me on the shoulder. I set my drink aside and turned around. Celeste stood behind me in the aisle of the kitchen. She smiled as I turned.

"Hey, James, could I steal you for a moment?" She asked. I turned to Tom and David, and they each held a subtle thumbs-up to me.

"Yeah, definitely." I smiled back.

"Come over to the couch." She said. She turned and gracefully parted the

143

crowd. I followed in her wake, moving through the fluid sludge of people who had crowded the space. She had her hand held back, as if asking for me to grab onto it. Still, I wasn't sure. I didn't want to risk making that move, so I didn't. Eventually she retracted her hand.

She took a seat on the couch and patted on the space next to her. I plonked myself down, and found that the couch was alarmingly firm. She shuffled herself closer to me.

"I just wanted to say great job on the fight. I know it was tough, and totally different to anything you've done before, but you did a great job."

"Thanks." I said, "But did I really?"

'Yes!" She insisted. "You really used your abilities to your advantage – dodging up the walls like that. I mean, you couldn't do more than burp four hours ago, but the battle put the armour and the hero right into you."

"If you say so." I said, "But really I was just fleeing…skilfully. And I feel bad for the woman."

"You shouldn't feel bad, James." She said. She lunged her arm forward and grabbed at my hand. Her palm was warm in mine. Her red, acrylic nails caressed my fingers. "She wasn't hesitating to sell us for a profit. The fact that you have such a strong heart is amicable, it really is, but not many others do. This is what it takes to be a Suneva on the streets."

"Anyway," she continued, "You're my hero tonight, and my hero deserves a drink." She released my hand and picked up two cups from the coffee table in front of us. She held one in front of me.

"It's some punch. It's really strong, I think Christi mixed it."

I took it from her hand and examined the contents. It smelled of strong vodka and tequila, but was blood red like bad wine. An orange slice floated to the surface and bobbed there.

"Thanks." I said, "But I can't drink tonight. Head of the River is in a week, and I'm the stroke of the eight…" Celeste seemed confused, "That's the front guy in a rowing boat. Anyway, coach would kill me if I was drinking this close to the comp. Hell, the boys would kill me. We're all watching each other tonight."

"Okay, if you insist." She said, and took the glass back. "But you're now personally responsible for whatever this second glass of punch does, and it might not be pretty." She winked at me, then took a sip of her glass. She put the second down.

"What else is there to learn about being a Suneva in the streets?" I asked her.

"See, I knew you'd ask." She said, "You just can't learn everything from a guy who's been dead for five-hundred years."

"I'd say it's more that you're a good teacher." I added.

"I'm sure I could teach you *many* things, James." Are the words which escaped her bright scarlet lips.

My leg moved towards hers, out of my control. Our legs touched. She didn't move hers away. Her hand migrated from her lap down to her knee.

"Like sensing other Suneva?" I asked. I was well aware that this was not her implication, but I had no idea what to say. She laughed, and took a sip of her drink.

Her drink.

I'm stroking the eight for Leslie Grammar in a week. The thought came into my head. *One week. Do you remember Toby Golding? The stroke of the eight when you were in your first year of rowing. Do you remember how much of a God he seemed like? That's your job in a week.*

"I could teach you that." Celeste's voice poked through my thoughts. "But I think the most important lesson to making your way around other Suneva is…"

*It's six whole minutes of excruciating pain. Two entire kilometres of it…*I could picture the start line in my head. I could see myself marshalling for the race, herded with the other boats like scared livestock. Staring down the whole length of the course. The people at the end were so small, they were unseeable. The drums would be pounding from the shorelines, a brigade of men marching to war. That's what it was – war. *You'll be out of breath, but everybody depends on you. It's going to be the hardest thing you've ever done.*

My hand rested on my leg, near hers. Slowly, I inched it across my thigh.

It's going to be so painful.

I reached out with my pinky, and made contact. Then, slowly, I rested my hand on the outside of her thigh.

You will be broken mentally.

She didn't flinch, or react. I could see her crawling her hand towards mine.

Just think of the line for the toilet before you have your team talk. The team talk for the first eight.

"…as I said to you before, *don't think, just do.*"

I felt like vomiting and peeing at the same time.

"Hey, I've really got to go to the toilet all of a sudden." I said, raising from the couch before she could grab my hand. "I've been busting this whole time."

"Oh, okay." She said. Her smile deflated. "I think the toilet is just around that corner…" She said, pointing past the kitchen.

"Thanks," I said, "And thanks for the advice. I appreciate your help and support…and stuff." I smiled roughly before jogging through the thick mess of crowd to the bathroom.

"Hey, Jimmy!" I was swung around by a meaty hand as I rounded the corner.

"Big Al!" I greeted as I recognised the face.

"Jimmy, my stroke-seat. You're not drinking tonight, are you?" He asked.

"No, man. Of course not." I said. "You're not either, right? I need my big six-seat to back me up."

"I've always got your back, man." He said. "In it together."

"Yeah, man. In it together." I smiled, and my bladder screamed at me again. I made a funny face and ran off towards the toilet. Al seemed to understand.

I pried at the toilet door, but it wouldn't budge. There was a woeful moan from inside. I could not hold it in, so I went into the bathroom, locked the door, and proceeded to piss into the bath tub.

Nervous piss number one. I thought to myself. *One week out, that's got to be a new record.*

It took me a moment to process what had just transpired on the couch.

Her hand…it was trying to grab mine. I realised. *I sealed the deal somewhere. This girl wanted me, I was totally smooth, but then my mind wanders?* I craned my head around to stare at myself in the mirror. My face was confused and defeated – just about the look I expected to see.

No, none of this bullshit. I asserted to myself. *You'll be a great stroke next week. You're a Suneva.*

I'm a Suneva. My passive voice seemed to come to the realisation. *I can do anything.*

You sure can, cheesecake. The assertive voice rocked my head. *Now you go back out there, grab that girl's hand, and stop screwing it up!*

I ran the water, flushing the tub, then marched my way back through the crowd to the couch.

I noticed that Natalie was sitting on the couch where Celeste was before. As I marched my way over, she stood up and blocked my path with a comically large smile.

"Hi, James." She greeted. She was actively blocking my view of the couch and the next room behind her.

"Hey, Natalie." I greeted sceptically, trying to meld my neck to see around her big, curly head of hair. "Where's Celeste?"

"She's gone to get another drink." She said. "I'm sure she'll be back in a bit."

"Another drink?" I quizzed, "But she had two…"

There was an uproar of cheers from several deep voiced boys behind Natalie. She rolled her eyes, slapped her face, and sighed. I got on my tip-toes to peer over her head.

There were two people making out in the portal between the TV room and the adjacent room. He had a meaty hand on her waist, grabbing tight – the other holding a cup of punch which I found familiar. She had her arms slung around his neck, limply hanging off his shoulders. Their eyes were closed.

They were Celeste Bouvé and Rhys Cameron.

"You *really* didn't have to see that, God damnit." Natalie cussed.

My eye twitched. My fists balled. My heart melted, slopped through my body's organ cavity, and fell out my ass. I could feel the air around me stir up as my face was painted in bright red. I was so embarrassed, so angry, and so regretful.

You had her, man. Was all I could think to myself.

"I think I'm going to go home." I said to Natalie.

"I'll come with you." She offered.

"No, it's fine." I said.

I didn't say goodbye to anybody as I walked out. I feared that in my rage, disappointment, and overwhelming sense of loss, I'd say something that I would regret. I was certainly thinking a few choice, regretful words.

Episode 3

A short guide to getting in trouble.

The drums pounded. A trumpet wailed. Blood rushed through my legs and my hot face. The sun was beating down on a glorious early autumn's day. Even sitting on the lake, it was hot.

I was already out of breath – or, I wasn't really, but it felt that way. In front of me sat the cox – Samantha Raywell. Behind me, my supporting man in the seven-seat, was Luke Hogan. A starter held our boat against the dock, ready to race.

I craned my body around, peering towards the end. It was so far away, just like it was this morning for the first race. But this race was *it*. Every single race I'd ever done in my life came down to this – my last chance to represent Leslie Grammar, and I held the keys to an engine of eight men.

My God, it's just so far away. I felt my world crushing down on me, everybody and everything drifting further away as if I was at the centre of expanding space-time. I was totally alone.

"Hey, Jimmy, eyes on me." Sam called, her hand covering the microphone. I stared at her with wide eyes, shaking from the feeling. To my left, Ire College had their boat grabbed by the starter. All boats were in the blocks now.

"Jimmy, this is your race, mate." Sam said, "Don't shit your pants. It's you, and everybody else in this boat. The first ten strokes come free."

"And what about the next one-ninety?" I squeaked.

"They come after. But they'll be done. I know you, and every man behind you, will do them well."

She uncovered the microphone.

"Eddie, light touch." She instructed, then covered up the mic again.

"Jimmy, you've got this. You're a rower. What are you?"

"A rower." I responded.

"Louder."

"A rower!" I banged the oar.

"You're a fucking rower, mate. You can do anything."

And I'm a Suneva. I reminded myself. *I have no limits.*

I felt the air in my rushed, panicked breaths. I felt the swirl of the gentle cross wind, which Eddie in the bow seat was fighting against. I felt the carbon in the oar and the boat. I was connected to this world in so many ways. I was bigger than my body gave me credit for.

The announcer's speaker buzzed. Silence fell.

"Drew College, Leslie Grammar…"

Oh sweet cheese.

"Saint Jerome's Grammar, Ire College, Melbourne College, Subiaco Grammar. Attention…"

I braced the oar, staring Sam in the eyes, not daring to break a gaze. Each millisecond passed with the anticipation of a lifetime. The banging of the drums and wailing of horns was silenced in my head. I hung on the word.

"Row!"

***

Before you ask, we didn't win – not by a long shot. The story of my life isn't one of prevailing victories in the sports field – that's my father's tale. We came fifth out of six. Making the A-final was already exceeding our expectations, but to *actually* beat another crew? Well, the crowd was going wild as we went past. It was neck-and-neck for fifth place, and we did it. We beat Drew College in the last two hundred and fifty metres.

In their deep burgundy blazers, Leslie Grammar supporters traversed the rocky shore to get into the water and splash us as we went by. We held ourselves at quarter-slide and let the boat glide by as waves of water enveloped us from excited fans. On the shore was Natalie, who gave me an extra big splash using subtle control of the water.

Standing on the other side of the crowd from her were Rhys Cameron and Celeste Bouvé. They gave up their grip on each other's hands to get into the water and splash us as we coasted by. For the first time, Rhys seemed happy. He wasn't hostile, he had a smile, and he was enjoying school spirit. It sickened me.

Surely, you're not falling for his bullshit, Celeste.

Past the crowd, I could see Mum talking to a few other parents. She waved at me enthusiastically when we locked eyes. I'd already started rowing away. I smiled. *I wish Dad could see how far I've come.* I thought to myself. *I've still got a long way to go to be close to him.*

We took the boat around the point of the island and into the landing. Our coach was waiting for us there. We had our final, emotional crew chat. We cheered, washed the boat, de-rigged and went to load the trailer.

As I masterfully dual-wielded ten-mil spanners, I felt a strong presence behind me. I turned from sectioning the boat to see Natalie in the rowers only area. I jolted in surprise, and passed the spanners on to Luke Hogan.

"Hey, you might want to get out of here before you get into trouble." I said.

"We'll be allowed out in a bit."

"I know, but this is pressing." She said. I looked around for eavesdroppers and nosy coaches who would push her away. The coaches were distracted with something on the trailer, so I entertained her little talk.

"Alright, shoot." I said.

"We're being followed." She whispered to me.

"That's a heavy accusation." I gulped.

"I've been feeling a Suneva presence all week. They've been leaving behind little trails of quatra in the quatra field – red snakes and blips around us."

"Maybe they just live around us." I said. "There's not much variation in our movement between home and school. School is near offices, it works out."

"That's what I thought." She continued. "But they're here, today. I can feel their red quatra around. They followed us, and they're watching us."

"Really? I don't feel anything." I noted.

"Not surprising…no offence." Natalie said. I frowned. "You haven't been feeling weird at all?"

"Well, I've been feeling claustrophobic – but that's because I was so nervous for the race. I once got so nervous for a race that I forgot to eat, and I fainted from exhaustion."

"Lovely." Natalie groaned. "But the feeling of being closed in could be their presence weighing on your soul."

"Sure." I half-heartedly agreed.

"I'll ask if Celeste can feel it, or knows this presence."

"Alright, you do that." I said. "Don't wait up for me. I'm going nowhere near Rhys Cameron."

"I wish I didn't have to either." She grimaced. I smiled at our mutual disliking of the boy.

"What on earth is she thinking?" Natalie laughed.

"I don't think it's a laughing matter…" I whined.

"Grey, what are you doing with hands off the boat?" My coach growled. I was knocked over by his voice. Even from a considerable distance, its harsh grizzle penetrated my very being. I scrambled back to the boat section.

"And you…" He said to Natalie. "This is rowers only. There'll be plenty of time to talk to our stroke-man later."

"Understood." Natalie said solemnly. She pivoted on the spot and left in an instant.

Just as scared of authority as I am. I laughed to myself. I plunged my arms deep into the boat section, and begun un-screwing.

"I didn't know you had a girlfriend." Luke Hogan said.

"Huh?" I poked my head up. "Oh, her? She's just a mate." My voice wavered, and my cheeks flushed red.

"Sure." He teased. "She was desperate enough to talk to you that she risked being yelled at by rowing coaches. Doesn't she know that they eat nails and cement for breakfast?"

"Clearly not." I said.

"You're embarrassed, aren't you." He prodded with a grin.

"No!" I objected. My whiny voice and determined objection caught the attention of the whole crew. Men rushed in to interrogate me with riggers in hand.

"She's cute James." Samantha said.

"No, she's…" I choked on words, trying to find some defence. Around me there was a resounding coo. I groaned. "You just watch me tonight, boys. I'll prove you wrong at the after party."

And I did.

I rocked up with a six pack of beers, but didn't end up drinking more than two. Drinks were passed around – shots on trays which seemed to all be handed to me. I was the stroke of the first men's eight. It was the first year that we didn't lose, and the first that I would drink at an after party. Everybody else started at the year ten rowing after party. I had intended not to drink at all this year, but here I found myself, in a party, being handed an inordinate amount of shots by my teammates.

I chatted to everybody, and danced like there was no tomorrow. In the blurred lines of the night, I was set up with Samantha. We kissed on the dance floor, and moved it to the outside bench. There were cheers happening around us all night, and we had to block them out to stay in the moment. I'm sure that I saw a disposable camera doing the rounds which snapped a flash photo of us.

Weirdly enough, I didn't like kissing her. It's not that she wasn't attractive, or that I wouldn't usually have done it. There was some other feeling, like I was holding out for something. It felt gross, and I felt almost like I'd violated myself in kissing her.

You're being stupid. I told myself in the moment. *She's gorgeous. This is a dream. Don't be an idiot, just keep going with it. You'll get into it in a bit.*

But I never did. And it never stopped feeling gross.

I went to bed very late that night, and was not prepared for the popularity of my story once I went to school on Monday.

"So…" Celeste came up to my locker on Monday morning. She held herself sweetly by the open door as I rummaged through my pile of sheets and books. "I heard you had a successful night after rowing."

"Yeah…" I laughed awkwardly. "Apparently, she's liked me for a while. I think that's the first time anybody has had a crush on me."

"It probably isn't." She said. "Girls keep secrets, and very seldom tell them."

"Sure." I said. "Well, I can say the same about your success a week ago, although I think you've extended the success."

"With Rhys?" She asked.

"Yeah, who else?"

"It's exciting, isn't it?" She smiled. "You and Natalie made him out to be such a bad guy, but he's nice."

"I'm sure he is, to you." I said with scorn. She frowned.

"Did Natalie talk to you about our stalker?" I asked her. I grabbed my books and closed the locker.

"She did." Celeste said. "I can feel them too. I just didn't want to scare anybody by jumping to conclusions."

"Sure." I responded. "So, you recognise them, then?"

"No." She said. "That's why I didn't think we were under threat. But the fact that they followed us to the lake - it's suspect."

"I'll say." I added. "What do we do?"

"I guess we just wait for now, and stick together." Celeste said. "If we wander off alone, we put ourselves at risk."

"Sticking together all of the time could be hard." I pointed out.

"It will be, so we'll just have to be *extra-best* friends." She smiled. "And I need you to tell Natalie something."

"What?"

"Get her to control her thread, James." She said, eyes serious. "I can sense her orange quatra from here like she's standing next to me. *The Umbrella Lady* was right. She oozes quatra. It makes us an easy target. I've already told her, but I think it would freak her out if you say that you can sense it. She'll put in extra effort to supress it."

"Sounds…dishonest." I said. "I'll see what I can do."

"It's for your safety too, James." She said. She leaned in, kissed me on the cheek, and was on her way. I was left bewildered, and immediately went to find Natalie.

I found her, as I expected, outside her homeroom, with all of her books in an incredibly neat pile in her arms. She wore her reading glasses, and was reading some textbook on top of the pile.

"Hey." I said to her. She was so engrossed in her reading that she almost didn't notice me.

"Hey James." She smiled. "I heard you had an interesting after party."

"Yeah…" I laughed nervously again, and scanned the hall. "How does everybody know?"

"It's big news, James." Natalie said. "Most of the rowers might go to the other campus. But the news gets here. Everybody knows Samantha."

"Alright, sure." I cringed. "Anyway, look, this might sound weird, and I can't lie to you, but you've got to use less quatra energy."

"What?" She quizzed, and leaned in closer, expecting me to whisper.

"Well, I mean, Celeste said that she can sense your orange quatra from the other side of the school. You need to control you thread."

"Alright…okay." She said, frazzled. I could see her eyes becoming glassy. Her locket glimmered around her neck.

"Oh, I didn't mean to upset you…" I said, but she backed off.

"No, James, it's alright." She said. "I, just…I know I'm the reason that we'll be found. I'm trying to use less quatra."

"Gee, Nat, it's not like that…"

"No, it is." She said. "I take that responsibility. My Yamitse is helping me to control my thread. I'm trying."

"Alright." I frowned. "But whatever happens is on all of us. Actually, it's mainly on Celeste…"

"No, we were on their sights. Didn't you hear the lady? Celeste is the reason that we'll survive. She knows the ropes."

"Maybe." I said. "But don't get down. You're inspiring – as a friend and a Suneva. Don't forget that."

She was taken aback that something so nice left my mouth. She smiled, and the happiness lasted past her confusion.

"I don't want to scare you, but the red quatra is strongest today." She said. "They're really close."

"We're all in it together then. Let's not worry too much." I said.

"Whatever happens is destiny, right?" She replied. I shrugged.

"Meeting you was destiny. Everything is destiny – so, I guess so." I reasoned.

We both smiled. Her blue-green eyes stared into my soul. "Anyway, I've got to get to my homeroom. I'll see you later…"

"Actually, James." She stopped me, grabbing my arm. Her glasses slipped on her face. "Would you mind sticking around me at recess and lunch. Maybe get Celeste with us…maybe we can all walk home together today?"

"Yeah, definitely Natalie." I said. "Don't worry, we're a team. Celeste says that we need to stick together." I patted her hand, then took it from my arm. I gave her a *'see you later'* as I headed off to my homeroom class.

Celeste, Natalie and I walked home together. The last warm, sunny day of autumn shone overhead. Natalie walked from the train station like she had her back strapped to a pole. She was trying to control her thread, as she put it, but Celeste whispered to me that she could still feel her energy. We didn't dare utter it to her.

"The other Suneva is nearby, too." Celeste told me.

"I have no idea how the two of you are feeling it." I said.

"You're just not connecting to the quatra field." Celeste said, "It's difficult to do. It took me a few years."

"So, what, when you were five?"

"Three." She smirked.

"Thought so." I rolled my eyes.

"This is another lesson of being a Suneva in the streets." She lectured. "And it's to use what comes naturally to you. You can't sense the quatra field, and that's fine, but the air is an extension of your soul and senses. Use that."

"Right." I hummed. She was right. The breeze distorted my ability to do it, but I'd always had the expanded sense to judge space and distance through my connection to air. I'd been doing it since before I was a Suneva.

I closed one eye as I walked, and keyed into the air around me. There was movement all around – from the eddies which swirled over leaves in the trees, to the branches that swayed, and the hair which shuffled atop Natalie and Celeste's heads.

There was something moving faster than the wind. Actually - two things. The first was a car, which came down the hill towards us. The second was a figure, walking a distance behind us. I turned to see a regular man with a brief case, just embarking on the bottom of the hill.

"That's not them." Celeste said. "But that's good use of your powers."

I smiled.

We were walking to Natalie's house first. The way we had to walk took us up the hill from the train line, then over the football oval at the crest of the street. Natalie became suspicious as we reached the top of the knoll.

"They're gone." She said, looking around. "Their signal faded quickly, and now it's gone."

"I felt that too." Celeste said. "Maybe they're just observing us after all. We could be safe."

We took steps onto the oval. It was a large field of grass, surrounded on all sides by tall, thick red river gums and pine trees. I became uneasy. All around, my senses were nullified by the great open expanse. But distantly behind us, I felt a disturbance in the breeze, right by the perimeter trees.

"I wouldn't be so sure." I said, looking around, "There's something wrong here."

"I'm getting that feeling too." Natalie said as we came to the centre circle. "It's too quiet."

"Not for long." The commanding voice of a London man rang from behind us.

"You were like a cat." Natalie would later joke to me. My eyes bulged from my skull, and my back arched. I immediately flicked my wrist to summon my staff, and ripped my armour from the void between *Omercronius* and I. Natalie and Celeste appeared to do the same, to become Zamelle and Genive. We turned to the voice.

Coming towards us were four Suneva. The one which spoke, I was sure, was the one strutting at the front of the pack. He had teal, squarish eyes and a triangular grille for a mouth. His armour was silver, purple and gold, and he held in his hand an axe-like staff. This was Vestas, Hesslik's quatra scientist who I had met earlier.

"To those who don't know me, which I believe is only one of you, I am Vestas – Hesslik's leading researcher into quatra science, mathematics, and quantification." He stabbed his golden axe-staff into the ground. Three teal rings emanated from it across the grass. Smoke rose from the ground where the staff had breached the earth.

"I know that you are Maiki, and you are Iva, but what is your name?" He asked Zamelle. "You must be a very talented Suneva for the amount of quatra you use." He noted. "It always makes it easier to find a Suneva when they leave such a thick trail of bright, orange quatra."

Zamelle slashed her weapons across the grass and howled at the remark. The cry was projected from her soul, and wailed the scream of a spectre. It was ghoulish, entirely inhuman, and it rattled my very being. I took a cautious step away.

Vestas smirked at the outbreak, although underneath his confident façade, he backed away a single step.

"This is my associate, Niskidin." He said, gesturing to a Suneva on his right. The Suneva had a severely hunched back, and asymmetrical armour. Their helmet resembled a massive, creepy grin, and one of their armoured legs appeared to be prosthetic. It had bundles of hydraulic tubes connecting to its pistons. They nodded a greeting, and threw their staff weapon into the dirt. They proceeded to sit cross-legged on the grass by it.

Niskidin…Kidin I considered. As I had the thought, my face became drenched or, at least, it felt like a bucket of water was poured over my head. I pulled a face at Natalie, then patted myself to realise I was bone dry. I dismissed the sensation with a quizzical eyebrow.

Kidin… I returned to my thought train, *what was that again? I'd heard of that power before.*

A mind reader. A foreign speaker reminded me in my own head. Their gravelly, harsh voice bounced between my ears. I stared at Niskidin, who had closed eyes, but smiled through his helmet.

Oh Gee.

"This is *Faravaer*, a new recruit from a Russian branch of the Argol gang. Iva, I'm sure you would know all about that."

Genive groaned and sparked a blue flame across her sword. Faravaer, a bright orange and incredibly sharp Suneva, stabbed their dagger *shath* into the ground.

"And this is Sirulik, my student. Don't be tempted to go easy on her. She's more than capable." Sirulik followed the gesture of their peers.

Stabbing a weapon into the ground – the classic Suneva greeting. I remembered.

From what I could tell, Sirulik and Faravaer were women. Their Suneva armour was more shapely, and their stature was shorter – if only by one or two inches.

"So," Vestas continued. "I'm giving you all the immaculate opportunity to be an asset to the benefit of the entire Suneva people. The three of you have unique threads which could vastly improve our understanding of quatra energy systems. If you join my study right now, you will live much more fulfilled lives. If you don't. well, I can't say…"

"Oh, shut up, Vestas." Genive called, "This isn't about studies. This is about selling me to back to Argol and getting your money."

"It certainly is not." Vestas rebutted.

"I don't know how many times I have to tell you idiots before it gets through your thick helmets, but I am *not* Iva Argol, and I put up a much better fight than she ever could have."

Vestas grunted. "I'm sure that's what you say to everybody, sweetheart. Even your friends." He chuckled, making a stupid smile beneath his helmet. "I'm guessing that's a 'no' from everybody then?"

There was no response.

"Fine." He sighed, "You've made your decision, it seems. By helping Iva Argol, the two of you have become co-conspirators of Argol corruption here in Melbourne, and as such, are enemies of the civilised Suneva community." He ripped his weapon from the ground and pointed it in our direction. "You *will* contribute to the cause of your brothers and sisters, but in a way which you could never imagine, and which I have long contrived. You have till the count of three to change your affiliations and *willingly* contribute to society, or I will *force* your cooperation. That includes you, Iva. Your hope is not lost."

"Beat it, Vestas." Genive hissed.

"One…" He grinned. His minions picked up their weapons – apart from Niskidin who sat on the floor. Zamelle and Genive stared with cold, unwavering expressions. We each raised our weapons to the circle of the standoff.

"…two…"

"Guys, why aren't we considering this offer?" I squeaked.

"…three…"

Boo! The voice of Niskidin shouted into my head. I shrieked in shock, and fired a bolt of quatra from my aimed staff. It flew towards Vestas, but was badly aimed enough that he did not have to dodge to avoid it.

"That's your decision, then." He snarled. He flicked his axe through the air, and an arc of pure lighting cracked from its tip towards me. I leaped out of the way and rolled through the mud. When I stood, quatra bolts were firing in every direction. A teal one came towards me, and I jumped over it to see it crash and bubble into the dirt.

I fired one back at Vestas in retaliation, and tried to think strategy.

There's no places to hide. I thought, glimpsing the totally flat oval. *And no places to jump to, or from.*

Not much use to being a Kiin on an open oval. Niskidin crackled into my head.

I growled. A bolt of Vestas' teal quatra zoomed past my head, and I spun into action. I extended my soul through my pronged staff, and gripped into the air by its end. I leaped off the ground and threw the air in the direction of Vestas and Niskidin.

The grass blew over, a glob of mud flung into Vestas' helmet, and he had to plant one foot back to fight the gentle breeze. My jump was deflected by the force of air leaving my staff. I landed on my knees, skidding in the mud.

"That's it?" Vestas cooed. "Boy, are you in for a treat…"

Sparks accumulated between his fingers. I backed up, and fired a bolt of quatra, which missed. The sparks merged into liquid electricity, which dripped and oozed from his fingertips. He lunged forward with his open palm and an arc of blue power surged from it.

I ran from its path, and it scorched the ground as it hit the earth. As I ran, a screaming bolt of lightning surged just a hair from my helmet and crashed into the ground in front of me. I pushed on the air to stop immediately.

The lightning hung in the atmosphere, roaring with power. I stepped away, to have another arc of electricity corner me on my back side, buzzing in deadly delight. I turned to Vestas, to see that he had me trapped.

Straining at the power of the arcs he commanded, he used all of his might to draw his hands together. I glanced about in horror as the walls of electricity closed in on me. I forced a gust of air towards an arc, to see that air had no effect. I could feel the intense heat of the surging arcs as they kissed my shoulders' blades. I clenched every muscle in my armoured body.

A helix of bright, blue flame licked Vestas' angular head. His eyes glowed in surprise and he rolled out of the way. His arcs of electricity dissolved into the air, and I leaped for dear life away from where he had fallen.

"Thanks!" I squeaked to Genive. "I thought *I* was meant to be helping *you* out here."

"You've got a lot to learn." She said between quatra blasts. "Take out the *Kidin*."

Take out the Kidin… I processed what she'd said.

To dinner, preferably. Niskidin said in my head.

Only if you're paying. I replied, lining up my shot on his cross-legged body.

Pain engulfed me. I seized up, my biological body – wherever it was, screaming into shock. My spine stretched itself out. My arms spasmed in their sockets. Hot, liquid agony raced through my body. I could see it pouring from my staff end as electricity. The grass by me caught alight.

Vestas was in front of me, fighting Genive. Niskidin had distracted me, and I realised that I had no idea where anybody was. I wasn't tracking anybody in the battle except for Vestas. It was his student, who I couldn't remember the name of, who was behind me, frying me.

I convulsed to the ground. If my helmet had a mouth, it would have been foaming. My hand landed in front of me, and a bolt of green quatra involuntarily leaked from it. It flew across the field, through the battle, towards Vestas.

Vestas leaped into its path. A marbled green-and-teal bolt of quatra emerged from his axe, and it flew back in my direction. I could see Zamelle step out in front of me, and fire back. Mud flung from the ground, commanded by her dual-swords. Fire and lightning boomed overhead. Vestas' bolt traversed the field of flying debris. It hit me square in the face.

It ran through my head like hot gas in my veins. It made it to my thread, and I convulsed trying to fight it. It zipped up the pipeline – into the void between *Omercronius* and I. My whole body became hot. I felt my connection to everything around me wavering, and fading. I cried to *Omercronius*, but my calls went unanswered. My vision faded to black. I passed out.

I was in a white room. It was dark, bar the soft glow of my teal Suneva eyes. The room had a linoleum floor, and tiled walls. There were rows of computers and machines set atop tables, with wires bundled between each. The monitors' screens shed some light into the room. They beeped every so often. I'd been working around the beeping so long now that I barely noticed it.

I was nervous. I was standing before a white table with a monitor and small device upon it. In my hand was a clip board, and atop the clip board was a piece of paper harbouring a long equation. I'd spent a long time making this equation. I was proud of my work, but anxious to present it.

Surely it will work this time. It's the tenth iteration, but I'm certain of it, this time.

The door behind me creaked open. Glorious, white light poured into the room from the crack in the door. It revealed the walls to my left and front, which appeared to be made of glass, and written upon in whiteboard marker.

"Vestas." The voice behind me called. I quickly swivelled to face it. Hesslik walked into the room. His cyan eyes cast a haze across my armour. He fumbled for the light switch.

"Are you a vampire, are you?" He joked. "Even Suneva as brilliant as yourself need some light to work."

"I like the dark." I replied. "It's easier to shed light on the subject when there's less light around."

"Interesting." He quizzed, closing the door behind him and stepping towards me. "I didn't think you were a spiritual man."

"I'm not." I replied. "That's just an interesting anecdote. I usually work with the lights on."

"You're an interesting Suneva, Vestas." Hesslik smiled beneath his helmet. "Anyway, show me what you've come up with."

"Right." I fumbled with the papers on my clipboard. I flicked through the working, to get to the final equation.

"Don't be nervous." Hesslik said. "Even if it's wrong, we'll just try again."

"Sure." I mumbled. I handed him the clipboard.

"The problem we encountered previously was creating a wave which could replicate all quatra signals in aggregate. As Sarakidin's studies demonstrated, the individual connections in a thread have different wavelengths and frequencies…"

"And the wavelengths are independent of the energy of each wave." Hesslik finished my sentence.

"Right." I continued. "Which is unlike the electromagnetic spectrum. As we discovered, the energy of quatra is set, as it can be quantised, and the energy of a Suneva is determined by the quatra *velocity* in the thread."

"We did." Hesslik said, flipping through the papers.

"And none of this helped me, actually." I admitted. "The waves we've been capturing in threads were periodic, but seemed to be repeating random sequences. That is why it's been so hard to create a wave which mimics *all* quatra forms."

Hesslik stopped flipping through the notes. He looked me dead in the eyes.

"And you think you've done it now?" Hesslik asked me.

"Yes." I said, confidently. "I took a simpler approach. I studied a flying bolt of quatra, and found its energy excitation to look like this…" I grabbed the pages on the clipboard, as Hesslik held them, and turned the papers. On the next sheet was a perfect sine wave.

"Then I did two more things." I continued. "I graphed the response of a thread after being hit with a foreign bolt of quatra…" I flipped to the next page. There were several plots, each more random in appearance.

"That doesn't look useful." Hesslik said.

"It's not." I said. "It shows that quatra absorption cancels the thread by creating unusable quatra signals. This isn't our answer, as it's not permanent."

"Okay." Hesslik noted. "So, what is our answer?"

"I got stuck here, but then I noticed something…" I flipped the page over. It showed four identical, random looking waves. "If you take the flying quatra wave away from the thread wave, you get this one. It's identical for each connection in the thread."

"Interesting." Hesslik mumbled. "What does it represent?"

"I do not know exactly." I replied. "But as you can see on the next page, it was identical over one hundred individual Suneva, of different connections, all black holes, and ethnicities."

"That's very comprehensive." Hesslik said, getting a closer look at the diagram. "It must be some base signal of connection."

"That was my thought, also." I said. "It's only present in the thread, so must be some qualifier of having a thread. Therefore, this would be the wave to model for our purposes."

I let go of my work and turned around to pick up an object off the table. It was a small, black, hand-held device which had a handle on one side, and two prongs on the other. There was a single button, just above the grip.

"These devices are programmed to output that base wave-form when you power them. I'll give you the honours of the first test." I said, handing Hesslik the device. He caressed it curiously in his slender, gunmetal hands.

"I must admit, Vestas, we're making some large assumptions here." Hesslik said. "But I'm curious as to the outcome. If you have solved this mystery, Vestas, then nothing in quatra-science is beyond your limits."

Hesslik, with the device comfortably in hand, strutted past me and across the room. He lingered by one of the glowing monitors, but continued through the rows of desks to the back, glass wall.

He flicked a switch by his left hand, and the room on the other side of the glass was thrown into brilliant, white light. It was a white tiled, white walled, dazzling spectacle of a laboratory room. Splashed in the pool of pure spotlights was a grey Suneva with blue eyes. Their armour was twisted, and stained dark. They were restrained in a bulky, steel chair.

They strained at the lashes – crashing the restrains against the bare metal- and howled a departed, haunting wail. The glass vibrated with its force. They were lost to the world – a rotten soul rattling in the shell of a Suneva.

"My goodness, Vestas." Hesslik exclaimed, turning to me. "Where on Earth did you find this one?"

"Narsus brought them in."

"Give that girl a promotion." Hesslik coughed. "And let's save this Suneva…"

He swung the door handle and pulled the door open. The harrowing shriek of the constrained Suneva blasted into the room. It rattled the equipment in the technology lab. The monitors of the computers buzzed in fear.

"Dear *Amasos*." Hesslik coughed. He held the door and ushered me in. I skipped across the lab, careful not to trip on wires. At the sight of me, the Suneva was rabid. He banged and howled and cried against the firm constraints.

"Where do I apply the shock?" Hesslik yelled over their phantom shrieks. I pointed to the back of my neck, where the thread meets the body. Hesslik nodded knowingly, and attempted to place the device on the grey Suneva's neck. They lashed their head around furiously, and growled with lethal intent. I rushed over to their side, and yanked at the leather neck strap. They gasped as their metal neck was pulled and tightly bound to the chair. Their wrists flailed. I stood back.

"For the future of all Suneva, Vestas, I hope this works." Hesslik said to me.

"It will." I replied. "I'm sure of it."

Hesslik pressed the device up to the grey Suneva's neck armour. He sucked in a deep breath, through his armoured form, and directed electricity from his palms. Blue lights on the signal generator lit up in sequence. It whirred, and buzzed, and finally arcs of electricity danced between its prongs.

The Suneva seized. The brief electrical shock should not have travelled through them, unless I had built the device incorrectly. I panicked as their limbs lashed. I went to grab Hesslik's hand, to stop him from hurting himself, but the violence stopped. I sighed in relief.

With my exhale, the light which poured from the spotlights increased two-fold, as if they'd only been half-on. The heavy atmosphere lifted, and with it, through the vents, floated the smoke of the grey Suneva's armour. It raised off his skin like black smog from a campfire. It tracked dully through the air, and dissipated out of existence.

A thick blanket of silence fell upon the bright, white tiles of the lab. The only sound that remained was the purr of the device, and the relieved breaths of Hesslik and I. The man beneath the armour slumped in the chair. His eyes were closed. He looked dead.

"Vestas..." Hesslik quizzed.

"Not dead." I said. "You can feel the charge in his nerves."

"Of course." Hesslik stepped back. "I think it worked, but you should be certain."

"Yes, let me test it." I said.

I stepped over to the chair-side bench and grabbed my thread-analyser. I held it to the unconscious man's neck, and pressed its button. The display lit up. I waited.

"And?" Hesslik asked.

"No thread." I replied, looking at the output. "It's been perfectly destructively interfered."

"What about the biology?" Hesslik asked.

"It should be intact." I replied. "We removed the thread only. We couldn't have destroyed the quatra pathways. Although, perhaps a long-term study on the health of the pathways is in order."

"Of course. That's a good idea." Hesslik's smiled.

"I've got many of them." I said. "We'll also need to test this on other thread types. This man had an average thread for somebody so possessed by quatra, but there are stranger connections out there."

"Vestas, you are absolutely brilliant." Hesslik said after a pause. His grin grew. "Thread removal technology...in our grasp. It's unfathomable. This is the future of our society, you do understand that?" Hesslik asked. He grabbed me by my arm and led me back into the computer lab. I was swung around in his grip, and landed in one of the lab chairs.

"Of course I do." I stated. "We can heal possessed and sick Suneva like that man. We can finally clean the streets of those lawless Argols. We can have proper punishment for abuse of power. This is exactly what you envisioned, my *Fara*."

"Yes." Hesslik smiled. "Exactly as I *envisioned*."

I turned my head curiously to his inflection. His grin faded.

"*Envisioned*, my *Fara*?" I asked. "It's not still your plan?"

"For the meantime, yes." He said. The joy had faded from his voice. The cyan in his eyes and partition muted.

"What do I need to add to this?" I asked. "At this rate, anything is possible."

"This *alone* will not tie together our future, Vestas." Hesslik said. "I have an idea. It involves the wireless transmission of electrical waves – like Tesla tried to do."

"Transmitting electrical energy through the air?" I asked.

"Perfectly. Transmitting it *perfectly*, around the globe."

"That's ambitious." I replied. "No losses, even with our technology, would be almost impossible. We could get near enough – which for power generation, would be close enough."

"Not for my purposes."

"It should work for your purpose…" I said, confused. "Unless you weren't talking about free energy…"

Hesslik wore a guilty smirk beneath his cyan partition. He held his hands behind his back and faced away from me, looking through the glass to the unconscious man.

"Free energy would be a lovely gift to human society, Vestas. Much like a housewarming, it would set the scene for our generosity, but it would do little in the long run for our relations"

"Sure." I ummed, "Then what do you propose we do with wireless transmission to solve the problem?"

"It really depends on how you define *the problem*." Hesslik said. He turned his head sharply to me. His eyes were blank – or, rather, a sea of conflicted feelings. No one intention shone clearly through his expression. I stood, and took a single step back.

"This man right here is – or rather *was* – part of *the problem*." Hesslik said. "He could not handle the quatra which he sucked from the black holes, and he paid with his sanity. He is a reason why we will never be perceived as entirely *good*.

"The energy which we hold is so dangerous, Vestas, and surely you know that We control it, but on a level, it controls us – just as the black holes do through destiny – and it is much more powerful than us. Suneva fall to it, and succumb to corruption Self-preservation turns to ambition, which leads to supremacy. Dangerous ideologies surrounding quatra are being hatched every minute Vestas. How people choose to use quatra is out of our control…"

"Yes, but we're working on the education programs right now." I interrupted, "They could be very effective in managing the majority…"

"The *majority*." Hesslik enunciated, turning to the glass. "But not *all*, and our problems stem from the few who can't be swayed. One bad apple spoils the bunch, my friend. I'm afraid we're swimming in a rotten barrel."

"So, you're suggesting your aforementioned proposal." I insisted. "If we remove the threads of the bad Suneva – those who inadvertently fight against our freedom – we'll only be left with the good."

"If only it were that simple…" Hesslik sighed.

"Vestas, you're a smart man." Hesslik continued. "Our problems are caused by the fact that we are us. If we were not us, we would not have our problems, yes?"

"Yes…" I whispered. I felt dread growing in my heart.

"If we want to get rid of the problems we face us Suneva, all we have to do is stop being Suneva."

"You want me to build you a transmitter so you can transmit this thread-killer signal globally, don't you?" I stumbled over my words. Hesslik turned from the glass to face me. He took steps towards me, and I backed away, into the darkness of the poorly lit room.

"It's the only *logical* solution, Vestas."

"It's madness, Hesslik." I squeaked. "This is treason."

"This is *saving lives*." Hesslik raised his voice with fierce passion. My foot stumbled on a wire, my body spasmed to keep balance. "Did you see that man in there? He was almost dead from his quatra use. We *saved* him. We could save everybody, before they even need it."

"Hesslik, I won't build this for you. Even if I could, it wouldn't work. You can't transmit this signal over the globe. You won't win."

"Vestas, you will make this device. Perfect or not, I will save us all. This will be done by the time of the great gathering of our nation. I will be the Suneva to liberate all."

"The great gathering…." I panicked. "That's meant to be the great triumph of our work! This is genocide, Hesslik. Hell, look at everything we've accomplished scientifically with *liktas* abilities. It's more than genocide, it's smothering all future human progress."

Hesslik laughed. He livened the pace of his advance, and flicked his wrist to draw his jagged sword. Sparks of electricity spurted from its edges – liquid charge dripping from its metal. Cyan energy roared through his helmet, and the sparks consolidated. They clumped together and formed a frightening red rope of superplasma. The room was bathed in a hot, red glow. The plasma hung limply between the sword and the floor, the tiles melted and caught fire under it. Hesslik continued to advance, drawing a charred line in the floor.

I backed into a desk, and in my rush to get away and keep my eyes on Hesslik, I pushed it over. A cable wrapped around my arm, and I went down with the table, landing between its legs and benchtop. The computer atop it smashed across the tiled floor. I became a tangled mess in the wires under the table, squirming for freedom. I yanked at the cables and flailed my hands, but I couldn't escape. I was splayed across the bottom of the bench.

"It's clear…" Hesslik said, steeping towards my trapped body, "…that you don't agree with me, Vestas. I thought you were a logical man, but maybe I was wrong."

He held the thread-killer device in his left hand. It whirred and purred, and an arc fizzed between its prongs. I cringed, and kicked my legs. Hesslik knelt down to my level, staring through my eyes, into my soul. The rope of thick, red plasma dove into the floor as he knelt. Toxic fumes burst from the bubbling ceramic floor.

"This is a great invention, and you have many more up your sleeve." He said. He let the arc linger between our faces, then put the device down by my feet.

"Hesslik, people will hear of this!" I shouted.

"Will they?" He asked. The heat of the plasma threatened to melt my leg. He let sparks dance between his long, grey fingers.

"Of course they will! I'll tell everybody. There's no way I'm working for you anymore."

"See, there's not much to tell if you don't remember it." He grinned.

His free hand lunged for me. He wrapped his sparking talon around my skull. I kicked and squirmed, but there was no escape.

"Neural editing – I believe it's an assertion of your own, yes?" He quizzed. "Your memory of this day might be…non-existent, soon. I'll re-enact this whole scene with you. We'll discover that your equation works, and we'll set to work curing the possessed and ridding the world of criminals."

A shock roared through my brain. I passed out.

***

I woke up, my arms flailing wildly and my mouth agape.

"Oh my goodness, I'm not Vestas…" I shrieked, before analysing my situation.

"Woah, you're alive." Natalie jerked in surprise, throwing some book half way across the room. She leaped across the bed to grab my hand. I was in my bed. Celeste was there too. She was using the house phone, but excused herself as I sat upright

Natalie sat over me on the bed. She held me up as I flailed my head around.

"What was that about Vestas?" Celeste asked me. She put the phone down and sat down on the bed, opposite Natalie.

"Holy…holy cheese, just let me comprehend what just happened…" I gasped. "Actually, why don't you two tell me what's just happened."

"You've been passed out for an hour." Natalie said.

"An hour?" I exclaimed.

"You were toxicated, and you didn't take it well." Celeste said. "I'd already taken out the *Ivaer*. Natalie and I took on Vestas and his student, and won. We grabbed you and ran. You've been in bed for about an hour now."

"Jesus…thank you." I said. "Really, you two…I can't believe it. You took on three Suneva by yourselves?"

Natalie smiled in my approval, still holding my hand. I let it go. Celeste grinned. She knew she was talented.

"Now, what was that about Vestas?" Celeste asked.

"I was in a crazy vision." I said. "I was Vestas, and I was presenting a discovery to Hesslik."

"What kind of discovery?" Natalie asked.

"They made a thread-removal device." I said. "They used it on a guy, and it worked. Then they said they had to test it on strange threads…"

There was a synchronous gulp in the room.

"Then Hesslik said that he wanted to use it to remove all of the threads in the world, using a free-energy transmitter."

"That sounds ridiculous." Celeste said. "Why would he want that? And why would Vestas go along with that?"

"Vestas didn't." I said. "Hesslik altered his brain. He put electricity through it, and edited his neural pathways."

"Goodness…" Natalie gasped.

"Yes," Celeste urged, "But why would *Hesslik* want that?"

"He said that the only logical solution to the Suneva's problems was the end the Suneva."

"*Holy cheese*, indeed!" Natalie mimicked my previous outburst.

"Well, sure. That *is* logical." Celeste said. "But devious as all hell, and disloyal to absolutely everybody. Of *course* he'd do this. I never trusted him – and that made *me* crazy…" Celeste sighed and pouted.

"So, what do we do?" Natalie asked.

"I don't know." Celeste said. "But I'll never stand by whilst somebody threatens my livelihood."

Natalie and I looked at her quizzically.

"Lots of prejudice against Suneva in France." She clarified. "I'd had enough of it over there, people telling you to give up your soul to be normal. Hesslik is threatening to strip us of part of our identity, and I won't let that happen. But I don't know what we can do. I can't get too close to Vestas, or Hesslik, or anybody right now."

"Let's take time to think about it." Natalie suggested. "We'll think of something – even if that answer is doing nothing."

Celeste almost growled at the suggestion of doing nothing.

"That won't do. This isn't something to be passive about." Celeste grumbled, then sighed. "You're right though, it's too big of an issue to think of a solution right now. We'll need time."

"A *lot* of time…" I added. "This is, like, a global issue. It's *way* bigger than us. Stopping Hesslik requires influence."

"Let's talk about it later, then." Celeste said, picking up her bag and slinging it over her shoulder. "I have to get going."

"Where are you off to in such a rush?" Natalie asked.

"Seeing Rhys…" She choked on her whisper. "I'll see you guys tomorrow."

"Yeah, see you tomorrow." I said.

"Have fun." Natalie called after the girl as she left. We looked to each other, our faces were bleak.

"I don't think Rhys Cameron solves much, do you?" I asked Natalie, and she hummed.

"I think Celeste deserves some fun after everything she's been through, even if Rhys is a terrible human." She said. "I don't think she takes the stripping of her core identity lightly."

"She wouldn't." I said. "And then, neither do I. I've only been a Suneva for a few weeks, and already it feels like years."

Natalie nodded, and stood from the bed. "We'll find a way to stop Hesslik." She said. "I'm sure of it."

Natalie and Celeste left my house, not a few minutes before Simone burst into the front door. She skipped her way down the hall, giggling giddily to herself. She tried to hide her elation, but from my lazy position sprawled across the couch, contemplating my existence, it was all too obvious.

"Good day at Uni?" I snuffed as she bounced her way towards the kitchen.

"Hah." She laughed, "Terrible day at Uni."

"Sarcastic happiness?" I asked.

"No I'm just happy about stuff you…" She paused, swivelling on her foot. "…stuff you actually do know about."

"Oh, really?" I asked. "I haven't heard anything about any boys, and I thought you said men were trash."

"They still are." She said, matter-of-factly. "No, this has got to do with Suneva."

I had to hold my eye to stop it twitching. Her revelations now directly affected me. Hell, they could even *involve* me. I broke a sweat.

"Oh, the Suneva?" I asked. "What *revelation* did you come up with?"

"You must have stopped chasing them, if you're not dead." She noted, standing over me now.

"Well, you're not dead and you looked for a hell-of-a-lot longer than I did."

"True." She hummed. "But I can see their danger more than most people."

Can you? I snorted.

"What did you find?"

"I wouldn't want to spark your curiosity again, lest you go searching and hurt yourself. *But…*" Her concern turned to a face-wide grin. She unzipped her bag, and withdrew from its largest pocket our family video camera. She pressed the eject button, and the cassette sized tape popped out. She caught it, and put everything else down.

"Watch this, I'm telling you, this is the find of the century. I'll go down in very real history."

"Simone the historian, what the hell did you find?" I asked, covering my nerves. She put the cassette into the converter VHS, and shoved it into the player. The TV buzzed and crackled to static.

"I think I've got the first video footage of Suneva powers in action."

The static melted from the TV, and in its place a picture formed. It was fuzzy at first, being a bright, grassy scene, but then the picture settled. It was a paused frame of seven figures, standing in a grass field, surrounded by trees. There were four Suneva who had their backs to the camera, and three facing them. I immediately recognised the blue flames of the *Ivaer* girl and the dual-pronged staff of the green and silver figure. This was a video of Zamelle, Genive and I facing Vestas.

"Oh sweet cheese!" I gasped, flailing my limbs. I recovered myself when Simone turned to face me.

"I know!" She said. "I mean, photos have been taken before, but how scary is this?" She was elated. My muscles were seizing in fear – the fear for my life in the future. "Now you'll see why I was reluctant to let you investigate this."

"You were?" I whimpered. "You must have been right. Damn *scary* looking stuff."

"I'm just ecstatic. I mean, finding footage of the paranormal is, like, a paranormal investigator's life dream."

"Do you know who they are…in the footage?" I asked.

"Well, that's another reason why this footage is so amazing." Simone gawked. "Do you see the girl with the flame?"

"The *Ivaer*?" I asked.

"Good memory." She smiled. "I'm pretty sure that's *Iva Argol*. I don't know how much you've read, but that girl is worth some serious money. I don't know who her friends are, but the other guys are with Hesslik and *The Empire of the Black Suns*. They think they're good guys…" She chuckled, "That's Hesslik's scientist, Vestas."

"How the hell did you find this all out so easily?" I squeaked.

"Iva Argol is underground knowledge, but Vestas is public information. Didn't you find the link to the Empire's website?"

"No!" I said.

"Oh, well, get better at research, James." She scolded. "Anyway, this will rock your socks off…"

She rewound to the start, then hit play. The sound of wind rushing by blew through the speakers. She zoomed in to the scene, from her position on the other side of the park. Zamelle came into frame, and her deathly howl filled the lounge room. The hairs on my neck stood up.

Then I fired my bolt of quatra, and the fighting started.

Zamelle was sparring with Vestas' *Liktas* student. Zamelle was amazing. She clawed at the mud under the grass and flung it with ferocity. She twirled on her clawed feet, dancing into position and dodging bolts with the fluidity of the running river.

Her aim was impeccable, but her opponent was fierce. Zamelle slid under an arc of electricity, and swung herself around. She fired a bolt, whipped with a snake of water, and redirected her opponent's blast. A burst of fire came from behind her back, and it didn't even surprise her. She turned around right away and attacked with a wave of water and mud.

"Hah, now look at how quick the green guy goes down!" Simone said, pointing to the other side of the screen. There I was, getting struck by an arc of electricity from behind and convulsing. The screen went black.

"Hah, yeah, what a loser…" I laughed nervously. "Did you see anything after this?"

"Nah, the tape ran out of room." She sulked. "I ran as fast as I could away. I went straight to the photo store to convert it to digital."

"Convert it to digital?" I gulped. "What are you going to do with a digital version?"

"Oh, plenty of stuff." She smiled, ejecting the tape and turning the TV off. Her grin was positively toxic. "Once this goes online, people can't reject the issue at hand. The Suneva are a public problem, and they're *real*. We can say it with certainty."

I bit my lip and cringed. I couldn't be more uncomfortable if I tried.

"What's up?" Simone asked me. She sat down on the other couch, her tape still in hand. I sunk down.

"What would you do if one of your friends turned out to be a Suneva?" I asked. "Like, I can guess why you wouldn't make a Suneva friend, but what if an existing friend came out as one?"

"I wouldn't be their friend anymore." She said flatly.

"But, they're still the same person." I said.

"Sure, but they wouldn't be once they get a glimpse of the Suneva community coming forward – and they'd have to."

"Hesslik's ideals seem pretty well-rounded to me." I swallowed my words.

Simone sighed and shook her head.

"He preaches as if he's the fairest, most self-aware oppressor that ever existed, but even his men still attack Argols." She ranted, "He talks to everybody about peace, and about joining the community together, and respect for all, yet I've got footage of Suneva under his orders ambushing other Suneva. He's the biggest advocator for social justice changes, yet not even he can follow his own rhetoric. How can I trust him to withhold his promise to protect me as a normal person? If I can't trust him, then why would I trust any other Suneva?"

"Jesus, you've really thought about this." I jerked. My hands clenched together. My unease was palpable. "Well, I sincerely hope nobody you know comes out as a Suneva. They're in for a shock."

"Sure." She said. "But the community of Suneva is also dangerous.
Communities like that are where hatred and ideologies get bred really quickly.
Circular thinking."

"Ironic." I coughed under my breath.

"Pardon me?"

"Nothing…" I insisted, squirming away.

"Good." She smiled at me. I was sweating bullets harder than I had been a week ago at the race. Every word could be a misstep. I was glad when Simone stood up and left, disc in hand, to the computer. I sunk into the couch.

I held onto my conversation with Simone until the next day – letting the horror of the footage and its eventual spread to the internet ferment in the pit of my stomach.

I told Natalie and Celeste to meet me in the library, in the computer area. Natalie was there even before I was, and I had the joy of witnessing Rhys Cameron kiss Celeste goodbye as he let her go from his sight. I had no right to be angry – because not making a move earlier was my mistake, but regret burned in my stomach like a fire. It burned right next to the fermenting doom. My head was too full of conflicting terribleness to know how to feel. I pulled up a seat next to Natalie and logged on whilst we waited for Celeste.

By the time she was sitting next to us, I already had *fairysmogsblog.org/Suneva* loaded and ready to go.

"Ew." Celeste commented on the screen. "Why are you on that site? It's the biggest hate spot on the internet. The creator is an absolute disgrace."

"Because they've got this…" I said, and scrolled down. Embedded in an article by *fairysmog* themselves, cited to Simone Grey, was the video Simone had showed me. I pressed play, and immediately paused it to let it load.

"Excuse me, James, but is that *us?*" Natalie gasped at the image. She tried to cover the screen with her hands to make it go away. Celeste pulled them from the monitor.

"Yep." I said flatly. "My sister took the video and sent it in. Perfect place, perfect time. To her, catching footage of Suneva is the holy grail."

Celeste groaned in fury. Her face flushed red.

"Despicable." She spat. "We're people, not zoo animals. Now, give me that…" She took the mouse from my hands and scrolled past the video. She read the description given by *Fairysmog*.

"She calls me *Iva Argol.* Unbelievable!" She growled. Her teeth ground and sparks of flame shot from her tongue.

"This is really putting a target on our heads…" Natalie laughed nervously.

"Yep, it sure is." I agreed. "We're done for, I recon."

"No, that's bullshit." Celeste said. "This description says nothing more than *Melbourne*. They're not trying to sell our location – they're just trying to spread their propaganda."

"That's still too specific for my liking." Natalie added.

"Let's not get hopeless until we see the video." Celeste grunted. She mashed the mouse button, and the video played.

"See," Celeste said after the first viewing. "A Suneva can't do anything with this. You can't smell the quatra field through a video. They don't know our quatra signals, and they don't know what we look like normally."

"Okay, that's much more comforting." Natalie agreed.

"Still," I said. "We've got a reputation. Hesslik knows we're against him now – so does everybody."

"I'm not so concerned about that. With Hesslik's plans as you saw them, James, we'd have to be publicly opposing him at some point." Celeste said. "If anything, it's a slight upgrade for me. The world gets to see my skill."

"That's well for you, but I'm too innocent to be the enemy of thousands of people." I protested. Natalie shared my grim realisation.

"Look, not to draw the conversation away, but I had something to bring up today, before the bell rings." Natalie said. "I think we should follow the red trail to the Suneva who's been following us."

"You do?" Celeste and I asked in unison.

"Yes." She said. "They weren't present at the battle."

"So, they were a scout." Celeste said.

"No, look. I know it sounds crazy, but I've had the urge that we need to follow the red trail to the Suneva on the other side. I feel like they need our help, and we definitely need theirs. Not only could they help us defend ourselves from Hesslik, but I know that they can help us bring down Hesslik's plans. I don't *know* how I know it, but I do."

"The call of the void." I said.

"The call of destiny." Celeste sighed. "I still think that's a terrible idea, we don't know *anything* about them, even past this intuition of yours."

"And this is the only way to find out, then." Natalie argued. "I know you're sceptical, and you have to be to survive, but I really feel that this is the way to go. We can't know who they are until we meet them."

"I kind of agree, actually." I said, surprised to hear those word from my mouth. I waited for what else my brain had to back them up. "Apart from Kuvalik and Lilawelle, where else do we have to turn for help? I've never felt threatened by the presence, anyway…"

"Because you couldn't feel it." Celeste bit.

"Yes, but…I don't know. I think it's worth a shot. I mean, they're our observer. They must know something that we want to know, if they're watching us."

Celeste pouted and crossed her arms.

"I just don't know if I trust destiny right now." Celeste said. "It's because of destiny that I got betrayed so many times by so many people. It's hard to trust it's calling."

"Or," Natalie rebutted, "It's due to destiny that you escaped every time, and that you're here, right now, to have this conversation. Everything happens for a reason, isn't that the philosophy?"

"Sure, but…"

"And the lessons you learned from each near encounter turned you into a street smart, powerful *Ivaer* of the blue flame. It's was all meant to happen." Celeste pouted harder this time, but gave up.

"I hate to admit it, but you're right." She said. "I'm here now, and arguably better for my experiences. It's just so hard to trust the world." She sighed. "But I swear, if this goes the way I'm expecting it to…"

"It won't." Natalie said. "I promise. I have a really good feeling about this."

Chapter 19

Hooked on a Feeling

That Friday night, Natalie, Celeste and I were about to set out from my house to follow the trail. We each had a bicycle, a backpack full of food and water and a single mobile phone between us. Natalie was visibly excited to be following the red trail to her destiny. Celeste was quiet, not talking much as we ate dinner. I was curious to see where this would lead us, but Celeste's nerves made me slightly uneasy. She'd seen a lot in her time running from hunters. It's possible that we should have trusted her destiny-contraire instincts for this instance.

We'd each given our parents and guardians an alibi. Natalie's Dad and Yamitse were out that night, and so we'd told my parents, and David's, that Celeste and I would be studying with Natalie at her house – possibly to become a sleepover. It was a happy, wholesome idea, and gave us a lot of time to play with.

From my front porch, our bike lights flashed into the night. It was autumn now, and the days closed earlier, making way for an unfamiliar chill of darkness. I had originally questioned the logic to do this in the night, and did so again as we walked our bikes beyond the edge of my house and into the dark.

"Suneva operate in the night, James." Celeste insisted. "It's why your sister's video is so rare. We don't like for others to see us. I've always wanted that to change. We should be able to be ourselves in daylight."

Natalie held her hands out beyond my fence. She held them in the peace-sign pose, her fingers twitching in the wind. Her eyes were closed, and her nose was up. She let the quatra field envelop her.

"Alright, let's walk up the street." She said. "I can't sense their trail here, but I have a feeling that it's close."

"If you say so." I said. "Can you feel the trail, Celeste?"

"*Non.*" She said. "But I think Natalie is right."

"Alright, fair enough." I agreed, feeling useless. I'd supplied the snacks, at least.

We walked our bikes up my street, then Natalie led us west, past the local shops and over the railway line. She led us from some instinct – not using her eyes or hands, but letting the forces which guided her string her along. However, once we reached the mouth of Kuvalik's street, her body snapped like a dog desperate to smell the grass. She kicked herself around, led by her posed hands, to the centre of the nature strip. She stood there, eyes closed, fingers twitching, examining something.

"Here's the first bit of trail." She said, "This is their quatra, alright – and there's plenty of it. They've gone that way." She pointed down the street.

"Towards Kuvalik's house?" I asked.

"Seems so." Natalie said.

"I sense that too." Celeste said. "I can feel the trail now. It's strong."

"Let me see that…" I said, bustling past Natalie and Celeste to the spot on the nature strip. I made the pose with my hands and wriggled them around in front of me. I felt absolutely no different. "I want to know how you guys do this stuff. What do you do to *sense* the quatra here, Natalie?"

"I don't know that I can teach it, exactly…" Natalie ummed. She shot a glance to Celeste, who sighed.

"I'm not sure why the two of you think *I'm* a better teacher for this. Natalie's clearly more skilled at it…" She groaned.

"I am?" Natalie's face lit up.

"Well, you've taught me so many good lessons already." I said. "You're a great teacher."

Celeste smiled. She stepped over to where I was.

"Alright…" She started. She got into position, sensing the field. She considered her words for a minute. I waited patiently. "You're familiar with the feeling on quatra in your body, *oui?*" She asked.

"Yes." I replied.

"Well, all you have to do, is feel it *outside* of your body…"

My face scrunched.

"Okay, maybe that sounded obvious…" She reconsidered. "The quatra field is all around us. Quatra in the field can feel like a stain in the world, which you can feel in your palm – almost like you can hold it. There's a stain here, below us, and it points in a direction because it was *smeared* into the field that way."

I huffed. I held my hands in front of me, in the pose, but I got no sense of a greater field. I could only sense the air which surrounded me and the carbon in everything else. I groaned.

"Oh well. It was a good thought that I could be taught, but I truly *am* useless." I huffed semi-sarcastically. "I can't even get the first feeling of the field."

"Feel it, and do it." Celeste reminded me. "It's there, just believe that it is."

Believe. That was something I hadn't heard before with this Suneva stuff. I'd taken everything so for granted that I'd forgotten how absurd it all was. A stain in an energy field was no crazier than throwing fistfuls of high-impact air.

I closed my eyes, and with my hands before me, I summoned the power of belief. *It's there.* I told myself. *It's there, because they said it is.* I felt nothing. Not even belief could summon a false firing of a neuron. I sighed.

"Damnit, guys, there's noth…"

My whole being was sucked into a singularity. A great wind swept by my soul, casting it off into a storm. When I opened my eyes, I found that I was not where I was standing before.

I was in front of a large iron gate, cast in the brilliant white pool of two looming industrial lights. The gate was made of thick steel beams, like prison bars. Behind it, also lit in blinding white, was a massive warehouse. It extended far to the left – further than the light shone upon it, and had a massive roller door adjacent the gate.

I looked to my left – the smoke of the vision distorting as I did so. I saw a Suneva covered in warm bronze and silver. They had a chain tied to their back, and meaty paws with which they saluted somebody standing past me. I turned around, to the guard's hut. The guard did not notice the Bronze Suneva standing there, so they looked up to a camera resting atop the gate's right-hand pillar and waved into it. The security guard jolted in surprise, and shook into action.

"*Lion's Foot…*" The guard gasped, "Didn't notice you there, go through."

"Thanks." The Bronze Suneva said. Their helmet was squarish, with sharp angles. Their eyes were crimson red, bordered in the centre and on top by a thick, black line. It extended down their face, like a striking nose. They had an American accent, like something from an eighties TV show about a small town.

A motor whirred, piercing the black night and the white light. The gate creaked and groaned, shifting on its rollers.

"Try again, James." Celeste said. I shook my head and opened my eyes – even though I was certain that they were just open. I stood bolt upright as my eyes and ears spun in their sockets. The haze of dizziness drowned from my skull in a rush of blood.

"Sweet cheese…" I moaned as I gathered my bearings. "Wow."

"What happened?" Natalie asked.

"I know where they are." I said.

"Oh, so you read the pattern?" Natalie chuckled.

"No!" I burst, "God, no, I couldn't figure that out. That's your thing."

She frowned.

"I had a vision. I saw them by a warehouse. They're a tall, bronze Suneva with a mean looking face. They go by the name *Lion's Foot.*"

"*Lion's Foot?*" Celeste huffed. "That's not a very traditional name."

"And I know where the warehouse is." I continued. "Or, I think I do. It's down by the other train line, near the bike path that way. I swear it's the same one. I recognised the gate."

"How do you know they're there now?" Natalie asked.

"I…I…" I stumbled. Nothing about the vision told me this, really. But I was so *certain* that I was just there, witnessing them, that it had to be true. "It was night in the vision. But, that's not good evidence…I just *feel* that they are."

Natalie and Celeste shared a quizzical glance. Natalie shrugged her shoulders.

"It's too good of a lead to waste. Which way is it?"

"North-west. Once we hit the bike track it's easy."

"We should stop by Kuvalik's on the way." Natalie said. "Just in case he's seen anything. They've been so close to his house."

"Good idea." I agreed. "You'll finally get to meet Kuvalik, Celeste."

She smiled.

"I'd be honoured to meet him." She said.

We made our way down the dark street, under the damp orange street lights which stained the road and pavement. I stepped past the porch – collecting my key from the rusty bike's pouch – and opened the front door. Natalie and Celeste entered behind me. There was no electricity in Mr. Finneck's house - when it was dark outside, it was dark inside. I held my bike's front light in my hand, and waved it down the corridor.

"Kuvalik?" I said as we stepped through the door. Shadows danced across the hallway as my light swung. I led the girls further into the house.

"Kuvalik?" I called again. My light scanned past the back door at the end of the hall. Shadows scurried from the torch beam, except for one, inilluminable, and in the shape of a man. It stood still, against the leaping, distorting shadows around it.

"Ah!" I yelled, and stumbled back. Natalie flipped back, drawing her twin swords. Celeste shrieked, stumbling further than I.

"Hello children." The inilluminable man said with a cheery voice.

"Oh, cheese. You scared me, Kuvalik." I panted. Natalie put away her twin swords, and Celeste stepped up to where I was. She pushed past me, between Kuvalik and I.

"*Meyafara Kuvalik.*" She greeted. She drew her sword and stabbed it into the ground before her feet. Kuvalik smiled, his purple eyes appearing on his smoky head.

"You must be Celeste Bouvé – Genive, the young *Ivaer* whom I've heard so much about."

"You have?" She asked, surprised.

"Yes, James talks very highly of your abilities, and your approach to being a Suneva." He said. Celeste turned to me and smiled, her cheeks flushing red.

"Why don't we all sit and have tea?" He asked. "I can put some more on…"

"Oh, no, we're in a rush, Kuvalik." Natalie said. "We just came to ask you a question…."

"Where do you keep getting tea from?" I asked, bewildered. "I thought we've been drinking it all."

"I go to the store and get more." He replied.

"But you're a ghost."

"A ghost can travel." He said.

"Really?"

"James, I'm a six-hundred-year-old *Liktan Fara* from Sparta. How did you believe I got here?"

"Oh…yeah." I chuckled.

"But it is hard to buy the tea." He said, floating past us to the kitchen. His smoky essence blew past my shoulder, lingering in the air. "Often the clerk screams in fright on the sight of floating tea, and I just walk out." Natalie, Celeste and I laughed at the image. Kuvalik grabbed the tea from the top shelf and dissipated his apparition, becoming invisible and leaving us with the spectacle of floating tea.

"And he's making it anyway…" Natalie sighed to Celeste and I. "Kuvalik, we were wondering if any Suneva came to visit you recently?" The tea set itself gently upon the table. Wisps of charcoal smoke coagulated from the thin air, and whipped around to create his form. His purple eyes filled from their sockets up.

"Apart from the *Welle* who gives me running water, no."

"Would this *Welle* happen to be a tall, bronze Suneva with an intimidating face?" I asked.

"…with crimson red quatra?" Natalie added.

"Uh, no. They're your *Yamitse*…" He said. "I don't know any Suneva here by that description."

"They came by your house." Natalie said. "There was a stain of their quatra by the pavement outside your fence."

"I did not feel them come by." Kuvalik responded. "Ghosts sleep too. In fact, I sleep quite a lot – through almost anything."

Natalie frowned.

"I don't think I'm making a very good first impression on my powerful *Ivaer* guest." Kuvalik chuckled.

"Oh, no. You're doing very well for a man of six hundred years." Celeste smiled.

"Thank you." He glowed back.

"We'd better get going, then." Natalie said. "We know where they are, just not *who* they are."

"What guides your interest in them, then?" Kuvalik asked.

"The call of the void." Natalie said. "Destiny, the pull of the universe. I've felt the compulsion to follow their trail."

"Hesslik is planning to destroy all of the Suneva threads, and already has a thread removing device. Plus we're about to get targeted by Hesslik's agents." I blurted to Kuvalik. "We think this guy knows something that we don't, and he can help us do *something* about the whole situation we're in."

Kuvalik didn't seem shocked. Instead, he sat upon the kitchen bench and pondered. He fondled a bag of tea between his ghastly fingers.

"That's quite a situation." He said. "But I'm not surprised. Hesslik has so much charm with the people, he could get away with murder and convince the world it's part of his good agenda.

"Still," He continued, "it's brave of the three of you to follow it up, especially in the face of his agents, but I wouldn't put the task beyond you."

"You wouldn't?" Natalie asked.

"By *Nerios*, no." He said. "The three of you make a powerful team. From three separate black holes – *Omercronius*, *Amasos* and *Veritas* - of three *macro elements*, and each connected to a *micro element*. A team doesn't come more formidable, or *destined*." He added. "If your feeling of compulsion is right, Natalie, then I could only assume this other Suneva is of the black hole Nerios, connected to *raduk* – earth – and of some micro element. I have long felt a great path for James and yourself, and now you too, Celeste."

"Good to know." Celeste said.

"Of course…" Kuvalik continued. "They could be any kind of Suneva from any black hole. But if they are as I predict, then I wouldn't put it down to pure coincidence."

"Why do you think we have a clear path like this?" Natalie asked.

"Who said it's a clear path?" Kuvalik turned her question around. "Destiny can be felt, but never predicted. The path is whatever you chose it to be, or wherever you feel you're being pulled towards. It's never clear what the ultimate result of the amalgamation of our compulsions will be."

"Yes…of course." Natalie agreed, after pondering the words.

We left Kuvalik and I led the girls through my home neighbourhood on our bicycles. We cruised north-west, dodging between the few suburban travellers to the bike track. Once there, Natalie picked up on the strong scent of our stalker's quatra trail, and confirmed that we were on the right path. We pedalled down the track, and came off just before the other railway line. We stopped by the mouth of an alleyway on a no-through-road. The alley bored its way between two cottages, and revealed a parking lot and large iron gate at its end, bathed in white light. Behind it, illuminated by industrial lamps, I could see the outline of the warehouse against the cloudy night's sky.

"This is definitely it." I said. "That's the gate from the vision."

"Good." Natalie smiled. She put her bike against the face of the alley and started to stroll down. "Destiny is on our side, apparently."

Celeste cringed at the comment. I lay my bike up against Natalie's and jogged after her. Celeste followed.

"Don't just stroll in, Natalie." I warned, grabbing her by the shoulder. "There's a guard and a camera by the gate. We'll have to sneak."

"Why?" She asked. "He knows who we are. He wants to talk to us – or else he wouldn't have been following us this whole time."

"And what if they're against us, Natalie, but we're still meant to meet them?"

"They haven't attacked us yet, remember?" She asked.

"*Non*…" Celeste said, stepping forward to Natalie. "You're making a lot of foolish assumptions right now, Natalie."

"Am I?" She asked. "If every other Suneva we've encountered is right, I leak so much quatra that they'd *have* to know we're out here anyway."

Celeste huffed. "Don't be so defeatist *or* idealistic, then. Right now, I'm putting a lot of trust in your *feelings*, Natalie, to follow the two of you out here on this suspicious trail. I trust *you*, but I do not trust a stranger, nor this place. We enter in our armour, as our *alis*, and without being seen, or we do not enter at all."

Natalie rolled her eyes. "We've beat Suneva two-on-three before. It's good to be prepared, but I don't think there's much to worry about. We're already targets. Wouldn't being in our armour make our presences stronger, anyway?"

Would it? I turned to Celeste, but she didn't notice my glance.

"I agree with Celeste." I noted, anyway. "We don't know why he's here, or who's in there. It doesn't look like a personal home, not even for a Suneva."

Natalie huffed, reassessing the scene. She flicked her wrists, drawing her twin swords.

"What do we say, then, when we get caught *sneaking* in to the building. Anybody who sneaks around is doing something they know is wrong. That's the whole point of sneaking. Anybody we come across will think we're there to harm them."

"With this level of security, I'm not sure it matters." I said. "They clearly want people out. Even them wanting us *in* is risky, given everything that's happened with us."

Natalie frowned and huffed. "Fine," She said. "I don't think it's so silly to *try* walking in first, as I've had no bad inclinations about this place..."

"You might not, but others here *do*." Celeste noted. "This is a team effort, and it hinges on trust."

Celeste flung her bag aside and tilted her head back. Her armour spread from her thread, encapsulating her body in crimson red and gunmetal grey.

"Armour it is, then." Natalie sighed, giving in. Together we became Maiki, Zamelle, and Genive, left our bags tucked under our bikes, and stalked along the shadow of the alley's fence towards the carpark.

Everything about the property appeared clean, even the gutter. Not a speck of rust hung on the gate's large bars. On the right gatepost, above the security hut, was a security camera. The gate and the fence were topped with sharp, barbed wire. There was nobody in the hut.

"Looks clear." I said. "How do we get past the camera?"

"I could handle that." Zamelle said. From the shadows to the left of a gate rose a snake of water. It slithered through the air slowly, wrapping around itself and twisting as it hovered. It snaked its way around the gatepost, and entered the camera through a conduit.

Sparks buzzed from behind the lens. The red recording light dimmed. Zamelle released her soul's grip on her connection, water leaking from the camera. She led us forward. We came into the carpark, and sleuthed around the edge of the light white's pool. We ducked into the security hut, and I smashed its light out with my silver fist.

There was a large, glowing, red button, sitting right in the middle of the control board. It had "GATE" printed on its face in black letters. I shrugged at the girls, and stomped my palm upon it. An AC motor behind our heads whirred and spat. Iron creaked and dust crunched in the mechanism as the gate rolled away from the hut. Sticking to the shadows, we slipped into the compound.

Huge industrial lights shone onto the warehouse, cutting through the darkness of the night. The large roller door of the façade basked in the field of white. I looked up to the towers and cursed.

"You're sure that he's in there?" Genive asked, although to whom I wasn't sure.

"No…" I said, but was cut off by Zamelle.

"He's in there." She said, her hands hanging by her side in the Suneva hand pose. "I don't know the layout of the room, but he's directly that way…" She pointed straight through the roller door.

"Good." I sighed. "Now we just have to worry about the lights."

"*I* can handle that." Genive smirked beneath her helmet. She extended her crimson hand towards the nearest light. Her fingers twiddled at their ends as she focussed on her connections. Her fingers balled up into a fist, and a disc of shade projected onto the ground. She tugged with her arm, and the bulb smashed within its housing.

"Oxygen is everywhere, and elements can be manipulated from afar." She told me, pre-empting my question. "Although, this is the extent of my soul's reach. Let's keep moving."

She ushered Zamelle and I along the perimeter of darkness to the next light post. She committed herself to the same ritual – extending her soul out to oxygen in the lamp, and using it to tear the wire in the globe. A path to the warehouse roller door was thrown into darkness, and we ran through it towards the entrance.

The door was still lit by a bulb mounted over it. With ease, Genive extinguished it, and we sleuthed along the building's face to the roller.

"Do we knock?" I asked, joking. I peered up to the height of the door. It had to have been seven metres high. "Because there's no way we're getting through here stealthily."

"There's no way around the side." Zamelle said. "I looked when we came around. There's a wire fence blocking off the side."

"Like, a fence topped in barbed wire, or a fence made of criss-cross wire?"

"Both." She clarified.

I flicked my wrist, and from my bone and my thread my staff formed. Its long green blade glimmered in the moonlight.

"I think it's finally a job for *me*." I grinned.

I slipped around the right side of the building, with Zamelle and Genive sneaking at my heels. I saw the fence Zamelle was talking about – and just past it was a switchboard and a door. *Beauty*, I thought.

The blade of my staff was thin. I did not craft it – I did not know where it came from – but it was made of single-atom-thick diamond. Still, I doubted that I could cut clean through the wire fence.

"What's your plan?" Genive asked me. I stood before the fence, and pondered. I extended my hand to it, to feel that there was carbon in the metal.

"It's an alloy." I said. "So, if I take the carbon from it..."

I gripped with my soul and ripped my hand backwards. Black rocks were torn from the fence's structure. They coagulated in my hand. I wrapped the black mass around my arm for later use.

"...the structure should be weakened." I raised my staff above my head and swung down upon the fence's links. They sheared immediately, and I pushed aside the broken fencing to give us a path. I stepped in, and all followed.

I walked up to the door, set into the corrugated wall by the switchboard. I tried to obvious solution first – to turn the knob.

"It's locked." I frowned. "But that shouldn't be an issue."

I put my palm over the lock mechanism. The door's jam was made of steel. I grinned, and yanked the carbon from it. I added the black mass to the other pile I had accumulated before. I slipped my staff into the door crack, and wedged it down. The door's bolt snapped, and I levered the staff to force the door open.

The door opened onto a clearing in a factory floor. The dusty concrete bathed in slowly sinking, blue moonlight which fell from the corrugated Perspex roof. This central space to the factory was voluminous, and eerie. Our footsteps rang into the empty hall. We stalked out into the centre of the clearing.

To our right were rows of floor-to-ceiling shelving aisles, and a lonely forklift. To our left, between us and the roller door, was a floor of metal-working machines, laying in shadows. Opposite the door we entered was a mezzanine, which held an office. Light oozed through cracks in the visible back door of the office, and clung to its dusty observation windows.

"Somebody is here." Zamelle pointed out. Somewhere, a door opened. Light flooded into the mezzanine office behind the shadow of a figure. My mind screamed, and I froze up, looking for a place to hide in the barren opening. There was a stack of palettes to our left, and Zamelle, Genive and I all ducked behind it. We fought to squish in together out of sight. Silence fell, bar the sound of shuffling feet above. We dared not make a sound.

A computer's growing whir echoed in the space. In the office, hands tapped away at a keyboard. A mouse clicked.

"What a surprise to see you here…" A voice came from my right – between us and the roller door. I jumped into the air in sheer fright, without even seeing who had spoken. I kicked off a blast of air, and landed with a skid of my metal feet across the concrete. Genive stood and her sword flamed. Zamelle stood ready to strike. Amongst the factory equipment stood Vestas. He strode towards us.

"Zamelle, Maiki…what the hell?" Genive growled. Her blue helical flames doubled in size.

"I thought the three of you would be hard to catch, but it seems you've reconsidered my offer."

"We've done no such thing." Zamelle snarled.

"Then why are you here?"

"We didn't know *you* were here!" I shrieked. "Oh cheese…we're done for."

"Done for?" Vestas asked. "Maiki, there are only good things in your future, *Lion's Foot*…" He called over our heads, "…help me show our guests to the lab."

Behind me, metal clanged, a chain unfurling onto the cold, concrete floor. It echoed sharply. I stiffened up, and against my will, turned to face it. In an aisle, bordered on either side by tall stacks of boxes, was a tall, Bronze Suneva. Their eyes were blood red, with black lining forming a menacing face. Their red gaze broke the blue glow of the night. Their bronze and silver armour was bulky, and sleek. Their lower right leg, in its armoured form, appeared to be prosthetic. They held their gaze on mine. Their chain, at its full length, hovered before them.

"Oh, *shit*." Zamelle cussed. Vestas' student Suralik ran out from the office onto the mezzanine balcony, followed by their *Ivaer* friend, Faravaer. They leaped down from the looking platform to join us on the floor.

"Ha, I wouldn't give up the high ground so easily." Genive spat. "You'll need it, you red-flamed *saletha*."

I didn't know what her insult meant, but it sure as hell riled up Faravaer. Plasma of red, hot flames dripped off their armoured fingers like molten metal.

"Now, nobody said anything about fighting…" Vestas said, but was cut off by Genive.

"I did, right now. You want me, come and get me."

She shot two bolts of bright blue quatra in quick succession, one at Vestas, and the other at Faravaer. Both dodged, but Faravaer fired in retaliation.

A bolt of hot, crimson quatra streaked past my helmet. I turned to the Bronze Suneva, his palm returning to his side. He stomped a massive, bronze foot down onto the concrete and gripped at the world around him through his soul connection

A crack ripped through the stone floor, extending from his toes. He heaved upwards, and suddenly my knees were rocketing towards my chest. The ground had burst open, and a platform of rock blasted upwards under me.

I jumped from the pile, using its momentum and blasting off a jet of air. I soared high over the factory floor, towards the tall metal shelving above *Lion's Foot*.

I extended my claws, and gripped into the first bit of metal I could touch, clinging half-way up the shelving. The massive unit lurched under me, threatening to topple. I leaped from it, pushing my way over to the next stack. A bolt of red quatra flew to where I had just been. A patch of metal burned hot and melted as the energy dissipated through it.

I landed on the next wall, only to see another bolt flying towards me from below. As soon as my claws had gripped onto a shelf, I found myself pushing off again. I vaulted just as the wall swung back to the aisle centre, narrowly avoiding the bolt which crashed into a box by my feet. It set on fire.

Something cold wrapped around my ankle as I flew. It wrenched at my foot and tore it backwards. I yelped in pain and surprise; Lion's Foot had me by his chain and pulled me from the sky.

I was whipped into the concrete flooring like a ragdoll. I tried to blast air under my body as I landed, but it didn't do enough to lessen the impact. I smashed across the ground, coughing and spluttering. I could feel my right shoulder screaming in pain under the armour of Maiki. I flopped onto my back, wanting nothing more than to lay there and wallow in my pity.

I saw him there, *Lion's Foot*, bearing over me. He was tall, and he was thick. He had strength beyond what I knew was possible.

I can't beat this guy with air, who am I kidding? I spluttered.

The chain yanked again at my leg, and it kicked me out of sleep and into action. I swung my torso off the floor and smashed my blade down on the chain. The link cracked, and as *Lion's Foot* pulled at the chain, it snapped. I jumped up, landing on my feet, and kicked the excess linkage off. It soared through the air – like a well-aimed shot on goal – straight into his hand.

"Thanks," he said, attaching it back to his end - melding the metal together like putty in his fingers.

"No worries." I said, with a smile. We were both smiling. We both caught ourselves smiling through our helmets, and frowned.

He grasped before him with his left hand, and flung it in my direction. A boulder tore from the ground by his foot and slammed towards me. I kicked a blast of air at it, but nothing happened. I scrambled out of its path, flying onto the wall of shelving as it crashed down the aisle.

Behind *Lion's Foot*, down the aisle, I could see Zamelle and Genive being drawn apart from each other and shepherded away from exits. The same had been done to me I realised — we'd been isolated. All free Suneva rushed to where Genive was drawn. She was being ambushed, hard. Blue flames tore across the roof of the building. Their light spilled into every corner.

I have to help her. I thought. *But air is useless against this guy. It's too weak. It won't work. I need a strong stance, like him.*

Like Dad. An intrusion echoed in my head. I blinked, stunned by my own thoughts.

Big and strong, like Dad. I agreed.

A pillar of concrete cracked towards me. Like a game of dodgeball, *Lion's Foot* threw the distraction, and fired his deadly bolt just as I leaped away from the stone. I extended my hand towards the bolt, but missed. It sailed over me as I crashed into the wall. I got straight up, almost to be rammed in the guts by another boulder. I swatted at it with my diamond-edged blade, and it cracked into two pieces. Their bolt came at me again, but this time, I spun my staff in front of me to catch it. It raced hot through my veins, and pivoting on my back foot, I rejected it with a dose of my own quatra and sent a toxicated bolt back his way.

He whipped the bolt out of the air with his chain. It burned hot where it was absorbed, but he held the linkages together with his connection to their metal.

I whipped my staff around my body, digging my feet firmly into the ground, and threw a blast of wind towards him. The force was enough to make my metal feet slide. I gritted my teeth behind my helmet and gripped in. Not an ounce of the bronze Suneva was moved.

Okay, fine. Air is useless. Ignore it. I've got carbon. I have to be strong.

I clawed at the carbon I'd wrapped around my arm. A quatra bolt came by and I had to shift my attention again.

No time for that. I cussed. *Fuck it.*

I lunged to my left and dug my claws into a sizeable box. Digging my feet in, adopting my new, unwavering stance, I ripped it from the shelf and launched it at the Suneva. He was shocked by my decision. He was used to dealing with electricity, the elements, and bolts of quatra, but not a box. He tried to swat it out of the air with his bulky, bronze arm, but the weight of it was more than he'd expected. He stumbled as it crashed into him.

By the time he'd regained himself, I had a palette on the tip of my long, dagger-like fingers. I threw it straight at him. This time, prepared, he flicked his armed hand and struck it with the end of his chain. The chain whipped around the palette and cracked it in half. It crashed to the floor.

He grinned at me, and gripped into the world around him with his meaty, metal mitts. He heaved across his body.

A pillar of concrete rushed from the ground to my right and jammed itself into my hip. I stumbled off my firm footing, but replanted my foot, determined to be strong. Another pillar punched me in the back, and I fell forward, onto my face. His foot stomped down on the ground, hard, and I feared his next move.

My mind was desperate. *Boxes are full of carbon*, I reasoned, Ms Gordon's lessons flooding in, *amongst hydrogen, nitrogen, oxygen, probably other stuff. If I pull at the carbon, will all of the boxes fall?*

I felt the earth shifting, I didn't have time to further reason with myself. I focussed on my soul's reach, and used it to rip at the carbon in all of the boxes it could grab. I rolled over and pushed myself away from *Lion's Foot*.

Chunks of graphite flung towards me. Behind them, in their wake, was a powerful explosion of plasma and flames. The fire roared bright yellow. Metal groaned. Pieces of boxes, like hot lava, rained from the shelves, which bent inwards above my head.

Shit. I ogled the mess. My instinct was to jump, but the air made me weak. I didn't need it. Carbon made me strong, it seemed. I gathered the graphite from the boxes and crudely formed it onto a disc, leaping to my feet. Like a battering ram, I held it in front of me and charged at the shelving to my right. I burst through the wall of fire, protected by my shield, and skidded across the floor of the next aisle. I kicked into a sprint, heading towards Genive and the clearing.

Behind me was a mighty roar of metal. Shelving collapsed as fire blazed under them. The walls crashed halfway into the aisle, before being ejected back out. Large footsteps stomped behind me. A chain cracked in the dust.

I spotted Genive. Three Suneva surrounded her, backing her into a corner. She swung her sword, and sparked a whip of blue, hot fire. It did little to deter her attackers, who advanced further. Zamelle was just to my left, amongst the machines, fighting somebody else.

"Run!" I yelled. I blasted a bolt at Zamelle's attacker, and two towards Genive. One of Genive's attackers turned, and engaged me in fire. I sprinted towards them, fearless. They fired a foul shot, I fired one just as inaccurately. Another Suneva turned, *Faravear*. They cast a bright red jet of flame towards me, but I held my shield to it and defended with a bolt of quatra. The graphite shield went up in flames faster than I could hold it together.

Damn it.

I launched its remains at my attackers, hoping to bowl them over. Just steps from the action, steps from tackling one of the Suneva and saving Genive, I heard the distinctive crack and rumble of concrete. I sensed the protrusion – a disturbance in the air in front of me, a huge blip on my radar – as it rose from the ground. My reluctance to accept the help of air had caught up to me. There was no time to think of what it could have been before the pillar of earth rammed into my stomach with the force of a truck. It hit me front on. My body slopped over it, and I was flung backwards through the factory.

I landed on my back with a hideous thud. I scraped across the concrete floor like nails across a chalkboard. My head slumped onto the stone. Heads turned to me.

I don't suppose you've watched T.V shows and movies, where the main character gets thrown halfway across the room by an explosion and just grunts, or makes a noise to indicate mild irritation? I wish I could report that I grunted, stood up, brushed myself off, and got back into action, but that's a bullshit expectation. I screamed.

The pain was overwhelming and infinite – my concept of time blasted from my body. I gasped for breath between my weak cries. I had been winded. The armour on my stomach wasn't dinted, but it had been badly scratched. I grasped at it with my claws. I couldn't ease the pain. Beyond that, it felt like my *soul* had been injured. I felt depressed, both emotionally and energetically. My mind was filled with sorrow. I wallowed on the floor, groaning.

The distraction of my dramatic demise gave Genive time, and a chance to strike. She brandished her sword in both fists, and used it to backhand her attackers with its flaming edge in one swoop. They each spun and stumbled, grasping their helmets. Genive used a clawed foot to kick Faravaer back into the others, then kicked off like lightning, sprinting for the side door.

She ran, and skidded on her insectoid feet to face me. She looked to me, then back to the captors – who appeared to be getting up. I could see her bouncing between feet, considering what to do, before choosing to run.

She blasted at Zamelle's attacker, forcing them to face Genive, which allowed Zamelle to toss them aside with her twin swords. Zamelle paused, staring at me. She went to run in my direction, but Genive grabbed her solidly by the arm and yanked her away towards the door. It slammed behind them, and nobody followed.

Crashing footsteps caused me to bounce on the hard floor. I spluttered, the vibrations doing nothing to take the pain. I stopped screaming now, and was just wailing. Much manlier, it seemed.

Lion's Foot knelt beside me. "Don't fight it." He said to me. A bolt of quatra ran straight from his hand into my armoured chest. It raced up to my thread, and I did as he said. My armour shattered off my body and the intense emotional pain followed it, crumbling to the floor like broken glass. I wheezed, sucking in a huge breath.

My stomach was bruised, I could feel it. Most of the pain was gone now, but there was still enough that I sat up to spit out bile.

"They'll be back." Vestas said, eying the side entrance. "I could see it in Zamelle's gaze."

Chapter 20
Capture

I sat in a cell. The walls were blue and silver – covered in metal sheeting. It was cold, which was nice, given that it was still a warm autumn. The bed they'd given me, surprisingly, was comfortable. My armour was gone. Despite the fact I had my connections available, I didn't see a point to it. There was no escape.

I'd found myself wrapped up in comfy sheets until only a moment ago. Voices outside my door had woken me. I sleuthed over to the door to listen to them. There were no windows to the hallway. I could have no way of seeing who was talking.

I pressed my ear up to the metal door. The voices had stopped. I frowned.

Pneumatics steamed inside the door. I felt it through my connection to the gasses before I heard it, but the sound still stunned me. My ears rang. The door swung open and I stumbled backwards.

The Bronze Suneva stepped into the room with me. I shook my head and regained my senses. I drew my staff and got low, ready to strike.

"Calm it, my main man." He said. His voice was American, and jovial. Just as the vision had shown me. I raised an eyebrow. He closed the door behind him. "I'm just here to chat."

"Okay, sure…" I quizzed.

"Relax, man." He smiled. His armour fell off his body. Revealed underneath was a tall, blonde man in his young twenties, of a godly build. His face was chiselled and, despite my unwillingness to admit it, incredibly attractive. He moved with an acquired charm and grace, taking a seat on the bench in my room next to the door. I relaxed my stance, and put my weapon away.

"It's hard to relax." I said. I lifted my shirt to show him my bruise. "It bloody well hurts."

His face dropped.

"I…Jesus." He stuttered. "I'm sorry."

"Why'd you do that?" I asked, although I knew why. He didn't want me to escape. It was simple.

"I thought you'd dodge it, or stop running. But you just held your ground." He frowned.

"Will it hurt when I go back in my armour?" I asked.

"It might." He said, "Your soul will have healed, but your *alis* won't. It doesn't heal. The dints just build up."

I bit my lip nervously, touching my stomach.

"But the pain in your *alis* won't subside if you haven't got your armour on. Maybe whilst you've got time in here, become Maiki. Let the pain pass. Meditation always helps."

I considered the advice. It seemed like a good idea.

"Why'd you come in here, anyway?" I asked.

"I honestly came to see how you were doing." He said. "And also, to tell you to keep up the good work."

"Good work?" I asked. A confused smile spread across my face.

"Yeah, man." He continued. "I mean, you're a pretty good fighter, for somebody who apparently hasn't been a Suneva all that long. I just feel like you weren't being yourself out there."

"How would *you* know *that*?" I asked. My face went red. He saw my offence and slouched himself back into the bench..

"I didn't mean it in a bad way." He said. "I just don't think the style you had going was *yours*. It felt like you were trying to match your stance with mine."

I went redder, this time blushing.

"I get it, man. *Kiin* isn't exactly matched to *raduk*. I'm not sure what I'd have done in your situation either."

"*Raduk?*"

"Earth." He smiled.

"Earth…" I repeated. Gears meshed together and started turning in my head. My brain whirred, trying to rip a thought from the tip of my tongue.

"You're not a Suneva from the fourth Black Hole, are you?" I asked.

"The fourth one?" He quizzed.

"Shit…" I pondered, trying to remember the name. "It starts with N…"

"Nerios?"

"That's it!"

"Yes." He said.

Cool. I frowned to myself. *There goes our destiny. The black holes just wanted us captured.*

"What are you doing working for Hesslik or Vestas, anyway?" I asked him.

"Why are you running with an apparent fugitive?" He asked me. I hummed rubbing my chin. His point was good.

"You seem like a nice bloke, though." I argued. "Vestas; not so much."

"I've got my reasons." He said. "Everybody has an asshole boss."

"True." I shrugged.

"Anyway, I'm needed elsewhere. I just wanted to keep you from going insane." He said, standing.

"Yeah, well, thanks, man." I articulated, poorly. He opened the door a sliver, and slipped his thick physique through it. He closed it behind him.

I sighed, and considered what I wanted to do now. I did not know what was in store for me during my capture here. I threw a pillow onto the cold floor, and sat upon it, cross legged. I let the armour of Maiki overcome me. It seeped from my thread, and limped across my skin, over my body.

It clicked into place, my green eyes illuminated, and I could feel the leftover pain- like waking up tipsy from a heavy night out. The pain was dull, and it throbbed. I held my stomach, glad that it didn't hurt more. I breathed deeply, trying to divert my focus from the pain. I'd meditated before with Kuvalik, and he would never understate its importance, but I wasn't sure how to do it right in this instance. I could meditate on my powers, but to *heal?* Instead of concentrating on *how* to do it, I let my mind run…

"Maiki!" A voice asserted. I was groggily swept from my trance. I rubbed my face, surprised to remember that my hands were metallic, and my face was a helmet. I sought the sensation of rubbing my eyelids, but I didn't get it.

"Nice that you're awake." Vestas remarked. He stepped into the room and closed the door.

I stumbled to my feet, startled, but slipped and fell back onto my ass. I could feel my heart kicking into overdrive, but there was nothing I could do. The door was locked, and he had electric fingers. I stood, finally.

"Are you ready to start your day as a useful Suneva to society?" He asked me. He had his hands interlocked, held before him merrily. A rotten sneer hung beneath the grille of his helmet.

"Not really." I said. "I mean, I don't trust you one bit, but there's no way out of this, is there?"

"Well, not unless your friends save you. I wouldn't recommend it to them, though. They'll end up in your position." Vestas' fingers pented. He strode up to my position. I backed from him, into the rear wall.

"In an hour, I'm going to run a series of tests on your thread. Things like wavelength, quatra velocity, strength function, and others, as you manipulate your element."

That's it? I scrunched my face. I was imagining probes and electrocution at a minimum. "That's…that's not so bad." I said.

"It's not hard, really." He agreed. "Then, if your friends don't come to collect you by the end of the day, I'll remove your thread."

"*What?*" I gasped. I whipped out my staff and went to aim it at him. My chances of escape were naught, but worth a try now. He raised his hand, like a gunslinger ready to shoot, and blasted me with a bolt of his teal quatra. I went to catch it in my free hand, but I missed its trajectory. It hit me in the armpit and raced to my thread. The armour of Maiki was torn from my body, shattering off me.

"Yes," He continued. I backed myself up to the wall. "I'll remove your thread. You might be a young Suneva, but you're a threat to security – and kidnapping isn't a light charge to have against my name. I'll remove your thread and set you free, never to bother me again."

"You're kidding." I burst. "That's…that's immoral, isn't it?"

"No." He said plainly. "You've chosen how you want to be a Suneva in the real world, and it's a threat to our image and our society. *Not* neutralising you would be immoral for *greater utility*."

I groaned. Anger boiled within me – blood rushing to my face.

"Hesslik altered your mind. You know that, right?" I spat.

"Excuse me?"

"The equation you made to remove threads, Hesslik is going to use it to remove all of the threads in the world."

"That's ludicrous." He dismissed, swatting a hand and turning away. "*That* is immoral."

"He zapped your brain so that you'd forget discussing it. He's making you build a giant electrical transmitter to send the signal globally."

Vestas, turned back. I could see the consideration in his eyes, but it was swept away. "You're insane." He sneered. "We're making free energy. You're mentally unwell, Maiki. Maybe I'll take your thread away early. Your friends have till nine o'clock tonight."

He snapped his foot down and pivoted to leave.

"You've got an hour before we start experimentation. Don't cry any more conspiracy theories or I will *not* make this easy for you."

The door slammed behind him. The thick metal of the cell rocked. I looked up to the skylight. It was barely morning – dawn light pouring in. I had time, but anxiety held me.

He didn't deny the free energy machine. I said to myself. *The vision must be at least partly true.*

I tucked myself back into bed whilst my Suneva sensations were stripped from me. I now had nothing else to do, and little will to fight the boredom. The bed was comfy. I rolled over to face the wall.

"Maiki!" An ethereal, holy voice whispered into the room and echoed off the metal. I was surprised to hear a voice when the door hadn't opened, and more surprised to have yet *another* visitor. I assumed I hadn't heard it, so rustled up tighter into the thick, thick doona.

"Maiki!" It came again. I snickered in disbelief, and turned over in the bed to see that I wasn't imagining it. There was a fully black figure standing by the bed.

"Ah!" I gasped, flailing wildly under the sheets. My heart burst through my ribs. My eyes popped out of their sockets. I looked at the figure again. It was smoky, with purple veins and eyes. It was Kuvalik.

"Kuvalik?" I asked. "How…how the hell did you get here?"

"I was getting my tea, when I sensed you were not home." He said cheerily. "So, I came to find you."

I sat up on the bed, slicked back my hair and I caught my breath.

"That's right…" I reasoned. "You can go places."

"That's right." He smiled. "What are you doing here, in the middle of Hesslik's compound?"

"I got caught. We followed the path of destiny, and the guy we were following works for Hesslik and Vestas. Destiny wanted me to be trapped."

"Interesting." He rubbed his smoky chin. "Although I wouldn't be so pessimistic about…"

"Vestas is going to remove my thread by the end of the day." I cut him off. His expression dropped.

"Oh.."

"Yeah, *oh*." I sulked.

"And even worse…" I continued. "I'm absolutely useless as a Suneva. I mean, air is so useless that I had to throw boxes in combat. Why is *kiin* such a useless power to have?"

Kuvalik huffed and rubbed his head. He took a seat on the bed next to me, and tried to think himself through a complete, convincing sentence. This took him a while, and I smugly waited.

"Do you remember the first thing I told you, James? I gave you a sentence, on the rules of being a Suneva."

"What?" I searched my mind. "Don't use quatra to hurt anybody?"

"That too," Kuvalik said. "But I also said that the point of quatra is not combat. The point is knowledge."

"So?"

"You're thinking about being a Suneva wrong. The powers aren't for fighting…"

"Well, that's all I'm using them for these days." I crossed my arms.

"Then you're using them wrong." He sat tall. "You don't yet have a proper understanding of what you can do, or what you are doing. When you use quatra for knowledge, you will learn the full extent of your abilities in the context of the natural world. Better manipulation of air will allow you to better defend yourself. Believe me, *kiin* isn't useless. You should have seen the warriors of the ancient *Kiin King*, the *Vochduvlad*. They were some of the most impressive Suneva to throw quatra, because they were so agile, reflexive, and acrobatic. They used their abilities as if they *were* the air. It was astounding."

"I forget that you're, like, six-hundred years old, sometimes." I noted.

"Don't forget it – I've seen it all." He smiled. "My point is, Maiki, that you can't try to emulate anybody else with your abilities. You've got to use the air like a *Kiin*, and like *Maiki*."

"So, how do I learn to fight like a *Kiin*?" I asked. Kuvalik rubbed his forehead.

"Maiki…" He sighed. The shadows leaked from his fingers from the force of his frustration.

"What?" I asked. "I'm in dangerous situations all the time, it looks like. I'm in one *right now*. Defence is important to me."

"It shouldn't be, it…"

"I don't want to be *weak*, Kuvalik." I burst. He shifted backwards, stunned by my admission. "I feel so weak. Amongst my friends, I'm weak. Natalie and Celeste, they blow me out of the water. I'm the human-hairdryer. Even socially, my friends are more influential than me. I've been given this power, but I'm still *weak*, and I hate it…"

Kuvalik wasn't sure what to say. His smoky fingers twiddled. My laboured, emotional breath was all that filled the room.

"You agree, then?" I asked.

"I think Suneva powers are reflections of the Suneva who own them." Kuvalik enunciated, picking his words carefully. "If you were bold and forceful, perhaps you would be a *Raduk* – a Suneva of earth. I think that you, James and Maiki included, are diplomatic, wary of conflict, and resourceful. I don't think this is a weakness, or indicative of weakness. I think you have a very unique way of finding solutions, and your power shows this."

"Right." I frowned.

"This probably wasn't the answer you were hoping for." Kuvalik said. "But it is the right answer. I said in the past that patience will help you become powerful like your friends, and that physical power *will* come with practice, but it is not going to be your strong point."

My expression was blank. I thought to Dad, the wall of a man, the exact opposite of weakness. It wasn't that I thought I was weak, it was just that I wasn't *him*. He is a man.

He was *a man.*

And you're a Suneva. My subconscious told me, but I didn't find it helpful. I wanted to be both.

"Thanks for the advice, Kuvalik." I said to the ghost. "Really."

"I'm sorry if they're hard words to hear."

"No, it's fine." I said. "Hard words are often what we need, you know? You'd never harden up in a world full of fluffy, pink pillows."

He laughed. I smiled.

"So, what will you do now?" He asked me.

"I don't know. Can you help me get out of here?"

"I don't think so." He looked around the room. "I barely got in here without being sensed. I hope you don't find it selfish, but I don't want to lose my consciousness today. I've been holding onto it for five hundred years."

"No, that's understandable." I smiled. "Go, walk through the walls, or something."

"But what will *you* do?" He asked me.

"I don't know." I said again. "But I've been thinking about everything wrong, anyway. Maybe if I try to solve this problem like the *Kiin* I am, I'll get an answer."

Chapter 21
Rescue Mission

Zamelle slammed the door of the factory and ran through the hole in the barbed wire fence. Genive was sprinting ahead in the darkness. She mashed the gate release button on her crimson claw, and slipped through the opening. Zamelle charged to catch up, but it seemed like the *Ivaer* was intent on getting away.

"Wait up, Genive!" Zamelle called. The French girl let her armour slip back into her soul. She picked up her bag from the alleyway floor and threw her bike upright. Natalie let her *alis* retreat too, and grabbed Celeste by the arm. She squirmed under Natalie's grasp.

"What are you doing?" Natalie asked.

"Getting far away, Natalie." Celeste said.

"And leaving James behind?" Natalie fumed. "He looked half dead, we can't just leave him in there."

"So, you're suggesting that the two of us should just waltz back in there and pull him out?" Celeste laughed. "Just you and me, against four Suneva and that bronze *thing* that you two led us to?"

"I don't know what to do, but we can't have left James there. I was about to grab him, I…"

"Oh, I knew this would happen." Celeste suddenly roared, smacking her bike with a hot fist. "Why Natalie?"

"Why *what*?"

"Why do we *have* to go back in there, right now, right into the centre of Hesslik's agents?"

"You'd rather leave James in their company?"

Celeste shook her head, a wide, condescending grin stretching from ear to ear. "I *know* you're not dumb enough to actually suggest that. Why did you have to prove me right?" Celeste grabbed at Natalie's hand and tore it from her arm. Her acrylic claws dug into Natalie's skin, drawing blood. Natalie stumbled back.

"What the hell am I proving? That I'm a better friend?"

"You're an Agent of Hesslik!" Celeste cackled. "The two of you. Oh, how I shouldn't have ever trusted you, leading us to that *fucking* Suneva. You *and* James leading us here. Now you're trying to lure me back in after I'd escaped? You almost had your money, too. To think I just tried *saving* you."

Natalie couldn't believe her ears. Did Celeste not understand the urgency here? They had *no clue* what Vestas was going to do with me. And what about the alibi we'd given our parents? This whole operation was only allowed to last one night.

"We…Celeste, come *on*." Natalie urged. "He just put his life on the line to get you out of there! You can't leave him there, here cares for you! We need to be back for…"

"You're not even denying it!" Celeste laughed. "And it makes so much sense, Natalie. I only had *one* agent on my tail until your fat thread offered to stick around. You were their bug, helping them find me."

"Celeste, I am not a bloody agent of Hesslik, get that out of your head!" Natalie growled. "If we leave him in there, we might never get him back. What the hell do we tell his mother? It's not about you."

Celeste laughed. She swung her leg around over the bike and slammed it on the pedal. Natalie, face scrunched with fury, lunged. She grabbed Celeste's shoulder and ripped her off the bike. Celeste's skin was hot to the touch – boiling hot. Natalie felt her palm bubbling, and she shrieked. They girls stumbled over each other, and the bike tipped under them.

"Don't you dare touch me, Natalie Athanas." Celeste warned, shoving her off.

"You can't just run off like this!" Natalie yelled.

"I'm not going *anywhere* with you Natalie." Celeste huffed. She thrust a finger at Natalie's face, causing her to back up. "You abused my trust, Natalie. I only had so much of that left. I trusted my urges to be your friend, to accept that you and James were genuine. But you used my belief in your earnestness to betray me! My God, I'd finally *opened up* for the first time in years…" She stopped to wipe a tear. "This world, for another, *fucking* time, has led me to my demise. May your soul *rot* in the void, and his too."

"Please don't believe that." Natalie urged, trying to find *something* reasonable to say. "I *am* your friend. I care for you, so does James. You're not seeing clearly. If I wanted you captured, wouldn't I have tried to neutralise you by now?"

Celeste's shook her head, her hand lunging for Natalie's throat. It gripped tightly about her windpipe and Celeste hoisted Natalie from the ground. The hot palm only got tighter.

"Don't you *dare* say anything more, Natalie Athanas." Celeste ordered. Natalie spluttered, sparks dancing in her vision. "You're stalling me because you can't defeat me alone. I know you have backup. I'm letting you off lightly, Natalie. Your friendship was false, but it felt real. You will leave this interaction without a burn so bad that they have to amputate the limb. That makes you the *luckiest* Suneva to ever cross me. *Never* follow me. *Never* contact me again."

Natalie felt her neck gush hot. A bolt of quatra slammed past her windpipe, into her thread, and attacked the void between her and Amasos. She gasped for air as a jagged blade ripped at her neck, tearing her soul and sensations out of her spine. The pain of it all rocked her body.

Finally, Celeste threw Natalie backwards, with no absence of force, onto the fence behind. Natalie's shirt tore on a splinter, her elbows grazing. She was winded, bloodied, and gasping for breath. Celeste finally mounted the bike and zipped off, flames sparking from her soles.

Natalie was shocked. Her sense of the world around her was dimmed. Without quatra, she couldn't follow Celeste even if she tried and she couldn't rush in to save me.

Not that it's possible. She thought to herself. *We never would have gotten out of there if James didn't get caught.*

She looked back upon the warehouse. It's huge, metal gate solemn in darkness. The only light came from the moon above.

I'll be back, James. She promised herself. *Celeste or not, I'll get you out. You're my friend, and we're in this together.*

Natalie looked down to her chest. Her locket hung over her shirt, gleaming in the blue haze of the autumn night. She grasped it in her hand, and spoke a prayer into it.

She dragged her bag off the floor and kicked her bike upright. The warehouse groaned against the night, and she peered back to it.

I hope you're alright. She thought. She gripped at the handlebars and pedalled off.

Natalie rode home, her light shining into the warm, blue night. She set an alarm, early enough to get out of the house before her folks got home.

If they catch me at home without James and Celeste, she reasoned, *Dad will know that the sleepover didn't happen. Then if James' mum calls, she'll know that he should be home. I can't be caught.*

She fell into her bed's warm embrace, but it gave her no comfort, she slept restlessly.

Natalie awoke as light shone into her face. Groggily, she tried to formulate a plan of attack for the day. She decided it was best to get away from the house, to cycle somewhere with a book, pen, carrot sticks and hummus, and write down her plan. She sat in the kitchen, with a piece of toast in hand.

A good street-Suneva… Natalie tried to remember Celeste's teachings. *…Always operates in the dark. Why is that?* She asked. *Good Suneva don't need light to know if another Suneva is around, they can smell the others' quatra. Darkness wouldn't even protect you from enemies. What useless advice…*

The front gate's motor whirred. The toast fell from her mouth, she scrambled to the front window, peeking from behind the frame. Her Dad's car was at the top of the drive, waiting. Her heart fell out of her mouth. She looked at the mess – things half in the bag, crumbs on the counter. Hot nerves flooded her system. She went into panic mode.

She scooped up everything she could need, and sprinted to her room.

The car door closed.

Surely Dad heard me. Her mind raced. She neatly folded the remaining items into her bag – not even in a hurry could she make a mess of it. She ripped the zip shut.

Keys entered the front door.

She looked at herself – she was in her lazing clothes. She didn't want to be seen in public like this, but she had no choice. She put on her runners and unlatched her bedroom window.

The front door opened.

Natalie threw her bag outside, then tumbled out after it. She gently let the window slide down, but it got stuck.

"Natalie!" Her Dad called for her. She fiddled with the window. It was truly stuck. "Natalie?" He called again. She could hear his footsteps coming for her room. Desperately, she tugged at the window.

It closed.

She ducked down.

Her door opened.

She sat in silence, back up against the house, not daring to make a sound. Her father's footsteps curiously treaded around the room. With each step, he pondered, and looked, and mumbled.

"Early of them to leave." He noted. His pace livened, and he left the room. Natalie sighed with relief.

She stalked around the house, back to where she'd left her bike. As she passed under her father's window, she had the acute feeling that he could see her there, sneaking around.

On second thought. She reconsidered. *Maybe there's some merit to operating in darkness.*

She kept looking over her shoulder as she ran out of the yard. She threw her leg over the bike, and pedalled it away as fast as she could.

She munched on an apple as she furiously spun her pedals. She found herself on the bike track, and, without much thought, knew where she was headed.

She cruised past the asphalt alleyway which led to the warehouse, to the street's end. The road was a court with a roundabout, but the two end houses left an opening between them. The path gave access to an overpass – a depressing, single biped wide skyway which gave glorious views of the freeway and the other railway line.

Natalie climbed it, and found herself at the pinnacle of the overpass. She parked her bike against the railing, and looked nervously over to the ground below. Cars moved so fast, that it appeared that the road was moving under her. She stepped back from the ledge, and looked to where she'd come. She could see the whole warehouse complex from here. The morning sun broke over her head, casting her shadow all the way onto its roof. She grinned, and dropped her bag to retrieve a pair of binoculars. She zoomed in to the building.

There's the side door. She thought as she spotted it. She shifted her focus left, to the chain link fence. It was still broken.

One possible entrance. She got out her notebook and pencil and started to sketch a plan of the building. She marked the side door with an X.

The building appeared to be shaped as an L, she noted as she drew it. The long warehouse part, where they had fought, ran along the freeway. The roller door, which she did *not* mark as a logical entrance, was on the front right of the building. The building continued along to the left of the roller, in a structure longer and thinner than the warehouse. There were no loading docks along the façade, or anywhere else. She could not stipulate what that part of the building was used for.

The mezzanine office connects that section to the warehouse. She thought to herself. *There must be useful rooms in there – probably where James is kept.*

There was an awning that ran the far length of the building. Near the awning, on the ground, was a low stack of boxes. On the roof, she could see an access entrance.

I don't think I can make those jumps. She hummed in thought. *James would be able to, though…*

Her binoculars swung by the roof entrance, and she noticed a security camera. Now that she noticed one, the rest appeared to her, as if painted in pink. Natalie noted their placements on her drawing. They heavily surveyed the front of the building. It would be difficult to enter from the front.

The back looks unguarded, though. The building's rear wasn't visible from the skyway, so another vantage point would be useful. She peered across the landscape, but could see no other high features. She frowned.

This is why darkness is useful. She huffed. *I'll have to check out the back without getting seen.* She got back onto the bike, and rode away.

Natalie found herself in front of a house which bordered the industrial property's backside. Behind it, she could see that there were no windows on this side of the building either, but only a closer look could confirm that and other details. Natalie examined the house between her and Vestas' warehouse. Without a doubt, people were home. A car rested in the driveway, a bike was on the porch, a light was on just past the door.

She huffed. She could see the back fence of this house. She could reach it if she tried, but it would be risky to climb it and weird to sit around in somebody else's yard. This whole operation was suspect.

She jumped and strained her neck, trying to see over the back fence, and caught what she thought was the top of a door frame, but nothing else. From what she could see, there was one camera here – easily disabled by a whip of water.

That's it, I guess. She thought. *That's my entrance.*

She was about to turn around, when a sensation tickled the tips of her fingers. The quatra field called to her with the presence of a nearby Suneva. Examining the house for onlookers, and once sure that nobody was watching, she stalked across the front lawn to the side of the house. The signal was stronger here under the cover of a side gate and switch board. She assumed the peace-sign pose with her hands and sat down on the grass, closing her eyes. Her mind was transported.

Her soul washed away, through her fingertips and into the sea around her. Natalie felt her presence spreading radially. The field dipped and waned, curving itself into large bodies, and expanding away in open space. In her mind's eye, she had a perfect map of where quatra was around her.

She felt the blood pumping in her body. The blood moved, and with it, quatra would flow in its veins. Her heart fuelled her sensations of the world, and of her soul. She relaxed. It's drum beat mellowed her mind.

She could sense Suneva now. They appeared as walking, coloured stains in a grey field. Somewhere between a dirty mark and a physical disturbance to the field, their presences rattled on her finger tips. She twiddled them, to get a better view.

There was one Suneva, walking through what must have been a hallway. It was one storey above the door. They passed another Suneva – whose scent she recognised as Vestas' student. They paused for a moment, to chat. Her sensations wondered elsewhere.

Another Suneva, further into the building, traversed diagonally. *Perhaps the corridor turns*. Natalie thought. She followed them. Their scent was familiar, but she was unsure of who they were. Their path turned parallel to the building face, and they stopped. Their quatra pooled in one place. The stain grew, their flavour becoming stronger on her palette.

The Bronze Suneva. She shuddered. Then she found me, next to where they had paused. To Natalie, my signal was weak. It did not shine, or stain like the others. It leaked weakly, like an injured animal. Apparently, it had always felt like that to her. She frowned.

Her concentration on me was broken by the sound of footsteps coming from the real world. One mystery Suneva, who roamed the halls, took large strides towards the back wall. Natalie was hit with a realisation.

If I can sense them, they can sense me… She reasoned. Her stomach dropped, falling out of her body like she was on a rollercoaster. Stress and nausea burned hot from its gaping hole, and climbed up her spine to her cheeks and eyes. She shot up. The Suneva was coming down a set of stairs.

She turned and ran, as fast as she could. The door to the factory opened. Heavy, metal footsteps paraded out of it. She glanced over her shoulder to see their long, sharp fingers curl over the wooden fence. They peered over the top, their silver helmet and blue eyes visible.

"Hey! You!" They yelled. Natalie sprinted. She tried to pick up her bike, but in leaning down, her bag fell over her head and spilled over the sidewalk. Her eyes bulged and her hands shook wildly. She looked back to the fence, to see the Suneva get their foot up, and over.

Natalie frantically palmed her possessions, jamming them into the bag. The Suneva was running now. She had packed this bag so well initially, that it seemed impossible that everything should actually fit. She rushed for the zipper, but it immediately got caught on the windcheater which hung half out. Her heart pounded.

The silver Suneva was past the house now. Their strides were long. Their weapon had summoned in their hand. It was pointed at Natalie.

She flipped her long, curly hair aside, slopped on the half-open backpack, and punched at the pedals. A bolt of blue quatra raced by her skull. A lock of her fringe disintegrated as the quatra blasted it into oblivion. She didn't dare look back. She got low to the handlebars and rocketed away. The Suneva yelled after her, and when she finally turned to look, she could not see them.

The bike skidded to a halt at the top of the next hill, and she held her hands out to sense any presence. There was nobody around. She cried in a sigh of relief, and sat by the roadside to regain herself.

Suneva need the darkness. She affirmed. Her head was dizzy.

***

Dusk set. I held a watch that *Lion's Foot* had given me. It was an old device Hesslik had given him, whose screen used to display videos until he broke it. Now it only told the time.

"Don't look at it too hard." He told me, when he last visited. "But spend your last minutes with your powers. Find peace in their presence. Do not take *kiin* or *maikess* for granted."

I held onto his words, like I did the watch, but I had no plan for escape. The whole building was too heavily guarded. I had observed the hallways as Vestas chauffeured me between my cell and the testing chamber. Not only would it be difficult to get through the pure-metal door of my room, but making it even a few metres in the building would have been a troubling enough task.

So, I sat in my room and looked at the watch. It ticked past eight thirty. I could feel my heart beating faster. I had to live my last half-hour as a Suneva at peace with my abilities. I took a deep breath. Destiny felt disturbed around me.

***

Natalie waited. She watched the sky from the dog park, with a faint view of the factory building. The sun had set, and its yellow and pink light had already faded from the sky. Moments ago, when the sun was on the horizon, it looked almost as if the heavens had been painted overhead. Now, even without the sun, the sky was blue and light. People were clearly visible in the glow of dusk. Natalie huffed, and glanced at her watch.

Eight-thirty, it read. She frowned, and looked back to the sky and the haze of the remaining day.

It's not dark enough yet. She thought. *But I've got to get him home. His poor mother…my poor Dad…*

Natalie hadn't been home all day. She couldn't break the illusion that Celeste, herself, and I were out the whole time. She sat in the quiet corner of the local library, meditating – concentrating on cutting off her quatra. She knew that her thread leaked. She knew that it would get her spotted, and that it already had put her friends in danger. Hours were spent today calming herself, and limiting the quatra which entered her body. Natalie couldn't be sure that she had control yet, but she didn't have more time to perfect it.

Natalie bounced on the spot, and looked to her watch again.

Eight-thirty-two, it read.

Screw it. She gritted her teeth. She mounted her bicycle, eyes intent on the warehouse, and pedalled off.

She ditched it by the front lawn of the house she'd stalked around this morning. It seemed that everybody was home – most of the lights were on, and even more cars were parked in the drive. Natalie, however, was intent. She didn't care. She marched into their backyard.

No quatra. She told herself, but when she spotted the camera over the fence, she remembered that *no quatra* didn't fit in with her original plan. She sighed, then focussed on letting go of her connections.

I'm strong without quatra, too. She reminded herself. *There's got to be other solutions.*

She jogged up to the fence line and got on her toes to peer over it. The camera faced the door, and gave a very limited view. Natalie was wearing all black clothes – a pair of leggings and a long, black skivvy. She had a black beanie on to hide her hair. She pulled it over her face, to reveal that she could see through it, just. She smiled.

She vaulted the fence like a dancer, lifting herself over with a fair amount of purely-human effort, and landed safely on the other side. She kept the beanie pulled over her face, and sleuthed towards the door.

The simplest solution is always the best. She told herself. She reached for the doorknob with her black, gloved hand. She didn't even have to turn it – the door wasn't closed, it seemed.

Natalie inched it open, to see that the deadbolt of the door had been sheared off.

She slipped into the crack in the door, and shut it gently behind her.

In front of her was a storage area. To her right was a staircase, which zig-zagged up to the next story. Her first instinct was to drop her hands by her side and feel for others in the room, and she had to grab her own hands to stop them from drawing quatra. She took a deep breath.

No quatra. Natalie told herself again. Keeping low, she slicked her way up the staircase, and peeked her head over the floor when she was high enough.

The décor before her was surprising. The walls were metal, with orange skirting, a grey midsection, and blue ridges. They resembled the kind of sci-fi, retro-futuristic buildings you'd find in eighties cartoons. There was nobody in this section of hallway, but there was also only one recession in the wall in which to hide. The reality of getting caught hit her suddenly, wrapping it's long, slimy tentacles around her chest and constricting. Her heart pounded. She looked at her watch.

Eight-forty-seven, it read.

She could feel panic constricting her further. It would force her to use quatra, and make a mistake. She took a deep breath, sat down on the step, and listened to her heart beat.

Relax. Natalie told herself. *Clear head.*

Her heart beat simmered down. She peeked back over the edge of the floor again. The coast was still clear. Her face now determined, she climbed up to the hallway. She listened for sounds.

There was indistinct chatter. It travelled down the hallway and filled the space, as if it came from everywhere at once. The words were unintelligible, but voices she knew. Vestas was talking.

Natalie squinted, trying to put the end of the walkway into focus. She could see a plant, which looked plastic, poking over the top of a low wall. She could see the wheels of a desk chair on the left of the frame.

She listened again for the voices. They danced in the air, further away now. Satisfied with the clear coast, she pulled herself up, and slipped down the passageway.

She edged closer to the end of the hall, with each step, checking that there would be no Suneva in the next room who could see her. As she came to the corner, she glued herself to the wall, and craned her head around into the room.

There was nobody in this room. She released her held breath, and walked in.

This place appeared to be an office. There were six cubicles, set up in two rows of three. Each cubicle had a computer and a desk chair. Around the room were plastic looking plants. Their green had faded, taking any joy the room had once possessed with it. Motivational posters hung on the wall, in between a bank of lockers. Natalie couldn't tell if the posters were satirical or legitimate. There was a closed doorway to her left, and an open one to the right.

That's the way that I sensed James before. She thought to herself. Although, in her drawings, she had noted this as a bend in the hallway, not another room.

A door swung open. The softly chatting voices became louder, and their metal footsteps clanked. The sound was consumed by the dull, grey cubical walls before it could deflect around the room. The voices were coming from the open doorway. It was not Vestas talking, she could distinguish. It certainly wasn't any Suneva she'd encountered.

Natalie's first instinct was to unleash her hands – to adopt a Suneva pose and sense their positions. Once again this forced her to grab her own hands and stop herself. Precious time was wasted avoiding her instincts - their footsteps approached, their voices amplified. She panicked, and dove under the desk of an office cubical. She balled herself up next to the box of a computer as their feet clanked into the room. Cords threatened to tangle around her head.

"Look, let's solve this once and for all." A male Suneva with a distinctly flamboyant voice said to the other. "I'll find the spreadsheet and we'll check."

"Look," the other protested. "I don't *need* a spreadsheet to know that I'm not on this shift. Vestas has been doing my head in. He makes up my hours, but I know what they are!"

"Then we'll prove it." The first Suneva responded. Natalie could hear them walking between the aisles of computers, coming her way. She tucked her legs in, and could feel her heart thumping through every cell in her body.

The complaining Suneva groaned, and their steps followed. Feet stopped in Natalie's range of sight. They rested in front of her cubical, facing her. She dared not breathe. One pair silver and dual-toed, the other bright blue and squarish. The two-toed Suneva took the seat. Their decorative, plated knee just inches from Natalie's face. She clung into the carpet.

Use your quatra. Her instincts screamed inside her head.

A hand reached down blindly under the desk, searching for the computer's power button. Natalie, resting against the box, held her breath. She watched the long, armoured finger as it searched. The hand headed straight for her face, when the thumb found the computer. The hand searched for the button. It pushed aimlessly into the plastic.

"Fucking on switch…" They cursed. Their chair scooted back. Their body bent down. Natalie smashed the button with her thumb. The tower whirred and purred. The computer made its boot-up noises.

"Oh, found it." They said, a smile coming across their tone. Natalie exhaled long through her nose, not to make a sound.

"Did you hear…" The complaining Suneva said to the flamboyant one, as the computer took its time to boot up. "…that they're taking that kid's *thread* tonight?"

"They're taking his thread?" They asked, shocked. His leg relaxed. "*Good.*" He said. "Stupid kids, running around with Argols. They don't deserve their powers if they're going to use them like…"

Natalie gasped, audibly, and immediately covered her mouth.

"…*dickheads*…" The flamboyant Suneva finished his sentence after a pause. He stopped moving for a second. The purr of the computer whirred into the room. Natalie halted her breath. She could hear her heart now. She wanted it to stop.

"Did you hear that?" They asked the Suneva who complained. Silence fell again.

"The thumping?" They asked.

"Sure," the flamboyant one replied. "That too."

They paused once more. Natalie's eyes bulged. Her mouth remained covered. The two-toed, flamboyant Suneva pushed back his chair. Natalie's internal monologue was screaming again. *Use your quatra. Use your quatra. Use your quatra.*

"Dude, it's these new computers." The blue-footed Suneva said. "I swear their fans thump and blast all of the time."

Natalie still held her breath. The two-toed Suneva remained still.

"Yeah." He agreed. "Especially this one. Noisy piece of shit." He scooted back to the desk. Natalie almost fainted from not exhaling as loudly as she could.

"See!" The flamboyant Suneva said after a few clicks and a whirr of the tower. "Your hours changed, honey. You're on with me from now on."

"*Oh Joy.*" The complaining Suneva deflated. They laughed together about it, although Natalie wasn't sure it was totally jovial. They shut off the computer, got up, and walked through the door which was previously closed. Natalie banged her chest and squeezed her hands. The action was stupid, but it relieved her nerves.

She rolled out from under the desk, and got up. Out of her pocket she pulled the building diagram she had drawn - I would be only a few metres down the right corridor. Her chest fluttering with nerves, Natalie listened for further sounds. There were none, so she sleuthed, light headedly, into the right-hand hallway. She reached the first door on the right. It had no peep-hole, so she held her ear to the door, and could only hear the relaxed bellow of a strong breath. Natalie held the knob in her gloved hands. She turned it, and threw herself into the room.

My cell door squeaked open. A girl in all black slipped inside, and pushed the door until it was almost closed. She turned to face me.

"Celeste!" I whispered. An amazed smile raced across my trodden face. I looked to my watch. *Eight-fifty-five*, it read.

Celeste said nothing. She flicked her mousy brown hair from her face. Her dark eyes looked glassy. Her scarlet lips trembled. She was giving me *that* look.

She pounced. Her arms fell around my neck. My hands, confused, flung themselves high into the air – as if my body wasn't sure what she wanted even as she took it. Her eyes closed, her lips met mine. Her lips were moist. Her breath was hot. Her mouth moved with mine, our noses touched, and our heads shifted.

My palms found their way to her hips. My hands felt so snug in the valley of her waist. I pulled her closer, her arms tugged behind my neck. Our kiss was passionate. Fireworks went off in my brain. Sparkles surrounded my head. I could feel myself becoming dizzy, barely comprehending what was going on. She pulled her face away from mine. It took my eyes a while to focus, but when they did, I saw her beautiful face.

"Wow…" I uttered. "Hi."

"Hi." She said. The universe was hidden behind her dark eyes. I was transfixed.

"What was that?" I asked. From the way I asked it, or simply the fact that I asked it, she raised an eyebrow. "I mean, I really liked it."

"You put your life on the line for me, James. I owe you that one."

"Oh, right." I scratched the back of my neck. My cheeks were flushed red. "And, for no other reason?" I asked.

She ignored my question. "I should have trusted you. You really believed in me. I can't believe I threw that away."

"Threw it away?" I asked. "When did you do that?"

"When I left you on the floor." She said, running and hand in my hair. "You didn't deserve that. Neither did Natalie. I should have trusted myself, instead of questioning everything."

"When did you throw Natalie aside?" I asked. "You saved her."

"It's a big story, James. Let's just go." She kissed me on the cheek, and grabbed my hand, dragging me to the door.

"Wait." I pointed to my watch. "Vestas is coming for me any minute. He's going to remove my thread."

"You want to stay around for that?"

"No, I mean, he's probably out there right now." I clarified. "We'll walk right into him."

"Better than staying here." Celeste squeezed my hand. "Come on…"

There was a scream. It ran through the hallways like a lost wraith – the ghost of a woman. It was chilling, settling between the inhuman shriek of a Suneva and the yell of a woman surprised.

"Natalie?" Celeste dropped my hand, her eyes wide. She held her posed digits by her side, and connected to the quatra field.

"Natalie?" I asked her.

"Natalie!" She responded. She gazed into my soul. "This is my fault - we should have done this together. Where would they have her?"

"The lab." I said, out of instinct. "Follow me."

I went to open the door, but it slammed itself closed, locking us in. My jaw dropped in horror, I looked to Celeste, her face was very similar.

"What did you do?" She asked.

"Nothing, I swear!" I rebutted. We both looked to the door, and hurriedly tried to pry it open.

A bucket of water splashed over my head. My ears were clogged, liquid pressing into my eardrums. My head felt full, like I'd dived too far into a reef. I clenched at my brain.

Boss will be happy with me. Niskidin boomed into my skull. *Caught Iva Argol and Maiki – and I didn't even have to try.*

Let us out! I yelled, although I knew it was a stupid thing to yell. I didn't sound nearly imposing enough, and he had no reason to open the door.

Tough chance. He said. *You two just have fun in the room. I think she's into you.* And with that, the feeling of pressure lifted. Water fell from my ears in torrents. My head was pulled from the depths. I held it as my brain spun.

"What was that?" Celeste asked.

"Niskidin." I said. "He trapped us in."

"Like hell he did!" She spat. "How much time does Natalie have?"

"Why are you asking me?"

"Because, Vestas experimented on you, right? How much time does she have."

I looked to my watch. "I've got zero minutes." I said. "Vestas didn't want hostages tonight."

"But he wouldn't remove the thread before running experiments." Celeste said "He's too…nerdy." She searched for the right word.

"No," I agreed. "He wouldn't – but nothing he did to me involved screaming like *that*."

Celeste huffed.

"She just got caught, then. A scream of surprise, not pain." She reasoned. "Would you say we have less than ten minutes?"

"Sure, it seems like ten minutes would give him all that he needs."

"Good." Celeste grinned. She rubbed her hands together and bit her tongue. When she released them, palms up, a powerful blue flame rose to a finger's height. It was thick, and vibrant.

"Do you see this flame?" She asked me.

"Yes." I responded. It looked like her usual fire to me.

"Third most powerful *Ivaer* flame in *existence*." She boasted. "Right behind the real *Iva Argol* and her mother, *Sanavaer*."

"That's impressive, but what's your point?" I asked.

"My point, is that whatever this door is made of, they didn't make it to withstand a bearer of a blue flame.

"So," She said, drawing her sword in one hand, holding the fire in the other. Helical blue flames engulfed the weapon. "The hinges were not made with withstand me..." Not afraid of being burned, she plunged her hand into the helix, and heated the sword directly. It started to glow red, way too hot to touch. Still heating the weapon, she lined up her shot with one eye closed. The door would open inwards – the hinges were on our side, but not the easily removable variety.

Satisfied with the sword – now on the verge of melting itself, she swung at the top hinge.

There was a crash of metal. Her sword dinted over the hinge. The hinge remained unscathed. She roared, and threw the sword to the floor.

"Okay, better idea." I said. "You heat the *hinge*, then I swing at it with my staff." Celeste's eyes were ablaze. Fire licked from her mouth – not metaphorically, but literally. She could breathe fire, and I only came to know it in that instant. She calmed, slightly.

"Fine. That's good." She grunted. She picked the dented sword from the ground and flicked it out of existence.

She pushed her hands up against the hinge – a little tall for her reach – and let blue flames gush from her palms. They splashed out like hot liquid, their tendrils flailing like a jet of water on a brick wall. She grunted to contain the power.

I summoned my staff. She pushed herself aside, and I swung on the hinge.

It was a clean cut.

"Yeah!" I pumped my fist. Celeste grinned with her fire grin. She too, was satisfied. She got to work heating the second hinge, and I sliced straight through that one too.

I stuck the prong ends of my staff between the door and its frame, and levered with all of my might. The door fell inward and slammed against the floor. On the other side was a very surprised Niskidin. Celeste and I both blasted him with a bolt of quatra before he could think. The first he redirected, but the second went straight to his thread. Celeste and I burst over the fallen door. Celeste grabbed the half-human Niskidin and shoved him over. He fell like a logged tree.

"Left." I said. Celeste nodded.

We dissolved our weapons and sprinted left down the hallway. Without any thought of being caught, I let my body spew forth into the office area. Two Suneva sat by a computer. They turned to me, and it took them a moment to process who they were looking at.

In that moment, Celeste smacked into my back. She bowled past my body, spotted the Suneva, and yelled. She grabbed the nearest object – a pot plant – lit it on fire in her hand, and threw it at them. It hit one of them square in the helmet. The pot rebounded, flew through the computer screen, and set fire to the screen's plastic shell. The hit Suneva slumped to the floor. The other had no idea what to do. He got up and ran through the side door towards the back exit.

"Keep running, James!" Celeste demanded. I kicked off the floor, using a small bound of air, and leaped over the cubicles to the opposite doorway. I sprinted through the hall, coming to the first door, and forced it open.

The door required far less force than I gave it, and I fell into the room, tumbling over the floor before kicking myself onto my feet. I assessed the lab.

The room had the white-tile, sterilised feel of a chemistry lab and a hospital rolled into one. This, I had realised today, was *not* the room I had seen in my vision. Natalie sat in the dentists' chair – strapped in by leather manacles at the wrists and ankles. Her head wriggled helplessly – she had barely noticed the intrusion. Vestas stood behind her, his right hand to the sky, wielding the thread removal device which arced with electricity. *Lion's Foot* stood to the left of the chair, he was stunned to see me.

Vestas' eyes caught mine. They angled upwards – he was grinning. He did not speak to us, as I would have expected him to, but he did appear to pause.

Carbon. The thought came to me. *The device is full of carbon.* I extended my grip to it, the world swirling in slow motion. I clutched at the carbon in the plastic casing, and in the circuit boards, and went to pull away.

Celeste slammed into the back of me. I stumbled on my feet, finally finding my balance. Vestas' grin broke through his helmet. Now he went to speak.

"This must be my lucky…"

"*Shut up.*" Celeste demanded. He frowned, but only slightly.

"Okay, then." He said. His hand began to plunge. I gripped again at the carbon in the device, and *pulled* on it.

Nothing happened.

It was the feeling of pedalling a bike with a toothless sprocket, or clicking a broken mechanical pen. Expectations of reality were slashed. Deep dissatisfaction, and the fire of anxiety, rushed through my body.

I tried it again.

Feel it and do it. I screamed in my mind – but that's exactly what I had done before. I reached, I pulled, and my quatra clicked over. I yelled. A fireball roared over my left shoulder. Disguised in the plume of flames, a bolt of Celeste's blue quatra.

Vestas would need to move to avoid the flames and the bolt. Vestas was standing behind Natalie. Therefore, the flames were headed for Natalie.

Patience and an open mind. The lesson from Kuvalik now ran through my thoughts.

I took a deep breath, flames roaring past my head at the speed of honey, and calmed myself. My staff fell out of my soul, into my hand. I used it to connect to the air, and I used my connection to give it energy, to rush towards me.

A gust blew through the room. The fire sat on the wind, deflecting away from Natalie, and up towards Vestas. He ducked behind the chair. Celeste's bolt singed Natalie's hair and crashed into the back wall. The paint on the tiles bubbled and boiled. Natalie screamed in fright.

Lion's Foot un-slung his long chain, and before it could hit the floor, he whipped it towards Celeste. The fire left her sword, and her sword left her hand as her arm was crushed against her body. The steel python constricted her, and wrapped her up tighter than she could hope to escape from.

Patience, and an open mind. I repeated to myself. I felt again for the carbon in the device, through my staff, as Vestas stood again. I held tight, and ripped away.

Black clumps flew towards the prong ends of my Suneva *shath*. The device went up in flames, a half-complete circuit board flinging itself away and skipping across the floor.

I shifted my attention to the chain.

Whilst Vestas scrambled to the floor for the remains of his device, I swung my weapon down upon the heavy metal linkages. My diamond blade made a sizeable slice into one link. I yanked it out, and stamped my chunky, silver foot upon it.

Fight like a Kiin. I told myself. *Be yourself.*

Who even am I? I questioned the logic. I looked down, and the chain was broken. I smiled, and leaped to Natalie.

I watched behind me, as the chain surrounding Celeste, broken from its master, constricted further. Celeste stumbled, and groaned. *He controls the metal, you idiot, not the chain.* I told myself off.

I wrapped my slim mitts around the leather strap holding Natalie's left hand. I yanked it tighter, then unlatched it, like a belt buckle. Natalie's hand screeched out of the blocks, slamming onto the other buckle. Behind her, Vestas rose. I blasted a bolt of quatra at his head, forcing him to duck, and clawed at the brace on Natalie's right foot. She kicked herself free – the wind of her booted foot scraping the tip of my nose – and jumped into action.

Vestas leaped from behind the chair and into the room. Celeste, held in the metal, telekinetic grasp of *Lion's Foot*, levitated by the door, Natalie engaged her armour, becoming Zamelle. She spun, conjuring water from the room into a deadly snake, and whipped at Vestas' face. His helmet spun on his head, and his body spun on its legs. He stumbled down to the floor again. I blasted a bolt of quatra at *Lion's Foot*. He had to remove a hand from his chain to avoid its path. Natalie blasted one of her orange bolts quickly after mine.

He lost enough concentration that Celeste, struggling against the heavy linkages, was able to break free in a fit of flames and rage. She tossed the chain back at its commander. The armour of Genive crawled over her body. I let myself become Maiki. We ran through the door, dissolving our weapons so that we could move faster.

"*After them!*" Vestas yelled. Electrical sparks crackled from the room. "*Strakos Kera!*"

Alarms sounded. Their sirens bellowed, bouncing between the retro-futuristic metal walls. The three of us piled into the office area, one by one falling into the first cubical. Genive went out of her way to sweep everything off the desk as we madly eyed for exits.

"That way!" Zamelle suggested, pointing left, to the back of the building. She ran, and before she could pass the cubical, a metal door rolled shut at the end of the hall. She spun on the spot, running back to us. There was only one other way – straight ahead.

"Come on!" Genive said. She sprinted, hands sparking with plasma embers. Plastic and cork-board walls melted in her presence. We burst through the opposite portal, into a metal hallway. The room we were running to had what looked like a huge television, and a couch visible.

A roller door slammed down, quicker than any of us could blink. It blocked the end of the hall. We skidded to a halt, looking behind us, back to the office. Vestas and *Lion's Foot* were fast in pursuit. Lion's Foot bowled through the furniture, transforming depressing plastic plants into paintings of depressing, plastic plants under his huge feet.

I pushed the group ahead.

"There's another way!" I yelled. I spotted the second exit – near the closed roller door and on the left of the hall. I was honestly making false hope when I yelled – it was pure coincidence that I was correct. I barged to the front of the girls, kicking off the right wall on a gust of wind to swoop into the secondary hallway.

There was a wooden door in our path. I summoned my staff and cut through it's deadbolt. It swung open, into the mezzanine lookout office.

With final, fate-filled bounds, I pressed off the floor into a sprint. The window slanted outwards over the factory floor. I built my momentum, and holding my pronged weapon like a spear in front of me, I leaped at the glass.

My weapon made the perfect hole for itself – like a machete in styrofoam – but did not make a hole for the wielder. Shoulder first, I crashed into, and finally through the window. I landed in a summersault on a pillow of air, on top of the plane of broken glass. I rolled, flipped up, and sprinted away. Two adjacent panes of glass fell next to me, crashing like cymbals and spreading deadly chips along the cold floor. Zamelle and Genive landed in the rubble. Together we ran directly away from the mezzanine, in a line towards the side door.

The alarm pelted and wailed. A red light fanned around the factory floor. Shadows ran in circles, splaying themselves far onto the back wall, chasing the beam of red around the room.

There was a mighty crack of rubble. The concrete by the side door roared. It was flung aside, to make room for a column of stone to block the exit.

I skidded to a halt, my metal feet sliding on the heavy dust. I kicked up and ran towards the machines, to escape via the roller-door. The whole factory shook as I shouldered past a mill. A dust cloud exploded from the roller's base, and a massive rock wall stretched up in its wake. I stopped, and turned, and stared at Zamelle and Genive.

Vestas stood on the mezzanine, guarding the broken glass office. *Lion's Foot* crashed onto the factory floor with a thud. The earth cracked under his solid figure. All around, Suneva were summoned by the warning bell's wailing. They slunk from the shadows, like manic hyenas. Their teeth bared, their weapons flared. In their indistinct chatter, they waited for blood.

There was silence, bar the whistle of hot, autumn wind, and the ambient buzz of alarms. Only Vestas' chuckle broke the stalemate. This was the calm before the storm – a moment to think. I examined the room. *How could* kiin *be useful here?* I asked myself.

I looked at *Lion's Foot*. He was too strong for me to confront head on – in fact I probably couldn't confront anybody in this room *head-on*. There were at least five Suneva here – Vestas, *Lion's Foot*, an indigo blue Suneva by the side door, and at least two in the shadows, between the huge, metal aisles.

I could feel minimal carbon around me in the machining area, but the aisles of storage were *full* of carbon. That, and they provided excellent high-ground for somebody who could bound between walls. If I could get up high, I could provide a lot of distraction, or even direct the battle. I smiled nervously.

Step by step, eager Suneva writhed from cracks and corners. Slowly, they advanced towards us.

"Okay…" I whispered to Zamelle and Genive. "You take the big, bronze guy, and I'll take everybody else."

"*What?*" Zamelle grabbed my arm.

"Okay, not *everybody* else." I admitted, "But if I can get high enough, I can distract them all away from you two. Do what you need to do. We don't need to take to take everybody down to get out of here – just the right Suneva."

"That actually sounds good." Genive admitted.

"Great," I grinned. "Then it's showtime."

I ran from the machines, away from roller door, towards the clearing. Wild quatra shots passed me, scraping along my figure as I bolted out into the open.

Lion's Foot skirted my left peripheral. He was preparing to do something as I ran in front of him. Two bolts, one orange and one blue, cascaded past his body. His attention was shifted. Vestas eagerly watched from up high, not involving himself.

On my right there was a godly crash of electricity. It was probably aimed at me – I could feel its tentacles caressing me. I tried not to think about it.

Standing before the centre shelf – its floor-to-ceiling mass of iron and wood obscuring my whole vision - I pushed down on the air around me. I blasted into the aisle, onto the adjacent wall of boxes. Bolts of quatra followed me. Some were very close, some were unbelievably poorly aimed – again, I tried not to think about it. *My distraction is working*, is all I told myself. I climbed up by bounding between the shelving faces, leaping the valley between the scaffolding stacks.

I had one more leap to get on top of the shelving. On a blast of wind I cast myself off, over the gap. Mind flight, in my hands, I felt a disturbance. Near me, air was superheated and ionised into plasma. A quatra bolt flew my way, and it would meet me as I gripped into the top lip of the scaffolding. I flailed my arms, pushing air upwards. I lost height, and tumbled just below my target. There were bags stacked on pallets where my hands would now land. My claws gripped into them as the bolt of quatra soared over my head-fin, and just managed to hold myself to the wall.

Thick powder burst from the tears my fingers had made. The powder was white, and totally opaque in the air. I blew it out of the way to see better, but that just stirred up more of it. Frustrated, I clambered to the top of the shelf, and slumped down on the structure, facing the ceiling. Wild quatra bolts ran up the side of the shelf. They could not hit me.

When I gained my breath, I rolled on to my stomach and peered over the side. A white cloud of powder slowly descended. A bright-orange bolt of quatra ripped through the cloud, disturbing it. The hole it tore revealed a Suneva on the floor, holding a staff in a loose grip, with silver, two toed feet.

You can't see anything through that cloud. I thought to myself. Now that I had locked eyes with the silver Suneva, their next bolt was incredibly accurate. I ducked behind the lip of the shelf, and fired one back on them.

An ambush feels like a Kiin *thing to do.* I reasoned. *Surprise, quietness, nimbleness.*

I blasted air into the valley, stirring up the powder which was already there. Reaching over the lip of the edge, I grabbed a bag from the top of the pile. My long fingers pierced it, and made it difficult to get a proper grip on it. I yanked it from the pallet, only then realising how heavy it was. I felt my weight shift and my stomach armour slide on the metal edge. I stopped dead, balancing on the corner. A bolt of quatra soared toward me from another Suneva in the aisle, standing directly below me. My first reaction was to throw the bag into its path.

The bag flew, and exploded in a cloud of dust as the bolt of quatra rammed through it. Thinking quickly, I unleashed a gust of air upon it, then used the blast to wrench myself comfortably back onto the shelf.

Powder spread over the valley of the aisle. It was thick, opaque, and drifted slowly. I stood tall, behind its cover, and blasted air downwards. The thick cloud descended like heavy fog. I had two Suneva in my trap.

But you can't see them. The thought came to me. I held my hands out to sense the air and carbon in the room.

Boxes glowed bright yellow on the heat map in my mind, they were full of carbon. Interestingly, the Suneva had no carbon in them, neither did the powder. My spatial senses were almost totally blocked by the dust. The air bounced around between particles. It was a field of pure chaos to my fingertips. I squirmed trying to comprehend it. Still, beneath the floor of the cloud were the waists and legs of Suneva, visible. I located my first target – the Suneva directly below me, and grinned.

I jumped from the edge, far enough into the aisle to land atop the enemy, but had failed to consider one thing – *how do I land?*

I peered, in horror, up to the ledge now too far away to grab onto, and down to the thick cloud, which raced towards my feet. Sure, I had jumped from heights before and landed on air, but never had I jumped from the near-ceiling of a factory.

This could ruin my perfect plan. I realised, as I pushed my hands and feet by my side. I used my soul to grab into the air around me, and forced it downwards. A vortex of dust cascaded around me. The powder turned violently turbulent, it spewed rather than ebbed. It churned like rapids. I couldn't see the ground now, or *anything*. I blasted once more, and felt the air surge against the ground. I bent my knees, expecting a crash, but receiving a gentle touch to the concrete. I wanted to sigh in relief, but also didn't want to give myself away, so I remained silent.

In the air, amongst the sickening powder which destroyed my senses, I could feel something more substantial. I slunk towards it. The object spun around, unsure of where it was looking. I lunged, pushing off the concrete, and wrapping my hands around whatever of it I could grab. I blasted quatra into the limb in my grasp. I heard the armour shatter, and I felt it dance away from my fingers. I let them go.

"Aw, *fuck*." I heard them curse. I grinned, and keyed into my sense of carbon around me. The shelves were lined with boxes, and where there was no carbon, presumably, was the aisle. I got my bearings, then snuck towards the roller-door end, away from my fallen victim.

The dust was thick. I used a gust of air in my direction of travel to stir it towards my target. I could feel them in the wind – like a wall jarring the flow. They coughed, their body moving from side to side. My footsteps were dead silent, the ground protected from the clank of my metal feet by small air jets beneath my soles.

The two-toed Suneva stumbled – I could *just* feel past the nauseating dust. I pounced onto them, my arms wrapping around their torso in a spear-tackle. They were driven into the concrete. I blasted them with a bolt of quatra, and leaped off. Their armour shattered, they coughed under the dust. Using all of my strength, I summoned a mighty gale in the aisle, which did what it could to clear the powder away. I followed the wind, leaping back up the scaffolding under the cover of the white cloud.

I hauled myself onto the top of a shelf and stood tall to observe the battlefield. Vestas stood behind the intact glass of the mezzanine office. Another Suneva, midnight blue with a copper whip, guarded the side exit. Their whip sparked and cracked with liquid charge. A bolt of quatra zipped up to the ceiling from the next aisle over.

In the open floor of the factory, *Lion's Foot* battled with Zamelle and Genive. It was the fight of mother nature – elemental forces meeting and crashing together. Pillars of earth were summoned, then charred by blue fire and slashed by whips of water. Bolts of quatra soared like bullets. Genive took cover behind a chunky lathe. Zamelle strafed the enemy, deflecting bolts from the whip-wielding Suneva and firing her own.

I have to shut down the door-guard's thread. I strategized. *The Suneva in the aisle doesn't matter, but I need to get the whipping guy away from Zamelle and Genive.*

I stepped back as far as I could and sprinted across the shelf. I pushed off its ledge with a gust of wind, and dug my claws deep into the wood of the adjacent ledge. I wrenched myself up, and crawled over to the other side.

A bolt of pink quatra grazed my head. I was stunned, almost actionless as a second, with better aim, roared towards my face. I flung my arm out before me, and took it through my hand.

It seeped through my system like hot gas with a powerful pump. It came close to my thread, I could feel it travelling. I tensed up with the feeling, finding myself unable, or my body unwilling, to summon my own quatra and flush it out. In the split second I had, there was only one action to do.

I closed the path to my thread.

I did it as if I'd done it a thousand times before. Finally, I had a connection to my own body – enough to direct my systems. The bolt skimmed past my neck, through the opposite shoulder, and down through my torso. It directed itself out of my foot, into the structure on which I stood. The wood beneath me exploded with the energy. It melted, caught ablaze, and my leg went straight through. I now straddled the metal ledge of the shelf. The Suneva below ran to me. They fired again, but it was badly aimed and I could dodge it from my position.

I flipped myself over, clinging on to the roof of the shelf. My leg dangled out of the hole. A quatra bolt entered, through my foot, and coursed through my veins. I pulled the leg through the hole, and closing off the connection to my thread, let the bolt redirect itself. It came out through my left hand, aimed to the sky, and dissipated itself through the roof.

I took a moment to find my head. I had a plan here. I felt for the carbon again. My soul, like all Suneva souls, had a limited reach. I had about a ten metre radius to work with – it was enough.

I stood tall, over the ledge. The Suneva prepared to fire. I gripped into the carbon, as much of it as I could grab, and ripped it towards me. Bonds snapped, trillions at once. The force of pulling yanked me off the ledge of the shelf. I fell, and a wall of fire, from boxes torn from their carbon, rose. The flames were so hot that metal buckled. The Suneva screamed – I screamed, falling head-first in freefall towards a wall of fire. They ran, I could not.

There wasn't enough time to reposition myself – to get my feet facing downwards, then cushion my fall to a stop. My weirdly aerodynamic shape streamed through the air.

Flight is the right of a Kiin, right? I reasoned. *How do planes do it?* More pressure down, less pressure up, that's how planes did it. I knew that from physics classes with Natalie.

My hands were by my side. Wind soared over them, on the top and bottom. I held on to the air. I'm not sure how I did it, but I twisted my soul through my fingers, and split the stream. At my command, the stream which flowed over my body sped up, and the stream below slowed down.

According to Bernoulli, slow fluids have higher pressure. It was intuitive in the moment, and the laws of physics backed me up. The tilt of my body shifted. My stomach angled towards the floor. I concentrated harder on the altering the streamlines over my body. Just moments from impact into hard concrete, I dug in hard, and pushed with all of my might on the overhead flow.

I swooped at the ground. My body pulled up, bursting through the wall of fire. As I charged through the liquid heat, the metal shelving buckled to failure. They collapsed over the aisle. It rained fire over my feet as I zoomed away at high speeds. I pulled up, soaring to the height of the tallest shelf. As I slowed, I veered left, landing atop the next shelf end.

I gripped my claws into it, breathing frantically, in absolute disbelief.

That wasn't flying. I reasoned, *but sweet cheese, if it wasn't close. That's gliding,* that's *fighting like a Kiin.*

I yelled ceremoniously, and pumped my fist. The section I was holding on to creaked, melting underfoot. I leaped from it as it crashed down, vaulting the gap and clawing into the side of the last shelf before the door.

Mr. Electric-Whip, now in range, cracked his weapon in my direction. The arc of liquid charge raced towards me. I ducked behind the corner, but the electricity couldn't touch me. It was grounded by the metal of the scaffold, racing towards the concrete. I climbed to the top, his thrown sparks flying at my feet.

I reached the top of the stack. By this point, I'd used every conceivable trick I could have conjured. I wasn't sure what else there was to do. I stood tall, looking at the whip-wielding-*Liktas*.

He snarled at me, the whip's cable arching with sparks. He flung the whip's end, and it clawed at the leg of the scaffold I was on. Straining with all of his might, he yanked the whip. It burst with brilliant blue plasma, melting the leg of the shelving and shearing it straight through. The structure creaked.

My eyes widened. I fired a bolt of quatra at him, but he whipped it out of the air with a crack of his cable. I fired again, and once more, he absorbed it through his *shath* with ease. I gulped.

Okay, solve this like a Kiin. I reminded myself. *There's no bags of powder around, no boxes to make fire, I probably shouldn't swoop at a man with an electric whip…*

The whip rounded the other leg of the shelf. He ripped again at the structure. This time, it shifted as he yanked away. I could feel the support of it crumbling under my feet.

I'm going to need graphite. I twitched, looking around. There was some carbon up here, although grabbing it would set a fire and force me to abandon the high ground, but it was worth it.

I hid over the ledge, out of sight of the *Liktas* below. He growled, and I could feel him ripping at the structure again.

From the wood in the pallets and shelves, and the cardboard in the boxes, I pulled a solid clump of carbon. A fire roared below as the black mass raced into my hand. I condensed it into graphite, and shaped it into a rod the size of my staff.

The shelf groaned under the fire and attack from below. It leaned, about to fall. Without a run-up, I dived off the edge head first, for my friend below.

His grin was maniacal. He licked his lips behind his helmet. His eyes keyed in on me. His hand shook, ready to strike with the cable. I held the graphite rod from its top at arms-length.

I controlled the air around my body, as I had done before. *I can't believe I'm doing this.* Was the thought to cascade through my buzzing mind. *I could barely pull-up before, and now I'm trying it one handed?*

The midnight-blue Suneva salivated eagerly. I swooped in close, preparing to pull up. He wrung his arm back, and slung it towards me. I re-adjusted the rod, and intercepted the dangerous copper whip as it coiled. Arcs of lightning roared through it, cascading into the ground and charring the concrete.

I lost half of my hold on the air while readjusting. I wasn't slowing down, or pulling up. I abandoned the graphite rod, the copper whip still attached, and held out my hand as I soared past the enemy. I shot a bolt of quatra right into his unsuspecting face.

I had but a moment to regain myself as he screamed in pure anguish. He foamed at the mouth, as if it were an attempt to distract me. I flung my hand back by my side, and tore it through the wind currents under my body. I tried desperately to grind the gusts below me to a halt, but in my haste, I did it unevenly.

The pressure differentials were in whack. My body twisted and spun, and I totally lost control. I flailed my limbs, pushing air in any-which direction to try and gain stabilisation. I crashed into the floor shoulder first, narrowly missing the machines on my right. Once on the floor, I blasted air to bring myself to a halt, and sprung up. My shoulder hurt, but not nearly as much as taking a pillar of earth to the gut. This was on the level of armour bruising, not denting. I needed to get up and help.

Over the machines, I could see Vestas, now desperate, joining the fray. He climbed down from the mezzanine – making sure to use the safety ladder.

This will be my last chance. I thought. *I don't think we can win a three-on-two against Vestas and Lion's Foot.*

I looked for high ground. I'd crumbled most of the rows of shelving now, through my *genius* use of my abilities. One end was left standing, looking over the battle taking place between Zamelle, Genive and *Lion's Foot.*

Could be risky getting there. I analysed. *But it's my only chance.* I ran, faster than I thought possible. My feet lightly tapped against the concrete. I tried not to draw attention – I needed *Lion's Foot* to be distracted by Zamelle and Genive.

I leapt onto the remaining shelf. Fire roared behind me. The crack of wood was drowned out, but the smack of my metal hands on the metal structure was distinct. I was sure that *Lion's Foot* would at least turn to the crashing sound, but he stayed engrossed. *Good.* In the distance, Vestas dropped to the floor, and began to run. I had no time.

I launched myself as high as I could, leaping twice up the structure, almost to the top. *High enough is good enough.* I reasoned. *Lion's Foot* was facing away from me, his neck exposed. I had the perfect opportunity to strike on a shot that he couldn't redirect – a tackle to the neck. A shot straight from my hand to his neck would have to be unstoppable – entirely unannounced and too close to the thread to redirect. Without thinking, I sprung from the shelf. The final shove of my jump forced it to crack and squeal. Behind me, it fell. *Last chance, buddy.*

Again, I controlled the air around my body. Without the proper height, I didn't gain as much speed as I would have liked. In fact, it became clear that I wouldn't make it all the way to him at all. I panicked. Vestas yelled, to warn *Lion's Foot,* and I panicked harder.

Desperately, I released a good portion of my grip on the air. I plummeted. *Lion's Foot* half glanced in a free second. I couldn't be sure if he'd seen me. I had to make this perfect.

Inches from the ground, at bullet speed, I tore at the air over my body. I pulled up violently, and pushed off the ground with a blast from my feet. From the bottom of my swoop, I shot off like a jet, pounding towards the enemy. I held my hand out. I opened my claws, ready to grab at his neck. Honing in with insane speed, I tensed for impact.

His hand flung itself up to meet mine perfectly. In a millisecond, the Bronze Suneva's meaty paw had wrapped itself around my wrist. I fired my bolt of quatra but it missed as my hand was jerked, instead nailing Zamelle straight in the face.

The Bronze Suneva's feet clung to the solid ground. His hand wrenched onto my wrist tightly. My velocity was whipped out of my control, and I wound in a circle around his head, hanging off my lip arm, until he released me like a hammer throw. My body rammed into Genive. I knocked her hard into the floor, and there was a quatra bolt waiting for each of us as we skidded to a halt. I was so dazed, that I couldn't be sure who had fired it. Celeste threw me off her. I rolled lazily away.

"Ha!" Vestas shrieked. Without quatra, I couldn't see the joy in his smile. He clapped his hands together, trying to stop himself from jumping around. "*Lion's Foot*, you're the best agent Hesslik ever sent to me." He patted the giant, bronze Suneva with the stern face. *Lion's Foot* did not respond.

Vestas ran over to us. He had cuffs on his arms, taken from the mezzanine most likely, and prepared to put them on us. Celeste jumped up to run, but she paused when he aimed his staff at her.

"This will hurt *way* more without the armour, darling." Vestas warned. "I'd choose carefully."

Celeste paused, then grabbed my arm to pull me up. Vestas' eyes narrowed. He channelled his energy, drawing on it from his thread. I could see sparks beginning to spit from the edge of his golden axe.

An iron chain wrapped around his waist. *Lion's Foot* pulled on it hard, ripping the scientist off his feet and nailing him to the ground. The bronze Suneva put his bulky, metal knee down on Vestas, wrapped his monstrous hand around the scientist's neck, and fired a bolt of quatra. Immediately, Vestas armour shattered off his body. He yelled in surprise, but unsurprisingly, couldn't move from under the great force of the Bronze Suneva.

"Unkind regards, Vestas." *Lion's Foot* said to the man — middle aged and skinny, with a bad taste in shirts. "Come on." He said to Natalie, Celeste and I. "We're getting out of here."

"What do you mean *we*?" Natalie and Vestas burst in unison. They glared at each other with red faces.

"You're abandoning me *and* taking Iva Argol? That's just greedy." Vestas sulked, still under the mighty, metal shoe of *Lion's Foot*. *Lion's Foot* huffed, dismembered his chain, and used its linkages to bolt Vestas into the ground.

"Firstly, you were planning to take my thread, so I'm not staying here. Secondly, I'm not *taking* anybody, and I'm not *selling* them either." He was adamant. His tone was so innocently defensive, that it seemed impossible that he was lying.

"I wasn't going to take your thread." Vestas insisted.

"I'm a Suneva of earth. I can hear your conversations through the floor."

Vestas quickly shut up. The red in his face turned from rage to embarrassment.

"Excuse me, but what makes you think that *we're* going with *you?*" Natalie spat. Her anger was palpable. Her hands shook in rage, as she found herself powerless against a Suneva of earth.

"Not to be funny…" The American Suneva said, slamming his palm downwards. The concrete blocking the door sunk back into the ground. "…but I don't know how you expected to get out of here without me."

"Oh, no you don't." Natalie held a finger to his face. Fear crossed his eyes. "That's not how this works. You explain yourself this instant."

He gulped at the stern demand. There was a ruckus behind us, and the last Suneva – the one I hadn't bothered to defeat, ran from between the flames in the aisle. Like a hero, spear pointed, they were ready to win the day. *Lion's Foot* stomped his foot down and shoved his hand upwards. A pillar of earth rocketed into their side, knocking them across the floor. He fired a bolt of quatra, which successfully neutralised them. *Lion's Foot* turned back to us, and let his armour recess. His face was more frazzled than it appeared before.

"Look, I can't explain here. Take me somewhere private, so we can talk."

"Sure, so you can abduct her…" Natalie pointed to Celeste. Celeste's face filled with offence.

"That's Celeste Bouvé, *Genive*, not Iva Argol. I know that. I'm not here for money." He pleaded. He was genuine, I was certain of it, but Natalie berated him further.

"How did you know that?" Natalie growled.

"Because I've been following you!" He pleaded desperately, then covered his mouth at the admission of his actions. "I mean, you knew that. You *had* to have known that."

"How much more do you know?" Natalie grunted.

"Enough." He guiltily admitted. "But I can't say anything here, or I'll put us in danger. Please, take me somewhere to explain."

"Boy, you're already in deep danger." Vestas said.

"Shut up, Vestas!" Natalie yelled. Silence fell. Her teeth were bared.

"Look, Natalie, we have to move quickly, before everybody comes back online." I pleaded with her. Her head snapped around to me, her rage following with it.

"You trust him?" She asked me.

"Yes, I do." I said. "If he wanted to take us, he would have overpowered us by now. He gave me good advice yesterday, and he saved our asses just now."

Natalie squinted, she turned to Celeste.

"I trust him too." Celeste admitted loudly, before Natalie could ask. "His aura is pure."

"You trust him, but you didn't trust James or me enough to come back and save him?" She asked, her voice quiet but laced with scorn. Celeste blushed.

"His aura is good, Natalie. I've been fooled before, but he is genuine right now. Your soul is genuine. So is James'. That's why I had to come back. You were never lying."

Natalie stared at the blonde-haired, American boy. Her eyes were fire, fuelled by a hatred losing its bearing. She growled, and gave up.

"Fine." She whispered, and ran towards the door. *Lion's Foot* ran past her, holding the door open for us. She didn't acknowledge him as she left. He closed to door behind us and raised the asphalt into it.

As he turned, Natalie pushed both he and I up against the fence. The American boy's arms flung into the air, his face was horrified.

"You." She said to me. "Where are we going?"

"The dog park!" I squeaked. It was near, private enough, and neither of our houses.

"You." She said to the American Boy. "What's your name."

"Chad Rogers – *Ferrad*…ma'am." He said.

"Have you got an ID?" She asked.

"What?" He burst. His face flushed white. "I…I don't have an ID…"

"Not even a passport?" She squinted.

"No…I never gave Hesslik my real name. The Empire doesn't know who I am."

"Very suspect, *Chad*." Natalie huffed. "But good, I guess…" She turned to me. "Let's go."

We each found our bikes, and reconvened at the top of the hill. I led the pack off, up the trail, to the dog park. The park's view overlooked the warehouse, the train line, and the neighbourhood. It was a sea of lights sprinkled onto a black canvas. In the distance, the flashing lights of a plane made up for the lack of stars in the dead sky. The moon hung low, and orange on the horizon.

We each took a seat in the secrecy of the spinning pod. Chad told his story.

Episode 4

Short Stories of Bravery

Chapter 23
The Man Who Roamed the Woods

Chad Rogers had the rising suspicion that Hesslik was trying to see to his demise.

The feeling boiled in his stomach, fermenting, gnawing at his mind for weeks, ever since he'd finished his mission in Manchester.

It had been a death mission, he was sure. Hesslik had sent him – his personal agent of investigation, the feared *Lion's Foot* – into the heart of danger. A software engineer and ally of the Empire, a Suneva of *kidin* and copper powers, was in trouble with the Argols.

Lion's Foot had a reputation. He was an agent of Boekidin's, before rising in rank. His work was good. Initially, his skill as a *Raduk* had startled his foes. Nobody had fought a *Raduk* in so long – he tore through enemies, catching all off guard. Those who survived to crawl back to their bosses spread the word of a Suneva in shining bronze, who struck with the power of his heavy chain.

Chad's connection to the earth also granted more subtle skills. Nobody had seen a *Raduk* in action for many years – nobody would know that he could hear conversations through the floor, from half a mile away.

Even though word of *Lion's Foot* spread, it would not help those who stood in Hesslik's path. To be faced with *Lion's Foot*, to have the hulking mass of earth-flinging Suneva find you in the night, was not only to be an enemy of the Empire, but a personal enemy of *Fara Hesslik* himself.

Still, all of the rumours in the world, all of the intelligence Chad could gather from afar, all of the fear he could instil, would not help him against the wave he faced in Manchester.

The Argols weren't more numerous than he could handle, but they were too well placed. They knew the exits and entrances of the building, they knew where to trap him, and they knew how he would fight. Chad was an intelligence officer, he did not think it unreasonable that they'd done their research, and he knew it would be thorough. But to corner him so perfectly? To expect his entrance just at the right time? *No*, they'd had to have had an Empire source. As Chad stood on the third floor of an office, no earth around him, witnessing the left leg of his *alis* sheared off at the knee by a great, flaming hatchet, he *knew* he'd been set up.

More condemning – Hesslik had been *surprised* to see *Lion's Foot* return. A hint of frustration came to his voice at the thought that his loyal ally, the software engineer, had survived the attack. The *Lion's Foot* in Chad could read the man.

He had a plan. Chad realised, using his Suneva connections to read the man's expression through his helmet. Hesslik was composed, but like all men, he would shake more when anxious. Chad could feel it through the earth. *He needed me and the engineer dead, and he needed it to look like an accident.*

Hesslik had been quick then to send Chad to Melbourne – to keep him busy gathering information. Hesslik had repaired the leg of Chad's *alis*, Ferrad, using his new limb technology.

When Chad reached the airport in Melbourne, he found himself consumed by thoughts of betrayal.

He thought back to when he had first found Hesslik – how different his life had been then. He'd just turned seventeen, having completed six months of hiking through the wilderness from his small home town in Oregon, to the railyard in Santa Fe.

The reason for Chad's departure was brash, but necessary. He'd grown up in a town in the centre of Oregon – nothing more than a strip of shops sandwiched between a lake, a forest, and a mountain. The valley of his hometown was lush, and through it ran a creek, which took the mountain sleet to the wide lake and the quarry.

His best friend growing up was a girl named Stacy. She was sweet, and cared for him deeply. Her father, the sheriff of the town, loomed over her like a thick shadow. When they played, the sheriff would always watch in the distance Disapproving.

Chad remembered the day which marked the turning point in their relationship. He and Stacy played by the creek on a freezing day of early spring. Chunks of brown and grey ice churned in the flurry of the storming waters. The thickly-scrubbed embankments crumbled underneath Chad as they played, and he fell in. A log burst from under the ice and delivered a dazing uppercut to his jaw. When he woke, the shadow of Stacy's father, Mr. Johnson loomed over him. Gun in hand, he blocked the sun. But he had saved him.

Stacy became popular, Chad did not, and as the seed of constant attention rotted at the empathy in her brain, their relationship fell apart. She was friends with his tormentors, and did not stop them – specifically Jimmy Nevis – from delivering their punishment.

This made it ever more surprising when Chad – the unpopular football lineman - got her invite to prom in junior year. He accepted the offer straight away, but was nervous. Had she changed, now?

The night came, and he strode over the creek, through the dense, twilight woods to her house. Both of their houses backed onto the forest, and through the thick woods was the fastest route between them.

Chad clambered his way over the low stone wall, and made his way around her pool, onto her deck, and to her back door. Chad wore his finest suit of charcoal grey, with an electric blue tie. Butterflies jittered in his stomach, but he found the confidence and composure to knock.

The door opened, and Stacy stood there in her electric blue dress, absolutely beautiful. Every day which he'd allowed himself to be smitten by her, despite her ignorance of him, had led to this. He approached the door, ready to hug her hello, when foreign hands grabbed her by the waist – Jimmy Nevis, from inside, waiting. Jimmy held her in full embrace and they kissed passionately, right there, in front of him.

Butterflies turned to lead in Chad's stomach. Joy sated to incomprehension. He caught Stacy's glance, and saw her malicious *joy* in the situation. Happiness, *evil happiness*, burned in her eyes.

Hands grabbed Chad – he usually could not be snuck upon when on the ground, but he was on a wooden deck – and hoisted him. Three sets, three boys, swung him into the air. Jimmy pulled out a camera.

A pile of dog shit, a massive puddle of mud, piss, spit, maybe? Chad thought as he fell, sure that he was to be launched into the most embarrassing situation of his life. All pretence of disappointment and heartbreak was suspended as his body tumbled.

He fell past the floor. He fell through the ground, and then felt a cold embrace. Back first, in his finest suit, with his hair done, Chad was consumed by the icy pool water. Like a stone, he sank.

Chad couldn't swim in the best of times. His mind fell into disarray, trying to contort his limbs to paddle upwards. The water numbed him wholly. The jacket constricted him boundlessly. His arms could be no use. Nobody came to help him. No air was in his lungs to lift him.

He pushed off the ground, and found that hands held him under the surface. The lead of despair in his stomach, Chad found, was not lead at all. It was a pit of charcoals, who now had a match struck to them. The intense fire of rage boiled in his guts. Water ran hot off his skin. His eyes shot red.

His mind wandered past survival, past the *need* the stay alive, and into the *need* the inflict revenge. Chad was broken, and these boys would be sorry.

He leaped off the bottom of the pool, and reached for the hands who held him down. He clawed at them, kicked off the wall, and dragged the boys in. Chad flailed off them, using their bodies as a solid platform to lift himself into the air, and breathe.

He sucked in a breath. The air was cold. A foot soared towards him, just as he comprehended the world, and kicked him in the head. Fire came to sooth the pain, he felt nothing. He grinned.

Chad's fingers slipped into the earth, and he felt that connection he'd always had. The ground was powerful. When he was away from it, he was weak, but with it at his fingertips, he was in an infinite position to fight for his freedom. He tore himself from the cold water, and rolled over the earth. Another boot hit him, but Chad tossed the feeling aside and stood tall.

The earth was still at his fingertips. In his state of pure, molten emotion – having its hot lava slosh through his systems – he felt the first inkling of his place in the world.

Jimmy lined up a punch. Chad gripped at the dirt – not touching it, but feeling as if the power of the ground was in his palm – and heaved upwards. A clumsy shaft of earth shot up and reamed Jimmy in the stomach. He doubled over, and slumped backwards.

Behind Chad, the two boys in the water clawed at the pool's edge. Their eyes spat fire, and they tossed themselves to dry land, intent on their own revenge. Chad yanked at the earth again, and gave it motion. Clumps of wet clay smashed each boy in the face, and they were projected into the pool. Blood spurted from one of the boy's noses.

Stacy stood, horrified, Jimmy's camera in hand, against the outside wall of her house. Her maniacal triumph had been replaced by fear. She scooted across the flowerbed, palming for the door. Chad, drunk on his own power, did not care.

The earth was at his command, just like he felt it always should have been. He raised a pillar of earth by her feet. It rose up to Stacy's neck, cupping it and lifting her up by it. She struggled for breath, clawing at the rock.

Chad was breathing heavily, simultaneously gasping for air and growling. His brain buzzed, too hyped on adrenaline, too obsessed with pure rage and revenge to think of words. All that came to him were concepts – deception, hatred, embarrassment, depression, Stacy's smug attitude, being taken advantage of. There weren't any possible sentences he could put together to describe the culmination of his feelings.

Stacy's skin turned blue. Her throat rasped. Her hands clawed, like a trapped mouse. Her neck was being crushed against the wall, and when Chad checked, his hand was still commanding the dirt to do it. He took a moment to look around. A section of the pool had been stained pink from a boy's broken nose. Jimmy had doubled over himself – not in any state to stand up. Another boy flopped onto the side of the pool, contempt with existence. Chad heard a car screech on the dusty track into Stacy's driveway, on the other side of the house.

Horror rocked his body. He'd assaulted four people today, with no witnesses to defend that they almost drowned him, and that it was self-defence. Even then, he understood that his actions couldn't be justified. The lava of his stomach diffused into his veins. Hot fear flushed his head. Images of his future in prison swam in his mind's eye.

He kicked the pillar of dirt which held Stacy to the wall by her neck. She collapsed onto the floor, and heaved for breath.

"You lost me today." Chad said, as if it meant anything to her. He wanted to help her, but they were both past that now. "You lost the only person who cared about you…"

He heard Stacy's father's footsteps as he disembarked from his vehicle. There was no way he could explain himself out of this one. There was no way that this story wouldn't spread regardless. In such a religious town, full of good, God-fearing, Christian families, he'd be burned at the stake if it was legal. Chad could command the earth. This – whatever he had just done, which he hadn't for a second comprehended or understood – was some serious Witchcraft. There was only one option for him.

Chad sprinted into the forest, and he never looked back.

The memory was painful for him, but that was why he left, he had discovered who he was. Lost, scared, and on the cusp of taking his own life a week later, he met the man who truly saved him. An old man, a *Liktas*, named *Vasilli Dimos*, from the city of Sparta. He was the man who took Chad to Hesslik.

They walked from Oregon to Santa-Fe, through the harsh wilderness. Vasilli taught Chad how to be one with the land, and the earth, by trekking him barefoot across it. He taught Chad of the soul, and spirituality, and of his place in the cosmos. He taught Chad to draw his *shath* – his Suneva weapon – a gleaming, silver battle-axe.

On their journey, they were welcomed into Native reservations, where Chad learned of the Native Suneva, and their understanding of the soul.

The Vasilli left him outside an old engine shed, waiting for an answer by the door. Chad held fondly the ancient man's last words to him.

"Take with you the knowledge of the earth. Strong, wilful and decisive. Rock depends, but is not dependant. Rock is strong, but not defined by its strength. Rock is great, but only by commanding greatness. Go into this world like the ground you control."

Moments later he met Hesslik and Boekidin.

Hesslik beamed at the sight of him. Chad told his story – a fake, but close enough story, with a fake name – as instructed by Vasilli. Hesslik leaped at the opportunity to tell Chad that his Empire was for Suneva like themselves – those who discovered powers beyond their comprehension and needed somewhere to turn.

Somewhere to be safe without judgement.

Chad adored the idea, and he thought Hesslik fabulous for making it a reality. Hesslik was keen on him too, and assigned him to Boekidin, to be an investigatory Agent under the name of *Lion's Foot*.

Chad cringed at the memory as he made his way to the Melbourne base of operations. *Hesslik is trying to kill me.* He couldn't understand why, and although his evidence was circumstantial at best, he'd done some further research of his own. Hesslik's personal operatives didn't last more than four months, usually. Hesslik made sure they disappeared without a trail. Chad had lasted one and a half years as *Lion's Foot*. He was well beyond the usual expiry. He shuddered.

Chad's next clue was the damning mission he'd received. He played it again as rolled up to the gates of the factory on his steel horse. The bike purred beneath his legs, rumbling as a beast. He put his headphones in.

"*Lion's Foot*, this is your mission." Hesslik's voice crackled through the half-dead earphone from the little black device – the one he'd handed me to use as a clock. "*Ms Umbrella* will deal with the Argols and assist Vestas. Vestas has been made aware of their arrangement. Your mission is of far greater importance to the success of the Empire. Keep this classified, as always.

"The Great Gathering of our nation is near in the future. To convince all Suneva of our nation's purpose and importance, we will need to have actions beyond our manifesto.

"There are stories, cornerstones of western Suneva history, about the three Legendary Suneva, of Teleportation, Time, and Gravity. In my library of Suneva texts, in Vestas' office in Melbourne, you can find books on them and how to find them. Whether you personally believe in the stories is irrelevant. You will find them.

"Not, however, without help. I have located three Suneva in Melbourne who will help you to form a diverse, fighting team. They are *Maiki*, the only discovered *kiin* of recent; *Zamelle* of *welle*, from the formidable *Menas* family, and *Genive*, of *ivaer*, a girl of a blue flame.

"Find these Suneva, *Lion's Foot*, and with them locate the *Nefarisos*. That is your mission."

It was a ridiculous mission, he realised. He'd been given nothing more than the location of the Hesslik's Library and Lab, yet was tasked with finding three specific Suneva in a whole city? Beyond that, they then had to find three specific Suneva across the whole globe, who may or may not exist, with absolutely no clues. It was a goose chase. He knew he was being played.

Vestas was all too happy to see Chad when he arrived. Vestas was a smart man, but was also an idiot, Chad discerned. Vestas' over-the-top fake enthusiasm for *Lion's*

Foot couldn't be missed – even without feeling the Suneva's anxiety through the ground.

Vestas set Chad to a task immediately, pairing him with *Ms Umbrella*, an operative with whom he had worked many times. They were to spy on some small time Argols. Vestas was quick to make a phone call after handing Chad this mission, outside in the carpark, for privacy. Chad delayed putting his things away, to spy on the scientist.

Chad hid behind the forklift next to the roller door. It was the only cover between him and Vestas. He wouldn't need to see Vestas, however, to eavesdrop. Instead, he tore off his shoes, and mashed his bare palms and soles into the asphalt. It was the height of summer heat – his skin screamed at him – but he subdued the pain. He listened.

"He's arrived." Vestas said into the phone. The clacks of his metal heels blasted into the asphalt atop his voice. Luckily for Chad, listening with hands was different than listening with ears. The loud sounds weren't jarring – they just covered up the soft ones.

"Yes," Vestas answered. "And I'd like you to tell me what you have in mind with him, Hesslik!" Vestas seemed stressed. Chad had missed Hesslik's opener. He concentrated harder, until he could just hear Hesslik's voice through the ground.

"He's a good agent, Vestas, the best I've ever had." Hesslik told him. Chad stiffened up, surprised. "He lasted well beyond what I expected. Most agents get shut down early on when they're eventually captured. Not this one."

"Yes." Vestas said, impatiently. "But that doesn't outline why you sent him here, to me. I mean…"

"I need you to eliminate his thread." Hesslik cut the scientist off. Chad's eyes bulged, he tried not to gasp.

"Hesslik…" Vestas trailed. "I appreciate the offer to have a test subject, but your personal agent?"

"He knows too much, Vestas." Hesslik said. "They all get to know too much. They talk with Argols, they eavesdrop on conspirators and traitors. After a while, my agents can't be trusted. He's not jaded, like the others, but he soon will be. It's a demanding job, he did it well, but now he must be stopped before he intervenes."

"Right…" Vestas sighed. "Well, I understand that – but don't you think it *imprudent* to send a potential conspirator into Argol controlled Melbourne?"

"Not at all." Hesslik said. "The Argols cut off his leg. I know he hates them. He will help you bring all of the big players in. He will be very effective at it.

"*But…*" Hesslik warned, anticipating Vestas' response. "If you even get the *hint* of betrayal from him, you eliminate his thread. Understood?"

"Understood, *mina Fara.*" Vestas nodded.

"But do leave him be until I visit. I'm going to be running a recruitment and community survey soon. I'd like to see him in action one last time."

"Sure thing." Vestas said. He was nervous now – Chad could feel it through the ground. He could also feel his own heart, drowning out all else in his rage and disappointment.

He'd been had. He'd done the man's dirty work for one and a half years, and now his payment would be thread removal, rather than his likely numerous planned deaths? It was obscene.

No, Hesslik couldn't get away with this – Chad decided. The Empire was good, and it stood for promising ideals, but Hesslik was immoral – mad even. He couldn't win. Chad would stop him. He turned to the device in his pocket, with Hesslik's instructions. The mission might have been a goose chase, but it outlined Hesslik's demise if done against him. Find the Suneva, find the Legendaries, and use them to revolt against the leader. If Hesslik believed that people would follow the Legendaries, then surely it was true.

Ferrad, as *Lion's Foot*, did his work, wrangling Argols alongside *Ms Umbrella*, as Vestas had prescribed. In his free time, Chad snuck through the compound library, trying to find texts about the Legendaries – but his search wasn't very fruitful. Even the most mundane aspect of the mission was a goose-chase.

Soon after Hesslik and Boekidin came to town, Chad disregarded Vestas' missions, instead, choosing to follow the *Fara* and *Faraku* in their recruitment tasks. He huddled down by the foundations of Mr. Finneck's old house on the day I had been sitting the couch inside with them.

Maiki, Chad heard Hesslik address me – the first of the Suneva on the list. Hesslik was already gathering the group, it could be too late to act. Still, if Chad was seen out of line this early on, Vestas would have his thread. He had to stay quiet, but he did follow me home.

He followed me to school the next day too, where he happened upon a Suneva he could track. Their wide orange trail, like a richly decorated boulevard to the thread, was a welcome sensation. He could now follow more easily, and monitor us.

The new orange trail, combined with the frail sensation of my Suneva abilities, led Chad to Finneck's house a second time, when Natalie discovered her identity, and to David's house on the night of our date. Once he caught the name of Genive, he knew he'd struck gold – he had found Maiki, Zamelle and Genive. He didn't believe in destiny particularly – it did not call to him – but he had found us, and that was enough. He left a note for us which we would never see.

News of the reappearance of *Iva Argol* spread like wildfire through the compound. *Ms Umbrella* told of how the girl claimed to not be the Argol daughter, and how it was a blatant lie. After *Ms Umbrella* lost her powers, Chad was recruited to chase the supposed Argol daughter. Instead, he chose to ignore the mission. He tracked us during the days, to check that we were safe, not yet choosing to openly betray Vestas, but stumbled upon Vestas' ambush party.

He would have been called on such a mission, but was missing from the scene. Vestas would be suspicious of him, which meant he was on limited time. He helped at the battle after I'd collapsed, acting from a distance, shifting mud to favour Zamelle and Genive. Then, he made his story to Vestas, that he'd gone interrogating local Argols to see if the stories of Iva were true. Vestas bought the lie, but it would only be a matter of time. Chad needed to ditch soon and come to us – but he still didn't have the book he needed to find.

Unfortunately, we came to him first. Chad was caught between two forces – if he explicitly helped us in our battle to escape, Vestas would know he was sabotaging the mission, and he couldn't keep looking for clues in the library. If, however, he caught one of us, the rest would come back, and he would have one last chance to get the clue Hesslik wanted him to find.

Chad captured me, and bided his time. He found his information in the library, a single innocuous paragraph of text with a picture, amongst a whole wall of books. The time was right. Zamelle and Genive returned to rescue me. Zamelle was captured, but without the three of us present, he couldn't give up his guise in front of Vestas – not if he wanted to make it out of that room with his thread. In the last second – the moment he was preparing to act, Genive and I broke through the door.

Chad chased us, following commands. If he helped us even now, we would all have to run, and Vestas' crew could still give chase. He played his cards as an agent, and chose to keep his guise to eliminate every thread in the room. A strategy which proved effective at getting us out safely, but which didn't prove his trustworthiness.

***

"So, there's a Great Gathering then? And it's actually happening?" I asked him.

"There should be." He said. He smiled whenever he spoke, as if he had nothing to be sad about. This confused me.

"Do you know about Hesslik's plan for the gathering?" I asked, and looked to Celeste and Natalie. The cogs turned in their heads, and their eyes fell wide open.

"Why are you all looking like that?" He asked. "What do you know?"

"Hesslik is going to remove all of the threads at the gathering." I said.

"What?" Chad gasped.

"I saw it in a vision. He's having Vestas build a giant electrical transmitter. Vestas thinks it's free-energy, but he's going to put the removal equation into it, and cut all of the threads at once."

Chad's eyes narrowed. His breath was hard, and scornful. The ground shifted under my ass.

"He has the technology for it." He said, after a pause. "Right now, I wouldn't put anything past him – but did you catch why?"

"He can't fix the Suneva's problems. He doesn't think his society will work."

"That's cowardly." Chad huffed. "I believed in his Empire – I still do. It would work."

"Not everybody holds that view." Celeste said. "There's opposition – and Hesslik certainly isn't doing himself any favours by hiring *agents* and having an underground information ring."

"Your story is fine, Chad." Natalie added, jumping over Celeste's sentiment. "But it's too perfect. How do we know that you abandoned Hesslik? How do we know that you're not just doing as he told you right now? I don't trust Vestas' or Hesslik's word that you're a deserter."

"I guess you don't know." Chad replied. "You'll just need to trust me on that. I hope that you can trust me – although, the mechanical Suneva leg should give me some points, right?"

Natalie huffed, her arms crossed.

"Maybe if you'd saved us before you'd defeated us, I'd be more forgiving." She said, and turned away. Chad frowned in his disappointment, like a puppy who was rejected by a toddler. It was a look of genuine disappointment in his failure to please. I smiled at the face, like you would to a sad puppy. He smiled back.

"So, mate…" His eyes lit up at my use of the phrase. "…when did you say this gathering was?"

"Next June, although I don't know where."

"A year and a half to gather three Legendaries, it can't be that hard." I smiled. Celeste did not share my optimism.

"They're mythical, James." She said. "More than half of all Suneva don't believe that they exist. I don't even see why they're important. You said it yourself, Chad, you'd been fooled into finding them."

"I believe that we'll find them." Chad smiled. "This might be the only time in my life that I've felt the push of destiny, and maybe that means something."

"But why should we care about them?" Celeste asked again.

"Because if Hesslik can prove that figures of myth live among us – if destiny can guide him to find three Suneva so hidden that their existence is refuted – he must be one of the most powerful, destined Suneva on earth. That would make him *the* destined leader."

"So, finding them first would give us legitimacy over him?" I asked.

"Absolutely." Chad nodded. "Although, there's more to it that I've found. They're influential beyond the fact of their existence. I've got a stolen scripture which outlies it all."

"This plan depends on the people being swayed by impressive acts of destiny." Celeste huffed, continuing through my hurry.

"Weirdly, I think that gives it merit." Natalie chimed in, finally. She turned into the circle. "It's being suggested by a past loyalist to Hesslik, and somebody who believed in the Empire. *If* your story is true, Chad, and *if* the Legendaries would sway you, then that's all we need. We only need to turn Hesslik's supporters away from him."

Chad beamed to Natalie's approval, struggling to keep his cheeks from shining rosy. Natalie was still unimpressed with the whole situation. Her arms remained tightly crossed.

"We'd better get to work then." I said. "We've got to beat Hesslik to them to make this happen."

Chapter 24
The Boardroom

Vestas sat in his chair, in the castle of the old Suneva fortress. Hundreds of years ago, this is where Olomb had gathered and discussed war strategies. Even further back, it was where Kuvalik defended against foreign invaders, in the siege of the grand Electric Throne, and won in a victory so senselessly coincidental, that it seemed to prove destiny for anybody who did not yet believe.

Vestas did not believe.

Vestas was a man of science, and a man of his word. Hesslik had ordered him to remove the threads of the three dissenters, finally, to allow him to complete his studies on thread removal, and to eliminate their threat. He had been so close, too, but it was just his luck that the saboteur *Lion's Foot* was one of the wrong-doers.

I never should have let him near them. Vestas scrunched at one of his papers. He looked at it, and upon realising its importance to his coming presentation, lay it on the table and ironed it flat with him palm. He glanced around the room for onlookers as he did so, and once satisfied that nobody had seen his egregious lack of judgement and disrespect for science, he grinned.

The door to the boardroom opened. Vestas sat up like lightning, immediately swivelling his chair to sit tall at attention. Boekidin came through the door first – his large, metal sheeted wings collapsing into his back so that he could fit in. He did not expand them once through the constricting doorway. He strolled to take a seat, and stared at Vestas.

Boekidin made Vestas uncomfortable, he had decided after a few years of working with the Suneva. His beady pink eyes were emotionless, and there were no discernible facial features to be sensed under that raven-like helmet. Plus, the large, plate wings were enough to make anybody squirm. He sneered at the sight of Boekidin, and caught a smile on the black Suneva's bird face that he felt he must have imagined.

Vestas was about to slouch down again, to shuffle through his papers, when Hesslik entered, unannounced. Now he shot up to attention, more surprised than before. He bowed his head to Hesslik, and Hesslik did the same back. Hesslik was smiling, so Vestas relaxed, if only a little bit.

Hesslik quickly took his seat at the head of the long table. These executive meetings were too small for the table they had been appointed, Vestas always noted. Sure, there was room for guest speakers, but they rarely had a guest speaker. Perhaps Olomb's cabinet was bigger, he concluded.

There was a seat reserved for himself, *Na Naristo* – the head of research. There was a seat for Boekidin, *Na Nassaserman* – literally translating to the finder of secrets, but known as the investigatory head. There was the seat of *Na Faraku* - the right-hand man, also filled by Boekidin. There was *Na Fara*, clearly Hesslik. Since Muhrakiin's death, and Lilawelle's disappearance from the committee, the seats of ethical supervisor and spiritual leader were missing. An empty ethical supervisor chair irked Vestas. He worried that without somebody to appoint the rules, their vision of disabling the threads of wrong-doers could be crushed.

Into the room, after Hesslik, came a group of about ten-or-so Suneva, all in armour, like Vestas, Boekidin, and Hesslik, who occupied the empty chairs and standing room. They held important sub-committee positions. The level of bureaucracy made Vestas dizzy – although maybe his dizziness came from the nerves he was feeling. He took a deep breath.

"Right," Hesslik said. "Suneva. *Tano a Tona* of *Na Faras Nas Suns*. Let's get this underway without formalities, shall we?" There was a hushed agreeance, a rumbling gurgle of slack-lipped teenagers, which slipped across the room. Hesslik took this as his cue to continue. "There are many things to get through today, firstly, Vestas: How has everything been in Melbourne, and with your research?"

Vestas took in a sharp breath. He had not expected to be called up first. His lip quivered, but he managed to fold it into a grin. He straightened his papers, and sat tall.

"Yes, well, research has been going well." He started weakly. Hesslik smiled. "The most exciting revelation is that I'm now certain of the efficacy of my thread-removal equation."

"Really?" Hesslik marvelled. "How so?"

"We've had a steady stream of participants of all forms to gain quatra data off. The results have concluded that no matter how different we may *perceive* each other's threads to be, Suneva, as a whole, are very homogenous. At the end of the day, the noted differences in the thread qualifier wave were not significant, even for the most eccentric of threads."

"This is great stuff, really." Hesslik said. "Now we've got a blanket-effective last stand punishment for wrong doers."

"Yes, it is exciting." Vestas relaxed. Hesslik looked away, back to his papers, and Vestas was almost certain that he would be asked no further questions. He grinned, and leaned back in his chair.

"And what of *Iva Argol?*" Hesslik asked. Vestas' eye twitched. "Presenting her to Naxaer Argol would do wonders for relations…"

"Ha, yes…" Vestas coughed. "Do you remember the friends of hers I told you about?"

"Zamelle and Maiki?" Hesslik asked. "It's a shame that they chose to help her. I trust that you managed to remove their threads, as you *did* ask me for such permissions." Hesslik tapped his fingers. Vestas gulped.

"I did ask for permission, but they still have their threads." Vestas stumbled, "That agent of yours, *Lion's Foot*, turned traitorous. He'd just finished beating the three of them into the ground when he turned on me, and took them off. I have no idea what they're planning now, but the four of them are dangerous – to life and to our cause."

"If I'd have known *Iva Argol* was in town, I would not have sent a suspected fringe conspirator – no matter how unlikely it would seem that a fugitive girl would conspire with an agent of mine." Hesslik said. "I apologise. It's my fault that your plans fell through, and it is my fault that the Suneva people are now in danger. I will address this. It is not your burden."

"I…" Vestas struggled to say any words. An inordinately huge smile of relief plastered itself across his whole head. He could have sighed his armour away if he'd wanted to. He slumped in the chair, swirling his fingers in his fists. He laughed from his nose. "Thank you."

"Did you at least get to experiment on them? I heard that you had Maiki. It was a shame to order his thread removed. I saw potential in him."

"Yes, well, don't fear that my *Fara*, he's out there." Vestas groaned. "And yes, I did manage to get data from all three of the Suneva – even Iva, who I did not manage to apprehend at any time."

He reached into the bag by his side, from where he had produced his papers, and drew out a device, like the electric donut he used to read threads, but on the end of a radar gun.

"Another invention." He smiled. "Born from the fires of necessity."

"That's brilliant. You didn't tell me about this." Hesslik gleamed.

"In all truth my *Fara*, I had to have *something* positive to present today." Vestas joked – although, in his heart, he was not joking, and this meeting was going far better than he could have ever hoped. Those around the table joined in laughter.

"What did you find out about them?" Hesslik asked.

"A lot, although I'm not sure how useful it is." Vestas started. "Iva Argol is a producer of blue flames. Her thread appeared entirely normal, with an *energy density* and *quatra velocity* well within one standard deviation of the mean. Her ability to produce such high energy flames is, however, not due to any greater efficiency with the energy. *Faravaer's* physical efficiency of quatra conversion is almost identical, yet her flames are orange. There is something about the nature of creating flames which Iva Argol knows, that other *Ivaer* do not."

"An old family recipe, perhaps?" Hesslik joked. The board chuckled, then composed themselves.

"Nothing quantifiable by numbers, at least." Vestas noted. He looked back to his papers, his hands steady and confident now. He read off the rest of his findings.

"*Maiki* has an incredibly odd thread. I was able to study it in detail. Nothing about it was strong. His abilities appeared to be at a level under his peers, and his power was lacking. The quatra velocity of his connection to Omercronius is low, and his arbitrary connection, the one which we still do not know the purpose of, is low but steadily fluctuates. In other Suneva, similar patterns in the arbitrary connection lead to an abundance of hallucinations. He is no exception – having told me about an insane, treasonous daydream of his involving me.

"*Zamelle* is the most peculiar of the threads. Her quatra velocity, energy density, and connection strengths were all well above average. Her power level was high, and her efficiency within the average. This surprised me, as her thread has a significant distinctive leak. The cause is not inefficiency, but that she cannot use all of the quatra that her body demands. I have never seen such a quatra velocity in any Suneva, ever. There has been no comparable case."

"Is this worrying?" Hesslik asked.

"It might be." Vestas said. "More worrying for us, though, and not for her."

"Don't worry," Hesslik said, "This team of Suneva is within my sights, Vestas, especially since they have sabotaged an agent of mine."

"What will you do?" Vestas asked. The board leaned in, anticipating the answer of their great *Fara*. Hesslik held himself with confidence. He placed his palms upon the table, and grinned.

"For the moment, I will shift you around." He said. "You will bring your studies back here, to the Empire's Castle base. We will begin work on wireless power, away from the distractions of the Argols in Melbourne. Some Suneva missionaries will stay to guard the library."

Vestas sighed in relief. The labs in the castle of the *Electric Throne* were much nicer than those cramped quarters in Melbourne.

"Boekidin…" Hesslik summoned his chief intelligence officer. Boekidin's beaked head peaked up, his beady eyes locking with Hesslik's. "I would like you to follow this team of highly-dangerous fugitives. I want you to find out their plans, and stop them from completing them, by all means necessary…"

Hesslik reached under the table, and produced a set of black, hand-held devices. He pushed them across the smooth, waxed table to Boekidin. Boekidin palmed one of them. It was light, and sleek. On the top face there were two prongs, and on the front face was a red button. His long, black talon slipped, and he pushed the button. An arc of electricity cracked between the prongs. He dropped it atop the table.

"Do I make myself clear?" He asked.

"Yes." Boekidin said. Boekidin was a man of very few words. Vestas had the feeling that if Boekidin wanted to talk to you, he would never do it aloud.

"How is your quatra tracker?" Hesslik asked. Boekidin clipped the devices to a hook on his hip.

"Exceptional." Boekidin responded.

"And her illness?"

"Controlled."

"Excellent." Hesslik smiled. His fingers pented as his plan came together.

"Be prepared for anything, Boekidin." Hesslik warned. "I have a feeling that they've got bizarre plans in mind."

Boekidin dipped his head, and considered his mission. Vestas could see his wings rustling behind his back, as if they responded to his thoughts.

Vestas was finally at peace, now that the attention had been taken from him, and his presentation didn't end in failure. The rest of the meeting happened in the background of his mind, whilst he contemplated his own brilliance.

You've done it again, Vestas. He told himself. *Saving the world one boardroom meeting at a time.*

Chapter 25
The Power of an Angry Mother

I opened the front door of my house. It was late, at least eleven by now. The left-over smells from dinner and the aroma of home hit my nose, and I was transported into a peaceful world. My struggle was over, the emotional rollercoaster of the past month had come to a head, and resolved. There was more to come, but for now, there was home.

Errol barged through the back door. His body, a flying barrel propelled by legs, roared up the runner of the hallway. He circled me, leaping and yelping in the simple incomprehensibility of his emotions. I felt similarly to see him, after my long day, and slumped onto the floor to let him jump all over me. In truth, my legs had, in that moment, given up. My knees shook me to the ground, and I simply accepted the dog licking my face.

Mum poked her head around the corner from the lounge room. Our gaze locked, and her eyes burst wide open. Her cheeks went the red of mars, her eyelid twitched, steam poured from her eyes. I stood quickly and backed up to the door, and she marched upon me. Her footsteps were the strength of an army atop a single sole. The house rocked. I reached for the doorhandle with my hand, frantically flailing foolishly.

"James *Ivan* Grey." She growled. She addressed me by my full name, this was anything but deadly serious. I squirmed, becoming limp. Errol was confused. He didn't like the conflict, but didn't want to bark at Mum, who he was more loyal to. "Where the *fuck* have you been?"

My brain searched, buzzing, trying to comprehend an answer, some lie. All I could think of was everything that had *actually* happened. *What the hell could I have done for over twenty-four hours which is realistic?*

"I…I was, uh…" I started to smile. I wasn't happy, it just happened when I didn't believe my own machinations.

"Don't lie to me, not now." Mum ordered. I closed my mouth. "I called Natalie's Dad, and he said you all must have been long gone. I called Tom's Mum, I called David's house. Nobody has seen the three of you for a whole day."

"Oh sweet cheese…"

"Yeah, *sweet cheese* is about right, James." Mum mocked. "Now, where have you been?"

"I…" I searched for the way to word my answer. My brain was spaghetti, haphazardly slopped in cold Bolognese sauce. It did nothing, except command that blood be rushed to my face. Mum was standing close in front of me, taking up my whole view with her rage. I glanced around, behind Mum, trying to find Simone.

"Is Simone home?" I asked. Mum squeaked a sound like a record scratch. Her face shone her offence.

"Is Simone home?" She snapped. "That's not the question, and you don't get to ask about where anybody is. You've been going out all year James, to all of these parties, and sports, and study sessions, but now I can't trust any of it. We had a system, James. I trusted you because you've only ever told me the truth, and I gave you a lot of liberty to do whatever you wanted because of it…"

My face was uncomfortable, I was sweating. I tried to butt in, to raise a finger and make her stop talking so that I could explain myself, but Mum's rant kept rolling through.

"I mean, hell, I can't even believe you'd lie James, and about what? You're the straightest kid going around. You cried when a balloon hit you in the head. A cop tried talking to you when you were ten and you cried because you thought you were going to jail and confessed to stealing an ice cream from the freezer. I mean, *seriously*, what the hell do you have to hide from me? It's not drugs, I can be certain of that…"

"Mum, holy hell!" I burst. She squinted, crossed her arms, and prepared herself to listen. I exhaled, calmness coming through my body like cold water. "Do I get to talk now?" I asked.

"It's not drugs, is it?" Mum continued. "Because let me tell you, they're all useless."

"What? *No*, come on." I huffed. "Just tell me, is Simone home?"

"Why?" She enquired. She stepped closer in. I had no room to move or think.

"I'm a Suneva, Mum." I burst. "Simone will kill me. She will kill me, then burn the body, and throw it off a bridge somewhere if she found out. She wouldn't even be my friend."

Mum's face scrunched, her head tilted, and she stepped back.

"You've joined a gang? Is that what you're telling me?" She asked. Her mind was swimming, but no bells were ringing, nor gears turning.

"What? No…Suneva are types of people…"

"So, you're gay?" She asked. "That's fine, but you don't have to stay out for…"

"No, *cheese*, it's not a sexual orientation either." I flailed. Mum stepped back again, confused further. I tried to gather a sentence, something which didn't sound ridiculous, but the only thought I could conjure was that I had soul-based elemental powers – and that was purely ludicrous.

"Do you remember the *Argols*?" I asked Mum.

"So, it *is* a gang…" She made a connection.

"No, I didn't join a gang." I repeated. "The Argols are Suneva. Suneva are people with…well…*elemental, soul-based powers*." I sighed just saying it. I looked at Mum, with guilty, stupid eyes. She smirked, then rubbed her brow.

"Okay, you joined a witch cult." She reciprocated the sigh. She walked back towards the lounge. "What was last night? Your initiation? You know, if it was the French Girl that got you into it, then I picked it. She's not your type, Jamsey. Don't do this sort of stupid shit for a girl…"

"Not a witch cult, either." I groaned. "Here, look…"

I let the armour of Maiki take over me. It felt disturbing to do it in the walls of my house. Maiki lived in the darkness. He lived on burning metal scaffolds, and in my imagination. He lived in my soul, but he did not live in my house. Not close to Simone.

Mum gasped, and was near screaming when she covered her mouth.

"Hey, hey, it's fine!" I whispered, trying to calm her. Errol barked at me. He tried to nip at my ankle, but couldn't find it – the joint being impossibly thin. This confused his cattle-dog instincts. I let my armour crawl back into my body. Mum was frantic.

"James…" She shrieked.

"That might have been a bit much." I considered. "But it does get cool, I'm telling you. Is this any better?"

I blasted down into the floor, and leaped into the air. I jumped over her head, landing on the other side the room on a cushion of wind. The blast from my hands pushed her off her feet, and she fell onto the couch. I cringed, and went to help her up, but she refused my hand.

"James, this is insane." Mum said. She looked past me, through my eyes – but not into my soul like so many others had done. She overlooked my soul. She was looking into my eyes, but not at *me*.

"Mum, it's not that insane." I said. "There are lots of Suneva. Natalie is a Suneva. Celeste is a Suneva. I made a friend today called Chad, he's a Suneva."

She was regaining her breath. Her eyes darted around my face.

"This still doesn't explain where you've been." She said. "This asks *way* more than it explains."

"I've been in trouble, Mum." I said, unable to lie. "Natalie and I have been protecting Celeste. She's been running from bad Suneva. I got captured, and used as a bargaining chip, but she and Natalie came back, and our new friend saved us."

Mum was shocked. Her eye twitched.

"Wow…that sounds really bad out loud." I laughed, nervously.

"You are making this no better for yourself." Mum said, plainly.

"I know."

Mum pulled herself up from the couch. She tried to stand over me, to be intimidating, but I had half a foot on her.

"Where else have you been?" Mum asked. "Like every night after school, when you just come home late, and I've never known. And what about those parties?"

"Well, the parties were parties – and that should be the most surprising part of all of this, I didn't have to lie about how cool I was." I grinned, Mum did not grin. "But in the afternoons, when I haven't been rowing or at band, I've been at the abandoned house near the train line. I've been learning how to be a Suneva from the ghost of a Suneva leader, who died five-hundred years ago."

"Old Mr Finneck's house?" Mum asked.

"Yeah."

"Does he have your Dad's tools?"

"I haven't looked."

"Huh." Mum pondered. She had calmed down, descending from her tip-toes to regular height. "I'm surprised that I believe all of this, but you don't lie, do you?"

"No, I can't." I said.

"You just don't tell me things."

"Yeah, that." I frowned. Mum stepped around me. She found the TV remote, and turned the TV off. I hadn't realised that it was on, but I felt the impact of the silence between us. She could only just recognise the son standing before her, and she didn't dare mention it.

"Thank you for telling me, James." She said, finally. "I don't approve - *at all* - but I think you've made up your mind."

"What's that supposed to mean?" I asked. I went over to hug her, and she accepted it, only just.

"I mean that if I tell you to stop seeing your friends, or stop doing whatever you're doing, you'll just go behind my back to do it. You've been okay not telling me for however long already…"

I bit my lip. Mum wasn't even angry, she was deeply disappointed, and confused. I couldn't help but feel gut-wrenching shame. I'd let her down.

"I can be safe about it." I said. I didn't look at her as I said it.

"Like you've been safe about it so far?" She pushed.

"Look…" I said, trying to gain some logical argument as to why I should be allowed to continue being a Suneva with my friends. I didn't think the urgency of losing powers would be caught on Mum. She'd probably prefer Hesslik's plan. "I know that I got into trouble, *but*, for once, this is something that you don't have experience in, and I do. It's not stupid for me to say that I know better about these powers and the people who use them. I can promise you that I can stay safe."

Mum crossed her arms tightly. She was finally looking at *me* again, I could see it in her stare.

"Doing this stuff makes you happy, doesn't it?" She asked.

"Yes." I smiled. "I love it."

"It's not just for that girl, is it?" She squinted.

"Which?"

"The French one."

"No, Mum." I squirmed.

"Good, because she's trouble." Mum said. "I could see it in her eyes. Not the girl for my son."

"Point noted." I sarcastically saluted Mum. I definitely wasn't going to tell her about the kiss, then, and how good it made me feel.

"Now, come here." Mum said, and held her arms open. I went into them, and she gave me a great, strong, hug.

"Now," She pulled away slightly to look me in the face, "If you're going to be jumping over people's heads, the first thing you're doing is jumping up to the gutters and cleaning them out."

"*What?*"

"They haven't had a proper clean since your Dad decided to pass the job on to you and piss off forever." She said. "You're getting out there when Simone's at Uni and jumping up onto that roof."

"Oh *cheese*." I huffed. "Fine, that's a deal."

"And Simone never finds out." Mum nodded.

Despite her begrudging self-insistence that I continue to do what makes me happy, Mum didn't let me leave the house for a week. I went to school, I did my activities, and I came home. This was a productive week in the life of James Grey. I cleaned the gutters, like she'd asked, then swept the roof, as she'd added on for the sake of it.

Exactly a week later, on the Saturday following our ordeal, Celeste, Chad, Natalie and I met at my house.

There were several reasons for meeting at my house, the first being that I wasn't ready to test Mum, and the second being that I wanted Mum to see my friends' faces again, and maybe not hate them.

I had gone to the store to buy chips, dips and fizzy drinks. I had a few untoasted sandwiches ready, packed to the brim with my special recipe, ready to be shoved into the burning hot jaffle iron. I waited eagerly for the doorbell to ring, one hand tightly gripping the handle of the sandwich press.

"God, you're eager." Mum noted. She'd just come home from work. It was encroaching on the hours of late afternoon. She made her coffee beside me.

"I know." I said. "I am excited."

"Don't you see these people at school?" She asked.

"Yeah, but…well…I don't know. Home is more fun than school." I replied.

Errol barked. The doorbell rang. I jammed two sandwiches into the press and ran with the dog to the front door. I mashed my palm into the handle and yanked the door open with ferocity. All three of them stood there, squished on my porch, Chad at the back.

"Hi guys." I said, a big, dumb smile strewn across my lips. "I'm making toasties, and there's dips and chips and drinks and I've been excited to finally have fun for the first time this week."

"Yeah, we can tell." Natalie chuckled. I gestured the three inside, and they walked through the door.

"Wow…" Chad said. He craned his head around and danced on his feet to take in the full view. "You've got a great house."

"Thanks, man." I said. "I don't know, it's modest."

"Hi." Mum greeted. She waved to everybody around the corner of the kitchen. The clang of spoon against coffee cup drowning her voice.

"Hi Maria." Natalie sang. Celeste smiled and waved, and from the simple gesture of an improper hello, I could see Mum's eye twitch. I nudged Celeste, only just. "*Bonjour* Maria." She burst, jumping in surprise.

"Mrs. Grey." Chad said. He marched to the front of the crowd, his hair spiked up professionally, his hand meaty and strong, presented for a shake. Mum smiled.

"Where are you making friends, James? The international club?" She joked, and shook Chads hand. His hand was gentle, but firm. It was a respectable handshake of a well-trained gentleman. Mum was pleased.

"Please, Maria is fine." She said. "You must be Chad."

"That I am, Ma'am." He smiled, and held his belt. He wore regular jeans, high-top sneakers and an unbranded shirt. It was in stark contrast to the bronze-armoured, leather adorned operative we'd seen.

"Well, I think James has been busy preparing a feast for you all. I'll be in the study if you need anything, James. Why don't you all take a seat outside? Not too many good days left."

"Eat with us, Mum." I said. "I didn't make the fifth sandwich for nothing."

Mum's eyebrows dropped. She craned her head, and squinted at the kitchen bench. Surely enough, there was a single sandwich left out of the jaffle iron, waiting for the next round. She chirped to herself.

"God, I should make you feel bad more often if this is the son it gets me." Mum joked. Chad chuckled, and nudged me. I already liked this guy.

Afternoon snacks put Mum at ease. I could see it in her smile, and she talked to my friends. Chad made many jokes. His laugh was contagious, it was a low, belly chuckle with the right hint of joviality. He had the perfect joke for each line that was said – as if his brain was simply a ticking happiness machine, ready to spread its joy. I could see Natalie sceptically chewing on her toasty. She didn't want to be taken by his charm, but she was forced to, at one point, spit a whole slice of tomato across the table as she burst into laughter. Chad snapped finger guns at her and she smiled with a full face of embarrassment. She rubbed her locket.

After eating, when Mum retired to do the bookwork, we all piled into my room. Business faces came on as we settled down around Natalie's carrot sticks and dip to discuss future plans. We each slumped on a quadrant of the bed.

"So, we're finding Legendaries, then?" Natalie asked Chad. "That's your idea for stopping Hesslik?"

"I don't know much of western Suneva history." Chad said, "But as I said, they seem to be prominent mythical figures. They're a game changer for any Suneva ideology. I found this information on them…"

Chad removed a piece of paper from his jeans. It was folded, and dirty looking. He unfurled it to the size of a full page. It was written upon in cursive writing, with a fountain pen, in a language I couldn't read. Chad showed the page to us, as if we could interpret it.

The scripture was recognisable, at least. I'd seen it before, etched onto Kuvalik's cupboard. There was another place I'd seen it too, but I couldn't think of it. In the bottom centre of the page was a drawing. It had the symbol of the black sun – like an eight-armed cross, with an interconnected hexagon backing it. Hesslik had used a variation of this symbol for his pamphlets – one without the hexagon.

"It's *liktan*." Natalie said. "I can't read it, or speak it."

"*Liktan?*" I questioned, then I remembered where I'd heard it before. "Kuvalik and Vestas told me about *Liktan*. Suneva words like *quatra* and *alis* and *shath* are *Liktan*, right?"

"Yeah." Chad smiled, "But you guys don't speak or write *liktan?*"

"I speak it." Celeste said. "I spoke it at home before I spoke French. I can read it, too."

"Well, that doesn't surprise me." Chad smiled. "You're not new to the Suneva game. Maybe, Celeste, you'd like to read the passage to Natalie and James. You know…" He looked sheepishly at Natalie, "to show that I'm not making it up." He gulped. Natalie smiled, somewhat, at his devotion to prove his sincerity. She took the page from his outstretched hand and gave it to Celeste. Celeste inspected it. We waited for her translation.

"The Legendaries are a mythical set of three Suneva, of the powers *kida* – teleportation, *zirran* – time, and *vectis* – gravity. The three Suneva have only been found once each in Suneva history, at the same time, for the formation of the first nation of Suneva by *Fara Vinavek*. Due to the distortion of their stories over time, it's not known whether or not they actually existed…"

Natalie hummed critically.

"But multiple witnesses account for their feats of nature."

"See, it's all good." Chad smiled.

"*Vinavek* wrote that the path to finding the Legendary Suneva was through a strict following of her ideological text, *Na Kitos Keroseva* – The Code of Connections."

I hummed, taking in the information. We had a lead, although I recognised none of what was going on.

"This seems better, then." Natalie hummed. "We're not just finding Legendaries and hoping that the precedence of their existence sways people to follow us, they actually *have* precedence in the formation of societies."

"That's why I'm sure Hesslik wanted them." Chad nodded. "Those who know the myths will know that their presence calls the formation of a new, great Suneva community."

"And prosperity." Celeste added. "This is powerful. *If* they exist, and we find them, we should see supporters flock to whatever our cause is. *If* people are that simple…"

"And *if* Hesslik doesn't get to these Legendaries first." I added. "Although it looks like we've got to do this code to get there before him. I don't know about that." I frowned. "Strict following of some doctrine sounds…difficult."

"My father liked the Code of Connections, though." Celeste said reflectively. "As far as I remember, it was some self-improvement kind of text."

"I've heard Hesslik talk of it, too." Chad said. "Although, intermittently, and only a name-drop."

Natalie banged the bed with her open palms. Her face lit up. She rushed to her feet.

"I know exactly where I've seen *all* of this." She beamed.

"You do?" Chad asked.

"Yes, it was all in the book I found when James and I first discovered Suneva."

"Oh yeah!" It clicked for me too. "I don't remember the symbol being exactly like that – the front had the *Empire symbol* – but that's where I'd seen the *liktan* letters before."

"That *Empire Symbol* is *The Mark of the Black Suns*, probably the most recognisable Suneva symbol." Chad added.

"There was a reference to the *Code of Connections* in the English portion of the text, too" Natalie grinned. "It's all there."

"Great!" Chad smiled. "So, Natalie, where is this book?"

Natalie frowned. She rubbed her chin.

"I put it back before my *Yamitse* would notice it was gone."

"And we can't just take it out again?" He asked.

"No." She said, bluntly. "She doesn't like me going through her library."

Chad frowned now, too. Celeste sighed, and spoke.

"Then let me go in. I've been stealing things and sneaking through houses for years."

"No." Natalie said, more defiantly. Celeste appeared insulted. "Sorry, I don't want this to turn into a police report – and that's what a book thief would look like."

"Then what do you suggest?" Celeste huffed. She enunciated her words precisely.

"I think we need to sneak in, read the right passages, and sneak out."

Chad shrugged. We all shrugged. The plan seemed solid enough, although I could feel Natalie's heart beating through the bed. She was anxious.

"When is your *Yamitse* not home?" I asked her.

"Right now. She's gone to her water aerobics."

"Hah!" Chad burst in laughter, then covered his mouth. His face was red, his diaphragm giggled to spite his desire for it to stop. He couldn't hold it, and burst out laughing, falling backwards off the bed. Multiple confused gazes fell upon him.

"What's funny about that?" Natalie interrogated. Chad had to stifle his laugh. He hit his fist against his chest.

"A powerful *Welle...*" He squeezed out and chuckled, "A Suneva of water doing a water exercise class?" He eyeballed us all, to see if we found it funny. His eyes begged us to laugh along, or else he'd feel insane.

"Oh goodness." He deflated. "I'm sorry, I just had the image in my head of her pushing against the water, and it *flying everywhere!*" He burst again. "And all of the old people would be *getting splashed!*" He snorted and banged on the ground. "*water...everywhere!*" He was manic. Celeste rolled her eyes. Natalie snorted air from her nose, laughing internally at the fiasco.

"So, let's go now, then?" I suggested.

"Oh, sorry Mavis…I don't know what's gotten into me today!" Chad enacted the sketch comedy transpiring in his head. As soon as he was done with his lunacy, we set off.

"We're just going to Natalie's for a bit." I said to Mum. "We might be back, or it might just be me."

"Okay, James." Mum said. Everybody said goodbye to her, Chad the most enthusiastically of all.

When we arrived at Natalie's house, her Dad wasn't home. Natalie regained five years of her life as her nerves about the situation dissipated. She searched around in the pocket of her jeans for her key and pulled it out. She opened the front door of her white-pillar, red brick cottage.

The inside of her house was incredibly modern. The kitchen, which seemed to be the centre of the house, directly across from the entrance, was full of new, shining silver appliances. To the right were a set of black, leather couches around a TV, and to the left was a sitting area. There were two doors on the back wall, one to either side of the kitchen.

Natalie hushed us with a hand gesture as we entered.

"Yamitse?" She called into the day-lit house. The sound of her voice echoed, but there was no response.

"Dad?" She asked again. There was not a shuffle of a mouse. "We're clear." She said softly, and led us in. I closed the door gently behind us.

"Follow me." Natalie instructed. She tip-toed through the main room of the house, around the right side of the kitchen to the door on that side. Even though there was nobody else in the house, I felt obliged to tip-toe as Natalie did.

We came through the right-hand doorway, into a small hall. There was a doorway at the end – opening into a laundry – a closed door to the right, near us, and a closed door to the left, up near the laundry. Natalie held a finger to her mouth, to shush us, and creeped up the carpeted hallway. She signalled us to stay back, and we did so.

She held her hands by her side, in the peace sign pose, to scan for any Suneva presences. She wrinkled her brow after waving her hands around, and reached for the door near the laundry. She opened it, and poked her head of dark, curly hair inside. She did not re-emerge from the door. She slipped into the room and held a thumbs-up into the hallway. We jogged after her.

The bedroom was from another era. The bed frame was made of dark, fine-quality wood, carved intricately. The bed was an amalgamation of hand-knitted and ancient white cushions, stacked on top of each other into an organised, delightful mountain of comfort. The doona was floral, and pale pink, to match the curtain. The day cast pretty light onto the carpeted, simple room through the window.

"Okay, be careful now." Natalie warned. She stalked around the bed, making sure to touch nothing. "My Yamitse will know if *anything* has been moved. Her memory is pretty much photographic."

"Well, that's comforting." I mused. "She'll have to know that we've been through her books, then."

"That's why this is risky." Natalie looked at me. Her face, I noticed now, was grim about this whole prospect. "Now, come on." She continued.

She went past the bed, and slid open the door next to it. There was a walk-in wardrobe, which she entered. Celeste and Chad walked before me. I entered last, and closed the door behind me.

"Don't ask me how I found out about this." Natalie said. "I couldn't tell you, I just *knew* it was here." She squatted, then got to her knees, pawing at the wall on the back-right of the wardrobe. Her head rustled against a fur coat, filling her view with her thick hair. She blew it aside, and there was a click. A triumphant smile crossed her face. She carefully put aside a small panel, and reached into the hidden compartment to grasp at something. The whole wall cracked now, and shifted – it was a door, and Natalie held the handle. She pushed it away, to reveal a secret room and ushered us in. Chad went in first, followed by Celeste and myself. Natalie entered last, leaving the door open.

"It doesn't open from the inside." She noted. "So we'll have to be quick."

The room itself was incredibly skinny – only the width of the door which opened into it. The back wall was inset and unplastered, with a whole two rows of books and assorted texts taking up the space of its brick-built shelves. The room was entirely dark, bar what light could make it in from the closet. Natalie produced a small torch from her pocket, and pushed us aside to scan the library. Dust flew into the air as we shifted ourselves around. The books appeared to be in relatively good condition, although the room itself was uncared for. The floor was concrete. It was cold to touch.

"Here we are." Natalie smiled. She put the torch between her teeth to grab at the book. Its spine was thick, and white, like the front cover. Its cover had the so-called *Mark of the Black Suns* as its illustration. Torch still in mouth, she flipped through the tome, searching for the right page.

"Here…" She mumbled through the flashlight. She handed the book to Celeste, and spat out the light to shine it on the page. "What does the *liktan* part say?" She asked. Chad gathered around behind the French girl, and read over her shoulder.

"Vinavek's *Code of Connections* is one of the few adhered-to practices of the *narakis* Suneva era." Celeste read.

"*Classic* era." Chad translated further.

"It is written as a vague few sentences which form a guide for Suneva to achieve realisation. Traditionally, it is forbidden to write or speak of the code's true meaning. The reason for this is abundantly clear to a realised Suneva…"

"Oh, great." I interrupted. "I don't suppose either of you are *realised Suneva?*"

Celeste shrugged. Chad shook his head.

"Realisation is like *enlightenment.*" He clarified. "I met a lot of Native American Suneva who you'd call realised, but they don't tell their secrets."

"Good." I frowned.

"Okay, screw the *prologue.*" Celeste said, scanning the page with her finger. "Here we go: Realisation is achieved through understanding the three types of connection; *kerosvoul* – the connection to the self, *keroseva* – the connection to others, and *kerokosma* – the connection to the world around us. A Suneva who is realised will completely understand their place in the universe, their purpose, and their role in the lives of others."

"Realisation is a long way off, yet." A crackly, ethnic voice emanated from the doorway. The shadow of a stout woman loomed over us as we crowded the book. We each let out a gasp of fright. Chad slammed the book shut, and looked between Natalie and the woman. Natalie was locked up in fright. Her torch dropped to the ground, and it broke on the concrete. My face flushed red with guilt and embarrassment.

"*Yamitse*…I…" Natalie stumbled for words. She was almost tearing. I couldn't comprehend the reason for her fright – but I was certain that I was about to find it out. Both of her hands crossed her chest, clutching at the golden locket which hung there. Her grandmother looked on unapprovingly. She took a step into the room, which was now well beyond capacity.

"You come to learn about *Na Kitos Keroseva?*" She asked.

"Yes, *Yamiste.*" Natalie replied. Her eyes were wide. Her words were quick.

"Aren't you all a little *young* for realisation?" Her Yamitse asked. None replied.

"We're not after realisation, *Tona Menas.*" Celeste had the confidence to say. Her face was blank. She stood strong, without a hint of guilt.

"Then what are you searching for?" Natalie's Yamiste asked. Her face remained unimpressed.

"Legendaries." Chad said. "We were using the Code of Connections to find Legendaries."

The room fell silent, bar the breathing of four nervous teenagers and the rasp of an older woman. Birds chirped outside, audible through the brick walls. My eyes darted between the older woman's, but she looked at the floor. She was thinking.

"Oftentimes…" She started, "*keroseva* - the connection to others -is overlooked. In my time on Olomb's council, I found that my social connections granted me more abilities, information, and favours, than the other two combined." She smiled, and let her hands rest by her side. Natalie slumped to the floor, the shock of the situation not permitting her to stand.

"Olomb's council?" Chad thought aloud. "*Tona Menas*…you're not *Lilawelle Menas*, are you?" He asked expectantly.

"I am." She answered plainly.

"Oh boy." Chad lit up. "Hesslik has been looking for you for a long time. The whole council of *Na Faras nas Suns* really missed you…"

Her face was strewn with sullen disapproval. Chad shut up immediately.

"*Na Faras nas Suns?*" I asked.

"Hesslik's Empire of the Black Suns." Natalie's Yamitse spoke. "What relation do you have to the council?" She asked. Her voice scorned.

"I was Hesslik's personal agent, before he ordered my thread removed." Chad answered, undeterred. "I left him after I found out. I think that the Legendaries will be the key to his downfall."

Natalie's Yamitse hummed, then broke a war-time smile once more. Her look of joy wasn't particularly euphoric, more than it was a serious affair, but it was a smile none-the-less.

"You can all call me Tess." She said. "Or *Mrs Floros*, if you prefer. I seldom go by the name *Lilawelle Menas* these days."

"Yes, *Mrs Floros*." Chad smiled. Celeste and I nodded in agreeance, not as brave as Chad to speak.

"You're not mad?" Natalie finally managed to ask. She'd been caught red handed, doing something she knew would be risky, under the pressure of her friends.

"You're good to *Yamitse*, Natalie." She smiled wholly. "Many of these books are private to me. If you would like to find answers, I'd prefer that you come to me first."

"Yes, Yamitse." Natalie nodded. Her grandmother nodded back, then nodded to each of us, before she took her leave. She left us in the dusty concrete room. Natalie was clearly shocked at this, and everything else which had just transpired. She still faced the doorway.

"Are you alright?" I asked her. I put a hand on her shoulder. She clung onto it.

"Yeah, I'm doing well, James." She said, finally turning to face us. "Just in shock from all of the panic. Do you ever feel your heart race with hot blood?"

"Yeah, like when you forget your homework?" I nudged her. She cracked a smile.

"So, what does this all mean for us?" Celeste asked, taking the attention away from Natalie. She let go of my hand, grabbed the book, and put it back into its place on the shelf.

"I don't know." I said. "I don't see how connection to the self, or *realisation*, would help us find Legendary Suneva."

"Maybe only a realised Suneva can find Legendaries." Chad Suggested.

"Yeah, but why?" I asked.

"Well, it's there in the passage." Chad said. "*Realised Suneva* have a greater connection to others. Tess even said that the Suneva social web is powerful."

"Yes, but we could be moving up in the social web right now. Why do we have to be realised?"

Chad shrugged.

"Two birds with one stone?" He suggested. Natalie and Celeste both shrugged in agreeance. Natalie pulled a notebook out of her bag.

"Okay," she said, producing a pen from behind her ear which I'd failed to notice. "If we're going to follow a social web, we should probably map down all of the Suneva whom we know."

She put pen to paper, but found she had nothing to write. She looked up for suggestions.

"*Kuvalik?*" I said. She shrugged and wrote it down. "Although, I suppose all of his friends are probably dead."

"Lilawelle." Chad suggested. "Your Yamitse might know some powerful people."

"She might," Natalie agreed, noting the name *Lilawelle Menas*, "But she doesn't mix with many Suneva these days. She's removed herself from it all, apparently."

"Shame." Chad shrugged.

"We could try to find my mother." Celeste suggested. "I don't know where she might be, or if she's alive, but she would help anybody who brought us back together."

"Okay, now that's a solid idea." Natalie nodded. She wrote *Celeste's Mother* more enthusiastically than any other suggestion. "Is she a Suneva?"

"Oui." Celeste smiled.

"Good." Natalie smiled back. "Any other ideas?"

I pondered, but I had nothing worthy of saying.

"We could ask Simone…" I suggested. "I mean, only if we wanted to be nailed to a cross, but she might know Suneva."

"Maybe not." Celeste cringed at the idea.

"Okay," Natalie said, reviewing the short list. "This is good for now. We've still got time, right?" She asked, looking at Chad. He checked his watch.

"No, I mean until Hesslik's gathering…" Natalie clarified to the American boy. He smiled dumbly.

"Oh, right." He said, "Yes. The gathering is in June next year. We've still got over a year to do this."

"Good." Natalie smiled. "I think we've got some *okay* ideas at the moment, but maybe we'll take a week to brainstorm by ourselves and lay low, then meet again."

"Sounds good." I said. "I like the sound of laying low for another week."

Celeste and Chad enthusiastically agreed.

"Then it's settled." Natalie said. "This is a problem for future us." She laughed at the idea, and jumped back to her feet. She put her notebook back into her bag, her pen back behind her ear, and crawled out of the room.

"Let's get out of here. I don't like this closet." She said as she led us out.

We finished off the dips and carrots that I had taken from my house. We lounged around Natalie's sitting area, talking of unrelated things and laughing. As I prepared to leave – the first of us to go so that I would appease my mother – Mrs Floros pulled me aside.

"James." She called me in her blunt voice as I collected by belongings from the kitchen. I arose to see her handing me a full plate of pita. My eyes grew in delight. "For your mother and your family." She said.

"Thank you, Mrs Floros." I said. My mouth watered. "You didn't have to."

"I want you to have it." She said. "I did not come to your house after you lost your father. The guilt has stayed with me for many years."

I looked between Tess and her pita quizzically. I certainly wasn't going to reject the food, but this was an odd occasion for the offering.

"You knew my Dad?" I asked.

"Yes. John Grey worked with Suneva communities in Melbourne. He was a good, moral man, above all else."

"Huh," I squeaked. "I thought he was just a policeman who worked against Argols."

"He did more than that – although he may never have told you."

"Right." I grinned. This was new to me. I didn't know how it made me feel.

"Your mother, Maria, is a strong woman, though. And you were very brave that night, I heard."

He lay with his mouth open. His throat was green and his eyes were wide with fright, or stupidity. His breathing was laboured, and wrong.

"Thank you." I said, shaking the thought, "But I don't like being called brave. I didn't do anything useful."

Tess frowned. She couldn't necessarily console me otherwise.

"He loved you with all of his heart." She said to me. "Never forget that."

"I won't." I said to her. She finally released her grip on the tray of pita, and I loaded it into my bag with the other trays and leftover biscuits.

"Say hello to your mother from me." She managed to lift her old, wrinkled lips into a smile – a gesture which appeared so unnatural to her that she must have learned to do it from T.V. I smiled back, told her that I would, and headed for the front door.

"Bye, guys!" I called to my friends who sat on the sofas. Celeste had started flipping through a magazine. Chad and Natalie appeared to be talking intimately. I didn't have a lot of time to speculate the topic of conversation as I reached for the doorhandle.

"*Au revoir*, James." Celeste smiled. Her lips were bold and red, like always. They moved with such finesse. I wanted to kiss them again. I would have to talk to her about that kiss. I was too nervous to bring it up, and neither of us had yet.

"Bye James!" Natalie said, disengaging from her chat with Chad.

"See-ya, dude." Chad waved.

"See-ya!" I said once more, and walked myself through the door.

Sunset glowed bright yellow across the horizon. Above and before me, the sky danced with pink and orange light. The air around me buzzed, shuffling in a mid-autumn breeze. I felt it on my fingertips, and I felt it in my soul. I smiled.

Mum, you're going to kill me. I thought to myself. I unslung my bag, reached in, and took a fistful of pita. I crammed it into my mouth. This was not the reason that Mum would kill me.

You're going to kill me because I have an idea of where to search for the Suneva social web, and you won't approve of it one bit.

I grinned, my mouth full of oily pastry. There was no guilt in the feeling, only exhilaration. I threw my bag over my shoulder, and strutted off into the cool light of dusk.

End of Volume One: Call of the Void